THE MARTYR'S SCORN

Pamela Gordon Hoad

Also by Pamela Gordon Hoad in the Harry Somers series

The Devil's Stain

The Angel's Wing

The Cherub's Smile

*****

First published 2018 by Silver Quill Publishing

www.silverquillpublishing.com

Typeset in Georgia

ISBN: 978-1-912513-61-1

Silver Quill Publishing

In memory of Miss Ann Hartley, the teacher at the former Richmond Grammar School for Girls (Surrey) who long ago fired my love of history, with much gratitude

Acknowledgements

I should like to record thanks to the friends who have supported me during the process of writing and preparing *The Martyr's Scorn* for publication. I must pay special tribute to John Bryden, accomplished organist and internationally acclaimed musician, who lent me invaluable books on the development of medieval organs. I also owe a particular debt of gratitude to my son, James, who raised many useful points on the draft, both as proof-reader and historian, and to Oliver Eade, who advised on innumerable matters, technical and literary.

I am particularly grateful to readers of my earlier books in this series – *The Devil's Stain, The Angel's Wing* and *The Cherub's Smile* – who have expressed their enjoyment of those stories and encouraged me to continue the tale of Harry Somers. My thanks, as always, go to my husband, Peter Hoad, for his support and patience.

Any errors are of course my own.

CONTENTS

Cuthbert Percy, relative of the Earl of Northumberland
Richard, Duke of York
Roger Egremont, cousin to the Earl of Stanwick
Lady Jane Glasbury, wife to Gilbert Iffley
Leone, assistant physician to the Marquis of Suffolk
Alice de la Pole, wife to the Marquis of Suffolk
Katherine Devereux, attendant on Alice de la Pole
Thomas Chope, master carpenter
Grizel, wife to Thomas Chope and sister to Rendell Tonks
Edward Devereux, Katherine's brother
Lord Walter Fitzvaughan
Gaston de la Tour, Lord Fitzvaughan's companion
Steward at William de la Pole's London house
Barty, page at William de la Pole's London house
Philip Neville, Baron Thornton, courtier
Bess Willoughby, wife to Robin, Lord Fitzvaughan's bailiff
Syb, servant at William de la Pole's London house
Queen Margaret, wife to King Henry VI
King Henry VI of England
Anne Hopgood, wife to Stephen Boice
Sister Michelle of Thannington, Kent
Captain and crew of the *Nicholas of the Tower*

Part I Winchester 1447

Chapter 1

The Warden of the Works held the door open and we slipped into the great abbey church as, with a rustle of robes and grinding of joints, members of the congregation genuflected at the words of the unseen priest. Outside it was dusk and no daylight penetrated through the high windows so my first impression was of entering a cavern of darkness, its height impossible to discern and its length indicated only by the cluster of candles in front of the distant rood screen. The gilding on the screen sparkled but I could make out no details while my eyes were adjusting their focus. Then, from behind the carved partition the voices of the monks in the chancel deepened as they chanted the words of contrition and their proclamation of guilt and grief thundered along the nave and from aisle to aisle. Travel-worn and exhausted, burdened by my own measureless grief and guilt, I sank to my knees on the tiled floor, beside the black-robed monk who had welcomed me, and allowed my tears to fall unchecked onto my grimy mantle.

Only four days previously I had been in Suffolk, well over one hundred miles to the north-east, where my world fell apart, dreams shattered and prospects ruined, cruel fate vitiating my newly cherished hopes. Since then my escort had set a hectic pace to reach Winchester, where I had been summoned in my capacity as physician but also to save me from arbitrary and vindictive judgement. We had ridden with unremitting speed, far faster than I found comfortable, and I was saddle-sore and racked by aching limbs. The only advantage of my physical distress was that it distracted me from the more devastating agony in my heart. In the half-hour since I dismounted and entered the hallowed precincts of the abbey, my misery burgeoned anew and I regretted that I had accepted a responsibility for which I felt no enthusiasm. I had yielded to the urging

1

of my friends who wished to preserve me from a prison cell, when my disposition would have been matched more readily by ending my pointless existence for good.

The Warden of the Works, as he had described himself, straightened his stance and I stumbled to stand beside him but my head swam and I could not prevent myself swaying. Alert to my difficulty, he took my arm and led me to the side wall, where the infirm propped themselves during the service, and gratefully I leaned against the stonework, closing my eyes as the voice of the reader rang out from the chancel. Perversely, I had enough pride in my professional role to breathe deeply in an attempt to steady myself rather than give way to the weakness of my body. I rested my head against the wall and tried to concentrate on the words of the Sacrist when, suddenly from within the hidden choir, a piercing shriek cut across the words of the liturgy, its tone signalling protest rather than terror.

My companion tensed but when I looked at him sideways his expression was bland and then he shrugged with a half-smile. I had no wish to draw attention to myself by proffering my medical services if they were not required and I was relieved that there seemed to be no flurry of consternation from behind the rood screen and only a little within the congregation. I saw two tradesmen exchange questioning looks while a portly citizen crossed himself and sighed but seemed otherwise undisturbed. Then, in the choir, contrasting with the usual rhythmic chanting, three separate voices began to sing, one holding the line of the plainsong, one soaring above it and the other below, blending their individual melodies with great beauty; and behind this glorious sound there was a dim rustle of movement followed by the click of a side door gently closing. I reflected that in a religious house of perhaps five dozen monks there would inevitably be some whose age and wandering wits might cause them to behave in an unseemly manner even as they prayed before the altar.

2

Their colleagues would be familiar with their infirmity and how to calm the sufferer.

When the service ended and the townsfolk made their way back into Winchester's maze of streets, the Warden of the Works led me through a door out of the south aisle, into the cloister which adjoined the church. Both church and abbey had a proud history, as I had learned on my journey from St. Edmundsbury, when the priest accompanying me spoke in awe of the blessed relics of St. Swithun which the cathedral sheltered: relics venerated by scores of pilgrims who came to pray at the martyr's shrine behind the High Altar. The abbey, named in honour of the saint, had been established long ago to nurture his legacy of holiness and healing and it had become wealthy from the bequests and donations of the faithful.

The abbey was under the day-to-day supervision of the Prior, for its titular Abbot was the Bishop of Winchester, who had many calls on his time, both secular and spiritual. Indeed, twenty years previously Bishop Henry Beaufort had been elevated as Cardinal and throughout his long life he continued to be a powerful voice in the King's Council. He was a magnate of both church and state, half-brother, uncle and now great-uncle to successive Kings of England: a man who apparently relished his eminent position and disparaged the hostility he provoked from rivals at the royal court. I did not imagine he could spare much time for the quotidian activities of the religious house he nominally headed.

'You're exhausted, I can see, but Prior Aulton would wish to greet you before you retire,' the Warden whispered and I rallied my disordered thoughts to listen. 'We'll call at his house in the close, on the other side of the great cloister, and then I'll show you to the guest-quarters.'

'I need not go to the Bishop's Palace tonight? Does it adjoin the abbey?'

'It would be unwise to impose that challenge on you when you're so weary. There'll be time enough to meet

3

your patient and fellow physicians in the morning. Wolvesey Castle isn't far but it's outside the abbey precincts.'

I was glad of the breathing space but something in his tone concerned me. 'You think I won't be welcome?'

A monk passing from the other direction gave a start as I spoke and I remembered that silence was generally observed inside the abbey. I put my hand to my mouth and the passer-by smiled at me as he nodded.

The Warden rested his fingers on my shoulder as we rounded the corner beyond the cloister and approached a doorway. 'We, black monks, as they call us, may speak to guests as necessary,' he said,' and there is no constraint within the Prior's house. What we've gleaned of the Cardinal's situation is only hearsay but I suspect you'll face a testing time. Don't worry yourself, though. When you're refreshed by a night's sleep, you'll know how to handle it. Your reputation has come before you.'

I did not find that news encouraging but we had entered the house and were being shown upstairs to await the Prior's return from the church. In his parlour I sipped the ale we were given with caution, fearful that in my weakened condition it might go too quickly to my head, but almost immediately he joined us, with arms outstretched and a broad smile.

'Doctor Somers, welcome. My good friend, the Abbot of Peterborough, sent word you were coming. You are a brave man.'

I had no idea whether this plaudit resulted from recent events in which I had been involved or the commission with which I was now charged. 'The Abbot has been most gracious in aiding me. I'm grateful to spend the night here before going to the Bishop's Palace.'

'I wanted the chance to speak to you before you take up your task.' The Prior gave a chuckle. 'I won't dissemble with you. I'm anxious to know what's happening in Wolvesey Castle. If the Cardinal's as ill as they say, there are measures I need to take. But it might be injudicious to act prematurely. I'm sure you understand me.' He swilled the ale in his goblet before continuing. 'If you were able to send me word how things stand, I'd be obliged. I don't ask for anything to breach your physician's duty to your patient but some hint of his prospects would be appreciated. Brother Simon will arrange some means for you to send information to me.'

'Brother Simon?' I blinked in confusion.

'The Warden here. He has charge of all the fabric of the abbey and he has a bevy of workmen at his beck and call. They live outside the wall of our compound and can be helpful in conveying messages.'

The friendly monk who had accompanied me since my arrival looked down modestly and I felt myself grinning at him. It was the first time for many days I had experienced a moment of shared human empathy and I was startled at its strangeness but the sensation was fleeting.

No sooner had we heard the knock than the door flew open and a scrawny monk pounded into the room, his black robe flapping loosely round him. 'I must protest, Reverend Father,' he bellowed, 'I must protest.'

I admired the way the Prior stifled a sigh but acknowledged the intruder benignly. 'And what is the substance of your protest, Brother Lambert?'

'They say you have engaged a physician to oversee my treatments – to interfere with my prescriptions – to question my expertise – to...'

'And who exactly are "they" in this instance? And from where do you suppose they have acquired this wholly erroneous information? Can you be specific?'

'Everyone is saying so. They say he's to arrive imminently, some jumped-up physician from the court seeking an easy billet with nothing to do but criticise and parade his book knowledge...' he faltered. 'Erroneous information, you said?'

Prior Aulton permitted himself to sigh audibly. 'Completely false, Brother Lambert, and I must counsel you to temper your passion. Permit me to introduce Doctor Somers, Doctor of Medicine from the University of Padua and lately physician to one of the grandest households in the land. He is spending the night in our guest-house before taking up his commission at Wolvesey Castle. Doctor Somers, this is our worthy Infirmarian.'

I bowed while Brother Lambert eyed me with the utmost suspicion. 'Hasn't the Cardinal physicians enough?'

'That's not our concern,' the Prior said and held out a goblet of ale for the monk.

'From what I've heard,' I said, trying to show I had taken no offence, 'it won't at all be an easy billet.'

The Warden of the Works had stood in silence since his colleague joined us but he cut across my words with his question. 'How is Brother Joseph? Have you pacified him?'

The Infirmarian glared at his questioner before answering. 'I've given him a draught and he's sleeping peacefully. I'll keep him in the Infirmary. He won't disturb the Holy Office again.' He bowed his head obsequiously towards the Prior with his final words.

'Take good care of him, Brother Lambert. He's not of a great age and has always seemed robust until this recent trouble – it's most unlike him to be disruptive.'

Despite weariness my professional interest was aroused and I opened my mouth to enquire about Brother Joseph's ailment but the Warden moved in front of me and shook his head. 'Come, Doctor Somers,' he said, drawing me to the door.

As we re-entered the cloister my companion spoke again in a low voice. 'Our Infirmarian is immensely knowledgeable about herbal remedies. His physic garden would be the envy of any apothecary and all in the abbey admire his skill. Yet Heaven has not blessed him with an easy manner and his prickliness does not endear him to all his brethren. It would be uncharitable of me to suggest he might sometimes be driven by malice in his behaviour –

6

God forgive me for saying so – but I caution you to be wary if you have dealings with him.'

I thanked him for his advice but reflected sadly that even within the walls of a renowned abbey, among men committed to serve the Lord God in every aspect of their lives, human frailty was still evident. I wondered whether the enclosed nature of their existence encouraged some monks to cultivate perceived affronts with as much dedication as the Infirmarian probably devoted to tending his garden. At least, I comforted myself, I would not need to become involved in their squabbles but I was sufficiently clear-minded to know I would encounter other tensions in the Bishop's Palace, which I must learn to call Wolvesey Castle.

*****

Next morning I felt rested but still bleary when Brother Simon came after the office of Tierce to see me on my way. He escorted me in silence, passing between the Infirmary and the hall where crowds of pilgrims were assembling before they were admitted to the cathedral to pray near the relics of St. Swithun. In the angle of the wall there was a gate and outside it a workman was waiting: a nut-brown fellow with hair, tanned skin, jerkin and leather apron all much the same colour. The Warden introduced him as Master Ranken and his high-sounding name reminded me of the humbly born lad who had been baptised with similar pretention: Rendell, once my servant and now a soldier, an irrepressible and often outrageous force of nature, my assistant in so many adventures. The monk's next words drew me away from that recollection to one equally stressful.

'Ranken is our master carpenter, whose handiwork is to be admired in abbey and Bishop's castle alike.'

'My oldest friend, since boyhood, Thomas Chope, is a master carpenter,' I said without thinking this might seem improbable.

7

The craftsman raised an eyebrow and I felt bound to explain further. 'We grew up together in a noble household. I didn't come from distinguished stock. I was fortunate to receive an education.' Despite my awkwardness I had the wit not to identify the noble whom we served. My thoughts had strayed to how Thomas and his family were managing in their changed situation.

'Master Ranken will be your contact,' the Warden said. 'If you have news to report, as Prior Aulton requested, or if you believe we could assist you, speak to him. He is regularly at Wolvesey Castle.'

'Whole lot of panelling in the south-east tower there needs attention but I've also got repairs to the cathedral choirstalls to finish. I'll be bustling between the two.'

While he was speaking a groom had appeared leading a fine grey horse and he stopped beside us. Brother Simon took the reins and held them out to me. 'You should arrive at the Castle in fitting style. This good fellow will show you the way. On the instructions of the Abbot of Peterborough, the Prior is lending Cloudburst to you for as long as you need him. He no longer gallops with much enthusiasm but he's steady and well suited for a physician's use.'

I gaped. 'I don't know what to say. I've never had a horse to use as my own before.'

'Your physician's instruments and other possessions have already been sent to Wolvesey Castle.'

'But I was forced to leave them at...' I could not bring myself to speak the name of the manor I had held from the Marquis of Suffolk but which had been withdrawn from me as a mark of his displeasure when I was charged, unjustly, with murder.

'I gather the Abbot of Peterborough prevailed on your companion, when you were threatened with arrest, to fetch your belongings and he had them sent on.'

'Rendell. Of course.' I experienced a moment of panic. 'He hasn't followed me to Winchester?'

8

'No. I think he had other tasks to fulfil.'

'He did. I'm glad. He'll have gone to help his sister's family.'

'Here, take the reins. Cloudburst is yours to use.'

'I'm overwhelmed by such kindness.' I felt tears coming into my eyes and tried to blink them away but the Warden saved me further embarrassment by dismissing Master Ranken and giving me his blessing.

'I'd be happy to see you again, if God wills it,' he said. 'May the saints be with you in undertaking your commission.'

I mounted and, led by the groom, rode slowly round beside the city wall to enter the town. Then we made our way along narrow streets to the gate-house of an imposing castellated residence which many a warlike nobleman would have been proud to acknowledge as his bastion. It was intended to be intimidating, a symbol of secular power and heavenly might. I trembled as I crossed its portal.

*****

I was greeted courteously by the Cardinal's Chamberlain and was glad of the Prior's forethought when Cloudburst was led away by an attendant who complimented me on his appearance. I was escorted into the great hall in the eastern range where my brother physicians were waiting, if not exactly to welcome me, with curiosity and probable disdain. I bowed as I approached the pair and introduced myself to a rotund man with a sour expression and his taller, less obviously hostile colleague.

'This is Doctor Chauntley and I am Doctor Willison,' the tall man said. 'You've been sent to share your knowledge with us in treating his Grace, I'm told.'

I had considered how to reply to such an assumption, in the hope that my questioners were ignorant of my precise circumstances. 'I had the honour to make the

9

acquaintance of the Abbot of Peterborough,' I said, 'and he suggested I might assist your deliberations. The Cardinal is ailing, I understand.'

Doctor Chauntley snorted but his associate gave a thin smile. 'His Grace has been ill before and recovered but his condition recently gives us concern although a diagnosis is not straightforward. You are a young man. What experience have you had in the practice of medicine?'

This was another answer I had rehearsed. 'I've been physician to the Marquis of Suffolk's household for nearly three years. I studied at Oxford and hold a doctorate from the University of Padua.'

'Pah!' Doctor Chauntley did not disguise his feelings but Doctor Willison bit his lip without speaking and I decided that I must take the initiative.

'What are the Cardinal's symptoms?'

The plump physician looked annoyed but could scarcely refuse to share medical information with me. 'His bodily functions are disturbed and his urine is diseased. The prognosis is not promising. Naturally we are treating his symptoms and we have drawn up the Cardinal's horoscope to determine the best time to bleed him.'

He clamped his mouth shut but it was clear there was more to be explained so I waited and did not comment. After a pause Doctor Willison spoke, hugging his hands to his chest. 'It is his Grace's mind which is more severely troubled.'

'Possessed by demons,' Doctor Chauntley asserted. 'Satan will proclaim a great victory to carry the soul of so distinguished a churchman into Hell.

I watched as Doctor Willison suppressed a frown. 'The Cardinal's confessor has sought our help but it seems more likely he is the person best placed to sooth a distressed mind.'

'Are you describing the confused wits of an elderly man?' I asked. 'Or do I detect something more outlandish?'

'You are perceptive, Doctor Somers. Evil spirits plague him' Willison gave me an open smile and I was encouraged to pursue my questioning.

'Does his Grace confide the reasons for his distress to anyone?'

Doctor Chauntley chortled unpleasantly. 'Do you expect a Cardinal-Bishop, three times Chancellor of England, scion of the royal house, to share his reasoning with anyone other than his confessor? Demons have invaded his mind and distorted his judgement.'

'Come,' Doctor Willison said, 'the Cardinal is in his chapel. We can observe him from the gallery. You can make your own diagnosis.'

I followed my fellow physicians across the courtyard, into the Bishop's quarters and up some stairs onto a small internal balcony. Below us, spread-eagled on the steps of his oratory, the unmistakeable red-gowned figure lay crumpled, clutching a crucifix in his gnarled hands. I caught my breath.

I had encountered Henry Beaufort some six years previously when, alongside King Henry and Suffolk, he required me to infiltrate a conspiracy against the sovereign's life. I had gained a reputation for investigating crimes and my services were recommended to the King in all sincerity, although I had no enthusiasm for the honour. In consequence I did as I was bidden and nearly finished my life on the gallows for my pains, escaping into exile with the help of friends until at long last I received a pardon. The injustice and ingratitude of the dignitaries I had served then was closely replicated by the wrongful accusation made against me in St. Edmundsbury only a week earlier and I had little hope of cheating the hangman's rope a second time. I stared at the Cardinal and felt nothing but distaste for the pathetic figure.

With an unexpectedly rapid movement the suppliant in front of the altar rose to his feet and rushed towards the door of the chapel, while Doctor Willison led Chauntley and me in a scamper down the stairs to intercept him. He turned on us with blazing eyes, although I did not think he recognised us as physicians, and he waved his arms above his head.

'Why should I die?' he shouted in a frenzy. 'Why cannot my riches buy me release from Death? How is it I must bow to his dictates, I who have yielded to no rival and bent the knee to no enemy? Puny men die. I will not acknowledge Death!'

I exchanged appalled glances with Doctor Willison but Chauntley regarded me smugly. 'Behold your patient, Doctor Somers,' he said. 'We've done our best to soothe body and mind but with scant success. You are welcome to expend your wisdom and learning on the case. I suggest you spend an hour or so with the worthy gentleman so you may understand his complaints. We shall not interrupt your consultation. In here, your Grace, this eminent doctor of medicine will advise you how to evade the tentacles death has extended to entrap you.'

Chauntley flung open the door of a small vestry and propelled the raving but frail Cardinal inside. Then he pulled my arm so that I lurched forward and I felt his foot against my backside as I tumbled after the old man. The door slammed behind me and I could hear Chauntley laughing but my attention was fixed on the grotesque antagonist crouched in front of me brandishing a solid silver candlestick.

'So you have come for me, have you, Death?' he screamed. 'I know who you are and I am not ready to follow you. You shall not carry me away!'

Chapter 2

'Your Grace, I beg you to be calm. I am no threat to you. I'm a physician, come to see if I can ease your discomfort.' I manoeuvred myself beside a rack of vestments, hoping I could duck behind it if the Cardinal became violent.

'Lies. Lies! I know you can assume many shapes. I'm not fooled by your tricks. You came last night, half-naked and starving, like a chained man in a cell. Who were you then? Which of those I imprisoned did you pretend to be? I'll smash your skull; then you'll need to find another guise but I shall know you, however you are garbed. I will not yield to your blandishments.'

He took a step forward, cackling, and flourished the candlestick but his arm was trembling with the weight. Understanding the nature of his affliction, I stood my ground. 'Those you have punished in the past are tormenting you? Your mind is conjuring their likeness, your Grace, but they are not real.'

'You have sent them, Death. They are all in your domain. The French girl, the witch, you've summoned her from the bottom-most pit of Hell, and she accuses me.'

'If Joan, the Maid, is in Hell, your Grace, at the Lord God's decree, how can you be held guilty? If she has merited the torments of Hell, surely your judgement on her would have been justified?'

He could not comprehend my attempt at logic and his voice rose to a screech while he clutched his stomach. 'I sent her to the stake in Rouen– and I sentenced others to similar fates. Now you rouse them against me. They plague me every hour, waking and sleeping.'

'You need good dreamless rest to strengthen you and soothe your mind. I can prescribe a draught to help you.'

'To stupefy me so you can carry me away? Never!'

His fury increased but he staggered as he tried to lift the candlestick a second time so I moved forward to take it from him and lead him to the window-bench. I was

13

pleased to resume my natural role. 'Are you in pain, your Grace? Is your belly troubling you?'

He stared at me blankly for a moment. 'I have seen you before,' he said. 'Who are you?'

'My name is Doctor Somers. Your memory is robust if you can remember me. It was many years ago you encountered me. I was a very young man.'

'A cunning ploy to masquerade as a doctor.' He seemed content with this reflection and smiled to himself before gripping my sleeve. 'Can't we do business, physician? I'm ready to barter. I'll give you half my wealth if you will let me be: for a year or two – five years, perhaps. It's far too soon for me to leave my duties. The King and the young Queen need my guidance.' His tone had become wheedling.

I was unclear in what capacity he was seeking to bribe me, whether as a humble medical man or the reaper of souls, but I was glad he had become calmer. 'I can't defy Heaven by adding an hour to your allotted life, your Grace, but I can try to make your pain more bearable.'

He closed his eyes but quickly opened them again and they were panic-stricken. 'They say my nephew, Humphrey of Gloucester is dead.'

I hoped it would it give him comfort to know he no longer had to confront the taunts of his lifelong enemy. 'It's true, your Grace, he died a week ago.'

'How can you be sure?'

'I stood by his deathbed...' I faltered, realising the stupid error I had made, as Beaufort rose majestically to his feet.

He spoke with the utmost scorn. 'You have betrayed yourself, Death. You took Gloucester and now you seek to take me: two of the greatest in the land. How did you contrive Duke Humphrey's demise? Was he poisoned or smothered? At whose command did you slaughter him?'

I shivered at his question for it had suited Suffolk to let me be accused of asphyxiating the Duke to avert any

14

suspicion falling on him, although in fact no human agency had ended Gloucester's life. 'No, your Grace, he suffered a seizure. The Lord God took him when it was time for him to go to his rest.'

'Cunning,' the Cardinal said with a nod of approval. 'No human agency but Death's victory.' Then, abruptly, he howled with distress. 'So Gloucester is waiting for me in your dominion. There was ill will between us and there are scores to be settled. But I will not meet him. I will not.'

With a burst of frantic energy he leapt to his feet, seizing the candlestick and hurled it at my head. I flung myself to the side and it whistled past my ear to thud against the panelling but, to my joy, the crash alerted someone outside the vestry and the door creaked open. A short white-faced man regarded the scene with horror before dropping to his knees in front of the Cardinal.

'Harum-scarum, hocus pocus, what's this?' His voice was melodious and he looked at the old man with affection. 'Your Grace is overwrought. We'll soon put that right. I've come to play for you. Let's go into the chapel.'

Beaufort took hold of the newcomer's shoulders. 'See here, Robert, Death has come for me but I won't go with him. He's taken Gloucester. He impersonates a physician but he's an imposter. Drive him away with your holy music.'

'This isn't Death, your Grace. This is the new leech come to see if he can do you good. Couldn't do worse than the two you've already got, could he?' He stood and held out his hand to me. 'Robert Bygbroke, doctor: priest, organist and bringer of quietude to unruly spirits. Call me Robert.'

I grasped his hand. 'I'm Harry Somers. Your skills are urgently needed. I'd be glad to listen to your playing but my presence may undo the good it offers the Cardinal.'

Bygbroke turned back to his master and helped him to his feet. 'See, your Grace, Doctor Somers doesn't question the efficacy of music. That's wisdom rare in a physician. Don't shilly-shally now.' He bundled the

Cardinal through the door and spoke over his shoulder to me. 'If you stand in the vestibule, Doctor Somers, you'll hear well enough. It's not a big instrument but it has a rich tone. I've a fellow ready to pump the bellows and I'll play until his Grace's head is nodding. Join me at dinner. We'll share a jar of wine.'

I had heard pipe organs played in churches in England, France and Italy, but I had never encountered the instrument's versatility which Robert Bygbroke demonstrated in his recital. I sat on the stone floor of the lobby, leaning against the wall, captivated by the power of the music, letting it sweep over me and lift my spirits, freeing them in some magical way from much of the tension I had felt since I left St. Edmundsbury. I was profoundly shaken and my face was damp with tears I could not control but the experience gave me renewed hope that I still had a purpose in the world. For the first time it seemed possible that, although I had lost the joyful prospects I nurtured for so short a time, I might yet derive satisfaction from the practice of my craft in the service of others.

*****

The Cardinal's body-servant confirmed that, when his master had been sedated by the organist's music, he would be able to administer the posset I prepared with ingredients from the shelves of the physicians' room. The weary man expressed his gratitude if it would enable them both to sleep peacefully through the night, as he had been required to soothe his master during the early hours for the past two weeks.

Inevitably my brother physicians were dismissive of my actions and, as we entered the Great Hall for dinner, Doctor Chauntley ridiculed any attempt to bring our patient relief.

'There are dark deeds in his past without a doubt and it's not for us to interpose our medicine between him and his damnation. It's the Cardinal's confessor who carries the burden of preparing his soul for Heaven's judgement and he has advised us to close our ears to Beaufort's ranting. No piffling potion can ease a soul cursed to perdition.'

I was unwilling to acquiesce in this defeatist counsel. 'Certainly the Cardinal's soul is not our concern but it's our duty to treat his body. He has some serious malady of the guts, in my opinion, and his pain is likely to increase. We should relieve his physical suffering as much as we can.'

'A thankless task in my estimation,' Doctor Willison said, 'but I won't interfere. Do as you think best, Somers.'

Chauntley puffed out his cheeks and blew, without making further comment, striding away to take his place at table.

I had intended to join the physicians at the meal but at that moment the Reverend Robert Bygbroke appeared at my elbow, grinning broadly. 'Don't dilly-dally, doctor. Sit over here with me. Priest I may be but I'll be better company than those charlatans and there are questions I want to put to you.'

I followed him to his chosen trestle, amused by his frequent use of alliterative phrases with their rhythmic, almost musical, qualities, and I took a place at his side. He seized a hunk of bread and crumbled it on his trencher, all the time looking at me sideways.

'Tittle-tattle, that's what this is about. What you can tell me.'

'I don't understand.'

'I saw you arrive this morning. One of the grooms from the abbey escorted you. Did you stay in the guest-house there?'

'Just one night. I'd had a hard ride and it was late to arrive at the castle.'

'Did you meet Prior Aulton?'

'Briefly. He made me welcome.'

'He would, he's a good man. He didn't mention me, I suppose?' I shook my head and the organist gave a nervous laugh. 'No, of course, he wouldn't. My thinking's higgledy-piggledy. Did he say anything about the Cardinal?'

I was cautious in answering this question, uncomfortable about where I was being led, although it seemed innocuous. 'He was concerned to know how ill his Grace was.'

My words excited Bygbroke. 'Did he say why? Can you remember what he said?'

'Something like "there might be measures I need to take". He didn't want to act prematurely.'

My companion sighed and gulped his wine. 'You give me hope, Doctor, but you look perplexed. You don't know of course that I belong to the abbey although I'm a secular priest, not a monk. Nearly twenty years ago I was appointed organist and choirmaster there. I loved that great organ in the north transept gallery, though it was cumbrous to play and needed all my skill. The sound reverberated through the cathedral and you could hear it across the cloister outside. I loved training the choir too – we don't have one here – and I trained the choristers with fervour, men and boys as well, from the school. But the Cardinal would have me come to Wolvesey Castle, to play for him and not the monks. I had no choice, willy-nilly, he would have me.'

'How long ago was that?'

'Must be ten years. Mind you, I've been rewarded, done well out of it. I've travelled with the Cardinal, played other fine organs and I'm fond of the old tyrant. I call him that to his face – no one else does. But if he goes to his rest, I should like to return to the abbey and play that glorious instrument again: four times as many pipes as the one in the chapel here.'

'You're worried you'd be kept to serve the next Bishop?'

'After so long it might be assumed I belonged here. Then again, the Prior could ask for me to return. His request could be granted but he might not think to ask. He might believe I wanted to stay here and he'll have installed another organist to play at the cathedral years ago.' Bybroke gave a sob and his face was contorted by sadness.

I was coming to understand how poor communications between abbey and Bishop's Palace must be. 'I could let Prior Aulton know how you feel,' I said. 'I could get a message to him.'

The organist trembled and pressed his hands together. 'You will do this for me?'

'Certainly, but in return I'd like you to tell me more about the Cardinal's condition. Everyone's distracted by the confusion of his mind and horrified by his attempt to defy death but I suspect he has some grave disease in his guts and he senses it's mortal.'

'You're shrewder than those other make-weight quacks. He's had the collywobbles for months but they're getting much worse. He tries to hide it but he's in agony sometimes.'

'I thought as much. We're helpless to prevent his deterioration. We have no knowledge how to correct the rotting of his innards. All we can do is try to relieve his pain and you've already discovered half the prescription: music and sleeping draughts offer the best hope.'

'You don't give him long to live?'

'Impossible to tell but I'd guess a matter of weeks.'

'So you'll get that message to the Prior?'

I gave my assurance and our conversation drifted on to other topics but, while I was happy to offer help in securing Bygbroke's future, I was apprehensive about my own prospects if my patient's survival was to be as short-lived as I feared. In no way did I belong to Wolvesey Castle or the abbey and, once I left the protection of the church, I would be in danger of arrest by the King's officers or Suffolk's underlings. The trumped up charge against me could be revived.

*****

I was gratified to learn that my potion helped the Cardinal sleep more soundly and he appeared a little calmer in the morning. Grudgingly my fellow physicians agreed I should continue to administer the mixture but I appreciated it was only a palliative which could not lessen the worst of his mania. At least my modest achievement gave me a degree of credibility with my colleagues and I noticed that they were content to absent themselves from Wolvesey Castle, from time to time, leaving me to bear the brunt of attendance by the sickbed. I gathered from Robert Bygbroke that when they were in residence at Winchester both Chauntley and Willison were accustomed to undertake business outside the palace walls and I imagined they supplemented their incomes by attending other patients.

A few days later I was accosted near the gate-house by Ranken, marshalling a group of carpenters who were carrying planks towards the south-east tower. I gave him a sealed note I had written to the Prior and asked casually for any news from the abbey. He screwed his wrinkled face into a dolorous expression.

'Loaded with misery they are. You can tell the nature of their silence is different: full of grief and a bit spiteful. They buried Brother Joseph at first light this morning.'

'I'm sorry. His illness was quite sudden, wasn't it?'

'Not just sudden but peculiar, I'd say.'

'He had some sort of seizure, I suppose.'

'In the chancel or the Infirmary, that's what some are asking.'

'Whatever do you mean?'

'There's some with no good word to say for Brother Lambert, the Infirmarian. Thinks too well of his skill with herbs, that's what they say.'

'Even the most experienced apothecary can misjudge the dosage when he's treating a very weak man. It doesn't mean there was a malicious intent if his remedies failed to assist the invalid or hastened his inevitable end.'

'You don't know Brother Lambert.'

Ranken's aspersions were brought to a halt because the Chamberlain appeared and hurried the carpenters on their way to the furthermost tower where they were working. The reason for his impatience quickly became apparent when I heard the by-now familiar roar of my demented patient pursued anew by his demons, as the Cardinal staggered into the courtyard, clawing at his mantle.

'It isn't right that I should die! I am still needed. There's more for me to do. All my riches, I offer. I will buy exemption. It must be granted. Listen to me! Take my offer. Ah! Ah!'

I ran forward as Henry Beaufort subsided to his knees and spewed over the ground. His face was ghastly white and he writhed, screaming invocations to Death to spare him and take his treasure instead. A bevy of people came rushing from hall and kitchen, Robert Bygbroke among them, throwing on his cassock, over unlaced shirt and hose as he ran.

'Help him to the chapel,' he called. 'I'll play for him,' but he recoiled when he saw the filth dribbling down the Cardinal's robe.

'He's too weak,' I said. 'His condition has deteriorated. He must go to his bed. He'll struggle but he hasn't the strength to stand.' I knelt beside him and used my hanging sleeve to wipe his mouth as noxious bile dribbled from his lips.

Doctors Willison and Chauntley strode from the hall to take charge of the situation, endorsing my decision that their patient should be taken to his bed but insisting, despite my protests, he must then be bled. Unscrupulous, vengeful and cruel Beaufort had been throughout his life but I could not wish on him the additional torments he suffered at their hands now he was in his dotage and defenceless against useless interventions. For their part, it seemed to me they revelled in the opportunity to impose treatment with which I disagreed.

Even more disturbing was Willison's suggestion that more extreme measures might be attempted. 'If evil spirits have entered his head,' he said, 'there is a means to evacuate them. The ancients used it to create a flue for the vile humours to escape.'

'You mean trepanation?' Chauntley scoffed. 'You'd enjoy an opportunity to drill through a skull, wouldn't you? But you daren't try the procedure on the Cardinal. If he died, they'd hang you from the rafters and rip your guts apart.'

Willison raised his hands in surrender. 'True enough. But I'd like to see it done.'

I shuddered at the thought but held my tongue.

His collapse in the courtyard denoted a crisis in the Cardinal's malady but he did not die for several days and, even in extremis, he sometimes roused himself to struggle from his bed and attempt to buy off the invisible figure of Death who was so real to him. It was a gruelling time for all members of his household but most of them, I suspected, were cheered by the knowledge that soon they would be free forever from his exigencies, serving a newly consecrated Bishop from whom they might gain preferment – an outlook not available to me.

My despondency was intensified when, after forty-eight hours of watching by Beaufort's bedside, I was summoned from the sick-chamber because a caller at the gate-house had asked to see me. It seemed improbable that anyone I knew could have followed me to Winchester but, as I hurried across the courtyard, I dared to hope that Rendell or possibly Thomas might have come to bring me news and perhaps to help me escape my enemies after the Cardinal's death. Instead, as I entered the guardroom where the visitor was waiting, I felt nauseous at the sight of the elegantly dressed merchant who greeted me with an ironic bow.

Stephen Boice was a man I had good reason to detest. He had harmed me and those I loved and he was a close associate of the unprincipled villain responsible for the unjust accusations against me. I was tempted to turn my back and walk away but the surprise of seeing him made me hesitate.

'Doctor Somers, how gratifying to find you here. The Cardinal hasn't long to live, I imagine, but he could do no better than to enjoy your ministrations during his final hours. I am on my way to embark for Normandy and contrived to travel through Winchester so that I might call on you.'

'It will hardly surprise you that I do not wish to see you. Excuse me.'

'Then you will miss my news about your delightful lady.'

His words tore into me but they prevented my departure, as of course they were intended to do.

'That's better, Harry.' He seated himself on a bench and crossed his legs. 'I remained in the county of Suffolk after the Duke of Gloucester's death and, as you know, I have a network of acquaintances who kept me well informed of events in the neighbourhood. Your lady reached sanctuary safely and a week ago, just before I set out for the south, she was taken on board a vessel bound for France. The weather has been clement so we may assume she's arrived unscathed back in her own country, ready to marry the noble Count to whom she has pledged her hand.'

'I pray the Lord God this is true,' I said. 'Whatever else you have come to say, I give you thanks for that information.'

'Perceptive as ever, Harry. You appreciate I have not come solely to revive your lust with news of your whore. Don't pull that indignant face. She lay with you out of wedlock, did she not? Be that as it may, it's not why I've come. I'm on my way to join my good-brother, Gilbert Iffley, who is in Rouen. He has written to me and he sends you greetings.'

'That's a matter of no interest to me, Master Boice. Baron Glasbury has done me great wrong and I want no further dealings with him.'

The merchant disregarded my protest. 'Gilbert is now a valued follower of Duke Richard of York, who was the King's Lieutenant-General in Normandy. York was expecting to be re-appointed to that high office when his term expired but now Edward Beaufort, newly created Duke of Somerset, has been appointed in his place. Gilbert has been sent to disperse the household York left in Rouen and I am to help him. We are become trusted companions of Duke Richard. Does that surprise you?'

'Not in the least.' I could not keep the anger from my voice. 'Iffley acted as go-between for Gloucester with his cousin of York and plotted to promote their interests with no regard for anyone in their path.'

'Crudely put, Doctor Somers, but I concede there's an element of truth in it.' Boice gave a supercilious smile. 'Gilbert is most anxious that you should join York's circle. He has a high regard for your investigative skills and would happily let bygones be bygones if you would throw in your lot with him.'

'He must be mad if he thinks I would do that.'

'Don't be too hasty, Harry.'

'I don't want to hear any more. I'm needed here as a physician.'

'But for how long? And where will you go when Beaufort dies? You may rest assured that the Marquis of Suffolk knows where to find you when you no longer have the specious excuse of attending the Cardinal's sickbed.'

I understood this was a threat. 'And if I was fool enough to accept Iffley's invitation?'

Boice's smile became unctuous. 'Then, my dear fellow, you will be escorted with the utmost speed and security to cross the Narrow Sea, as I shall shortly do, and your arrival in Rouen will be celebrated. Despite this setback to his hopes in Normandy, the prospects for York's supporters are infinite.'

'I understand your message,' I said, 'but have nothing to say.'

'You won't have long to make up your mind, Harry, once Beaufort is dead. If you come to your senses, when that happens, send a message to Master Brill, cordwainer, by the market steps in Southampton. He will see that you are whisked to safety before Suffolk has any inkling that you are at his mercy.'

I took the paper bearing Master Brill's name, which Boice held out, and was relieved to watch him leave the gate-house. Our meeting had been distasteful but, paradoxically, it confirmed me in the risky course of action I had been pondering. To act with openness and honesty was rash indeed in a world where great men jostled for position and their acolytes boosted them with cunning and corruption; yet it was my choice. I might be signing my death warrant by my action but later that evening I penned my letter to William de la Pole, Marquis of Suffolk, preeminent counsellor to King Henry, Sixth of that name.

My Lord Marquis, I beg you to read my humble petition. You know well the circumstances in which I was sent, an innocent bystander, to observe the death throes of Humphrey of Gloucester but then became an object of suspicion. I know that when wicked and jealous men, looking to foment dissent among the King's advisers, accused me of murder, their aim was to blacken your name, for I was physician to your household and they could claim you were complicit in my alleged misdeeds. Accordingly I understand why it was necessary for you to deflect their base rumours by disowning me, thus placing me in peril of my life, although I was privileged to receive the protection of Holy Church. Since then I have attended his Grace, Cardinal Beaufort, as requested, but his end is drawing near so my future becomes uncertain. I have no wish to go into exile again, as I was once forced to do, and

25

I have refused to join those who have no love for your interests. All I seek now, my lord, is to serve humbly in my profession in some quiet town far from the seat of power and the activities of great men. I swear I shall never seek to involve myself again in affairs of state. I know you to be a just man and I ask you to consider my predicament and grant your clemency. When the Cardinal is gone you will be the King's only trusted adviser and your word alone would be my defence. I beg you therefore to judge me with equity and grant my request to serve out my days without hindrance in the modest capacity I have described.

If your back still troubles you, my lord, there is a jar of the ointment, which gave you relief when I applied it, in my old room at your London house. It is labelled "embrocation". You will always have my loyalty. I remain your faithful servant, Harry Somers.

I read it through and cringed at the grovelling tone but deemed it necessary if I was to have any chance of success. I wondered whether to refer to the offence I had given to Queen Margaret but decided this would be futile. Suffolk knew everything and he must determine my fate. So I gave my letter to one of the messengers who took news every day from Wolvesey Castle to the court and returned to my station beside the dying man's bed.

*****

When the final hours came, Beaufort was no calmer than he had been for weeks past, struggling from his bed to scream defiance and plead for his life while squirming with the agony which churned in his belly. It was clear to me that some rotting disease was devouring him from inside although Doctor Chauntley continued to insist his pain was caused by avenging demons which had colonised his guts. In practice our explanations made no difference to his suffering and we had no means to combat its extremity. It was a gruesome, alarming experience to watch as, despite his furious struggle, the Cardinal eventually expired after a torrent of abuse against rapacious Death, his servants, his physicians and probably his God. Even his confessor did not demur when Chauntley declared that unquestionably the wretch had gone straight to Hell.

In due course we filed from the room and my fellow physicians lost no time in turning their attention to me, as I expected. Perhaps surprisingly it was Doctor Willison who spoke first.

'You'll be on your way, now, Doctor Somers. You've no function here while we wait for the election of the next Bishop. Chauntley and I have our own business to pursue in the meantime. There's no guarantee the new man will want two physicians in his household, let alone three; indeed, he may bring his own doctor with him. You'd best pack your things and be off at dawn.'

It was far too soon to hope for a reply from Suffolk and I had nowhere to go but it would be pointless to argue. I was sensitive to the possibility that my colleagues might denigrate my care for the Cardinal publicly and I could ill afford to be blamed for another death. Acquiescence was my best defence against their malice so I ordered that my horse be ready for an early departure in the morning. Then I sought out Robert Bygbroke to explain my position and share my anxieties with him.

'Go to the abbey helter-skelter,' he said. 'They'll offer hospitality for as long as you want. If the Marquis's reply comes here, I'll see it sent on safely and perhaps you'd remind Prior Aulton of my hope to return to the cathedral. I'd be glad to find our paths crossing again. I've enjoyed your company and you'll have a better carousal with me than a parcel of monks will offer.'

I knew what he suggested was the best solution but I was hesitant about imposing myself on the abbey's generosity without warning and did not share the organist's optimism about the length of time the monks might be prepared to shelter me. Nevertheless I set my

27

worries aside while I joined him in a farewell flagon of ale and my last evening at Wolvesey Castle passed in a pleasing haze.

Robert Bygbroke came to see me off in the morning and I was touched by his concern for me when there was so much uncertainty about his own future. He told me it could be weeks before the Chapter elected a new Abbot and received the King's agreement to their choice, who would also become Bishop. He would be forced to rest in limbo until his place of employment could be resolved. I wished him well and rode through gate-house slowly, sorry to be leaving the haven which had given me respite from my personal troubles for so short a time. Then I became aware of a squat brown figure waiting in the roadway and hailed Master Ranken with surprise.

'Come to fetch you, Doctor, I have,' he said. 'We've heard the Cardinal's gone to his rest so the Warden's hoping you'll come to the abbey. He wants you there. He thinks you may be able to help.'

'I'll be glad to come.' I grinned with pleasure. 'In what way can I help?'

'Warden'll tell you,' Ranken said darkly. 'He has questions you could answer.' His voice fell to a whisper. 'It's not my place to say and I'd rather you didn't let on that I have, but my guess is he believes Brother Joseph was murdered.'

When I arrived at the abbey I was told Prior Aulton wished to see me immediately and I was hustled across the outer court to his house. In view of what Ranken had disclosed, I was not surprised to find Brother Simon, the Warden of the Works, was with him, looking agitated, but his superior was determined to observe the courtesies before introducing a potentially tendentious subject.

'You are welcome, Doctor Somers,' he said, 'and I was grateful to receive the message you sent me from Wolvesey Castle. I rejoice that the Reverend Robert Bygbroke wishes to return to his post as organist at the cathedral. As soon as we have elected the new Abbot I will make my representations to enable this to happen.' He paused and drew breath. 'I understand the Cardinal was sadly afflicted in his last days.'

I was interested the Prior knew this but reflected that Ranken's workmen had eyes and ears and were not inhibited from using their tongues when they left the Bishop's Palace. 'It was not a peaceful end, Reverend Father. His physicians did what they could to moderate his suffering but his mind was tormented.'

'His chantry is prepared in the retro-choir of the cathedral and we are saying Masses for the repose of his soul. The Chapter will convene in two days to consider the choice of his successor.' He walked across the room and stood by the window which faced towards the pilgrims' hall and the infirmary. 'You have had a thankless task since you came to Winchester, Doctor Somers.'

'Any physician is used to attending deathbeds.'

'Quite so but I believe you have other talents, tried and tested, above and beyond the practice of medicine. The Abbot of Peterborough has informed me how you assisted the Superior of his daughter house in Stamford by making certain investigations.'

'The Prioress of St. Michael's,' I said and could not supress my smile. 'I was able to help her by establishing

29

the whereabouts of a child who had been taken from the care of the nuns.' I hoped that was all Prior Aulton knew for I had also kept the reverend lady supplied with gossip from the court which she used to gain advantage and seek donations for her convent.

'A redoubtable woman, I understand. Have you met her?'

'I have. She is terrifying.'

The Prior threw back his head and laughed. 'So I've heard. Her reputation makes it the more impressive that she recommends your services – not merely as a physician but as investigator.'

Brother Simon had been fidgeting during this exchange but at the Prior's last words he became alert. 'We need your help,' he said.

'The Warden is inclined to impatience,' the Prior said with an indulgent nod towards the monk. 'It's to be hoped that all we need from you is the answer to one question – and it is of a medical nature. That may lay the Warden's wild imaginings to rest.'

'I'll do my best.' I felt uncomfortable caught between them but I recognised that we were coming to the purpose of this meeting.

'Our good Brother Joseph had served the abbey for many years as Almoner. It's my assessment he was taken from us in God's good time but there are circumstances which worry the Warden and some of his brethren. When the fit took him, while attending our holy service, he cried out angrily in a way that was most uncharacteristic.'

The Warden could restrain himself no longer.' What we want to know, Doctor Somers, is whether you are aware of a poison which does not seem to cause digestive contortions but brings about a seizure and throws the victim into a coma from which he never recovers.'

I thought carefully and did not reply at once. 'I have come across the effects of a dark deed when a compound of yew bark was used to kill a man by provoking a seizure. The difference, as I understand it, is that Brother

Joseph lingered on for a day or two whereas the unfortunate man in the other case died almost instantly.'

'Could the strength of the dose account for the difference?' The Warden sounded excited. 'Is it easy to formulate a lethal potion with yew bark?'

'It's possible a weaker dosage would take longer to prove fatal. A capable apothecary might know about such things.'

'Or an Infirmarian?'

'Brother Simon, I have counselled you not to put your malevolent fancies into words.' The Prior's tone was severe. 'There is absolutely no evidence that Brother Lambert had given the Almoner any potion until after the poor man's seizure. You must not suggest the Infirmarian had any culpable part in his death. You are allowing your uncharitable dislike of our brother to run away with you.'

The Warden bowed his head. 'I ask pardon, Reverend Father. But Doctor Somers should know that the Almoner spoke strangely as he collapsed. Those next to him in the monks' choir heard him clearly and it seems to me his words had significance.'

The Prior sighed. 'Very well. Tell Doctor Somers what he said although I suspect it was merely the fit unravelling his wits.'

The Warden lowered his voice as if he was pronouncing holy words. '"The hippocras": that's what he said. "The hippocras."'

'Is he likely to have drunk hippocras before the service?' It seemed to me improbable.

'In the refectory we drink our wine unflavoured by spices.'

'So if indeed he'd drunk hippocras it would have been somewhere else?'

'Such a thing would be irregular and reprehensible.' The Prior was irritated. 'It's unimaginable that Brother Joseph imbibed such a drink from an irregular source. It was merely the weird working of his

31

afflicted mind which brought the word to his mouth as the fit convulsed him.'

'It may be so,' I said. 'Have the brothers been questioned to see if anyone is aware that hippocras might be available somewhere?'

No,' the Prior answered. 'I am unwilling to give substance to this ridiculous notion. Doctor Somers has answered your question, Warden. The circumstances of Brother Joseph's death do not suggest his seizure was brought about by man's evil but by Heaven's will. You must let this rest now. That is my determination and I require your obedience to it.'

Brother Simon dropped to his knees. 'I obey,' he said huskily.

The Prior turned to me. 'Thank you for your help, Doctor. I know we can rely on your discretion to keep silence on this matter. You are welcome to stay at the abbey as long as you wish.'

That was a precious concession and I left the Prior's house with a feeling of relief but Brother Simon, at my side, was restive. We walked in silence until we reached the guesthouse when he took my arm and whispered in my ear. 'That was not what you said. The Prior read more into your words than was justified. You did not deny that the Almoner's death could have been induced by a potion, did you?'

I shrugged. 'It's beyond our knowledge or discernment to be certain.'

He looked at me straight in the eyes. 'So there is more to discover. I am sworn to obey my superior but you gave no promise to desist from enquiries. I beg you, Doctor Somers, do what is necessary to find out the truth.'

*****

When I roused myself next morning I realised there was an unusual bustle in the cloister and shortly afterwards I was requested to call on the Prior without delay. I hurried to his lodging and as I passed its entrance I was intrigued to see the Chapter House thronged with monks silently gesticulating to each other. I was admitted to the Prior's parlour and found him alone, robed in his formal vestments, his brow furrowed, clasping a scroll of parchment in his hand. For a dreadful moment I feared he had received a royal command to surrender my person to the officers of state.

'Doctor Somers, you are acquainted with the royal court. Can you confirm this is King Henry's seal?'

I was astonished but had no difficulty in complying with his wish as I had seen the King's seal on several occasions. 'It is, Reverend Father.'

'I should not have doubted but the contents are so unexpected, I needed to be sure. I am instructed, as is the Chapter, to elect William Waynflete as Abbot and Bishop.'

The name meant nothing to me and I repeated it blankly.

'He is currently Provost of the King's new foundation at Eton but previously he held a similar position at the College, here in Winchester. He's a worthy man and has clearly won the King's favour for his success in financing the buildings at Eton but I have to admit...' His voice tailed away in embarrassment and I finished his sentence for him.

'You wouldn't have considered him a candidate for the Abbacy?'

'May the Lord forgive me, no. It isn't usual for the King to be so prescriptive. Of course I haven't been involved in an election as Prior but I believe there are typically exchanges between the King and the Chapter before a mutually acceptable candidate is chosen. This letter tells me Waynflete has already been given custody of the temporalities. Our agreement is a bagatelle, taken for granted, compelled on our obedience to the King.'

'Provost Waynflete has obviously established an enviable reputation for his work at Eton.'

'He has adroitly ingratiated himself with our virtuous King.' The Prior shook his head as if repudiating what he had just said. 'I must compose myself to meet the Chapter. You will not repeat what you have heard, Doctor Somers?'

I gave him my pledge and felt sorry for him as he set off to confront his brothers with the unwelcome news. I speculated that men who spent most of their lives in silence would prove voluble when released from constraint to express their views on this infringement of convention.

I borrowed a manuscript of St. Augustine's treatises from the abbey's library and sat in the cloister to read it, observing how the monks scurried from the Chapter House, whenever it was the appointed time for a service in the church, with eyes downcast but heightened colour in their cheeks. I inferred that their debate was heated and their displeasure festering so I was not surprised when their deliberations extended into a second day and my solitude was undisturbed.

There were no other visitors in the guesthouse and, left to myself, my comportment was as silent and studious as that of a tonsured theologian. The peaceful routine was welcome to me and I began to wonder whether this was the way I should spend the remainder of my life, shut away from the hazards and attractions of the outside world. It offered a means to escape the malevolence which threatened my safety and I had no qualms about dedicating myself to a future of celibacy. The malicious fluke of fortune which deprived me of the woman I loved and was to have married had left me numbed and I doubted I would experience temptations of the flesh again.

I was indulging these placid thoughts in the forenoon of the second day when my reverie was shattered by a russet coloured figure hurtling into the cloister from the outer court. As soon as he saw me Master Ranken threw his arms in the air in a gesture of relief and propelled himself to my side. In the absence of the monks, he clearly felt free to break the rule of silence.

34

'Thank the Lord, Doctor, you're here. Will you come? One of my apprentices has fallen from a ladder. He's likely broken his leg.'

Even in my moments of quiet contemplation I had no wish to abandon my professional role and I set aside my book to follow the carpenter out of the abbey precincts and through the South Gate of the town. A short distance along the street beyond the wall, beside a much grander edifice, stood a low building with a sloping roof and two ladders propped against it. At the foot of one ladder a cluster of workmen surrounded a lad who lay crumpled on the ground. The scene reminded me horribly of the manner in which I sustained an injury in boyhood resulting in the limp I have always had since then.

I examined the injured youth and quickly confirmed his master's diagnosis. 'He's broken his ankle. It's a clean break. He's lucky it's no worse. Is there a bone-setter in the town?'

Ranken shook his head. 'Not since old Panton died. He would have done it. Couldn't you?'

'I'll do my best,' I said. 'I've managed before. Get me a rigid lath of wood and stout binding. Don't be afraid, lad. Young bones mend well and it's a simple fracture. You'll be up on your feet again before long.'

Ranken despatched men to fetch the materials I needed and while we waited the cathedral bell started to ring. I assumed it indicated the time for the next service but the master carpenter winked at me. 'Reckon they've chosen the next Abbot and Bishop – just as instructed. Bit galling for Prior Aulton, if you ask me.' I could not disagree.

I completed my work as gently as I could but the boy continued to moan while I handled his leg and when his comrades lifted him to return to their lodgings he screamed in pain. I turned to Ranken. 'Is here an apothecary who could supply primrose and chamomile – or some other herb to deaden the throbbing?

'Up beyond the abbey, near the market cross, there's a fellow dispenses remedies but you'd best ask the Infirmarian for something from his garden. It'd be quicker.'

I opened my mouth to protest that I was uncomfortable at the idea of seeking Brother Lambert's help when I realised that this would give me an opportunity to speak to him in a professional capacity, without any suggestion I was investigating accusations against him. Accordingly I hurried back through the South Gate and, on entering the abbey, met the Infirmarian, returning from the Chapter House, at the entrance to his domain. I ignored his frown when I accosted him and made my request without enquiring as to the outcome of the Chapter's deliberations.

'My remedies are for the monks,' he said as I followed him through his well-stocked garden. 'I have no remit to serve townsfolk.'

'Didn't Our Lord accede to a request for crumbs from the master's table? The injured apprentice and his colleagues carry out work for the abbey. I ask for your charity towards the boy.'

The Infirmarian's lip curled and he replied with sarcasm. 'Oh, wise physician, to seek the help of a humble Benedictine brother. How you must rue the necessity.'

I did not rise to his provocation but kept my eyes steady on his face until at length he shrugged. 'I'll give you a mixture of my own devising based on a smidgen of belladonna. It's of proven value in dulling the pain of injury.'

This was a test set for me. Belladonna in tiny doses could alleviate pain effectively but in a more concentrated form it would kill. I feared he would give me a concoction to harm my patient but I was anxious to secure Brother Lambert's trust. 'I should be greatly obliged to you but perhaps you would allow me to sample the mixture first to satisfy myself it is suitable,' I said.

'You're bold. What if I intend to prepare something like tainted hippocras so that you may bear the blame for the boy's death?'

The back of my neck tingled with apprehension at his reference to hippocras but, recognising this was intended to goad me, I stayed calm. 'Medical men should rely on each other's integrity. Besides, I think it unlikely you murdered Brother Joseph so the risk is minimal.'

A slow smile crept across the Infirmarian's gaunt face.

He led me into his dispensary and took a small pot from a cupboard filled with precisely labelled ingredients. He handed it to me with a twitch of his lips. 'May I ask why you exonerate me from responsibility for a foul deed when I am viewed with suspicion by some of my reverend brethren?'

I licked a morsel of the mixture from my finger. 'From the appearance of your garden and the remedies you store on your shelves, I deduce that you are both knowledgeable and meticulous in the practice of physic. I think that if you had wished to do away with the unfortunate Brother Joseph, using a modicum of yew bark, you would have contrived to do so more skilfully and suddenly than was the case. You would have given him a speedier death and prevented him mentioning hippocras or any other substance.'

The Infirmarian threw back his head and laughed. 'I begin to like you, Doctor Somers, and see you are your own man. This will benefit your patient, have no doubt. And if you're inclined to pursue the question of responsibility for Brother Joseph's death, I suggest you enquire into his links outside the abbey.'

I registered the implications. 'As Almoner he would have had dealings with pilgrims and poor supplicants, I suppose?'

'That's true and he had care of the Sustern Spital, where twenty needy women are housed, as well as the almonry where the boys who sing in the Lady Chapel receive instruction. His duties took him outside the abbey but he also had more personal contacts in the neighbourhood. Several of our fraternity come from the town of Winchester, as did the late Almoner, and he maintained his family links – with his blood brother in particular. I suggest Sir William might be consulted on the possibility that Brother Joseph had a murderous enemy.'

'You believe he was murdered?'

The Infirmarian nodded. 'It's possible. Get Master Ranken to take you to see Sir William Devereux. He owns lands across the River Itchen and is a prominent person in the locality. He guards the privacy of his family and, who knows, his brother's demise may have been organised to bring him grief. Now you'd best get back to your wretched apprentice, Doctor Somers. Good day to you.'

*****

Next morning, while the monks were still preoccupied, grumbling about their enforced subservience to the King's decree, Master Ranken met me at the South Gate to escort me on a visit to Sir William Devereux. He was intrigued by my wish to meet the gentleman, whose reputation for aloofness sounded daunting, and I tried to divert him with questions about the injured boy's condition although he brushed them aside.

'That stuff the Infirmarian gave you brought the boy relief. Trust the monks to have a trick or two up their sleeves, better than an ordinary apothecary can provide.' We had reached the riverside and crossed it beside a mill, bustling with activity. 'This is all part of Sir William's demesne: pasture, woods and half a dozen mills. The abbey gets much of its flour from here.'

As we climbed the flank of a slope leading uphill I began to formulate extravagant theories linking the Almoner's death to his brother's wealth. I even mulled over the likelihood of corrupt practices in the abbey's dealings with suppliers given preferential treatment because of their familial links to the monks, but my musing was interrupted by the arrival of a corpulent man on horseback, coming up behind us, who hailed my companion.

'Master Ranken, I'd not expected to see you here. Are you working for Sir William Devereux at present?'

The carpenter drew himself up and gave a courteous bow. 'No, Master Mayor, I'm showing this young physician the way to Sir William's house. He's acting for the abbey following Brother Joseph's death.'

This was not strictly true but I did not quibble and introductions were made while Mayor Cranshaw of Winchester muttered about the sad business with which I was charged. We reached a side path but Ranken ignored it, striding ahead towards a fortified manor-house we could glimpse through the trees.

'Sir William won't be at home,' the Mayor said, reining in his horse. 'He particularly invited me to meet him at his large barn beyond the wood. He sent a message at first light. I fear there may have been mischief afoot that he sent for me so urgently, although this side of the river is outside the city limits and beyond my jurisdiction. I hope his property has not been fired or raided by ne'er-do-wells.'

We followed the path past the house until the barn came into sight and we expressed relief to see the building intact. We advanced with confidence towards the entrance while the Mayor gave a halloo to announce his presence. There was no reply.

Visibly irked by the possibility that he had been misdirected, the Mayor flung open the door of the barn and came to an abrupt halt, squeaking in distress, while Ranken and I hurried in behind him. The spectacle confronting us was horrific. On a bundle of hay, two partly-clad figures lay in a pool of blood, the man collapsed, straddling the young woman whose dress was thrown up and her head askew. It was obvious what they had been about but, whatever impropriety had been committed, both were now dead. The man's right arm was bent, crushed under his chest against the girl and uncongealed gore dripped from his elbow.

'This is Sir William?' I whispered.

'Aye,' said Ranken. 'But, God forgive him, there's more to it. They are father and daughter.'

Chapter 4

'Merciful Heaven,' the Mayor wheezed. 'Why did he send for me?'

'He must have wanted you to find this,' I said, 'but it's scarcely credible.'

'He wanted to expose this unnatural filth to the Mayor?' Ranken was shaking. 'Dear God, how long had he been tupping the girl? Or could he no longer restrain his lust but knew if he took her, they both had to die?'

The Mayor drew himself up authoritatively. 'It's not for us to speculate but there's action to be taken. It's properly a matter for the Sheriff but I am on hand and will not shirk my duty. Master Ranken, I'd be obliged if you would hurry to fetch my bailiffs from the Guildhall. I charge you to say nothing of this business to anyone, not even the officers. Do you understand? Absolute discretion is needed.'

The carpenter gave his word and left us while I knelt beside the bodies, studying them at close quarters. I raised the man to reveal his right hand clenched around a small dagger plunged into his own chest, the wound positioned directly over his heart. The young woman was soaked in her father's blood but a quick examination showed she had not been stabbed. The marks of a ligature around her icy throat were evidence that she had been throttled and a knotted silk cord, probably her own girdle, lay by her side.

I described my conclusions to the Mayor and he nodded. 'Your first impressions support the notion that Sir William was overcome by guilt, killing Mistress Isabella and then himself. What appalling perversion!'

I eased the dagger from the man's chest and freed his hand from the hilt, extracting a thin thread of silk from beneath a broken fingernail. Then I sat back on my haunches looking at the Mayor, impressed by his demeanour and air of intelligence. 'There's no way to be

41

certain, sir, but it is possible things are not quite as they appear. There are inconsistencies.'

'Whatever do you mean?'

'I'm not convinced Sir William killed himself. Look at his hand which was enfolded round the dagger. Do you see the way his thumb is at an angle? It is dislocated.'

The Mayor lowered himself to kneel beside me, unconcerned at soiling his gown in the glutinous mess on the ground. 'Could it have happened as a result of the violent blow he gave himself?'

'Perhaps but, if that was the case, wouldn't he instinctively let go of the dagger when it dislocated? His fingers were fixed rigidly round the hilt and the blade was embedded in the incision it made. It's almost as if his hand had been forced round the weapon after it was thrust into him. And I wonder how he contrived his exact position while in his death throes. It may be fanciful of me but something doesn't seem right.'

The Mayor pursed his lips. 'You've experience of violent death, doubtless, Doctor Somers. I can only use my eyes. But you're free to make further inspection of the circumstances. What about the girl? Can you tell if they'd had congress?'

I lifted the man's body in order to examine his daughter and I peered at the untidy bed of hay on which they lay. The process was deeply upsetting to me, reminding me of a more personal occasion when a woman had been abused by a villain, but I concentrated on what I could determine from the sight before me while the Mayor watched me intently. Under the girl's fingernails there were also traces of silk thread, indicating how she had grasped the cord and tried to prevent it tightening round her throat.

When I had finished I rose to my feet. 'There are signs of intercourse with the girl but there's no way of proving that her father was responsible. We may presume she died before Sir William but I cannot say that with certainty. See how the hay has been scattered. I think she was dragged through it. Let's look outside the barn to see if there are any tracks.'

Mayor Cranshaw accompanied me and we inspected the churned mud in front of the doorway. 'A horse came here recently,' he said, 'and there's no sign of one now, except mine tethered over there. If it was Sir William's it may well have trotted home. There are scratches on the doorstep too as if something was dragged over it but we can't tell how old they are.' He faced me squarely. 'Are you seriously suggesting a third person could have been involved?'

'There's too little evidence to justify that assumption, sir, but it's conceivable someone knew of the vice they practised and appointed himself their executioner.'

The Mayor looked annoyed and turned back into the barn. As I followed him I bent to pick up a small squashed bundle of vegetation on the threshold. My companion pointed to Sir William and his daughter. 'You are rightly guarded in your diagnosis but I find it far-fetched to imagine that this foul tableau could be a contrivance by an unknown murderer. I was summoned here by Sir William, I assume in desperate remorse, so that I might be witness to his incestuous perversity and his act of self-inflicted penitence.'

I drew a deep breath. 'I agree it seems preposterous that a rogue should stage this revolting scene to tarnish the names of his victims but it is possible.'

The Mayor folded his hands on his stomach and addressed me sternly. 'I am mindful that I was summoned here, Doctor Somers, intended to make this discovery and to vouch for its disgusting implications. Your presence is fortuitous. I have a nose for misdeeds and what I smell here tells me that Sir William had succumbed to devilish temptations, perhaps incited by his own lascivious daughter. A Jezebel of his own blood.' The Mayor picked stray straws from his gown and flicked them aside. 'If a

43

third person had been involved, he'd be badly spattered with blood – difficult to disguise that, don't you think?'

'That's true. There are spots of blood around the bodies and as far as the doorway. Perhaps your men could enquire whether a bloodied rider was seen by anyone after the deaths.'

'I know my responsibilities, Doctor Somers, and I must ask you to say nothing of the theory you have advanced.' He caught my look of indignation and moderated his tone to one of ingratiating reason. 'If some villain is indeed culpable, let him believe he has succeeded in baffling us. He would surely have had a purpose in committing so vile a crime. Let us observe. He may betray himself by his future actions.'

This made sense and I agreed but I was startled by the Mayor's next words. 'My bailiffs will hold their mouths and we'll give out there was a sad accident in the barn without disclosing details. I must however ask you to accompany me to the castle to make a formal and confidential report to the Sheriff of what we have found.'

I did not hide my surprise. 'To Wolvesey Castle?'

Mayor Cranshaw chuckled. 'I forget you've not been long in Winchester. No, we must go to the royal castle, at the far end of the town, to report to the justices.'

My stomach heaved, for the prospect of entering the King's castle, even though the court was rarely in residence there, filled me with misgivings: but I had no option to refuse.

*****

Our visit to the castle passed without incident and I returned to the abbey shaken but unthreatened. The Mayor ordered his bailiffs to question Sir William's servants and seemed competent to conduct the necessary investigations, although I did not feel confident that he would consider all the possibilities. I was reassured when he urged me to call on him in two days' time to discuss the case further and I agreed despite my reservations about venturing again into the centre of the town. I had my own reasons to be intrigued by the death of Brother Joseph's relatives. I thought it too great a coincidence to be unconnected with the Almoner's demise and I wondered if Sir William had made enquiries about that unexpected event. Besides, when I straightened the stems and flattened the crushed leaves of the nosegay I brought with me from the barn, I had no problem in identifying lavender, lovage and foxglove – all of which would feature prominently on the shelves of any apothecary or in the garden of an Infirmarian.

*****

Now that the election of their new Abbot was concluded the monks had resumed their usual occupations and I took the opportunity to accompany Brother Simon on his inspection of the various maintenance works in hand on the premises. He explained he was permitted to speak in the course of his duties and took me to the kitchens, refectory and brew-house where repairs were being made to leaking gulleys, cracked plaster and broken vats. Then he conducted me through the pilgrims' door into the retro-choir of the cathedral, where the faithful waited to be allowed nearer the relics of St. Swithun behind the high altar. Stonemasons, aloft on scaffolding, were adding final flourishes to Cardinal Beaufort's soaring chantry and I could not prevent myself trembling at the sight of his painted effigy lying beneath its ornate canopy. His appearance was formidable, clad in robes of state, and I contrasted this with the afflicted invalid whose deathbed I had attended.

'The pilgrims can get closer to the saint,' Brother Simon said, commanding my attention. 'They can enter through the low doorway at the bottom of the stone screen over there and creep on all fours to crouch directly under the shrine. Some leave tokens there, to represent the

45

prayers they offer to the saint, gifts to remind St. Swithun of their pious requests. You might find the passage difficult with your limp but you're welcome to go through the door.'

'I'm happy to make my petitions to the blessed saint from afar,' I said and I knelt for a short time beside the Cardinal's memorial making wordless supplication for God's favour towards those I loved but might never see again.

The Warden bustled about scrutinising carving on the chantry pinnacles and newly laid tiles on the floor, chatting knowledgeably with the master craftsmen, and I realised that care of the great church was the passion of his life. I commented on this as we walked down the nave to the west door and he was delighted with my perception.

'It's how I can best serve the Lord God,' he said. 'My dream is to see the Lady Chapel remodelled and the retro-choir more fittingly embellished. I could imagine it filled with other chantries and a fine new screen, to God's glory, separating it from the monks' choir. Bishop Beaufort was not interested in my plans and the Prior says they cannot be afforded.'

'Is the abbey poorly endowed?'

'Not at all. It enjoys the revenues and produce of thirty manors but there are always other claims on our income. Brother Lambert is persistent in urging the need for expansion of the Infirmary and Prior Aulton is inclined to favour him.'

I noted the bitterness in the Warden's voice and imagined this might be the root of his antipathy to the Infirmarian. Perhaps, among men living a largely enclosed life, minor disagreements festered and sapped their judgement. It was a depressing thought.

We fell quiet as we left the church and crossed towards the guesthouse where, by gesture, I invited the monk to enter. 'I'd like to ask you something, if you're content to break your silence to assist a visitor.'

The Warden of the Works smiled. 'If it's in my power to answer in accordance with God's law.'

'I haven't forgotten your concerns about Brother Joseph's death. You may have heard of a further tragedy in his family.'

The monk crossed himself. 'News of the world reaches the cloister although in this case we've closed our ears to scurrilous rumours.'

So much for the Mayor's proscription against gossip, I reflected. 'All manner of possibilities must be examined and I need to ask if the Infirmarian ever leaves the abbey precincts.'

The Warden moistened his lips. 'I shan't enquire what lies behind your question. The Infirmarian is not one of the office-holders with licence to venture beyond our gates. He has no occasion to do so.'

'Could he absent himself without being missed?'

'It might be possible – if his assistants supposed him elsewhere in the abbey.'

'Any absence would need to be limited to the intervals between the prescribed offices in the church?'

Brother Simon suppressed a fleeting smile. 'The Infirmarian has permission to miss services if his patients require attendance. The Infirmary has its own chapel where, as an ordained priest, he can say Mass.'

'The Infirmary is near the south gate from the abbey. Would the gatekeeper challenge a monk leaving at an unusual time?'

'The gatekeeper is elderly and frequently asleep. Pilgrims are encouraged to pass through the gate so he is not required to query comings and goings.'

I sighed. 'Thank you, Brother Simon. I know you won't tell anyone of my enquiries but I must also ask that you don't dwell on their implications. I make no accusation, have no evidence to justify any suspicion. Please believe me.'

He bowed his head but I saw his smirk of satisfaction. 'I have confidence in your ability, Doctor Somers, and await the outcome of your investigation with earnest anticipation.'

*****

Later that day Prior Aulton invited me to take wine with him before joining the common meal. I expected he might interrogate me about the circumstances of Sir William's death but it was apparent he had already received a detailed account and was more concerned to offer me spiritual support if I was distressed by what I had seen. I assured him that, although the scene was shocking, I was familiar with the range of human depravity.

'Mistress Isabella was of marriageable age,' he said. 'Brother Joseph mentioned his worry that she should be suitably affianced before much longer.'

This was interesting and I was keen for the Prior to say more. 'I judged her to be around twenty years old.'

'Indeed. She was her father's sole heir and would have brought considerable wealth to her husband. I question now whether poor Brother Joseph suspected impropriety lay behind her failure to wed.'

'Surely there would have been suitors for her hand?'

'Brother Joseph did confide to me once that Sir William discouraged approaches from unworthy men. At the time I thought little of it but now I fear it concealed a base truth.' He paused. 'Yet Brother Joseph seemed to approve Sir William's caution. He was anxious his niece should not make an unfitting match. I even counselled him once not to dwell on such worldly affairs when his mind should be absorbed by heavenly matters.'

The Prior's words gave substance to the idea of incest between Sir William and his daughter which might mean the father, overwhelmed by shame, was guilty of murder and self-slaughter. On the other hand, if my theory of an unknown murderer was correct, this person was most likely to have acted in revulsion, adopting the role of an avenger for their sin. To an extent this reassured me, for it was difficult to imagine the Infirmarian in such a guise and I could think of no other motive for his involvement. I admitted to myself that I was loath to believe that Brother Lambert, a monk and fellow practitioner in medicine, was responsible for a heinous crime. Nevertheless, the anomalies I had observed in the barn remained but I did not share them with the Prior. Most of all the presence of that herbal posy troubled me and I tried to persuade myself it was simply something sweet-smelling Mistress Isabella carried in place of a pomander.

I had not responded to the Prior's comments and I became aware that he was looking at me closely. 'Don't trouble yourself, Doctor Somers,' he said with a smile. 'Perhaps our late Almoner had learned something of his brother's shame and that provoked his seizure. It would be possible, would it not?'

I nodded and he poured more wine into our goblets. 'Meanwhile, let me assure you I have written a deeply grovelling letter to our new Abbot, entreating him to release the Reverend Robert Bygbroke from Wolvesey Castle to return to his duties at the cathedral. I've written with such cringing sycophancy I fear I should make confession to the Lord God of extravagant but assumed humility.'

Welcoming this diversion, I joined his laughter but, while I hoped his meek epistle would elicit a positive reply, I remembered the failure of my own grovelling entreaty to the Marquis of Suffolk to achieve any response whatsoever.

*****

Nervous of being noticed outside the abbey, I hurried through Winchester to the Guildhall with my head down, hoping to be inconspicuous. I glanced quickly at the market cross as I passed, knowing that such locations were often meeting places for disaffected citizens addressing their complaints to the authorities, and was glad there was no sign of a disturbance brewing. It was strangely affecting to see goodwives with their baskets browsing at the booths which sold drapery and cooking utensils and I realised it was now a month since I had spoken to a woman other than in the most cursory manner. A doe-eyed matron gave a bob, seeing my physician's garb, and her smile reminded me of pleasures I was determined to eschew but it comforted me as well.

Nearby in the market place butchers' stalls displayed cuts of fly-blown pork and sausages dripping blood and I wondered if regulations were imposed, as they were in the City of London, to prevent the sale of rancid meat. The stench was unwholesome and I was uneasy about the effect of infected air on the poor people making their purchases. I averted my eyes but gave a start when I heard my name called and recognised Doctor Chauntley emerging from a side lane.

'I didn't know you were still in the town,' he exclaimed. 'You're not angling to secure a post in the new Bishop's household?'

'Absolutely not,' I promised him. 'Are you as yet unclear about his requirements?'

Chauntley shook his head and appeared distressed. 'We've been told he will want only one physician to serve his entourage. He invites Willison and me to resolve which of us it should be and he'll confirm arrangements when he visits us shortly.'

'That's awkward for you.'

Chauntley puffed out his substantial chest. 'Damned awkward. I thought Willison might seek a position elsewhere. He'd spoken of it and a few months ago I gathered he was likely to leave but he's still here and he'd like to take over some of the work I do outside the palace. He's a younger man. Bishop Waynflete might prefer him.'

'Would you think of going to serve some other noble household yourself?' I posed the question merely in courtesy, thinking how unlikely it was that he would be appointed to such a post and he shook his head sadly.

'I've no wish to leave the town,' he said. 'There's a woman I visit, lives near here. It's convenient. At my age I wouldn't want to make new arrangements.'

I wanted to laugh but controlled myself. 'I'm sorry but you must excuse me. I've an appointment I must keep.' I waved my arm vaguely in the direction of the Guildhall. 'I hope your problems are resolved.'

I was still enjoying the notion of Chauntley's clandestine mistress when I arrived to see the Mayor but it was pushed from my mind as soon as the civic dignitary, sitting opposite me in an ornately crested chair, outlined what his bailiffs had learned from their investigations.

'The Devereux servants were thoroughly cowed by their late master,' he said with satisfaction. 'Saw nothing, knew nothing, more or less. Sir William often walked round his estates at daybreak and it wasn't unusual for his daughter to accompany him. There's no doubt father and child were close although I admit no disgruntled scullion suggested more than that. Hands held up in horror at the suggestion of any impropriety between them. Still, you'd expect an incestuous scoundrel to conceal his ignominy from his minions.'

'Mistress Isabella's maid is most likely to have known if there was more,' I suggested.

The Mayor grunted. 'You'd expect so but the girl is a timid little thing, only been with the family a couple of months after the old one was taken with a seizure. My men got nothing useful from her except that Isabella slipped from her bed at first light that morning, to check on her pony which had been coughing. The negligent maid seems to have fallen asleep again after that. I directed she be soundly whipped.'

'Were you able to find out who brought you the message ostensibly from Sir William?'

He narrowed his eyes at my choice of words. 'My steward gave me a description of the boy who came here

51

but the officers found no one matching it at the Devereux house. I see no purpose in looking more widely for him.' I began to question his decision but the Mayor shrugged and stretched his legs in front of him. 'I've discovered one fact that might interest you, in view of your links with the monks. In the event of his daughter predeceasing him, all Sir William's lands and possessions are gifted to the abbey.'

My mouth fell open. 'That represents substantial wealth?'

'A huge fortune. Bishop Waynflete is a lucky man. When he was at the college here he showed great love for its buildings and at the King's foundation of Eton I hear he has created an edifice of beauty and renown. Now, as Abbot, he'll be able to enhance the cathedral and the abbey as models to be admired across Christendom.'

I did not speak but the implications appalled me – with such resources it might be possible to give effect both to the architectural ambitions of Brother Simon and the previously thwarted aspirations of a resentful Infirmarian. Could Brother Lambert have known Sir William's intentions? Could the late Brother Joseph have mentioned them?

Mayor Cranshaw crossed his legs and draped the skirts of his gown over his broad thighs. 'Sir William's body-servant is not the brightest specimen of humanity but he had one contribution to offer which will interest you, although I hesitate to nourish your imagination with it. He asserts that he had never seen the dagger his master clutched when he died. Sir William's usual weapon was missing from his belt.'

I held his gaze while I put my question. 'Sir William appeared to be a well-built, muscular man. If he'd been attacked would he have been able to defend himself?'

'Certainly. He fought in the French wars years ago and remained active in the hunting field. I knew it would tantalise you, Doctor Somers, but I see no significance in his use of any particular dagger. He probably had several and doubtless selected the sharpest.' The Mayor gave a chuckle which annoyed me.

'It could add weight to my suspicion of a third person's involvement,' I said. 'Sir William may have been taken unawares.' I stood up and strode about as I gave expression to an idea which had been incubating in my mind. 'Maybe we've been wrong in our speculations. What if Sir William had been lured to find his daughter raped and murdered? He'd have been desolated. Easy to attack a man when his whole reason for living has been destroyed.'

The Mayor sank back in his seat. 'That's too fanciful, Doctor. Do you really suppose some crafty villain devised a fiendish plot designed to blacken Sir William's reputation, not just to kill him but to darken his name with unnatural vice? At any rate if there is such a devious murderer, we're unlikely ever to find the wretch. He'll have made good his escape.'

'If there is such a fellow he must have hated Sir William with rare intensity. Surely someone would know if Devereux had such a vicious enemy?'

The Mayor cleared his throat as if considering whether to say more. 'Doctor Somers, I am unwilling to be beguiled by your ruminations. If there were any substance in them, the origins of such hatred would no doubt lie in the past – perhaps in Sir William's time in France – and such a murderer would be far away by now. I'm obliged for your assistance but it is my decision that we let the matter lie, concluding that the perverted father killed his daughter and then himself. I shall report to the Sheriff accordingly and I am confident he will accept my judgement. Bishop Waynflete will be visiting the town in the near future and he will not wish to hear of a murder left unresolved and the perpetrator not brought to justice. It is much better to draw a veil over the discreditable episode and let the observable sinners rest in their graves unmourned and quickly forgotten. Do you understand me?'

I understood his reasoning perfectly and was disappointed that the Mayor had proved so spineless but my position was too vulnerable to risk inflaming his anger, causing him to make enquiries about my presence in the town. I bowed my head meekly, acknowledging his decree, but I knew that if the opportunity arose I would investigate those deaths with all the rigour and intelligence I could muster until I was satisfied the truth had been revealed.

Chapter 5

News of Sir William's bequest spread rapidly round the abbey and the Prior ordered Masses to be said in gratitude by all the ordained priests among the brotherhood. Masses for the dead man's soul would be irregular in a case of self-slaughter and I learned from the Warden of the Works that some monks felt uncomfortable about benefitting from the murderous circumstances. Brother Simon was not among them. He argued that Sir William acquired his wealth lawfully and, whatever sins he had committed, they did not taint his gift which would be used for God's glory. He was already working on plans to remodel the Lady Chapel.

When Ranken sought me out by the pilgrims' hall I was ready to tease him about the years of employment this could bring him but he had more serious matters to tell me.

'There's something you should know, doctor,' he said, pausing affectedly to heighten the tension. 'One of my men was making his way to work on the day Sir William died, walking on the far side of the river, to cross by the mill, as he did every morning. He saw a figure in black riding furiously down the slope from the direction of the barn and heading upstream. He was too far away to attempt any identification but it's interesting, don't you think?'

My stomach somersaulted as I nodded. I had not shared my suspicions with the master carpenter and admired his insightfulness but I did not welcome his news. Any ne'er-do-well might choose to wear inconspicuous black to carry out a dark deed but the Benedictine brothers wore their black habits every day.

'There could be more than meets the eye about the whole business.' I spoke guardedly but I trusted Ranken and decided to seek his help. 'I'd like to know the identity of the boy who took the message to the Guildhall so he could be questioned. He didn't come from Sir William's household. The Mayor thinks there's no need for such enquiries. It's obviously distasteful and he's no wish to be dragged into more unpleasantness when there's an easy way of closing the case but I'm not entirely satisfied we know the whole story.'

Ranken rubbed his nose and winked. 'Leave it to me, doctor,' he said. 'My lads'll find the boy.'

*****

In the short time since the apprentice's accident, I had been asked for advice or treatment by a number of Ranken's colleagues who lived beside the South Gate of the town and had no other physician to consult. Mostly their queries related to injuries sustained at work or aching joints which inhibited their effectiveness but sometimes they asked about ailments suffered by their wives or children. The prospect of building up a practice among the townsfolk of Winchester was attractive to me but I decided I must limit this to those serving and living close to the abbey until I could be confident I was safe from Suffolk's vindictiveness. I remained wary of letting my medical activities become known more widely by frequenting the apothecary's shop near the market cross. Accordingly I decided I must visit the Infirmarian again to see if he would allow me to raid his herb garden regularly for useful remedies.

Admittedly, I was also intrigued to see how Brother Lambert would behave towards me, given the alarming possibility of his involvement in the Devereux deaths: the suspicion I could not dismiss now I was aware of an ostensible motive. With that in mind, I was unprepared for the form and fervour of his response when I mentioned Sir William's demise and the provisions of his will.

'It's wrong – the devil's work – to accept his money. I've heard how he was found, the flagrancy of his unnatural sin. I shall refuse to allow a groat of his legacy to be spent on the Infirmary.'

If this was contrived disgust, designed to deceive me, it was convincingly portrayed and I expressed my surprise. 'Surely, Holy Church has benefitted from many a sinful man's donations?'

'When a man expresses remorse for his past sins by making provision in his will in atonement: that is one thing. But for an incestuous murderer to slay himself, after carnal knowledge of his daughter, that is abomination and God's house would be polluted by accepting his filthy inheritance.'

'I don't believe many of your brothers share your opinion.'

'The more shameful for them. The Infirmary will remain free of contamination.'

Despite his outrage he was content to supply the herbs I required and even asked me to examine a rash on the chest of one of his patients. In fact his attitude towards me was friendly and this encouraged me to put a leading question to him.

'You suggested I should visit Sir William, implying he might know of someone who wished Brother Joseph harm. Were you aware then of Sir William's own apparent depravity?'

'Apparent! From what I've heard, it was explicit enough when you and the Mayor found him. But I had no intimation of his degeneracy. Nor, I feel sure, had Brother Joseph. I rejoice that our worthy Almoner was spared that misery.'

I swallowed a comment. Could his vehemence conceal deceit? His fury against Sir William seemed genuine but it might have pre-dated the man's death. Ranken's news of a horseman in the vicinity of the barn corroborated my theory that a double-murderer had arranged for the Mayor to find the bodies and proclaim their sinfulness. Had Brother Lambert sent me to Sir William Devereux for the same purpose? Could he have appointed himself as God's avenging angel to punish evil? Was it perverse fastidiousness, after committing murder,

57

which drove him to reject any advantage to himself and the Infirmary from his own crime? My meeting with the Infirmarian only increased my misgivings.

*****

A week or so later news was brought to the abbey that Bishop Waynflete had been provided formally to the see of Winchester by Papal Bull and he was to be consecrated shortly in Eton church. I thought it would have been more appropriate for the ceremony to take place in the cathedral but, when Prior Aulton invited me to call at his lodgings, he voiced no concerns on the matter. He complimented me on offering medical services to the workmen, urging me to continue in my practice, and then he extracted a sealed packet from among the papers on his desk and handed it to me.

'The Abbot of Peterborough has written and he enclosed this communication for you. I think you can guess its origin.'

For a mad moment I mused whether it was possible the Marquis of Suffolk had chosen this cautious route by which to send his reply to my letter but I soon relinquished that ridiculous idea. Instead, by the time I reached the guesthouse and broke the seal I knew who my correspondent must be and was cheered by the hope that the Prioress of St. Michael's in Stamford had not forgotten me. Nevertheless, her message took me back to a world I had abandoned and remembrance of it troubled me.

Doctor Somers, I rejoice that you are safe in Winchester. It is as well that you remain in the protection of the church. Suffolk is untrustworthy and self-seeking and I am sure you have learned not to rely on his good faith. He feathers his nest comfortably, following Humphrey of Gloucester's death. At the King's command, the late Duke's extensive lands are divided between Suffolk and Queen Margaret who has already taken possession of the fine Palace of Pleasance at Greenwich.

Not all I have to tell will be welcome to you but I thought you would wish to have news of your friends, so far as I have been able to gather it.

In particular, the Earl of Stanwick sends his good wishes. You will know he was instrumental in securing your escape, together with the Abbot of Peterborough, and he has your interests at heart. Unfortunately his health continues fragile and he has returned to his northern estates and his family. His Countess is a lady of most Christian forbearance and I pray for her daily. She cares for the Earl's natural daughter with loving devotion and now she has agreed to exceed even that generosity. You will share my pleasure that young Eleanor prospers under her guidance and it is imperative this continues.

Lord Fitzvaughan and his catamite have travelled across the Narrow Sea with the ambassadors seeking to renew the truce with the French King. I understand not all the nobles at King Henry's court favour continuance of the truce and some of his representatives in Maine are still refusing to cede their castles to the French under the terms agreed two years ago. Walter Fitzvaughan and his colleagues will have a difficult path to tread in the negotiations – but he is well used to that.

Your despicable acquaintances, Gilbert Iffley, Baron Glasbury, and Master Stephen Boice are both now serving the Duke of York. The Duke is offended that his commission as King Henry's governor in Normandy was not renewed and his disaffection is dangerous. I hope he will soon be appointed to some position where he can do less harm. I do not trust his intentions.

I am sure you already know that the French Countess, whom you rashly aspired to marry, is fittingly wed to a nobleman in her own country. I hope you are now sufficiently freed from lust and passion to appreciate your good fortune in escaping a union which would have brought you terrible repercussions.

I regret I no longer have the benefit of information which you were able to supply in the past, Doctor Somers.

I pray that your prospects will improve and I shall reap the advantage of your wisdom once more.

I read the letter a second time and a third, welcoming the news that young Eleanor, the Earl of Stanwick's natural daughter, was prospering in her father's household but failing to understand the allusion to the Countess's extreme benevolence. I understood too well the Prioress's concerns regarding both the Marquis of Suffolk and the Duke of York. The latter magnate, the King's closest living relative now Gloucester was dead, was held by some to have a claim to King Henry's crown and the presence of scheming rogues like Iffley and Boice at his side was disturbing. Tensions between the highest in the land, when the monarch was a gentle soul unable to dominate his restless advisers, fostered lawlessness and might lead to more dangerous unrest. I noted the Prioress's belief that I should remain in the protection of the church and it tempered my burgeoning hopes that I might ever live and practice medicine freely in the town.

I wished the Prioress had been able to give me news of my dearest friends but they were unknown to her and too humble to gain her interest. I was distressed to learn that the Queen had commandeered Gloucester's palace at Greenwich, where Thomas and Grizel Chope lived and served, and I worried for their futures. I wondered anew where Rendell had gone and whether Suffolk would still provide for my assistant, Leone, whom he was sponsoring at the university. I was relieved that the Prioress made no reference to Walter Fitzvaughan's wife, Lady Maud, but I was pained to think of her cast off or incarcerated by her husband for the outrageous trick she had attempted to play on him.

My sleep was fragmentary that night, interrupted by frightening dreams and wisps of thought which rapidly vanished but left a sense of desolation. I wished the Prioress had not pulled me back to the life I had left and could not resume. When I awoke I persuaded myself that a peaceful life in Winchester was now the summit of my ambition.

*****

Perhaps because of my own discomfort, I tried to convince myself that I must abandon further investigations into the Devereux deaths but Master Ranken had the bit between his teeth and was true to his word in pursuing enquiries. When he summoned me to meet him outside the abbey a few days later he was glowing with triumph and pushed a vacant-looking urchin in front of him.

'This is Dick who took the message to Mayor Cranshaw. Lives on a farm outside the North Gate of the town.'

I resolved not to be drawn into this development. 'You'd best present him to the Mayor,' I said.

'Not likely. If the bailiffs can't be bothered to find him why should I help them? You question him, Doctor.'

I hid my reluctance as the boy looked at me sullenly. 'Is it right, Dick? Will you tell me what happened?'

He frowned and began to hold out his hand but Ranken knocked it aside. 'Went to get the eggs from under the hedge,' he said. 'Do that every morning. Man on a horse called me over. Told me to go to the Mayor and tell him.'

'What were you to tell him?'

'To meet Sir William at the old barn. Right away. It were urgent. He made me say it twice. He watched me go through the gate into the town. Then he rode off.'

'Did you know the man?'

'Nah. Bit of a toff. Thought he must be Sir William.'

'What did he look like?'

'Dunno. He had a hood.'

'How was he dressed?'

'Dunno. In black.'

I extracted a coin from my pouch. I only want the truth, Dick. Is there anything else you can remember?'

'Horse were grey.'

I caught my breath. Was it possible Brother Lambert had taken Cloudburst from the Prior's stable on his pernicious expedition? The hood would have covered his tonsure.

Dick stretched out his fingers to take his payment. 'I ain't done nothing wrong.'

'No, I'm sure you haven't. Thank you for telling me what happened.' I turned to Ranken. 'The Mayor ought to be informed of this.'

'What's the point? I reckon he doesn't want to find out any more or he'd have had his officers combing the district.'

I agreed with this depressing conclusion but Dick's testimony fitted with the workman's observation of a black-clad rider and the speculation that a third party wanted the bodies to be found by a civic dignitary. It was material evidence. 'If the Mayor's men come to question you, Dick, just tell them what you've told me and don't make up anything that isn't true.'

The boy grinned, stroking the coin in his hand, and I left Ranken to escort him back through the town. I had no doubt in my mind that the anonymous horseman was responsible for the horrendous scene in the barn but his identity remained a mystery. Could it have been Brother Lambert? If he had ridden on, following the town walls, he would have been able to re-enter by the South Gate and return to the abbey before he was missed. I did not want to link the Infirmarian with the appalling crime but it was becoming more difficult for he had both motive and opportunity.

I knew Mayor Cranshaw would not welcome the information but I sent him a note summarising all we had learned from Dick and suggested he might wish to interview the boy himself. That salved my conscience; but I made no mention of possible suspects or the Benedictines' customary hooded robes because, I argued to myself, this was obvious. I was unsurprised that my letter received no reply.

*****

During the following days a rumour spread among the townsfolk that God's own hand had struck down the incestuous Devereux couple, in direct retribution for their heinous sin. A bolt from heaven, no less, had caused Sir William to slaughter Isabella and take his own life and all such sinners could expect similar punishment. People crowded into the churches to repent their own misdemeanours and several priests elaborated on the idea of God's instant justice in a way that strengthened their hold over their listeners. I imagined that although Mayor Cranshaw was unlikely to believe this intimidating fable he would utilise it as an acceptable explanation of why nothing further could be established. For the honour of his little town he had no wish to perpetuate gossip about unnatural iniquity in its midst, especially when a visit by the new Bishop might be imminent. Frustrating as this was, I dared not protest.

I concentrated on my modest physician's duties and welcomed the chance I was given to expand my role. The Warden of the Works considered that the new Almoner, Brother Titus, was an excellent choice for that position. He had started at once to review the full extent of his responsibilities and soon asked me to provide advice and assistance to the pilgrims when they entered the abbey, treating their various ailments with whatever remedies human knowledge might devise, complementing their intercessions to the saint whose relics they revered. He also enquired whether I would be willing to visit his charges in the Sustern Spital, where twenty needy old women were cared for by dedicated sisters but lacked a physician's guidance. I knew by then it had been outside the building where these women were housed that Master

63

Ranken's apprentice had fallen. It was conveniently near the abbey and under its charge so I was happy to comply with the Almoner's request.

I was well received in the hall of the Sustern Spital and found my new patients in reasonable health considering their dependency. Several of them were enthusiastic to have a visitor to whom they could chatter: especially, perhaps, a man who, despite the disfiguring birthmark on my cheek, was presentable enough for the elderly women to flirt with a little. I was amused by their reminiscences and had difficulty is extricating myself from their gossip as I moved round the room. Most of them were sitting on stools or benches against the wall but three were lying in their beds in the far corners and I noticed that one of these seemed not to move at all. As I crossed towards her the nun accompanying me spoke in a whisper.

'Mistress Woodman is nearing her end. She can still hear our voices but she cannot speak. She has lost almost all use of her limbs since her seizure.' These were familiar symptoms and I nodded but the nun had more to say. 'She knows of the tragedy although we tried to keep it from her. I think it is hastening her demise. Her family have served the Devereux household for many years. I will leave you with her but there is little to be done. She is not in pain.'

I gasped in surprise as understanding came and I remembered what I had been told. I knelt beside the pallet, leaning close to the old woman's face, waiting until the nun was occupied elsewhere in the room. It might be rash and not strictly professional but I decided to take advantage of this improbable opportunity, while chiding myself for having assumed that the woman's seizure had been fatal.

'I'm a physician, Mistress Woodman and I'm sorry to see you so afflicted. I don't want to upset you but you may be able to help me. I've been aiding the officers enquiring into the deaths of Sir William Devereux and his daughter.'

The blankness left her eyes and her mouth opened so I was sure she had registered what I said. 'I believe you served Mistress Isabella until you were taken ill.'

Very slowly she lifted her left arm from the bed-cover, bending her elbow as if it cradled something. 'You were her nurse?' I bent closer to her ear. 'And then her maid?'

Again the old woman's mouth twitched and her eyes filled with tears. It was my duty not to distress her and I must not prolong my questioning so I decided to pose one final, tendentious query and pray that it would not put her into another apoplexy. 'Good-mother, forgive me for asking this but, to your knowledge, did Sir William ever hurt Mistress Isabella?'

Her shoulder shook and she made a guttural sound in her throat which caused the nun to turn round and look at us. I feared I had gone too far and pulled back from peering at Mistress Woodman's wrinkled mouth. She could not shake her head but her jaw quavered with a slight sideways movement. Could she be indicating a negative reply? I knew I must not read into this miniature reflex what I wanted to believe and dared not pursue the matter further. I rose to my feet while the nun came to join us and with one quivering finger the old woman made the sign of the cross.

'She is blessing you, Doctor Somers,' the nun said. 'How pleasing! She may have thought you were a priest. You must rest for a few minutes, Mistress Woodman. I think you are to have another visitor. I glimpsed your niece from the window coming along the road. Please, Doctor, there is one more patient for you to see.'

She led me to a shrivelled little person with twisted, swollen hands who, despite her infirmities, was jovial and anxious to talk so I sat with her for several minutes. Then, from the corner of my eye, I glimpsed a young woman entering at the far doorway who handed over a bundle of clothes and a basket of bread to the nun before making her way towards Mistress Woodman. I rose and excused myself as politely as I could, contriving to meet the new visitor in the centre of the hall.

'Your servant, mistress. My name is Doctor Somers. I am sent by the abbey to have a care for those who are sick here. Are you Mistress Woodman's niece?'

She gave a bob. 'Yes, sir, but you'll be able to do little for my aunt. Oh dear! That sounds rude. Forgive me.'

She had a delightful laugh but I was staring at the yellowing mark below her eye and, aware of my attention, she touched it lightly and gave a dismissive shrug as if it was of no consequence. 'I wash my aunt's linen and bring her sweetmeats once a week - not that she can stomach them.'

'That's kind. I'm sure your aunt knows you are good to her. She understands what she hears and would say so if she could.'

The young woman's smile lit up her face and, with a pang of nearly forgotten pleasure, I thought how pretty she was. 'You're most observant, sir, though it's sometimes difficult to work out her meaning. I can probably do so better than most. Excuse me, Doctor Somers. She can hear my voice and is looking towards us.'

'May I know your name?'

She pursed her lips coquettishly for a moment and then laughed again. 'I am Mistress Dutton, sir, wife to Samuel Dutton, butcher of St. Peter's.' She gave me a low curtsey and moved, with an entrancing wiggle, to her aunt's bedside while I rallied my disorderly emotions and turned to the door.

If I had kept my wits about me and not been distracted by foolish notions, I would have asked her then and there if she could interpret her aunt's feeble gestures to me. It would have saved time and prevented some disagreeable occurrences but my mind was preoccupied with reminiscences of feminine charms from long ago and my concentration drifted.

*****

While I made my way back to the abbey my mood became mournful as the fleeting pleasure of Mistress Dutton's smile was replaced by memories of all I had lost. By my own fault, as well as the cruel exigencies of fate, I had forfeited opportunities and seen my dreams obliterated. It felt as if my hope of happiness had been doomed, ever since I was forced into exile six years previously and Bess, my first sweet love, believed a mistaken report that I was wed to another. She had become a contented wife to Lord Walter Fitzvaughan's bailiff and, if all had gone well with her pregnancy, was by now a mother. Over the years my wayward heart had played Bess false but I was cruelly punished for my faithlessness. The pain of losing Yolande de Langeais, my highborn promised bride, and the death of our tiny, secret son was still agonisingly raw. I could not envisage my future with any other woman.

The wave of grief swept over me, drowning my resolve to bury the past deep in the recesses of my soul and I could no longer withstand its battering. I stumbled blindly across the courtyard beyond the abbey gate towards the cloister and by the time I was climbing the stairs, in the privacy of the guesthouse, I sobbed aloud, indulging the misery I had tried for three months to keep at bay. I had never felt more desolate.

'Oh, hush and whist, Doctor Somers. Now's no time for skimble-skambles. Whatever ails you, cast it aside. I never thought you a wishy-washy sort. See, who's come to cheer you.'

I blinked through my tears as I turned towards the small man who bounded to my side and despite my anguish I attempted a grin. 'Reverend Bygbroke, Robert! Has the Bishop released you?'

'Not a moment too soon – if appearances are to be believed. I bring satisfaction to the Prior, the resonance of music to the brotherhood and whatever personal merriment I can offer to my lonely, sorrowful friend.'

My voice caught in my throat and I could not speak but as he slapped me on the shoulder and hugged me I knew that the companionship he offered might help rebuild my shattered resilience. If nothing else, oblivion could be sought in the convivial jars of ale we would share.

Chapter 6

Robert Bygbroke brought news that the Bishop was to visit Winchester in time for the celebrations on St. Swithun's feast day and this led to a flurry of activity to ensure he could be fittingly welcomed in the cathedral. The Warden of the Works bustled about, ordering tiles to be scrubbed, windows cleaned, woodwork oiled, choir-stalls brushed and candlesticks polished. Robert himself organised a team of blowers to pump the bellows and played thunderous voluntaries on the organ, after which he ordered new calf hides and ash hoops for the bellows, together with glue, wire, hinges and hooks. His jubilation was infectious and he expressed his thanks time and again to the Prior and to me, as intermediary, for bringing him back to the instrument he loved. I protested I had done nothing but pass messages to and fro yet he was insistent I was worthy of his gratitude.

'All right, Harry. I accept that all my supporters have been vehicles for God's grace towards me. Willy-nilly, it teaches me my duty. I shall pay my respects to St. Swithun's relics in earnest of my appreciation. I shall go on my knees, through the little door in the screen in front of the retro-choir and prostrate myself behind the high altar.'

'Rather you than me,' I said, laughing. 'It must be pitch-dark in the passage and you need to crawl on hands and knees.'

'It shall be done. I shall join the column of pilgrims snaking their way into the retro-choir.'

'I don't think there is one. Brother Simon has insisted no dusty feet or sweaty bodies shall befoul his immaculately cleansed sanctuary until the Bishop has seen it.'

'He'll make an exception for a priest though.'

I grinned and watched the organist stride resolutely into the cloister. I had no doubt he would persuade the Warden to admit him to the retro-choir. I walked in the opposite direction, towards the guesthouse, and was dismayed to see a visitor standing on the threshold, a soberly dressed man with an air of superiority, a man I had hoped never to see again. A cynical smile drew in the corners of his mouth.

'It is a surprise, isn't it? I didn't expect to find myself in this blessed spot, once more on England's soil, once more addressing the recalcitrant physician who has caused me such trouble.'

'Your memory deceives you, Baron Glasbury. It's I who have the right to rue our meeting. Through your devices I've suffered torture and faced death; those I loved have been taken from me and I've been branded a traitor and murderer. I have nothing more to say to you.'

I caught the flash of malignancy in his eyes. 'Stephen Boice told me I'd find you intractable but it's several months since he saw you, when the late lamented Bishop Beaufort was still breathing in the midst of his sycophantic minions. I hoped the tedium of living with the holy postulants in the abbey might have changed your perspective on what I have to offer.'

I turned my back on the man I had known as Gilbert Iffley until I learned of both his baronial title and his evil machinations but, to my horror, I felt his hand on my shoulder.

'Not so fast, Harry Somers.' He swivelled me to face him. 'You will pay me the courtesy of listening.'

'Courtesy? Take your hand off me or I shall shout for you to be removed from the abbey.'

'Didn't you hear the bell? It is the hour for Sext. The monks are gone into the church. The workmen I observed over by the pilgrims' hall are far away and will not hear you. Don't struggle, doctor, I should be reluctant to hurt you. I simply ask for your attention while I make my offer.'

I refused to answer and clenched my jaw but I could not prevent him from speaking.

'You are remarkably stubborn, Harry. I admire that, after all you've been through. My purpose is quickly stated. I bring you an offer of honourable employment, as a physician, to the highest in the land.'

'I hardly think you are come as emissary from his Grace, King Henry.'

He sucked in his cheeks and smirked at me. 'That worthless usurper may not wear the crown for much longer, Doctor Somers. I'm sure you know there is another of the blood royal with a greater claim to sit on the throne and the skill to fill it far more effectively if he chooses to press his rights.'

'That's treason,' I blurted, despite myself.

'And will you denounce me to the King's officers at the castle? I think they would put you under arrest and introduce you to their incomparable instruments of torment to ascertain the truth of your assertion. You are in no position to threaten me and if you have any sense left in your wilful head you will give my offer careful thought. Richard of York is in need of a new physician for his household and I have recommended your services. He is aware that you have served Suffolk in a similar capacity and the fact that you are now in bad odour with the Marquis only enhances your suitability in his eyes.'

I decided it was pointless to antagonise my oppressor by repeating the accusation of treachery. 'I'm content where I am.'

He released my shoulder and stood back, chuckling. 'Now York is back in England and his affairs in Normandy wound up, he can expect to take his rightful place at his royal cousin's side. The upstart, Suffolk, will be sent packing – if all goes well – to the gallows or at least into exile. Join us, Harry. Your intelligence and determination are appreciated and you will be rewarded richly. What an estimable record you will hold – to have served in the households of Gloucester, Suffolk and York, to say nothing of the late Cardinal.'

He was reminding me that years ago I had been compelled to switch my allegiance from Humphrey of Gloucester to the Marquis of Suffolk but I had been scrupulous in ensuring I did my former patron no harm. It was obvious the offer before me carried no guarantee with regard to Suffolk's welfare and Baron Glasbury read my mind.

'Why do you persist in nurturing loyalty to a man who has cast you off and allowed you to carry the blame for his own misdeeds?' When I did not reply he adjusted his gown on his shoulders and straightened the chain round his neck. 'I shall leave you now, Harry. Think about your prospects and how my offer could improve them. Suffolk may yet seek to scapegoat you for Gloucester's death and you may need to flee across the Narrow Sea. Remember Stephen Boice told you how to contact Master Brill, the cordwainer, in Southampton to arrange your passage to safety. But I recommend sidestepping the risk, Harry. Take up the place in York's household. Don't be a fool, physician. Consider where your best chances lie. I wish you good-day.'

I watched him pace elegantly along the path from the guesthouse while I clamped my arms around my chest. I would not wish him to see how I struggled to quieten my trembling limbs.

*****

That afternoon I went again to the Sustern Spital and was saddened but not surprised to learn that Mistress Woodman had passed away in her sleep. The wonder was that she had lingered so long in a world to which her frail body had such tenuous links. I remembered her attempts to tell me something which she had no way of expressing and it reminded me of the mystery I was impotent to solve. I returned to the abbey in sombre mood but Robert Bygbroke was waiting to entertain me with an account of his devotions directly beneath the saint's shrine and, although he could not have foreseen this, to reawaken my disquiet and curiosity about Sir William Devereux and his daughter.

'It's awe inspiring, Harry, believe me. All in the darkness, crouched low like the wretched sinners we are, and then at the end of the passage a glint of light comes through a gap in the stonework and you can glimpse the gilding on the shrine above you. I knelt there and sobbed, I don't mind telling you, full of joy and gratitude.' His eyes were moist and he looked at me plaintively but then he gave a giggle and shattered the solemnity of the moment. 'Someone ought to tidy it up, though. The Warden of the Works hasn't sent his cleaners underground. It's a danger to the unwary. Look: I cut my hand. It could have stopped me playing the organ.'

It was not a deep wound but the slash ran across his palm and the rag he had wrapped round it was mottled with blood. 'I'll bind it more securely for you,' I said. 'How did you do it?'

'The pilgrims leave offerings under the shrine. I took a fragment of the broken casing from round the organ. Master Ranken is repairing it.'

'You cut your hand on a piece of jagged wood?'

'No, no. Some fool had left an unsheathed dagger on the pile of gifts in the dark corner. It's a mercy I only touched it lightly.'

I froze. 'A dagger? Near the top of the pile?'

'Quite a fancy thing, with scroll work on the handle. I felt the pattern. No surprise really. They get rich and poor paying their respects to the saint. Could have been a soldier's weapon. Maybe he'd killed someone with it.'

Robert chortled with merriment but I could not join in laughter. I had not told him of my involvement with the Devereux deaths or the uneasiness I felt about them and I was not inclined to dispel his cheerful humour by introducing such a miserable subject. I was relieved when he excused himself to check the work which had been done to improve the efficiency of the bellows and eliminate the squeak from one of the organ stops.

Nevertheless I had no intention of ignoring what Robert had told me and early next morning I accosted

Ranken as he made his way towards the cathedral, a bundle of measuring poles under his arm. I described what the organist had seen and was not disappointed when the master carpenter quickly construed it as I had.

'You think it could be Sir William's missing dagger?'

'It's worth checking. Do you think you could go and look?'

'Of course. I'll tell Brother Simon I need to inspect the struts in the passage. Nothing easier.' He tapped his nose in that knowing manner which reminded me of my former servant, Rendell.

*****

I expected that Ranken would return to report his findings without delay and when he did not appear I assumed he had concluded the dagger was of no interest. I was irritated by his failure to explain his reasons, which seemed out of character, and I began to wonder if the dagger had been removed from the pile of gifts since Robert Bygbroke saw it. Who could have done such a thing? Was it fortuitous or of malicious intent? I was troubled by the alternatives and took a walk along by the town wall, past the Sustern Spital, in an attempt to calm myself. Then, as I approached the mill by the riverside where we had crossed on that fateful morning, I spotted the very man causing me this mental turmoil scuttling down the grassy slope opposite.

'Master Ranken, I didn't think to find you here?'

'I could say the same thing about you, Doctor, but wait until you've heard what I've learned.' He was panting and took several breaths before he continued. 'The dagger was Sir William's. Not a doubt. I've seen his body-servant.'

'You've been to the Devereux house?' My tone betrayed my annoyance.

'Belongs to the abbey now though.' Ranken was unperturbed by my peevishness. 'They've put in a steward

74

to run the estate and Matty's long nose is out of joint having to serve such an inferior man after being Sir William's personal retainer.

'He recognised the dagger?'

'At once. I never had any doubt when I saw the silver scrollwork on the hilt and Matty confirmed it instantly. Sir William always wore it in his belt, apparently. Someone must have taken it when he knifed the poor man with another weapon.'

'And forgot to switch them over when he wanted us to think Sir William killed himself. Then he hid the evidence in a place unlikely to be disturbed, below St. Swithun's shrine.'

'Perhaps he suffered pangs of guilt and went to do penance there.'

I was not inclined to be so charitable. 'Did you leave the dagger with Matty?' There was a hint of sarcasm in the way I emphasised the name of the hitherto nameless servant.

'What do you take me for, Doctor? Course I didn't. Here it is.' Ranken extracted it from his boot and held it out so I could see for myself the accuracy of his description. 'Will you deliver it to the Mayor?'

There was no purpose in persisting with my truculence and I shrugged. 'I suppose I should but he won't welcome it.'

'Listen to what else I heard from Matty. Then you can decide what to do. Those officers the Mayor sent didn't question him properly at all and he didn't like their insinuations so he only told them what they asked – not other things he knew.'

Ranken now had my full attention and my bad temper had dissolved. 'Please tell me.'

He gave a cunning grin. 'Thought you'd be interested to hear my news. Sir William wasn't quite the recluse we'd been led to imagine. He had one old friend in the neighbourhood. Matty said they'd fought together in

France and they often shared a jug of ale and talked of the old days. Matty reckons if anyone knows the secrets of Sir William's life, it'll be Master Woodman.'

'Woodman?'

'That's right. He's the brother of the old dame you met in the Sustern Spital. He's even older than she was and he's been lodged at Holy Cross for the last few years.'

'Where's that?'

'A mile or so downstream to the south. It's a hospital for indigent old men, just like the Sustern Spital for the women.'

I wondered why I'd never heard of it. 'Does it come under the aegis of the abbey too?'

'Not of the abbey but the Abbot. Bishop Beaufort took a great interest in it, enlarged its buildings so more old men could be accommodated. A Master lives there and runs the place from day to day. The Prior isn't involved, nor any of the monks. I thought you might want to pay a visit there and meet Master Woodman.'

I shook Master Ranken's hand with enthusiasm. 'Absolutely but I can hardly go there as a physician without an invitation.' I was already thinking of Mistress Dutton as a possible channel to make contact with her uncle.

'I'm sure you can sort out something, Doctor.' Ranken winked and once again he tapped his nose.

*****

After my initial excitement at the information Ranken had gleaned I considered in more sober mood how I could encounter Mistress Dutton. She had no occasion now to visit the Sustern Spital so I would have to go in search of her but that should not be too difficult. She had told me the quarter of the town where she lived and I knew St. Peter's was near the market square where the butchers traded from their stalls. An enquiry in the neighbourhood should lead me to her. The difficulty for me, of course, was my nervousness about venturing so far from the abbey's protection but I resolved it must be done.

Next morning while the monks were at the service of Tierce I set out, walking with one of Ranken's assistants until we reached a wood-yard where he had a bundle of laths to collect. I was not wearing my physician's gown because I thought I would be less conspicuous without it and the early sun promised a hot day, so I was pleased that no one paid me attention when I struck out alone towards the market cross. I soon came in sight of the butchers' booths and nearly burst into a trot when I recognised Mistress Dutton herself at one of the furthest counters just before the roadway began to climb the hill. Then I realised she was arguing with the burly fellow at her side and I slowed my pace, fearing to interrupt a disagreement between man and wife. Although her words were indistinguishable her shrill tone carried along the street while Master Dutton's angry growl left no doubt they were exchanging insults. I noted that salesmen and customers at other stalls ignored the confrontation and I conjectured it was a regular event.

I hesitated by a bench on which items of haberdashery were displayed, all the time watching the scene along the road, and I gulped when I saw the butcher raise his hand to his wife. He did not land a blow, however, and Mistress Dutton tossed her head and darted away into a side street. I hastily excused myself as the haberdasher approached, scenting a sale, and I hastened after the butcher's wife.

I caught up with her just as she lifted the latch on a door and I called her name a little breathlessly. She turned in surprise, looking me up and down, and the frown vanished from her face.

'Why, Doctor Somers,' she said with a very fetching curl of her lip. 'I haven't seen you in town before.'

'I seldom go far from the abbey. I came to look for you, Mistress Dutton. I need your help.'

She glanced along the street and pushed the door which opened directly into a small simply furnished room. 'You'd best come in.'

I felt it more appropriate to speak to her in a public place but she swept into the house and if I was to question her I had to follow. 'I simply wanted to ask you something.'

'Will you take some ale?' She picked up a jug and poured into an earthenware beaker without waiting for my reply. She lowered her eyes modestly as she handed it to me but when I thanked her she gave a flirtatious giggle and, conscious of her charms, I stumbled over my words in trying to explain my errand.

'I w-wanted to enquire... to ask you about your uncle, Master Woodman, who lives at the hospital of Holy Cross.'

She pressed a knuckle to her lip before answering. 'I don't have contact with my uncle. Years ago he quarrelled with my mother who was his younger sister and I know nothing about him. My aunt who was older than my mother stayed close to him but I expect you've heard she's gone now.'

I nodded. 'I'm sorry for your loss, Mistress. I only learned of your uncle recently and believe he might be able to help me solve a problem. When we met before you mentioned where you lived so I thought I might come and ask you to introduce me to him. I apologise for troubling you if that's not possible.'

'Did my aunt tell you he lodged at Holy Cross?'

I stared at her in puzzlement. 'How could she?'

'She was clever at finding ways to show her meaning. She always made the sign of the cross when she wanted to refer to her brother – for Holy Cross, you understand.'

I groaned. 'If only I'd had the sense to ask you at Sustern Spital, I'd have saved a good deal of time. Mistress Woodman made the sign of the cross and I thought she was blessing me.'

Mistress Dutton gave a delightful trill of laughter. 'I'm sure she would have done that too. Oh heavens...'

Heavy footsteps outside the door interrupted her words before latch was raised and the hinges swung open. In a moment Samuel Dutton was towering over me, his blood-stained hands grasping the neck of my jerkin. 'Have I spoiled your enjoyment, my lusty little fellow? Did the whore invite you into my house to drink ale with her?'

'What nonsense is this, Sam?' Mistress Dutton's trembling voice belied her efforts to stay calm. 'Doctor Somers has come to ask me about my uncle.'

'Doctor, is it? Where's your physician's gown then?'

'It was too hot to wear a gown.' I knew I sounded foolish and false.

The butcher released me. 'I don't doubt the heat is in your prick. You identified her as the slut she is. What did you want with John Woodman?'

'I'd like to see him. I thought Mistress Dutton might be in touch with him and could arrange it.'

'Christ Almighty, do you take me for a ninny? I've heard men invent excuses for their rutting but never anything so gutless. Your brother physician who serves Holy Cross could take you there any day.'

Mistress Dutton saw my look of bewilderment. 'Doctor Chauntley at Wolvesey Castle cares for the residents at Holy Cross.'

I winced at my stupidity. The hospital was in the charge of the Abbot-Bishop so it was logical his household physicians would minister to the old men who lived there. 'I apologise for troubling you,' I said. 'I should have realised.'

Master Dutton blocked my way to the door. 'Chauntley keeps a harlot along the road and I fancy my sweet wife has a yen to learn the trade. Full of simpering smiles, isn't she? I've had cause to thrash her often enough for rolling her eyes at another man but I've never known her let one into my house while I'm away. I'm tempted to carve you into pieces, you fucking lecher.'

He hurled me across the room to crash against the wall and to my horror he drew a knife from his belt, but as he took a step towards me his wife seized his arm. 'It's not true, Sam. He's an honest man.'

Her words infuriated the butcher, as doubtless they were intended to do, and he sprang at her, punching her face, while she cried out, urging to me to escape. When I hesitated she shouted again. 'Go! I beg you. Go!'

I prayed he would do her no serious injury, while squirming at my cowardice, but in the moment when he was distracted I obeyed her command and burst through the door, running to find one of the Mayor's bailiffs at the Guildhall. This fellow laughed at my concern for the safety of one he called a notorious female, assuring me Master Dutton had every right to beat his wife. My palpitations increased as I made my way back to the abbey and I staggered against the wall of the graveyard, catching my breath. My revulsion at the situation I had escaped was matched only by shame that inadvertently I had provoked it.

*****

In desperation to engage my mind on something more constructive I paced on more staidly, after drawing breath, and entered the gateway of Wolvesey Castle. A moment's reflection might have suggested this was unwise, without thinking through what I should say, but I was in no condition for abstract reasoning. The gatekeeper remembered me and waved me through, confirming that Doctor Chauntley was at the palace, probably in the great hall, so I made my way there but it was Doctor Willison whom I encountered first. He looked unwell, his face gaunt as if he were in pain.

I greeted him but he seemed cross, asking curtly what I wanted. 'It's Doctor Chauntley, I'd like to see.'

'He's gone to the kitchen. The boy who turns the spit has been scalded. He'll be slapping goose fat on the wound. Does he know you were coming?'

I shook my head. 'I came on the spur of the moment, to ask him something.'

Willison drew himself up to his full height. 'I've heard tales of you since you left us. Quite a crony of the Mayor, it seems.' There was an edge to his voice which made me wary. 'Ingratiating yourself to secure a physician's practice in the town, I suppose?'

'Not at all. I happened to be with him when the bodies of Sir William Devereux and his daughter were found. I helped Mayor Cranshaw record the details. He hasn't asked me to do more.'

He bit his lip and sighed. 'A cut and dried case, it seems. And a filthy one too.'

I had no wish to discuss those deaths with Willison so I changed the subject. 'I understand Doctor Chauntley has charge, as physician, of the hospital of Holy Cross?'

Willison narrowed his eyes. 'Why does that interest you? Are you angling to win the Bishop's favour and a role in his household, despite your protestations to the contrary?'

'Certainly not. There's a resident I'd like to meet at Holy Cross and I thought Doctor Chauntley might arrange it for me.'

Willison sucked in his cheeks and I deduced he imagined my request would be peremptorily dismissed but at that moment his colleague appeared. Chauntley nodded briskly to his fellow physician but gave me a friendly smile. 'I heard that exchange,' he said. 'Is it still true, Doctor Somers, that you have no designs on my position?'

'You have my assurance. I just want permission to visit Holy Cross.'

Chauntley gave a sideways glance at Willison and moistened his lips. 'No harm in that. I'll give you a pass to show to the gatekeeper.' He took my arm and drew me aside while Willison span on his heels and stamped out of the hall making no attempt to disguise his irritation. Chauntley gave a sly grin. 'I told you how he's trying to oust me from the palace. He's tried to persuade me he should take over care of Holy Cross – ease my burdens, he says. I have to keep alert and forestall his contrivances. He'll be furious that I'm letting you cross its portals with my blessing when I've barred him from the premises. I count it a victory to discomfit him.'

Chauntley gave a snigger but, having seen the force of Willison's wrath, I wondered if he was wise to rile his associate in such a gratuitous way. Nevertheless I was happy to benefit from their mutual mistrust and I left Wolvesey Castle joyfully, clutching my authorisation to enter High Cross and speak to its residents. The success of my appeal to Doctor Chauntley pushed aside the embarrassing memory of my encounter with Master Samuel Dutton and his abused wife.

Chapter 7

In the evening my chagrin returned and I told Robert Bygbroke an abbreviated version of the incident with the butcher, expressing my anxiety that Mistress Dutton had been murdered by her husband after I abandoned her to her fate. I was put out by the organist's mirth at my sorry tale and then, assuming a solemn expression, he cautioned me against unsuitable relationships.

'Jiggery-pokery requires discretion, Harry. It's most unwise to tangle with tradesmen's wives.'

'I wasn't tangling with her in any way.'

He brushed aside my protest. 'Appearances are what count. Jealous husbands are the butt of most unsavoury jokes and your butcher is affronted. Oh dear me, physician, you've given the poor man some bitter medicine. It will only increase his green-eyed itch.' Robert burst into infuriating laughter and I soon left him to walk in the cloister, hoping to compose myself before seeking my bed.

On the far side of the covered walkway I followed the path past the Prior's house and to my surprise I heard raised voices coming from the building. The shutters were thrown open as it was a warm evening and I could hear Prior Aulton was annoyed. I had no wish to eavesdrop but as I registered what he was saying I could not resist the temptation.

'Bishop Waynflete will not understand your intransigence. He has welcomed Sir William's bequest to the abbey and asked what plans we have to use it. Brother Simon has a detailed scheme prepared for refurbishing the retro-choir, including provision for the new Bishop's own chantry when the time comes – may God grant him long and productive life. It's obvious the Infirmary is inadequate for our needs with so many elderly brethren to care for. You've said so often enough yourself. The Bishop will expect you to bid for a proportion of the legacy.'

'I will not taint my office by taking money from an incestuous murderer.'

'You are presumptuous and arrogant, Brother Lambert. You dare to usurp the Lord God's judgemental role and set yourself up as an avenging angel.'

I shivered and crept on my way on tiptoes. The phrase the Prior had used was one which had come to my mind in considering the possibility that the Infirmarian was guilty of double murder, taking it on himself to punish the sin of incest. I had tried hard to dismiss the idea that the monk could have perpetrated the crime but if his superior, who knew all his weaknesses, believed inexcusable arrogance might lead him to execute vengeance on those he judged culpable, perhaps I was wrong. It was profoundly troubling.

I was hardly less irritated next morning after a restless night when the organist bounded to my side with a jovial titter as I broke my fast in the guesthouse. 'Fret no more, good friend,' he proclaimed. 'I've been to the marketplace and can assure you Mistress Dutton is vivaciously alive, albeit sporting several blemishes to her face. Her husband has an angry scratch across his cheek so can't have had things all his own way but he's more chastened because the Mayor's bailiff knocked on the door to say there'd been a complaint about a disturbance in the house.'

'You've seen them? You went for my sake? The Mayor's bailiff called? I didn't think he would.'

'Yes, yes, yes and you obviously have more credit at the Guildhall than you surmised. You're too tender-hearted for the hurly-burly of illicit assignations, Harry. I shouldn't have teased you.'

We were soon firmly reconciled and I was delighted that Robert said he would walk some of the way towards Holy Cross with me as the morning promised fair. I had told him nothing of my purpose and he did not enquire but treated the occasion as a jaunt to be enjoyed before he held a practice with the choirboys at the abbey. We set out while the mist still hovered over the water meadows and we strolled for a mile or so by the side-streams which threaded their way across open ground to join the main river. We passed through a stand of trees and emerged to glimpse the buildings of Holy Cross for the first time, pausing there for a moment to admire the tower and gabled transept of the church soaring above the wall which encircled the hospital. I had not expected anything so substantial, so dominating in the landscape.

I turned towards Robert to express my surprise when from the corner of my eye I caught movement across the river and the words froze on my lips. A black-clad horseman riding a grey horse had appeared, making his way parallel to us on the other bank of the Itchen and, after drawing rein for an instant, he spurred rapidly downstream out of our sight.

'Someone you didn't want to see?' Robert asked.

'Did you recognise him?'

He shook his head. 'Too well swaddled and my sight's not good at a distance. Nice horse. Like the one you rode when you came to Wolvesey Castle. Is it one of the monks?'

I attempted to sound unconcerned. 'I don't know. I can't even be sure if the horse comes from the Prior's stable.'

'One grey horse is very like another, unless you're close to it.'

I tried to take comfort from that observation. 'True. I mustn't imagine perils which don't exist.'

'Perils?' Robert looked at me quizzically. 'Related to your reason for coming here?' He was altogether too sharp in his deductions.

I forced myself to laugh. 'I'm being fanciful. It's of no consequence. I'll go to the gatehouse and seek admission. You'd best return to coach your youthful charges in the choir. It's only two days until the Bishop will be here to listen to them.'

He held my eye for a moment and then shrugged. I'll see you at dinner. I hope your business prospers.' Then he set off at a trot and I guessed he had lingered too long away from his duties.

*****

Master Woodman was a slight figure, afflicted with curvature of his back, and he lacked the lower part of his left arm. He told me that he sustained that injury many years previously outside the walls of Orleans when he had fought in the French wars alongside Sir William. He insisted that despite this disability he had served as cupbearer to his lord after their return to England until the constriction of his spine prevented him moving freely.

'Sir William had me admitted here through the good offices of the late Cardinal and visited me every few weeks until his untimely death. Brothers in arms, he was pleased to call us.' He narrowed his eyes at me. 'Did the Mayor send you?'

A half-truth would suffice, I decided. 'I had the misfortune to be with Mayor Cranshaw when the bodies of Sir William and his daughter were found.'

'Taken his time, making enquiries, hasn't he? Still, I suppose it was clear enough what happened and he's got more pressing things to look into.' The old man wiped moisture from his nose with the back of his hand. 'My poor lord, that he should be driven to uphold his honour in such a way.'

This was not the reaction I expected and I realised that, shut away in Holy Cross, Master Woodman might not have heard the scurrilous tales about the Devereux deaths. I must proceed cautiously with my questioning. 'Upholding his honour?' I repeated.

'Such a sweet little girl she was. I mind her well. Gave her piggybacks and picked her posies. God help us, they're all daughters of Eve when they grow to womanhood. Avid for a man between their legs, luring unsuspecting fellows to indulge their basest feelings.'

'You blame Mistress Isabella for what happened?'

'She betrayed her family's good name, trampled their reputation in the dirt. Sir William had no choice.'

'You mean he was bound to kill her? You don't hold him blameworthy in any way?'

'What else could he do? Must have broken his heart to do it. He loved her with a father's fiercest passion. I can see it all in my mind's eye – the misery he suffered when he saw her dead in his arms. Her pale face lifeless. Her breathing stilled. That's why he did for himself. He couldn't bear what he had done nor, dear Lord Christ, could he live with what she had done. God grant him rest.'

I was appalled by Master Woodman's attitude but instinct told me I must question further and perhaps challenge the interpretation which seemed obvious to him. It was almost certain he knew nothing of the two daggers and the evidence that a third person had been involved: but I did and I was obliged to seek resolution of these conflicting versions of the tragedy. I must let him take his time and not prompt him.

'I wonder, good father,' I said, patting his uninjured arm, 'if you could bear to tell me the whole story, what Sir William told you of his daughter's behaviour and the pain it caused him.'

*****

An hour later I reeled into the courtyard of Holy Cross, cursing myself for a purblind idiot, lacking faith in my convictions, too ready to accept the deductions others laid before me. What old John Woodman had confided was restricted to those things he knew with certainty, for he refused to speculate about alternative explanations, but I was confident I could complete the picture and draw conclusions which now made perfect sense. I needed time to reflect, to plan how to respond to this new understanding, but I doubted I would be given that luxury. I watched a cart move away from the door to the hospital kitchens across the yard and trundle out through the gateway. Then I followed it, standing in the shadow under the arch for an instant before stepping into the sunlight. I half closed my eyes against the brightness and peered round intently. I was not mistaken. He was waiting for me.

He stood on the edge of the trees across the meadow with his horse tethered to a stump beside him. When he saw that I had found him he raised his right hand as if in benediction and began with long slow strides to walk towards me, his black gown rippling the long grass. He had drawn a blade from the scabbard hanging on his hip and I presumed he was resolved to kill me. My hand fastened on the hilt of my small dagger but I had no stomach for fighting even in self-defence. This was not the confrontation I would have chosen but I advanced to meet him.

'Congratulations, Doctor Somers, I take it I am unmasked.' I underestimated your tenaciousness.'

'I've been slow in my deductions but now I've learned a little. I suspect I don't know the full story. I'd be glad if you'd enlighten me.'

He laughed. 'I don't think you ask from salacious curiosity. I suppose you find my involvement in such an affair improbable.'

It seemed probable he intended to taunt me before lunging forward with his knife. Yet delay gave me an opportunity to prepare myself and I loosened my dagger, hoping he would not guess how feeble a swordsman I was. Besides, playing for time might be to my advantage for the gate to Holy Cross could creak open once more and witnesses emerge to thwart his murderous intentions.

'I would wish to give any man a fair hearing. I've seen enough of life to realise crucial circumstances may not be apparent to the casual onlooker.'

Doctor Willison grunted. 'Have you ever loved a woman with all your heart and soul, longing to make her your wife? That is my story.'

My pain was still raw when the scab covering concealed grief was picked but I must give no hint of this and keep my tone neutral. 'It's one I understand. Mistress Isabella returned your devotion?'

'She would have defied her father and fled from his house to wed me but it was not so simple.'

'He would have disinherited her?'

'You make it sound a squalid transaction. It wasn't that but I'm not a rich man and Isabella wished me to benefit from the wealth which would rightly be hers. Her father refused to consider me as her suitor.'

'You continued to meet her?'

'In the barn at first light. We lay together. I thought if I got her with child her father would relent.' He shook his head with a groan.

'Instead when he discovered you together he throttled her.'

'He must have hidden outside the barn. I left first and was riding down the hill when I heard her scream. I was too late to save her. But not too late to be revenged. I felt I'd been martyred along with my beloved but I could give vent to my scorn for her murderer. Can you understand what it is like to be mad with fury, every rational thought subsumed into the need to kill?'

Too well, too well; but I must not let myself be diverted by my own recollections. 'Killing was not enough for you. You determined Sir William's honour must be tarnished and with it his daughter's virtue rubbished, the woman you loved.'

'God forgive me. I've suffered for that sin in the weeks which have passed but at the time I was driven by demons in my soul to strike down the villain and destroy his good name. I carry with me next to my heart the proof of his turpitude. Its existence gives me some comfort that my violence was justified. Look, look – I've shown no one this letter. He drew a crumpled paper from inside his gown and held it out. 'Read, how he spurned my offer.'

I flattened the short note and read its message with increasing distaste.

Never is my answer, Willison. Never. I charge you to make no more approaches to me. As for the wishes of others they can go hang. I's appeal to me is rejected absolutely and without compunction. William Devereux

I looked up at Willison. 'Mistress Isabella had begged her father to permit your match and his reply was that she could go hang?'

Willison's thin lips trembled. 'Exactly. Perhaps I should have realised he would do her harm if she defied him and I failed her. That's why I sought to traduce his name even after death. Yet I have felt the need for atonement.'

'You sought forgiveness at St. Swithun's shrine.'

'Ah! You found the dagger I carried away with me. I wondered how you made your deduction that I was guilty. In our tussle Sir William's weapon fell to the ground and when I stabbed him I was too overcome to think of switching the blades and fixed his hand around the hilt of mine. A foolish error. All I could think of was ruining the wretch's reputation and I rode on until I could send a message to the Mayor so he would find the bodies as if in shameful congress. I trusted there was nothing to link me to the scene. I always suspected John Woodman might know I'd asked for Isabella's hand but I thought that, once her father's name was blackened, his rejection of my suit would only confirm the evil perversity of his own lust.'

'Yet you tried to visit Master Woodman at Holy Cross.'

'I intended him no harm. I would have wept in front of him for my lost love and tried to win his compassion.' I frowned, reflecting that Doctorr Willison lacked understanding of Master Woodman's loyalty to Sir William, but he mistook the reason for my grimace. 'You'll think that coldly calculating, Harry Somers, but I've been troubled by what I did. I swore on St. Swithun's shrine, to devote the rest of my life to physic and healing, to atone for my fatal passion. You, it seems, have been sent to prevent me fulfilling my vow. Heaven's will be done.'

To my astonishment he held out his weapon with the hilt towards me. 'I shall not resist arrest,' he said.

I was unprepared for this turn of events, confused by my own response. 'Have you told me the truth, Willison? All the truth? What about Sir William's brother, the Almoner?'

He scowled. 'I had good reason to dislike the monk because he encouraged Sir William to repulse me, but I had no part in his demise. I believe he suffered from an excess of choler in the spleen which brought about his apoplexy in God's good time.'

This was certainly plausible, as I had never discounted the chance that Brother Joseph died of natural causes, and it appeared that Willison had made a frank confession of his involvement in the Devereux deaths. He could not know how easy it was for me to feel sympathy for a man who had killed in righteous anger, avenging the mistreatment of the woman he loved. I reached out and took the dagger from him.

'I've no wish to see a fellow physician's carcase on the gibbet but you cannot remain serving the Bishop's household unless you're prepared to confess your sin to him.'

He shook his head. 'You're right. I couldn't stay in Winchester. I'd willingly make confession to a priest and seek to do penance if I was far away from here but escape isn't open to me now you know everything. I submit myself to your will. I want no more blood on my hands.'

It occurred to me that this suggestion of moderation on his part might be intended to win my gratitude but it was of no importance; he had already stirred the anguish in my heart and drawn the comparison with my own experience.

I spoke slowly. 'I wouldn't impede your passage if you sought to leave the country with immediate effect.'

He gasped. 'You'd let me go into exile? Now, on the instant? If I could cross the Narrow Sea to Normandy..., I have a cousin in Rouen. I could build a new life there.'

The coincidence seemed preordained and I smiled. 'I suggest you go at once to Southampton and seek out a cordwainer called Master Brill who lives by the market steps. An acquaintance told me of him in case I wished to cross the Narrow Sea. He'll find you a berth to cross to Normandy.'

'You mean it?'

'Go now.'

I walked with him to his horse and watched him ride away, his outpouring of thanks ringing in my ears. I had no right to grant him this remission, no power to confer the exoneration only a justice or priest, in their different ways, might bestow. I had grossly exceeded my remit but I knew why I had done so. I saw myself in his predicament, subject to unutterable torment, and I believed in his sincerity. I promised myself that I too would acknowledge my repentance, praying near St. Swithun's shrine to beg forgiveness for my presumption and giving thanks that Brother Lambert was blameless of any crime.

*****

When Willison was out of sight I gazed round. I registered the stationary cart on the track to the town, far to my left, wondering for a moment whether our encounter had been observed by the tradesman who set out from Holy Cross ahead of me, but the vehicle appeared to be unoccupied. I thought no more about it and wandered back, through the trees, to emerge onto the water-meadow beside a muddy branch of the Itchen in a deep trench. There was no one ahead of me or visible across the river and I heard nothing but the clucking of the fowl in the stream and the rustling of the reeds. My mind was filled with contradictory interpretations of what I had learned and what I had done, uncertain whether I could justify even to myself the clemency I had no authority to offer.

The dark shape rose from the channel beside me just as I had passed the spot where my attacker must have been crouching and I did not comprehend what was happening. The blow which cracked open my head felled me instantaneously and threw me headlong into the swampy ditch so, with my last wisp of consciousness, I was aware of my mouth filling with water and slime before blackness obscured everything.

Chapter 8

When I first opened my eyes I had a bleary impression of dazzling light and my head was throbbing. I had no strength to do more than blink but I registered that I lay on a raised bed, enfolded in soft linen sheets with a feather pillow easing the ache in my neck. It was enough to reassure me although I had no notion why I was there and I drifted into sleep once more.

Next time I stirred I was conscious of someone lifting my shoulders slightly and applying something soothing to the back of my head. He was murmuring encouraging words and I knew who he was before my heavy eyelids fluttered.

'Doctor Chauntley.'

'Good, good, my boy. Don't try to sit up. You're on the road to recovery now but take it gently. It was a vicious blow. Lucky you've got a skull like a rock. Do you remember what happened?'

I concentrated and the sorry details sorted themselves in my mind into a coherent account but I was not ready to talk about them. 'Am I at Wolvesey Castle?'

'Indeed you are and have been these three days. The Reverend Robert Bygbroke had you brought here after dragging you from the brook. It would have been ignominious to drown in two inches of water but you were incapable of saving yourself.'

'Robert found me? How? He'd left me long before.'

A movement to my right alerted me to the presence of another person in the room. 'Hush, you restless flibbertigibbet. Don't worry about it. After we parted I started off along the path back to the abbey but then I saw that horseman we'd seen ride south, splish-splashing across the river near Holy Cross and making for the stand of trees opposite the gatehouse. I retraced my steps to wait in the undergrowth and see what the fellow was up to. I thought he might do you harm but when you emerged you seemed to converse quite amicably with him, not a sign of hanky-panky, though I couldn't see too well or make out who he was. When he rode off and you began making your way back to the town I felt stupid so I stayed hidden until you'd passed me. I didn't want to confess my namby-pamby fears on your account. But then this villainous giant heaved himself out of the ditch and clobbered you with a club. I assumed he was a cut-purse but he ran off as soon as he'd floored you and I managed to drag you clear of the filthy water which was choking your windpipe. You spluttered like a wheezy bellows when you drew breath again.'

The excitable account and attempt at humour focused my mind. 'You saved my life, Robert, but your choirboys must have missed their practice.'

'Good, good, you have your memory intact.' Doctor Chauntley fussed over me, insisting I must continue to rest, but there was one fact I needed to know.

'Did my attacker get away?'

The organist gave a trill of laughter. 'He did at the time but he's lodged in the prison at the King's castle now. When he turned to run off I recognised him as that purveyor of foul offal which pollutes the market square with its stink and I knew he resented your attentions to his sweet helpmeet. He's sworn to the Mayor that you'd lain with her in unlawful intercourse and he was entitled to impose punishment. It's the talk of the town and the cause of much hilarity. Samuel Dutton's not popular and there's many a lewd fellow envies the randy physician who's boarded the butcher's enticing wife. You're celebrated, Harry, but Prior Aulton is troubled about your continued residence in the abbey. Still, you can stay here until you're better.'

I buried my face in the pillow, groaning at this horrid turn of events, so that Doctor Chauntley, misinterpreting the cause of my distress, drove Robert from the room and plied me with a disgusting potion which he said would help me sleep peacefully. In my weakened state I hoped it would bring lasting oblivion.

95

Despite my disinclination to face the situation confronting me I made good progress and within the week Doctor Chauntley declared I was well enough to leave Wolvesey Castle and resume my physician's duties. The wound on the back of my head was healing, covered by a dressing under my cap which also hid the patch of bare scalp where my colleague had hacked off my hair to expose the gash I suffered. Reluctantly I expressed my willingness to return to the abbey and abide by Prior Aulton's determination as to whether I could remain there. Doctor Chauntley looked amused.

'You're to be interviewed by a more august personage than the Prior before you leave here. The Bishop has summoned you to attend him and I expect he'll have a question or two to put to you.'

'Bishop Waynflete is here? What does he know?'

'As much as I do, which may be partial. His visit is to be brief. He'll return for his enthronement in the cathedral on another occasion. Come, I'll take you to him.'

I entered the Bishop's private quarters in consternation, not moderated by Doctor Chauntley's knowing wink as he left me at the door. Waynflete was seated at his desk, a scroll bearing seals unrolled in front of him, but he glanced up at once when I entered and beckoned me to a stool. He was a lean, sinewy figure with piercing blue eyes which he fixed on me.

'I give Heaven thanks for your recovery, Doctor Somers,' he said and as I murmured 'Amen', he continued. 'You are satisfied with the treatment you have received from your medical colleague?'

'Most certainly, your Grace.'

'Good, Chauntley will be my household physician in Winchester. I'm glad to hear he has the approval of one trained in Padua with all the latest learning.'

I shook my head in disclaimer but noted that the Bishop knew more about me than I would expect or probably welcome. He raised an eyebrow with disarming amusement. 'Did the butcher have cause to doubt his wife's unsullied virtue?'

I took a deep breath. 'She has in no way been compromised by me, your Grace. I do not know the root of Master Dutton's jealous suspicions but he had no justification for doubting her honesty so far as I am concerned.'

'Yet you entered her house alone and accepted ale from her hands?'

Uncomfortably I bowed my head. 'A misjudgement I have sadly rued. She was courteous and I meant no harm.'

'You've been used to the freer exchanges between men and women among the nobility and did not appreciate conventions might differ among the townsfolk of Winchester?'

I was alert now to his assumed insouciance. 'I don't claim that, your Grace. I come from humble stock and am used to mixing with all ranks.'

'Why were you so anxious to speak to her that you ignored propriety?'

It was the question I dreaded because the answer could lead me onto a subject I must avoid. 'I had met Mistress Dutton at the Sustern Spital where her aunt lodged until the old woman's death. There was something about the aunt's condition I wanted to ask.'

Bishop Waynflete's gaze did not waver but I sensed his disbelief although he did not challenge my assertion. 'Mayor Cranshaw believes you are a troublemaker in the town,' he said. 'Does he have reason to think so?'

'We took divergent views on a particular matter.'

'The Devereux deaths?'

I tried to show no surprise while cursing the breadth of the Bishop's information. 'Yes, your Grace. But the Mayor had responsibilities which I did not.

'Quite so. He displayed prudence in handling a distasteful business. I remember young Mistress Isabella when I was at the college here. She would come down to the mill with her duenna while my scholars were at their exercise in the field by the river. She proved a notable distraction for the boys and I fancy she was fully conscious of her charms. Ripe for marriage even then, she was: a pity her father did not pack her off to a suitable husband.'

I was unsure what the Bishop implied but, to my relief, he did not pursue the circumstances of the deaths although I hoped there was no link in his mind between that subject and the news he gave me next. 'I've received a letter from the other physician who served my revered predecessor at the castle: Doctor Willison. He has relinquished his post and tendered his apologies for not explaining to me in person why he'd decided to leave.' As Waynflete paused I struggled to hold a bland expression. 'I think you know an opportunity has arisen for him to join a relative in Normandy. Indeed he speaks appreciatively of your advice in helping him decide to go there. I too am grateful because it has saved me from an invidious choice as I require only one physician in my episcopal household. Chauntley will serve loyally, will he not?'

'Assuredly, your Grace.' Of that, at any rate, I was confident, but the Bishop had other questions to put to me.

'You've not been tempted to seek a future in Normandy yourself?' I shook my head but did not conceal my surprise and Waynflete flicked up his eyebrow once again. 'You've had visitors from across the Narrow Sea, I hear. I thought they might have brought you offers of employment with the King's former Governor in the Duchy?'

It was unnerving to realise I had been spied on but there was no purpose in prevaricating. 'A suggestion was made, your Grace, but I declined it.'

'May I ask why?'

'I am King Henry's loyal subject and would not wish to serve...'

The Bishop cut across my stumbling words. 'You imply that Richard of York is not loyal?'

'I didn't mean to suggest that but some of the Duke's acolytes are not to be trusted. I've learned that to my cost.'

A broad smile spread across his bony features. 'I too. I pray that Baron Glasbury will amend his life and find favour with our Lord God but, until he does so, you are wise to be wary of his deviousness. Would you serve Suffolk again if he asked you?'

The switch in tone caught me unawares and I stumbled in replying. 'He wouldn't do it. I have no expectation... I can't hope...'

'Quite so,' the Bishop said again as if what I had stammered made sense and gave him his answer. 'The Marquis is consolidating his position at the King's right hand. I counsel patience.' He reached out and rolled up the scroll in front of him so, assuming our interview was at an end, I stood but he gestured for me to sit down again. 'I have full confidence in Prior Aulton to run the abbey here, Doctor Somers, but it is incumbent on me to take an interest in its affairs. What is your view of the Infirmarian, Brother Lambert?'

I rallied my wits quickly. 'He is knowledgeable and dedicated, your Grace. I respect his skill and his integrity.'

'Interesting. Can he be persuaded to use some of the Devereux money to benefit the Infirmary, do you think?'

'I believe if his Abbot were to offer him guidance he would do so. He's genuinely troubled, thinking it would be wrong to accept tainted money, but he'd be honoured to receive your Grace's counsel.'

Bishop Waynflete rose and extended his hand for me to kiss his ring. 'God keep you, Doctor Somers,' he said 'and bring you to a happier future. You show wisdom and understanding. I hope we shall meet again.'

My expression of gratitude was sincere and I returned to my room full of admiration for the man who now held the See of Winchester. His experience as a teacher showed in his quick perception and interest in people but he was no narrow pedant, nor a blinkered penny-counting administrator. Instinct told me he could offer qualities which would be invaluable in supporting timid, pious King Henry, buffeted between rival advisors. I hoped he would be able to use his skills to resolve simmering differences and to prevent unchecked animosities from deteriorating into open conflict. It was heartening to think that the King's insistence on his appointment as Bishop was not some royal caprice but thoughtful recognition of Waynflete's worth.

*****

My subsequent interview with Prior Aulton was, as expected, more awkward than the meeting with the Bishop. He was courteous, even apologetic, and made no overt accusations as to my moral behaviour but said he could not countenance the abbey being associated with ribald jokes and smutty innuendo. I spared him embarrassment by accepting that I should leave its precincts and he agreed that I could find lodgings outside the south gate, where Master Ranken and his colleagues lived, conceding that I might still offer physic to pilgrims as they waited to enter through the gatehouse. The arrangements would suffice to provide a roof over my head and give me a little income but my link to the protection of the church would be tenuous and I could not rely on safety from arrest if forces of the state were to move against me. I had no better alternative.

I was greatly disappointed that Brother Simon, the Warden of the Works, who had been so friendly and sympathetic when I first arrived, became distant towards me. His disapproval was evident, although he spoke no word of criticism, and as I had no appetite for him to make his censure explicit I kept out of his way. By contrast and to my pleasure the Infirmarian sought me out and assured me I could continue to avail myself of herbs from his garden to treat my patients outside the abbey.

'That's more than generous.' My tone probably hinted at surprise.

'You thought I'd be appalled that you'd spoken with a woman? Some of my brethren denigrate all women as inheritors of Eve's sin. Narrow lives, they've lived. I know differently and only entered the abbey as a novice when the pure young woman I loved succumbed to a fever.'

He brushed aside my murmur of sympathy. 'It was long ago and I'm reconciled to my calling. I wanted nothing else after Ellen died. I was apprenticed to her father, an apothecary, and he looked kindly on our affection for each other. He understood why I wished to abandon my articles when we were both bereaved. Perhaps the loss rankles still and makes me morose sometimes but serving in God's house helps me feel closer to Ellen who is in God's keeping. The Prior would chide me for such ideas but I don't believe them sinful.'

Much became clear to me with Brother Lambert's words and I asked him to bless me when I left the abbey. I wondered if I should have taken his course of action, cloaking my own grief in dedication to a holy, secluded life as I had contemplated briefly, sitting in the cloister months earlier. I knew that was not my God-given vocation but this knowledge, when my future was so uncertain, made me more unsettled and disgruntled.

I tried to disperse gloomy thoughts by insisting to myself that the change forced on me was beneficial, giving me the opportunity to expand my practice in the town which I had coveted, and I was cheered by Robert Bygbroke's support. Ranken found me lodgings with an elderly widow and the following day I entertained the master carpenter and cathedral organist to a stoup of ale in my garret room looking towards the outer abbey walls. We indulged in jovial badinage and Robert made merry, disparaging the quality of the liquor I supplied, comparing it unfavourably with the choice wines to be found at Wolvesey Castle.

'This sour piss is good enough for rough labourers or uncouth physicians,' he teased, winking at Ranken, 'but I have a more refined palate and appreciate something sweeter. Ah, the days when I could enjoy a bowl of fragrant hippocras!'

I had no wish to abandon the frivolity of the occasion but could not let this casual reference pass. 'When did you drink hippocras?' I asked, dreading the reply.

'It was the favoured tipple of Doctor Willison,' Robert gurgled happily. 'His medicine of choice, he said, and he entertained his visitors with it whenever he could.'

'Did he have many visitors?' I held my breath.

'Now and then. He'd taken to inviting the Almoner from the abbey to call on him – that poor Brother Joseph who died. I couldn't imagine what they discussed. They didn't seem on friendly terms. Here let's refill our glasses and drink the health of all hospitable physicians and confusion to all narrow-minded monks.'

My stomach contorted and for a moment I feared I would spew up what I had drunk. I was terrified Ranken would pass some comment indicating he had heard the rumour that Brother Joseph's death had been brought about by tainted hippocras but he said nothing. Despite that reprieve I sat long after my companions had left me, agonising as to whether I had misjudged Willison with culpable naivety. I had absolved him from a crime of malicious premeditation, believing he killed Sir William in maddened passion after the woman he loved had been murdered by her father. He had evoked my sympathy. Yet if he was in fact a calculating poisoner who plotted to destroy the monk he saw as his enemy and then lied to me, I had made a dreadful blunder by allowing him to escape from justice. I could not know the truth of the matter but shame at having arrogated to myself the role of judge and guilt at my possible gullibility deprived me of sleep until the dawn was breaking.

In the next few weeks, despite my troubled mind, I had an outwardly placid existence, but it was overshadowed by the prospect of attending the Assizes when Master Dutton would be brought before the Justices. I had no wish to be paraded in public as a victim and, as I did not see my attacker when he beat me to the ground, I tried to persuade myself that I had no relevant evidence to give. I advanced this argument to Robert Bygbroke who relished his own role as star witness for the prosecution.

'Fiddle-faddle.' He replied. 'You'll be asked to remove your cap and exhibit the grievous wound you suffered. I know the scab's healing nicely but you can see where your hair's only beginning to grow again. It'll be a moment of pathos for the court. Comedy too perhaps: the regrowth is still quite spikey.'

I growled amusement but I dreaded the butcher elaborating his account of my alleged misbehaviour with his wife. He would no doubt plead that he had not planned the attack in advance but acted opportunistically when he happened to see me at Holy Cross Hospital, although he was unlikely to be exonerated on any grounds of mitigation. I knew the wretched fellow was bound to be sent to the gallows but if he asserted that the assault was unpremeditated, it would be horribly reminiscent of my attitude to Doctor Willison's offence. I found it difficult to sympathise with my vicious attacker and accepted the law must take its course. Yet the notion disturbed me that perhaps, in some way unknown to physicians, Master Dutton's unwarranted jealousy indicated an ailment of the mind which we could not comprehend. I comforted myself by rejoicing that charming Mistress Dutton would be freed from the physical abuse her husband inflicted but I am ashamed to recall I gave no thought to the vulnerability of her new status.

The location of the trial in the King's castle only intensified my unease and I was sweating when I was summoned into the courtroom and saw the judges arrayed before me. I saw the prisoner too, standing between warders, more gaunt than I remembered and showing signs of ill-treatment on his bruised face, but more importantly, as it proved, he saw me. Immediately he snarled and had to be restrained from leaping forward while he raised his bound fists and shook them at me.

'There's the adulterous swine! Devil take his luck in escaping. If I'd had my cleaver with me, his head would have parted company with his shoulders, I can tell you.'

I retched in revulsion but as one of the Justices spoke I realised Master Dutton had condemned himself with these incautious words.

'You admit your guilt then, fellow? You don't deny causing this physician grievous harm?'

When the prisoner roared pride in his crime I understood that I was reprieved. No witnesses were needed and sentence was passed expeditiously. He was condemned to hang and I was free to leave. A tremor of relief passed through me but my ordeal was not quite at an end. A throng of townspeople had gathered at the gate to the castle and there were muted catcalls from some tradesmen as I made my way out although they were drowned by the cheers of labourers I recognised as members of Ranken's workforce. I had become a symbol of divisions which existed between neighbours in the small town and this grieved me.

Two days later Ranken reported that the butcher had been executed, evidently expecting me to celebrate his demise. In fact I was full of regret that I had inadvertently occasioned the fellow's death and pondered uneasily how a man's irrational urges could prove self-destructive. I kept to my room for the rest of the day, in gloomy contemplation of humanity's contrariness and ignorance.

The light was beginning to fade when my landlady knocked on my door and she could not keep the disapproval from her voice. 'There's a caller, Doctor Somers, asking for you.'

'A patient?'

'No, that Dutton hussy who caused all the trouble. Shall I send her away?'

I rose, shaking my head, but I had learned to be cautious and insisted that the landlady stayed in the room during the meeting despite my visitor's protest.

'My request is personal, Doctor Somers, not a matter to be shared with one and all.' The new widow's appearance was suitably modest but she pouted at me prettily and I was reminded how attractive she was.

'My landlady will be entirely discreet but I'm unwilling to risk further harm to your reputation or mine by meeting you alone. Why have you come?'

'To implore you to take pity on the woman whose name has been traduced, along with yours. Have you considered how I am to live, bereft of a husband and breadwinner?'

I experienced a qualm of anxious guilt for not thinking of the woman's quandary but I responded dispassionately. 'It's two months since Master Dutton's imprisonment. How have you managed during that time?'

She tossed her head in a sign of pique which did not fit well with her guise as a supplicant. 'Friends have helped me,' she said. 'They cannot do so permanently. Isn't it your responsibility to provide for my sustenance?'

I caught my breath but forced myself to reply calmly. 'I'm sorry for your situation but I have no obligation towards you and my means are very limited. I can spare you a few pence in charity but nothing more.'

She looked over her shoulder at my silent but glowering landlady before stepping nearer to me and fluttering her eyelids. 'You misunderstand my meaning, Doctor. I am asking you to restore my honour by taking me as your wife. I will serve you well at bed and board.'

I stepped back in alarm, colliding with the wall, as Mistress Dutton cupped her hands under her breasts and thrust her bosom towards me. My outraged chaperon could contain herself no longer. 'You impudent slut, how dare you? Get out of my house!'

The butcher's widow was unabashed. 'I've surprised you, Doctor. Forgive me. I ask only for what is right.' She smiled, stretching out her hand to stroke my cheek, and she must have felt me tremble. 'I've always known you had a yen to lie with me.'

'Mistress Dutton, this is absurd and you must leave. Your painful loss has turned your wits.' I pushed her aside roughly and flung open the door. 'When you are more composed you will regret your behaviour and we will say no more about it. My landlady will show you out.

The older woman needed no second bidding and propelled the importunate widow down the stairs, leaving me in great distress. The incident would have been upsetting in any circumstances but my shame was heightened by the treacherous throbbing of my manhood which, as Mistress Dutton had so accurately divined, longed to take her in lechery.

*****

The next two weeks were a purgatory of conflicting emotions. I dreaded leaving the house in case Mistress Dutton lay in wait for me or made a more public assertion of my alleged duty towards her, while all the time frustration fed my lust for the body she had offered. In weaker moments I even brooded over the possibility of taking her to wife, despite knowing full well how unsuited we would be, and I prayed for my good sense to return and bring me equanimity. I continued to treat injured workmen and coughing infants but I was largely oblivious to the outside world and paid little heed to Ranken's announcement that, now the Assizes were finished, men from the court had arrived at the royal castle.

It was not until my landlady appeared at my door one evening after the curfew horn had sounded, with news of a visitor asking for me, that I appreciated the doom-laden implications of these arrivals. She saw my start of alarm and grinned to reassure me. 'It's not that strumpet, Doctor, never fear. It's a well-turned out soldier.'

I shut my eyes as understanding came and resignation swept over me. Instinctively I gathered up my doctor's gown and carried it while I descended the stairs, holding the bannister tightly in case I should stumble. A compact figure of medium height awaited me at the foot of the staircase and I recognised the crest on his armour instantly, accepting I could no longer withstand the fate I had avoided for more than half a year. The embossed clog and chain gleamed in the light of the lantern the soldier carried and marked him as a servitor of William de la Pole, Marquis of Suffolk. I had no doubt I was to face the deferred reckoning which my former master considered my due.

Part II Winchester, Stamford, Yorkshire, Dublin and London 1447-1448

Chapter 9

The soldier clicked his heels, banged the shaft of his pike on the ground and saluted, while I nodded without looking at his face and concentrated on sounding unconcerned.

'You're to escort me to the castle, I take it?'

A peal of laughter greeted my question. 'Cor blimey, Doctor, is that all the greeting I get? Is this what six months with the holy brothers has done to you? Turning your nose up at old mates, are you?'

My voice came feebly, disbelieving, as I grasped the newel post. 'Rendell?'

'That's me name, same as it always was. Glad you've not completely forgotten me.'

'Of course I've not forgotten you. It's just that I can't believe you're here. You're serving Suffolk?'

'Yeah. He offered all Gloucester's bodyguard a place in his suite. I ain't fussy if the pay's good enough. But you were right guessing what I was here for. I'm to take you to the Marquis, not under arrest but with no quibbling, under escort.'

I clutched at the straw of his presence. 'Were you specially selected for the duty?'

He pursed his lips as if musing how to break bad news but he could not hold the guise and began to grin. 'Yeah. Suffolk summoned me and gave me instructions. He said you're not to be anxious but he wants you brought to him after dark and by a secret entrance.'

This was not wholly reassuring. 'I suppose he thought I wouldn't try to get away from you, as my old friend.'

'Be a fool if you did, Doctor. For all our old friendship I'd skewer you without a second's pause if you disobey his Grace.'

I could not be sure if he was in jest or earnest and, at that moment, I did not want to find out. I put on my gown and smoothed down my cap. 'Lead on halberdier, I am at your command.'

'This here's a pike, not a halberd,' he corrected me, 'but I can use both and the bill which has a hook for yanking riders out of the saddle. Handy that.'

I nodded meekly, uncertain how I was meant to relate to this competent and self-assured young soldier, but, as we walked, I pressed him for news of our friends. 'I've been worried about Thomas and Grizel. Do you know how they are?'

He looked at me sideways with a mischievous grin. 'They're fine. Didn't stay long at Greenwich after Queen Margaret claimed the palace. Live in the City now, they do. Thomas's set up as master carpenter on his own account, not a hand's throw from the Tower. Only been there a month but he's picking up good business already. Just as well because Griz is in the family way again: drops a whelp every year. I can tell you being an uncle is losing its novelty.'

In the old days I would have cuffed him for speaking of his sister with disrespect but I did not dare to behave so casually in our new circumstances. I murmured satisfaction at his news and quickly lowered my head when we were challenged by one of the town guard for being abroad after curfew. Rendell produced his authority and answered the man with lofty disdain, receiving an obsequious salute in return. It reinforced my nervousness.

As we approached the cobbled slope leading up to the castle entrance, Rendell took hold of my elbow and impelled me towards a shabby low building on our left. He produced a key and opened its door which gave onto a flight of steps descending into the darkness. He ushered me through and handed me the lantern while he relocked the door from the inside. 'Keep close behind me,' he said. 'The steps are uneven and slippery.'

'This leads into the castle?'

Rendell turned his head and tapped his nose. 'Yeah. For use by those not meant to been seen going in or out. Quite a network of passages, there is. Don't worry, I know the way.' He adopted a sterner tone of voice 'When we come out into the courtyard you'd best keep your mouth shut. You're to look like a physician come to attend one of the nobs. Think you can manage that?'

*****

I obeyed my instructions and Rendell escorted me in silence through the castle to Suffolk's private chamber. Sounds of merriment echoed up stairways and the aroma of succulent delicacies, roasted meat and rich sauces, hung in the air, reminding me of culinary delights which I had not tasted since joining the monks in their humbler fare. Distractions tempted me all the more because I was terrified of what might lie in store when I faced the King's favoured adviser, the man who had disowned me after I obeyed his bidding.

An attendant announced me, Rendell gave a rueful smile before turning on his heels and I was admitted to the presence of William de la Pole, Marquis of Suffolk. I bowed low and as I straightened I observed that he was sitting on an upright chair with his hands clasped tautly on the desk in front of him. For a moment he did not speak.

'You don't look in the best of health, physician,' he said at length. 'Perhaps the constraints of the cloister don't suit you and I'm told you've recently suffered a nasty attack for straying from the paths of celibacy. That may have contributed to your pallor.'

'The allegation was unjustified, my Lord.'

He grunted. 'Maybe; but dalliance is not out of character, you must concede, although you've lowered your sights if you've been sniffing round a butcher's wife. You've displeased the tradesmen of the town, Harry. They've sent me a petition protesting at your presence here.'

'I'm sorry...I'd no intention...'

He cut across my stammering. 'You've also irked Mayor Cranshaw. He's made complaint that you've caused mischief by interfering in a case he was investigating.'

'We did not see eye to eye, it's true. I thought him negligent when he chose not to pursue information I gave him but the responsibility was his and I did not intervene.' This was not strictly correct but I was exasperated the Mayor was seeking to get me into trouble.

Suffolk pressed on the table and rose to his feet. 'You could not desist from chasing after the truth, any more than you can stop yourself breathing. What I consider a more serious charge is that you wrote to me in inappropriate terms, implying I had knowledge of your attendance at the Duke of Gloucester's deathbed. How could you expect me to respond to such an assertion?'

I bowed my head, stifling a sigh. Over the previous three years I had watched the Marquis's pride in his achievements develop from modest and justified contentment to vaunting self-satisfaction, yet I believed him basically honest. Now, it seemed, he was willing to sacrifice considerations of honour to his own continuing advancement. My apology was husky. 'I didn't mean to cause you embarrassment, my Lord.'

'Have you forgotten the danger that letters I send might be intercepted? Your communication reached me safely enough in the episcopal pouch but I could not be confident that any answer I sent to you would escape the attentions of those who wish me ill.'

I must have looked surprised. Three years previously Suffolk's correspondence with the King had been diverted and read by men opposed to the truce he was negotiating with France but I had no idea the privacy of his messages was still at risk. 'I didn't expect the threat continued,' I said

'That was disingenuous, Harry Somers, when you knew Gilbert Iffley and his cronies were still active. Both he and Stephen Boice have visited you, I understand.'

111

'I didn't know I was under such scrutiny.' I bit back a sharper retort but my anger was growing.

'It was their movements, rather than yours, which were monitored but when I received report that they had seen you it seemed possible you were sufficiently aggrieved with me that you would choose to join their enterprise.'

My temper flared at this and I no longer cared if I lost all hope of the Marquis's goodwill by my vehemence. 'Your Lordship may have noticed that I have remained in Winchester, despite the overtures made to me to serve the Duke of York. I would have hoped you knew me well enough to credit me with loyalty to my King, despite the injustices I have suffered for my pains.'

Suffolk lowered himself stiffly onto his chair and fixed his eyes on mine. 'You haven't lost your spirit. That's good. I concede you have some reason for your annoyance with me but I never intended to abandon you utterly – unless I had no alternative. You speak of your loyalty to King Henry. Do you believe the Duke of York disloyal?'

'I've no knowledge of the Duke's allegiance and would not presume to question it but I'm well acquainted with the men you've named who now serve him, as they once served Gloucester. Iffley and Boice are dangerous malcontents and you are wise to keep them under scrutiny. I fear they may yet cause harm in the King's realm.'

Suffolk shifted awkwardly on his seat. 'Are you turned prophet now, physician? I will add to your prophecy. If we cannot contain and neuter the threat these reprobates present the King's realm is at risk of being torn apart.' I was astonished by his frankness and merely inclined my head before he spoke again in a gentler manner. 'I've had to tread carefully since Gloucester's inopportune death at Saint Edmundsbury. I've been accused of having him poisoned, through your agency, and without doubt I have benefitted from his removal from the King's Council. I'm not quite secure enough yet to admit you back into my household but in a year or so, if all goes well, I hope to welcome you in your old position. If you're able to overlook the injustice you perceive you've received at my hands.'

Once I would have dropped to my knees in gratitude and relief at this offer but I had learned to be wary in giving my trust to an incomparable opportunist. 'I'm grateful, my Lord, but can't commit myself so far ahead.'

'I don't expect you to, Harry. I've engaged an elderly quack to serve at my London house for the time being and your young protégé will help him when he returns from the university.'

'You're still sponsoring Leone in his studies? That's generous.'

Suffolk gave a thin smile. 'Take it as earnest of my good intentions towards you. I assume you'll have no objection to leaving Winchester in the current circumstances? I can oblige the worthy tradesmen, pacify the tedious Mayor and make use of your talents in a way far more fitting for a man of your ability.'

This was unexpected and I wondered what he had in mind. 'My Lord, I've been content to live in the town until recent events soured the atmosphere. Where would you wish me to go?'

'An old acquaintance of yours is nearing death but you may offer him a degree of ease in his last months. He's requested your attendance and I suspect he has some specific task he wishes you to undertake. The Earl is confined to his estates now and you will need to travel far to the north.'

My intake of breath was audible. 'The Earl of Stanwick?'

'The same. You should set out tomorrow. Three of my men will escort you to ensure your safety on the road. Tonks can be one of them.'

It took me a moment to register that this was Rendell's name and begin to express my pleasure but I was diverted by an expression on Suffolk's face which I remembered. 'While you're in the north,' he said, 'I'd be indebted if you'd look a little wider than the affairs of Stanwick's household. The great families of those parts, the Nevilles and the Percys, are always at each other's throats and their constancy can never be taken for granted. I'd welcome some information from an impartial observer on how things stand between them, bearing in mind that Richard of York is married to a Neville.'

He flicked up an eyebrow as he faced me and I comprehended perfectly what he was about. I was to play the part of his catspaw once again; it was the price of my escape from present difficulties. 'I will do so on one condition, my Lord,' I said, my voice quavering more than I wished. 'Mistress Dutton, the butcher's widow, faces poverty without support. If you would make provision for her to live in decency, it would be a charitable act.'

He sprang to his feet slapping his thigh and wincing at the movement. 'By God, Harry Somers, you are incorrigible. Charity be damned, you incriminate yourself by your concern for the slut. Condition indeed! Never mind, I'll provide for the woman's future until she inveigles another enamoured buffoon to the church door.' He gave a great guffaw of laughter.

I did not challenge his assumption but bowed my thanks. 'My Lord,' I added as he waved me to the door, 'I think you may have used up the ointment which eases the pain in your back. If Rendell accompanies me back to my lodging, may I give him another jar to bring you? I can then set out for the north confident that you will not be inconvenienced by aching joints.'

'Devil take your impudence, physician, but send me the balm by all means. You've a long ride ahead of you. Prescribe something for your own saddle sores.' He was still chuckling as I left the room.

*****

Suffolk's jest was well aimed because I had never enjoyed riding for days on end and the journey to the north of Yorkshire was a daunting prospect. My companions clad in Suffolk's livery were soldiers used to hours on horseback and they set a challenging pace which I was loath to complain about, knowing that Rendell would delight in mocking my inadequacy. Fortunately the sergeant who led my escort soon noted my discomfort and enquired whether I would wish to take a day or two's rest anywhere on our route. Only then did I dare to suggest we might seek lodging at the hostelry of the Raven in Stamford.

My mind was in turmoil after my hasty departure from Winchester and I regretted there had been time for only the briefest of farewells to the friends I had made there. Prior Aulton and Brother Simon were courteously cool but I was touched by the Infirmarian's sincerity in lamenting my departure. Ranken and his workmates were understandably rueful at the loss of their physician but Robert Bygbroke was soon in tears, begging me to return.

'Such a mish-mash it'll be here without you, no mistake. No one to raise a glass with, only namby-pamby monks. Don't dilly dally, Harry; come back when you can.'

I promised I would but had no confidence in my ability to choose my future. The further I rode from the abbey which had offered me sanctuary, the greater my uncertainty grew. I was returning to a way of life familiar to me from boyhood, serving in a noble household, undertaking assignments for my lord beyond the scope of my profession, yet in circumstances which lacked hope of permanence. During my time in Winchester I had mourned what I had lost and longed for my former freedom; now I was unsure whether I was sufficiently hardy to face the trials which would await me.

My request to call on the Prioress of St. Michael's convent was granted on the day after our arrival in Stamford and I waited to meet her in the parlour where I had last seen her more than two years previously. I did not recognise the nun who admitted me from the gatehouse and she regarded me with suspicion, checking that the door from the room to the cloister was locked on the outside. When it clanked open a few minutes later and the Prioress strode in with a swirl of leaves around her feet, I was relieved to see that I was welcome and there was no need for formalities. The aquiline nose shotup as if to sniff the atmosphere but her shrewd eyes were gleaming.

'So you have extricated yourself from the protection of Holy Church, Doctor Somers. I expected nothing else. What does Suffolk want you to do?'

'Attend the Earl of Stanwick's sickbed, Reverend Mother, – and assess relations between the Nevilles and the Percys.'

She clapped her hands with glee. 'I could tell him that. You may recollect that I'm kin to Henry Percy, Earl of Northumberland, who keeps the northern Border of England safe against the depredations of the Scots. He does so alongside his neighbours, the Nevilles, and there's as much bad blood between those English fellow subjects of King Henry as with King James's men. One day swords will be drawn to settle their enmity.'

'Is that day likely to come soon?'

Her lips twitched without smiling. 'That's what you are to assess, I imagine. Don't underestimate the rivalry between them. If it ever became linked with the wavering ambition of Richard of York, there would be real danger.'

'The Duke is married to a Neville.'

'So is the Earl of Northumberland: sisters cleverly distributed between the great houses of the land. One at least will weep bitter tears in the future, I surmise, probably both. Tread warily in the north. I understand your old acquaintance Stephen Boice landed at Hull not two weeks ago. That won't be with innocent intent. No doubt when he's fulfilled his mission he'll join his chagrined master and decamp to Ireland.'

I did not disguise my confusion. 'Ireland?'

The Prioress seated herself on the window bench and smoothed her skirts. 'I wondered if Suffolk had told you. Richard of York is appointed to be the King's

Lieutenant in Ireland, although he's yet to take up the post. Demoted from the grandeur of his position in Normandy and effectively exiled from the royal court. Suffolk must believe it's an astute move but I fancy it will rebound on him. York holds extensive lands in Ireland and there is logic in his appointment but I fear he'll feel aggrieved and humiliated. His unpleasant followers whom you've encountered may well urge him towards open belligerence. Your commission in the north takes place amid fascinating uncertainties.'

'The Marquis didn't judge it necessary for me to be aware of this. Is it true that the Earl of Stanwick has requested my presence, do you think?'

The Prioress nodded sadly. 'Definitely, although I couldn't say what he wants you to do. The poor man's suffering is nearing its end and he formed a high opinion of your talents as a physician but it's credible he has something else to ask of you.'

'Young Mistress Eleanor is still with him?'

'With the King's consent, he's made her heir by adoption for all his wealth and his beneficent Countess cares for his bastard as if she were her own. That's a most happy outcome.' She stood and I bowed, accepting that our interview was at an end. 'You will resume your letters to me, I trust, Doctor Somers. I'd welcome knowing what you discover, if you may properly disclose it to me of course. I've valued your wise judgement greatly in the past.'

'I'm honoured Reverend Mother.' I owed her no less and was glad to renew our communications.

She moved to the cloister door and put her hand on the latch. 'One other detail you should be aware of, Doctor Somers, as you're to venture into the Stanwick household. Eleanor's wretched mother has been given shelter there since the woman's rift with her lawful husband. The Countess is uncommonly generous to harbour the Earl's old mistress but I suspect that scheming hussy is as untrustworthy as ever. I counsel you to be wary, physician, for Lady Maud Fitzvaughan will have lost none of her wiliness nor, I imagine, her brazen allure.'

She swept from the parlour without looking back while I absorbed the horror of what she had told me.

Lady Maud's presence in Yorkshire was unexpected and puzzling. Her husband, Lord Walter Fitzvaughan, had confined her to his estates in Norfolk after she engaged in a pernicious plot to trick him and I had thought her still incarcerated there. Years before I first met her, during her girlhood she had been ill used by a malicious guardian and prevented from marrying the young man she loved: the man who became the Earl of Stanwick. She had borne his natural daughter, Eleanor, who had been cared for in St. Michael's Convent for many years. Now the child had been acknowledged as the Earl's heir and embraced by his bountiful but childless Countess. It was indeed a happy outcome but Lady Maud's presence in this amiable home was an anomaly which could not augur well for the comfort of its members.

Knowledge of this history was burdensome enough but Lady Maud posed a more personal problem for me, overlaid with guilt and infused with lust. During the years since I met her we had lain together, both before and after her marriage, half a dozen times. The carnal temptation she represented had been easily dismissed when I met the woman I planned to marry but now, thwarted of that happiness and after enduring long months of celibacy, I knew I would be vulnerable to her charms if she chose to offer them again. All reason and good sense insisted I must resist her but, if she sought to renew our intimacy, I had no confidence I would succeed.

Chapter 10

No journey across open country is free from danger but the road north from Stamford was well frequented by merchants, pedlars, pilgrims and itinerant tradesmen, with the occasional entourage of a noble lord moving from one of his residences to another requiring other travellers to move aside. The stretches of track which made me feel uncomfortable were those through heavily wooded land where it was easy to imagine bands of ruffians erupting from the trees and seizing our goods and persons. Fortunately the valour of my escort was not put to the test but it may be that their martial appearance deterred ne'er-do-wells from approaching. On the other hand we did not look as if we were conveying expensive merchandise worth stealing. Whatever the cause, we faced no hindrance from vagabonds but the deterioration in the weather, as autumn drew towards winter, brought its own problems and slowed our progress. The mellow gleam of the sun shining low across stubble-pocked fields was replaced by heavy rain screening our surroundings from sight for almost a week. Then, on the penultimate day of our journey, the wind increased in strength and our horses whinnied with unease at the turbulence around us as leaves danced madly across our faces and twigs snapped under nervous hooves.

The small habitation of Northallerton was to be our resting place for the night before we left the principal road and struck across more rugged terrain towards our destination. I was glad to reach shelter in such raw conditions but the inn offered few comforts and after supping a dish of indifferent broth in a noisome parlour I decided to brave the gale by pacing round the courtyard. Rendell accompanied me but the howling wind curtailed our conversation. Throughout the long ride we had been cordial but circumspect with each other, exchanging jokes and reminiscences but conscious of ambiguities in our relationship since he had become Suffolk's sworn follower and I was liable to be sacrificed as Suffolk's pawn.

There were half a dozen trees at the back of the inn and we heard their branches cracking when a gust caught them so we turned back beside some outhouses and ducked as a tile from the roof skittered loose and crashed in front of us. I saw Rendell gesticulate but could not make out his words while a roaring noise above our heads intensified and I was startled when he hurled himself against me, pushing us both into a doorway. Stones thumped around us and we were showered with fragments of turf, escaping serious injury although my cheek was grazed by flying debris, but Rendell shouted with urgency for his companions. When they emerged from the inn he pointed and sent them running behind the outhouses while he returned to me, as I wiped a smear of blood from my face. He picked up a jagged piece of rock and held it out.

'I spotted there were a bundle of tiles stacked on the roof where it's being repaired. The rope holding them must have been ripped apart.'

'Well spotted,' I said, looking with curiosity at the object he was holding.'

'This ain't no roof tile though. This were thrown at you by the bugger on the roof. Expect he cut the tiles free to disguise what he was up to.'

I opened my mouth to doubt the existence of a rooftop attacker when Rendell's colleagues rounded the corner dragging a whimpering fellow between them. I recognised him as the ostler who had led away my horse when we arrived.

'Best go inside,' I said drily, registering that unwelcome truths were likely to be disclosed in the ensuing interrogation.

My fears were fully realised for the man was so terrified of the soldiers that he readily confessed his part in my attempted murder, insisting that he had misaimed intentionally and begged forgiveness. It soon emerged that he had been bribed to watch out for my arrival and ensure I never left the inn alive.

'Who bribed you?' Rendell had assumed the role of inquisitor and when the prisoner hesitated he signalled to the soldier gripping the man's arm to apply force. The fellow squealed and began to sob.

'I don't know his name. God's truth, I don't. He stayed here a week back. He said you'd likely come – a physician with an ugly mark on his face. I don't know more.'

'I think you do,' Rendell said. 'We could put you to the instruments if you're stubborn.' The ostler's arm was twisted more sharply.

'No, sir, no sir. I don't know – only one thing I did hear. He was speaking to his servant who was with him. Something about Normandy. That was the place they said.'

I groaned and assured Rendell I was certain of the villain's identity. There was no need for the worthless ostler to suffer further and I insisted he be freed, although the soldiers declared he must be given a beating first.

They dragged him away while Rendell cocked an eyebrow at me. 'Who?'

'All I know is that Stephen Boice landed at Hull a few weeks back. He'd been in Normandy. He and Iffley have been trying to persuade me to join them under Richard of York. Maybe they've lost patience and decided to dispense with me altogether.'

'Either that or they're trying to terrorise you into joining them.'

Rendell's shrewd alternative was not in the least consoling.

*****

One other unsettling incident occurred before we reached the Earl of Stanwick's demesne and it was not dissimilar to the attack at Northallerton. We were riding along a track carved into the hillside, below a steep incline and above a sharp drop into the ravine on our right. I happened to glance up and saw, far above us on the hillside, masons working on a tumbledown building, when suddenly there were shouts and a clatter of stones down the slope. The noise and debris caused the horses to shy and one of my escort needed all his equestrian skills to prevent his frisky young mount dashing into the precipitous chasm. Fortunately I had been provided with a well-travelled mare of equable temperament and she merely scuffed her hooves on the loose ground and neighed loudly in protest.

Rendell scrambled from his saddle and clambered uphill, shouting to the posse of labourers above him, while the rest of us advanced to a more sheltered corner and waited for his return. I was ready to accept that the rock-fall was an accident but when my erstwhile servant came clattering back to us I could see from his face that I was not to be humoured by this comforting conclusion.

'They swear it weren't one of them caused the landslide,' he said. 'Some ragged-looking wayfarer ran out of the bushes further up the hill and set the pile of stones sliding.'

'A likely story,' the sergeant snorted but Rendell was shaking his head.

'Nah, I saw the bugger. By the time I got up to the workmen he was just disappearing back into the undergrowth.'

'Why didn't they grab him?'

'Reckon they were scared. He's a big fellow.'

'Shall we go up and search for him?' The sergeant sounded half-hearted.

'No,' I said. 'He's probably a witless clown who thought it would be fun to startle a party of riders without understanding it could be dangerous. We've not far to go now. Let's get on.'

The sergeant saluted and we moved off but Rendell stayed close by my side. 'You don't believe that, do you?' he mouthed at me.

'I'd like to. Let's hope it's not put to the test.'

Rendell winked. 'I'll wager it will be.'

Ravensmoor Castle stood on a bluff projecting towards the north above the valley. It was strongly defended by the natural gorge below its walls on three sides and the stream curving its way through the trench. When it had been built danger was seen as coming from the Scots, although it was many years since their raids had penetrated so far into England. On its southern flank a well-used track led straight to the gatehouse and an assembly of buildings had grown up beside it, housing the dependents of the castle and their animals. These dwellings and byres were well kempt and the courteous competence with which we were escorted through the gate confirmed that, despite its remote location, this was an efficiently managed demesne.

After the ambiguous events of the last two days, Rendell and I both noted the presence of three chained guard-dogs acknowledging our approach with ferocious growls, until they were quieted by their keeper. For prospective residents of the castle they were reassuring protection but Rendell had once been savaged by such creatures and we were wary as we passed their station.

Countess Stanwick met us in the courtyard and made us welcome, explaining without embarrassment that the Earl was resting but would greet us after we had dined. She was short in stature but self-possessed in her bearing and it was immediately clear that she commanded the respect and obedience of her husband's servitors. I recalled the Prioress's appreciative words about the lady's virtues and this first impression affirmed her insight. Nevertheless it was the Earl I was anxious to see and that inconvenient guest, Lady Maud Fitzvaughan, I was even more concerned to avoid. I observed gratefully that Eleanor's mother was not to be seen when we sat at table in the great hall.

The young girl herself was present at the meal. It was two years since I had met her briefly and she had matured into a pretty maiden of nearly thirteen years, with all of her mother's attractiveness but no hint of Maud's wilfulness and guile. I had not expected her to remember me but as the Countess began to make formal introductions she smiled and clutched the woman's arm.

'I know Doctor Somers, Mother. We met at Stamford when Father took me there to thank the Prioress for her care of me as a child. Father spoke highly of him and told me to think of him as a friend.'

I bowed, hiding my uneasiness at hearing Eleanor address the Countess as her mother. 'I'm honoured you remember me, Mistress Eleanor. I shall try always to be worthy of the Earl's good opinion.'

'You've come to be his physician. Will you be able to make him better?'

'I haven't seen him yet, mistress, but I'm told his condition worsens. It's in God's hands whether his decline can be halted but I hope to relieve the pain he suffers.'

She nodded. 'She said you were an honest man.'

The Countess shooed the girl to her place at table, leaving me unclear to whom Eleanor had referred but speculating that the Prioress might write to her former charge, as she did to so many correspondents.

After the meal I was conducted to the Earl's chamber, high in the main keep from where he had views to north and south, out to the hills and into the courtyard. I was horrified by the change in his appearance since I had seen him early in the year and was glad that natural caution had prevented me from promising his daughter any improvement in his health. His shrewd eyes peered at me from their sunken sockets and I saw he read my thoughts.

'I rejoice to see you again, Doctor Somers, as a free man. My household will benefit from the skill and knowledge you bring to moderate their ailments. I am well aware what you can do for me is limited.'

'Mistress Eleanor asked if I could make you better.'

He gave a wan smile. 'It is for her sake that I wanted you to come.'

'Is she unwell, my lord?'

'No. no, I thank God she seems robust. It's a different matter. Now is not the time to explain. I'm weary. Doubtless in a day or two I shall feel stronger – it's the pattern of this debility, I have a day's respite now and then. Settle yourself, Doctor Somers. Make the acquaintance of the folk who live in the castle and the village beyond the gates. I hope you will minister to all of them. If you have a potion to lessen the nagging in my belly, let my body servant have it, would you?'

As I gave my assurances he closed his eyes and I retreated from his chamber, down the winding staircase. Where it gave onto the landing beside the great hall Rendell was waiting with a face like thunder.

'You knew she was bloody well here, didn't you? You're a fucking disgrace.'

His truculence irritated me and I pretended not to understand his assertion. 'Whatever are you talking about?'

'Lady bloody Maud, Lord Fitzvaughan's wife. When did you know she was here?'

'The Prioress of St Michael's informed me at Stamford.'

'Why didn't you tell me?'

'Because I knew you'd misunderstand and make a fuss. It has no bearing on my position here.'

'No bearing! Christ, you'll be bearing down on that bitch soon enough, if I know you. How can you even think of it when you nearly had Madame Yolande to wife?'

Rendell had reason to revere the woman I loved and had aspired to marry but his words made me furious. 'Be quiet with your filthy innuendo. I've no interest in Lady Maud and it's no business of yours anyway.'

'Crap! Thought we was mates, like we used to be. Please yourself. We're off tomorrow, back to the south and

Suffolk's service. I'll think of you fucking that whore and then I'll forget I ever knew you.'

He stamped down the stairs and I was too angry to call him back.

By evening I regretted allowing him to rile me, although I refused to admit to myself that his strictures were well intentioned – and well-aimed. I looked for him, ready to apologise for my bad temper, but he and his colleagues had left the castle to visit a hostelry outside the walls and I had no appetite to follow him there. When I rose in the morning after fitful rest I was told my escort had already departed on the first leg of their journey to re-join Suffolk. I was given a message from the sergeant explaining their haste and wishing me good fortune but there was no word from Rendell. Throughout my sojourn in Winchester I had missed the lively companion who shared so many adventures with me in the past and I had rejoiced to see him again. Now I was sorry and ashamed that we had parted on bad terms.

Later that morning my chagrin deepened when a waiting woman I remembered knocked at the door of the small room where I was to dispense my remedies. I knew her as deaf Marian who had observed but not overheard several of my conversations with her mistress and once had been dismissed from the chamber to save her from witnessing what she should not see. She handed me a folded paper, carelessly unsealed, and the neat writing was familiar to me. *Come to me an hour before sundown, Harry. I need your counsel.*

I longed to refuse the summons but could not be discourteous to a lady who was to be one of my patients. I nodded and spread my hands wide in enquiry.

'Lady Fitzvaughan is lodged in the Middleton Tower,' Marian said and she narrowed her eyes, 'in the far corner of the courtyard. It is not overlooked.'

'She is confined to the tower?'

Marian read my lips and shook her head. 'She is free to come and go as she wishes, to join the household at dinner in the hall and ride outside the castle walls. It is her choice to remain in her own quarters much of the time, except when she walks with Mistress Eleanor in the courtyard.'

Despite my ill humour I felt a pang of regret that Lady Maud felt compelled to suppress her natural and provocative vivacity.

*****

I assumed a professional demeanour as I approached the Middleton Tower, resolved to deal with the wretched woman dispassionately, but my first sight of Maud confirmed that there need be no artifice in my physician's role for she was obviously unwell. She had lost weight and her face, although still beautiful, was marked by furrows beside her eyes and mouth. She was propped on cushions in her bed but to my relief she was fully dressed. She stretched out her hand as I walked towards her.

'Ah, Harry, how we have both suffered since we last met. You have lost your French paramour and I am banished from my husband's company.'

She was always excitable but rarely sensitive to another's pain and her words took me by surprise. Her recognition of my loss was unexpected while the distress at her own dilemma seemed affected and contrived. 'Lady Maud, I'm sorry for your difficult situation. I had thought you still in Norfolk. How long have you been at Ravensmoor?'

She pouted and lay back on her cushions. 'Two months I suppose. I am part of the bargain.'

'Bargain?'

'No one has told you yet? They said Ralph was poorly; otherwise I imagine he'd have informed you. I don't see him of course. It would be indelicate.' She rolled her eyes on her final word and gave it an inflection loaded with ambiguity.

127

'The Earl is very weary at present. He indicated there were things he wished to explain when he felt stronger.'

She looked down for a moment. 'Poor Ralph. It's a cruel business, this incapacity which is eating his vitals. He offered me sanctuary here and Countess Mary begged me to accept. She is a woman of supreme kindness and virtue.' These last words were spoken with such scorn that I was unsure whether Maud was deriding the Earl's wife or implying that her generosity was false.

'Does Lord Fitzvaughan know you are here?'

She trilled with laughter and some of the old mischief flashed in her eyes. 'Naturally. How could I have escaped captivity in Norfolk otherwise? I told you I was part of the bargain.' Seeing my bewilderment she stopped teasing me. 'The bargain concerns Eleanor. That's why I had no option but to assent to their terms. After Walter realised that I was barren and had been planning to foist another's infant on him, as if I had borne it, he determined to rid himself of me. You know he's desperate for an heir to save his inheritance becoming forfeit to the King if he dies childless and he was tempted to cast me off so he could take a fruitful bride. Not that he would relish his duty in her bed any better than he did in mine. His affections lie elsewhere as you are well aware.'

I nodded, thinking of Gaston de la Tour, his favoured companion, whose attitude towards me had proved ambivalent in the past.

'Walter believed he'd found the perfect way to rid himself of me when he learned of Eleanor's existence and the relationship I had with Ralph in my youth. He intended to claim I was pre-contracted to the Earl and therefore our marriage was void and could be annulled by Holy Church. There was hearsay evidence to support the fact of my betrothal to Ralph and if the Earl had been willing to confirm the circumstances, I would have acquiesced with Walter's plan.'

I watched her expression carefully and I read the resentment which clouded her eyes. 'That would have meant the Earl's marriage to the Countess was also void and he would not agree to shame her.'

She smirked. 'You comprehend the lofty concepts of honour which I find meaningless. Ralph refused to comply with Walter's proposal but he suggested an alternative arrangement. He and the Countess have adopted his natural daughter, my sweet Eleanor, as their own and with royal consent she is confirmed his heir for all his land and chattels, except his title. Ralph pointed out to my esteemed husband that if he retained me as his wife, in name at least, he might also be able to recognise my bastard as his heir. Eleanor is now a wealthy heiress and her wardship will fall to the Crown on Ralph's death so, with her father's blessing, Walter has petitioned King Henry to be appointed her guardian in that event. The King is well affected towards my husband and is expected to grant consent. A neat solution, don't you think? It will save my sweet sodomite of a spouse from forcing himself to bed another woman. It was as part of their gentlemanly accord that Ralph offered to house me at Ravensmoor and so free Walter from all unwelcome encumbrances.'

The bitterness in Maud's voice was audible. 'Surely the Earl also had in mind that the arrangements would mean you could be close to your daughter as she grew to womanhood, in a way that's never been possible before?'

'I don't doubt it was his intention but he reckoned without the Countess, beatific Countess Mary. She has stipulated that Eleanor shall never know I am her mother. The child uses the term to address her and calls me simply "Lady Maud" Eleanor does visit me and enjoys my tales of life at the King's court but to her I undoubtedly seem a woman of dubious virtue, cast off by her husband, not someone to be admired.'

'That's hard for you.' I was upset by Maud's evident hurt. 'It's affected your health?'

'I have no purpose here but I've nowhere else to go. Walter has all my inheritance and I have no means to live elsewhere, unless I chose to take the veil. Walter would welcome that, I think – as would Countess Mary.'

'I could not repress a slight smile. 'The Prioress of St. Michael's might grant you refuge if Lord Fitzvaughan paid over some of your dowry to her house. But I don't think it's a life which would make you content.'

Maud drew herself into a sitting position and I noted that colour had come into her cheeks. 'You are impudent. I've had no lover, physician, since you took me in the solar of Suffolk's London house. How long ago was that? Two years? I think you will remember.'

'After you'd threatened me with a knife as I recall.' I regretted the rashness of my response as soon as the words were out of my mouth.

'The titillation fired us both, did it not? Since then you have probably slept with a dozen as well as impregnating that French noblewoman, while I have kept to my chaste bed.'

I controlled my instinct to rebut her assertion. 'Lady Maud, it's helpful to appreciate your position. A physician can treat ailments better if he knows what troubles his patients. I could offer a mixture to lift your spirits. Marian can fetch it for you.'

She leaned forward and touched my hand. 'Something else you might lift to please me, Harry.'

I pulled back and bowed, pretending not to understand the innuendo. 'My Lady, I must go. I trust you will regain your vitality and contentment. Try to rejoice in the good fortune which has come to Eleanor.'

She giggled and the tip of her tongue crept between her lips. 'Come again, physician. You have the means to minister to my needs and I shall welcome your attention.'

I fled from her room trembling. Maud was as enticing as she had ever been and I could not prevent myself feeling sympathy for her predicament. All her life, while men had controlled her actions, sometimes in

130

despicable ways, she had struggled to serve her own interests and to preserve some semblance of dignity. However misguided she was, I could not help admiring her perseverance and fortitude. In my mind I prayed to the Virgin to give me strength to reject her advances but, since Mistress Dutton re-awaked my senses, my body had begun to yearn for the physical comfort she offered and I did not know whether my basest longing would overcome my finer resolution.

Chapter 11

A week passed before the Earl was ready to speak to me again and by then winter was hard upon the countryside, branches and bushes rimed with frost. I was glad to stay within the confines of the castle and village in such weather and used the time to acquaint myself with my new patients. There were fewer dependents than Suffolk had in his great London house where I had served but they included a variety of outdoor labourers, farm hands and herdsmen with calloused knuckles, strained muscles and swollen joints, often differing from those suffered by cooks, carpenters and masons with which I was more conversant. It was satisfying to treat such a range of disorders and seek to extend my knowledge but the people of Ravensmoor, who were not used to having a physician continually at hand, did not always welcome what they saw as my intrusiveness.

When I was summoned to the Earl I had momentarily forgotten his promise to share some confidence with me and entered his chamber intent only on playing my physician's role. He looked more wizened and wracked with discomfort than when I had seen him before and I hastened to examine him. He did not resist but soon brought my prodding and pressing to an end.

'There's nothing to be done, Doctor Somers, I know that and I welcome the potion you have prepared for me which dulls my pain. My time is growing short and there are matters I must see concluded before God calls me to account for my life. Most importantly my concern is with young Eleanor and her future.'

'I understand you have provided for her richly, my Lord Earl.'

'All I could endow her with will be hers but she is near marriageable age and what is hers will become her husband's. It is imperative the match is suitable in all respects.' He paused.

'You have someone in mind?'

'Yes, I thank God, there is a pleasant lad of noble birth whom she has known since she came here and there is affection between them. He's kin to the Percys, indeed he's the Earl of Northumberland's ward, and I'll be content to see Eleanor bound to a family I've always esteemed. Henry Percy has agreed that they should be betrothed next summer when the boy, Cuthbert, attains his fourteenth birthday. When I saw him on my return from Saint Edmundsbury earlier in the year the Earl promised to give me written confirmation of his commitment but, despite my letter to remind him, nothing has been forthcoming.'

'You think he has changed his mind?'

'I don't know why he should have done so. The marriage would bring the Ravensmoor lands within the purview of the Percys and safeguard them from the Nevilles of Raby Castle to the north from here. There may be good reason for Henry Percy's dilatoriness but I'm anxious to see the arrangement formally endorsed. I shall not survive to attend the betrothal ceremony but I want assurance it will take place.'

'Will you write to the Earl again, my Lord?'

'I shall but I won't entrust my letter to an ordinary messenger. I'd like you to take it, Doctor Somers, and seek an audience with Henry Percy so you can explain with discretion why I beg him to put his agreement in writing. You're fortunate the Earl is currently at his castle of Topcliffe, not his main seat at Alnwick many leagues to the north from here, so you won't have too far to travel.'

Far enough, I thought, with the first flurries of snow in the air. 'Do you fear there are men who would seek to prevent the marriage unless it is firmly contracted?'

He looked at me with rheumy eyes. 'My renegade cousin, Roger Egremont, who will inherit my title although not my lands, may have other plans for the Stanwick heiress. Roger has ingratiated himself with Duke Richard of York and may use my death as an opportunity to make mischief.'

I drew in my breath slowly. Your cousin was with the Duke in Normandy?'

'And has returned to England with him.'

'Has anyone visited you on his behalf? A man named Stephen Boice, perhaps?'

'I know Boice. I saw the havoc he created in Saint Edmundsbury with his good-brother Gilbert Iffley, Baron Glasbury, at his side. I would drive both of them from my gate should they attempt to visit me. Why do you ask?'

'Boice is said to have landed at Hull a while back and I have reason to think he bribed at least one rogue to murder me as I was journeying here.'

'They recognise your worth, Doctor Somers, and since you will not join their cause, seek to eliminate you. A strong posse of my men will accompany you to Topcliffe.'

I bowed my head. I had not intended to imply I was afraid and could not understand why Boice might want me dead, but the provision of an escort was welcome. 'If you'll pen your letter to Henry Percy, I will leave in the morning.'

'I'm obliged,' he said with a weary nod, 'I will endeavour to postpone my demise until your return.'

I noted that the Earl made no reference to Lord Fitzvaughan becoming Eleanor's guardian but I thought it likely this proposal was merely a safeguard in case the marriage plans miscarried. At all events I had no intention of disclosing that Lady Maud had made me privy to such delicate information.

*****

The journey was uneventful, despite the leaden skies which threatened to unload their store of snow on us, and I took the precaution of insisting that we skirt the town of Northallerton rather than seeking lodgings there overnight. I had no wish to encounter the ostler bribed to do me harm. We arrived at Topcliffe Castle in the late afternoon and even in the fading light it was an impressive sight, built on a tongue of land between the confluence of the River Swale and its tributary, moated and standing on a mound, flanked by extensive terraces and outworks. It far surpassed Ravensmoor in grandeur and I reflected that, if the Earls of Northumberland now came there only occasionally, their preferred seat at Alnwick must be of unmatched splendour.

I was made welcome but told that Henry Percy was away in York, expected to return on the morrow. I did not object to an evening at leisure especially when, after we had dined, a trio of travelling musicians entertained the company with a recital of melodies from those northern parts. The leader of the group played both the citole and the fiddle but it was his mellow voice, singing of love and gallant deeds, while his companions accompanied him, which enchanted me. When he sang the old ballad of Agincourt, *Our King went forth to Normandy,* with its proud endorsement of God's favour for the English, men stamped their feet and echoed the refrain at the end of each verse. I wondered how many listeners were contrasting the glory of that victory in our fathers' day with what they saw as England's shameful capitulation by seeking a truce with France in recent years.

'I've seen you before, physician. I never forget a face, especially if it's marked so notably as yours is.' The otherwise insolent reference to the birthmark on my cheek was softened by the musician's jovial expression.

'Thank you for your music. You have a fine voice.'

He sat on the bench beside me and rubbed his knuckle across his lips, peering at me. 'I have it!' he exclaimed after a few moments 'The late Duke of Gloucester's Palace of Pleasance by the Thames. I sang there several times in my youth.'

'And I grew up and served there.' I felt a warm glow of happiness to remember Duke Humphrey's patronage of the arts and learning. 'My name is Harry Somers.'

'And mine is George Wilby. Do you serve Earl Percy now?'

'No, I've travelled afar since my days at Greenwich and am come here with a message for the Earl. Most of the year I've spent in the south, in Winchester.' I had no wish to discuss my background and mentioned Winchester only because I thought Master Wilby would know nothing of the town. It provoked an unexpected response.

'You've been in Winchester! I don't suppose you encountered my old friend who served the late Cardinal, God rest him: the priest and organist, Robert Bygbroke?'

I exclaimed with delight. 'I account him my friend,' I said. 'What jiggery-pokery has led me to meet you in this northern fastness?'

He roared with laughter. 'He still speaks with alliteration, does he? You capture his tone well. Oh, this is a joyous meeting. Come, let's share a jug of ale.'

It came as no surprise to learn that Master Wilby and his colleagues frequently played at court and it was there that he had met Robert when the organist accompanied Cardinal Beaufort on his visits. We exchanged merry anecdotes about the man we both liked and as we drank deeply I became nostalgic for Robert's company but Wilby's next words shattered my benign mood. 'You must have been in the town when that unpleasantness about the Devereux knight and his daughter came to light. Nasty business.'

'How on earth do you know about that?'

Master Wilby winked. 'Nothing like a salacious story for spreading round King Henry's court. It had to be kept from royal ears of course – our pious King would have soiled his small clothes if he'd heard about such goings-on. I think one of the local justices reported it to someone in London. Gave the nobles a chance to indulge a feeling of moral superiority over country gentlemen. I suspect the story grew with the telling.'

'Probably,' I said. 'You're right. It was a nasty business.' To my relief he didn't enquire further and I was not going to admit I knew anything in particular on the subject. I cursed Mayor Cranshaw's inaction which had allowed libidinous accounts to spread but felt uncomfortable about my own part in suppressing the truth. It was strange to ponder those events when so far away from the scene.

Henry Percy returned to Topcliffe the next morning and later in the day I was summoned to meet him and deliver the Earl of Stanwick's letter. He waved me to a stool while he read it and I was able to study his fine features and robust build. I could imagine him taking the palm on the jousting field and I was aware he had fought for his King in France on several occasions. He took his time thinking about his fellow Earl's request and then addressed me directly.

'I didn't realise Ralph's condition was so serious and this matter urgent. He speaks of his early demise. You are his doctor?'

'Newly come to his household, my Lord Earl. I regret his prospects are not good. That's why he's so anxious to provide for Mistress Eleanor's future.'

'He fears another suitor for her hand may intervene – one he would not favour? He is shrewd. The Nevilles are restless and Richard of Salisbury is quite capable of seizing a bride from under my kinsman's nose. We must be on our guard. Even a betrothal can be vitiated by a cleverly staged abduction.'

I remembered that the Earl of Salisbury was a leading member of the Neville clan, long-time enemies of the Percys, but it had never occurred to me that Eleanor's father feared for her physical safety. 'He hasn't confided his precise concerns but certainly he is looking for reassurance.'

Earl Henry fixed his gaze on me. 'The girl will be a considerable heiress but the bequest may be challenged by Ralph's cousin who will inherit his title. She will need the backing of powerful interests to uphold her cause if it's referred to the King's Council. I've never heard who her mother was but Ralph claims she was of noble birth.'

I noted his use of the past tense and although I felt discomfort it was not for me to correct him. 'I understood so from the Prioress of St. Michael's convent at Stamford where the girl was cared for as an infant.'

'There's no prospect of a further inheritance from her mother's family, I suppose?'

I exhaled, realising that this northern potentate who lived in semi-regal style might be swayed by the opportunity to acquire influence over a wider area. It was dangerously outside my brief but I took my chance. 'It isn't generally known but Lord Walter Fitzvaughan has petitioned the King to be granted the girl's wardship her on the Earl's death.'

A slow smile softened Henry Percy's expression as he voiced his thoughts aloud. 'Is that so? The girl is his kin? Walter has no direct heir of his own, I believe, so his lands will fall forfeit to the Crown unless he is granted permission by the King to bestow them elsewhere. I would hazard that King Henry's high opinion of Fitzvaughan's service would secure agreement to such a request. His lands are in Norfolk, are they not?'

'Near Attleborough in Norfolk, my Lord Earl'.

'Am I right in my surmise, Doctor Somers? Might the girl also inherit the Fitzvaughan demesne?'

'My Lord, such a possibility is well beyond my knowledge – but I have heard it mentioned.' I shocked myself at the risk I was taking, referring anonymously to Lady Maud's gossip. 'If his Grace, the King, were to indicate he would approve such an arrangement Lord Fitzvaughan might find the proposition attractive.'

The Earl of Northumberland rocked with laughter. 'What an excellent, discreet physician you are, Doctor Somers! Walter Fitzvaughan would be spared the necessity to visit a woman's bed in order to procure an heir and that would please him well, while the girl will be one of the wealthiest heiresses in the realm. You've convinced me.'

Suddenly alarmed, I sought to moderate what I had said. 'My Lord, I should stress that what I report is hearsay only, I can give you no certainty...'

'It's enough. I shall write the letter Ralph seeks. The young people may be betrothed in the summer when Cuthbert is fourteen and married a year hence. I trust it will give the poor man comfort. See my clerk in the morning and he will give you the written undertaking over my seal.

I bowed and expressed gratitude while the Earl rose and patted me on the shoulder. 'I can see why both Duke Humphrey and the Marquis of Suffolk have esteemed your service. Take care you don't enmesh yourself too deeply in the rivalries of men who jockey to speak privately in the King's ear. It's a dangerous game, physician. I wish you well.'

This message was hardly original but nonetheless disturbing. I knew that I was tangling with affairs I would do best to leave alone. Nevertheless, as I had pledged I would, I penned brief, factual accounts of my visit to Topcliffe for the information of the Marquis and that intimidating holy woman at Stamford.

*****

It was as if I had brought Earl Ralph the rarest medicine to alleviate his pain. He took my hand as he read and re-read the letter, then lay back against his pillows and sighed. 'It is all I could hope for. I have done my best for the girl. It's in God's hands now.'

He shut his eyes and after a little I assumed he had fallen asleep but when I made a slight movement he stirred, gripping my fingers more tightly. 'Promise me, Harry,' he said, 'promise me you will stay with them – my unfortunate womenfolk – at least until the marriage has taken place. Henry Percy will protect them once Eleanor is wedded to his kinsman.' He sensed my hesitation and was alert to its meaning. 'Save only if his Grace, the Marquis, commands your presence before then. Will you promise me that?'

I inclined my head. 'Yes, my Lord, I will promise that.' It did not seem a burdensome commitment and in truth I had nowhere else to go.

The Earl's next words were troubling and made no sense but I dared not question them. 'I know Walter Fitzvaughan is an honourable man but I fear to put temptation in his way. God bless you, Harry, and guide you to defend my womenfolk from all who might abuse their trust.'

*****

There were three weeks until the Feast of the Nativity and at Ravensmoor they passed in sombre peacefulness. Everyone knew the Earl's life was fading and went about their business quietly, lowering their voices when outside his muffled door or below his window and noting when I or the chaplain was called to the invalid's bedside. The Countess was admitted to his chamber several times a day and Eleanor also visited frequently, emerging tearful but tight-lipped. Senior members of the household were summoned to make their farewells to the Earl and on the Eve of the Blessed Nativity I watched with foreboding as a veiled lady was escorted from the Middleton Tower across the courtyard to the main keep. I was pleased for Lady Maud that the only man she had truly loved gave her the opportunity to part from him forever in this world but she would comprehend, from the fact of his invitation, he had little time remaining.

In the early hours of the Feast Day the Earl's body-servant roused me to say the long ordeal of pain and debility was over. The priest was in attendance but needed only to repeat the prayers for the dead since Ralph Stanwick had slipped away in his sleep without disturbing his attendants. He was much respected and deeply mourned so the following weeks were filled with necessary duties and sorrowful reflection.

Letters were sealed and consigned to the care of hardy messengers ready to brave the icy ground and frozen rivers as they rode east to Topcliffe and south to the royal court. The Countess called on my advice in wording some communications and, although she controlled outward expressions of her grief, I saw the weariness in her eyes and recommended a cordial to help her sleep more easily. I was not asked to visit the Middleton Tower but, meeting deaf Marian in the courtyard I gave her to understand that if her mistress required physic I would attend her. Eleanor was pale but gave no sign of great distress and, appreciating that young people can be resilient, I did not trouble her. I was occupied with the ailments of others in the household willing to consult me about persistent coughs, shortness of breath and constriction of the lungs, chilblains on chapped toes and fingers, abscesses which would not heal and more serious injuries from tumbles on the ice.

The first hint of a short-lived thaw encouraged me to walk outside the castle walls, welcoming the appearance of washed-out, crushed grass visible below the grubby slush, although the wind still sliced through the layers of cloak and gown. A figure was crouched beside the fishpond and I recognised Eleanor peering into the water where the bailiff had broken the ice. It was common courtesy to greet her and I started to approach when a movement of her hand made me realise she was wiping tears from her cheeks. I hesitated to intrude but she looked round and jumped to her feet.

'Doctor Somers, don't go. I'd welcome your advice.' Her cheeks were flushed and her words tumbled out quickly as if she had released them from habitual constraint. 'Do you think it wrong to grieve? The chaplain says I should be glad that Father is gone to his rest. He was a good man and should find himself with the blessed souls. It's selfish of me to regret his going for my own sake,

141

because I miss him. Do you think such sorrow is unhealthy?'

She had never spoken to me on such a personal matter before and I was glad she was willing to consult me. 'Mistress Eleanor, I think your sorrow is natural and it's beneficial to shed your tears. Only if you were to dwell on your grief to the exclusion of all else in your life, would it be unhealthy.'

'Thank you, Doctor Somers.' She blinked and smiled. 'You've answered my next question because I felt guilty letting my thoughts stray sometimes to Cuthbert Percy and our betrothal, even while I wept for Father.'

'The Earl would be joyful that your betrothal brings you happiness. He told me it would please you.'

'I've known Cuthbert since I came to Ravensmoor and we've always liked each other. I feel fortunate I'm not to be yoked with a stranger.'

'It's a good prescription for a successful marriage. You've seen the example of the Earl and Countess. Your parents...'

'The Countess is not my mother.' Her words cut across mine and I was too startled to respond at once. 'I call her Mother because I have no other and she is loving and kind. But my real mother died when I was a baby and I have been told almost nothing about her.'

I swallowed my denial. 'Have you always known this?'

'No, although I suspected it was the case. The nuns who cared for me at Stamford revealed nothing. Father told me as he lay dying. He begged me to continue to honour the Countess as if she were my true mother but he wanted me to know that the woman he had loved in his youth was both beautiful and unfortunate, misused by cruel people but glorious in her fortitude. Those were his words.'

The apt description stung me and I longed to tell the girl that her mother lived and was near at hand but it was not my place to speak, at least not then. 'Treasure that thought, Mistress Eleanor. It's a mark of his love for you and for your real mother, that the Earl had courage to tell you.'

I held out my arm to help her across the stones bordering the pond when I heard, almost simultaneously, a shout and a growl behind me as Eleanor gasped. She jerked my arm and I skidded on the frosty stones, hurtling forward and falling face-down in the ice-cold water, while she stood resolutely facing the beast pounding towards us.

'Rusthead, let be, she said in a commanding voice.

I dragged myself, dripping, from the pond, the weight of my sodden gown dragging me down, and saw the white-faced keeper snatching the animal's collar as it hesitated by the water's edge, still snarling. 'Mistress,' he panted, 'are you unhurt?'

'Of course I am,' Eleanor said cheerfully. 'It's hardly likely Rusthead would hurt me. But how did he get loose?'

'That's what I want to know.' The man patted the agitated hound. 'Lucky the boy spotted it; he shouted and I ran after the dog as it broke away. They're chancy beasts, these guard dogs, trained to kill if they're sent after their prey.'

I was already shivering while we made our way up the slope to the castle and I knew I should get out of my freezing clothes as soon as possible but I felt deep unease about the incident and had to find out how the dog had escaped. When we reached the growing crowd by the lowered drawbridge the Countess was questioning a lad who enjoyed his moment of glory.

'I see'd him, my Lady. He came slinking round the corner and he had a cloth in his hand. He went straight to the dogs, let them nuzzle the cloth and slipped Rusthead's chain. Then he ran off and I shouted. He was that crazy big man that lives in the woods. The guards have gone to catch him.'

'You mean it was intentional?'

'Oh yes, my Lady. He knew what he was about. He dropped the cloth. I picked it up.'

I rocked on my feet as I identified a rag which I had used to mop up spillages in my dispensing room and threw out when it was saturated with liquid. It carried the scent of the pharmacy, as did I. The Countess turned to me in alarm.

'Great heaven Doctor Somers, what are you thinking of? You should be out of those wet clothes and drying yourself by the kitchen fire. You're chilled to the bone. Get him inside, good man.' She beckoned a serving man who took my arm.

'I should like to question the fellow who loosed the guard dog,' I said before I was led back into the castle but my voice shook as a bout of shivering seized me and my words may have been lost amid shouts.

It was true I should have known better than to stand about chilled to the bone and I paid for my foolishness with a fever which kept me to my bed for two days with a raging headache and aching limbs. I felt stupid and sipped my infusion of coriander and pennyroyal like the dutiful patient I aspired to be. I had been told the man who let loose the dog had been caught and I was content to regain my strength before interrogating him. I wanted to defer the moment when he named his pay-master and confirmed my fears that Stephen Boice was still seeking to contrive my death.

When I woke on the third morning feeling clearer headed and able to leave my bed, I could not justify further delay so I asked the attendant to arrange for the prisoner to be brought under guard to my room. He stared at me as if I was delirious, mumbling. 'I can't do that, sir.'

'Why not? I want to question the rogue.'

The serving man scratched his chin. 'The Countess and the Steward questioned him and found him guilty of a wicked act. He's swinging on the gibbet, down the valley, now. He won't trouble you more, sir.' My look of horror made him pause and he spoke deliberately as if to a child. 'He was a known vagrant and ne'er-do-well, sir.'

'I thought someone might have paid him to attack me.'

'They say he did ramble on about a man from Normandy but he was a great liar and it made no difference to the verdict. He was lucky not have hanged years ago for the mischief he's caused hereabouts. You're not in any danger at the castle, sir. The Countess'll tell you.'

I shut my eyes as if accepting his message of comfort. There was nothing I could do about it.

Chapter 12

Within a few days messengers and carriers, delayed by the weather, arrived at the castle bringing belated condolences to the Countess and consignments of goods ordered weeks before to her minions. Among the contents of letter-pouches were two missives addressed to me and as soon as I saw them I took them to my room to read in private. One, in a clerkly hand, had been redirected from Winchester. It bore a seal I recognised and I dreaded the news that it might contain, setting it aside until I had quieted the pounding in my chest. The other had been brought with correspondence for the Countess and carried Gilbert Iffley's crest. I broke it open roughly preparing myself to read an outpouring of malice enlivened with menaces.

Dear and esteemed Doctor Somers, I trust we may lay aside the difficulties there have been between us in earlier days when different conditions existed. I write at the behest of Richard, Duke of York, who bears you no ill will for your reluctance to join his entourage. Rather, he expresses his sincere gratitude to you for sending to him Doctor Bertrand Willison whose services have already proved most valuable. The Doctor joined us when I met him in Normandy and he is now with us at York's castle of Fotheringhay, where the Duke holds court until he chooses to visit Ireland as the King's representative. Willison has manifold talents from which we shall benefit. It is my hope that, before many months are past, you too will take your place alongside your former colleague. This letter conveys his Grace the Duke's good wishes, those of my good-brother, Stephen Boice, and my own humble regards. Your friend, Gilbert Iffley, Baron Glasbury.

I stared in astonishment at the document. How could it be reconciled with the attempts on my life undoubtedly organised by Boice when he was in the north of England last autumn? It would be consistent with Iffley's mode of operation to accompany flattery with threats but threats were entirely missing from the letter. I had no answer to the puzzle but was deeply worried to know Willison had joined York's company. It had never crossed my mind that he might do so for he had mentioned Normandy as a refuge where he had a cousin and might rebuild his life. Iffley spoke of him as a valued colleague with manifold talents and I shuddered, wondering if that phrase indicated the Baron was acquainted with the physician's murderous expertise as well as his healing skills. Above all I admitted my responsibility for his freedom: misled perhaps by sympathy, beguiled into accepting he had no part in Brother Joseph's death. I already felt guilt at my impetuous action in letting him escape; now it seemed he was at the service of men I knew to be unscrupulous and the implications were alarming.

I took up the other letter with a strong presentiment of unhappiness, although anxious to divert myself from Iffley's effusion. It came from Sir Hugh and Lady Blanche de Grey and I could picture them at their small manor of Danson in the County of Kent. Many years previously I had held my tongue about their involvement in less than honourable activities and they had favoured me in gratitude since then, above all by providing my mother with a home in her old age. I had not visited Danson for two years and had no recent news of my mother's well-being but a letter from her benefactors was likely to mean one thing.

So it proved and I sat in mournful reminiscence recalling the woman I had neglected for too long, whose joys and sorrows had depended so much on my successes and failures. Had she died grieving for my disgrace, disappointed that I had lost the trappings of my previous position as Suffolk's privileged retainer? It was painful to acknowledge this must be the case and to convict myself of responsibility for yet another reprehensible act. I put my head in my hands and soon felt moisture trickling through my fingers. I had never felt more alone.

*****

Next morning the Countess summoned me to her late husband's study, in company with her Steward, and after a brief enquiry as to my health she proceeded to unfold a letter, prodding at the broken seal with her finger.

'He has wasted no time in the fashioning of a personal seal with the Stanwick crest. I have never met Roger Egremont but his behaviour in sending this missive bears out everything I've heard of his deplorable character.'

'My Lord's cousin...?' the Steward began.

'The new Earl of Stanwick. On that there is no dispute.' Her voice was crisp. 'But, as we might have expected he proposes to challenge my husband's bequest to Eleanor. Propriety might have suggested a decent interval between hearing of his cousin's death and asserting a claim to the possessions of which he is deprived but he has sent me this outrageous proposition, with not a word of sympathy for my loss.'

'My Lady, the late Earl was confident his arrangements were secure. King Henry has assented. Roger Egremont's shortcomings are well known.'

The Countess waved her hand impatiently at the Steward's attempt to re-assure her. 'Since when has the primacy of the law been sufficient to uphold a maiden's rights when powerful men intend otherwise? Egremont is currently lodged with Richard of York and his discontented followers but he proposes to travel to Raby Castle in the near future.'

'Raby? The Nevilles' stronghold?'

'You grasp the point, Doctor Somers. His intentions are clear. He will seek Neville support and they will give it with enthusiasm as a way of baiting Henry Percy. Raby is but half a day's ride from here.'

'They will attack Ravensmoor?'

The Countess turned to her Steward. 'Our defences must be strengthened and men assembled from the countryside ready to fight if need be. I charge you to put in hand everything necessary. Consult with the captain of the guard and follow his advice. I will prepare a letter to be taken to the Earl of Northumberland within the hour.'

The Steward bowed and left the room but the Countess signalled me to remain with her. 'There is more, my Lady?' I asked.

She did not reply at once but turned the paper in her hand so I could read the sentence she indicated. 'Roger Egremont displays more subtlety than I expected. After expressions of bombast and threats, he offers a means to safeguard Eleanor's inheritance and prevent bloodshed.'

I raised my eyes to hold hers for a moment, sharing her disgust. 'He seeks Eleanor's hand in marriage. Has he no wife already?'

'He has buried two wives. We should have realised why he was in no hurry to take a third, knowing Ralph was near his end. Note his blandishments: if I am willing to sacrifice Eleanor I may remain at Ravensmoor for the rest of my life, an honoured dowager, and the positions of all our household members will be guaranteed. Peace and harmony will prevail. How enticing! Many a young girl's future has been bartered for less.'

I was uncertain whether she was tempted by the proposal. 'The Earl of Northumberland would be deeply offended by the slight to his kinsman if you granted Egremont's request.'

'Indeed he would and when the smouldering animosity between Henry Percy and the Nevilles erupts into violence, as it will, Ravensmoor would be on the battle-line. Egremont's promises are worthless and I will not sacrifice my husband's child in the vain hope that they might be sincere. It would vitiate all Ralph's intentions when he made Eleanor his heir.'

'Can her betrothal to Cuthbert Percy be expedited?'

'I shall entreat the Earl to agree. It is all I can do.'

She sank back in her chair, leaning her head against the carved backrest and for a moment I studied her pained expression in silence. Then I spoke hesitantly. 'My Lady, is it for you alone to make this weighty decision?'

Her head shot forward. 'Are you suggesting I consult that wretched woman who bore Eleanor out of wedlock? Her status is not acknowledged.'

This glimpse of the Countess's rigidity was chilling and I experienced a frisson of compassion for Lady Maud, destined to count for nothing in any manoeuvring about her daughter's future. 'I accept Lady Fitzvaughan has no role in the matter,' I said, 'but on the Earl's death Eleanor's wardship will have passed to the Crown. Royal consent to her marriage will be required.'

She gave a rasp of irritation. 'Do you take us for fools, physician? Henry Percy will have sought King Henry's consent as soon as he learned of Ralph's death.'

I held the Countess's angry gaze until she lowered her eyes. 'My Lady, I understand Lord Walter Fitzvaughan has petitioned the King to be named Eleanor's guardian, under a grant of wardship. If this has been confirmed it will be for his Lordship to agree her marriage. I can see no reason why he should object to a union with Cuthbert Percy but...'

'Who told you that?' The Countess's voice cracked with annoyance as she cut across my words. 'It was a foolish passing fancy Ralph had when he was weak.'

If this was true and Lady Maud had invented a certainty which did not exist, I had committed a blunder in speaking out of turn at Topcliffe but something in Countess Mary's tone sounded false. I decided to build on my indiscretion rather than deny it. 'The Earl of Northumberland knows of the arrangement,' I said.

She blanched but did not challenge my assertion 'I didn't know. Ralph didn't tell me he'd proceeded to implement the idea. He must have yielded to the smooth talk of that slimy snake Lord Fitzvaughan sent here.'

I did not hide my bewilderment. 'Lord Fitzvaughan sent his representative here?'

The Countess snorted. 'Representative is not the word I would use but he did send his degenerate crony. Only a week or so before you came here, Doctor. I know he brought papers from Lord Fitzvaughan but I supposed they related only to his lordship's depraved wife whom we had sheltered. Are you telling me Ralph was prepared to support Walter Fitzvaughan's petition to be accorded rights of wards-ship in respect of Eleanor?'

'I think it likely, my Lady, but I've mentioned it only because, if I'm right, we might turn the position to advantage. I assume Roger Egremont will have no inkling of this wardship but, if it is explained to him in inoffensive terms, surely he will make his overtures to Lord Fitzvaughan in the hope that he can secure agreement, man-to-man, for the disposal of Eleanor's hand. This will buy a little time.'

I did not doubt her intelligence and she nodded slowly. 'In the meantime I shall ensure Henry Percy sends his fastest messenger to the royal court seeking consent not merely to a betrothal but an honourable marriage. If Walter Fitzvaughan has any role in this, King Henry will remit the matter to him but I don't doubt our noble King will indicate his own wishes. The Percys are loyal and valued subjects whereas Roger Egremont is a known renegade.' She rose to her feet and held out her hand for me kiss. 'I'm grateful for your wisdom, Doctor Somers. I shall write with the utmost grace and reasonableness to the new Earl of Stanwick.'

I left the Dowager satisfied that I had done what I could to secure Eleanor's interests and her father's objectives but I was uncomfortable about one piece of information I had gleaned. No one had mentioned that Gaston de la Tour visited Ravensmoor shortly before I arrived and although this omission was not necessarily sinister it worried me. The one constant in Gaston's life was his commitment to Lord Fitzvaughan: all others were catspaws, to be used and discarded when their purpose was concluded. This would most certainly include Lady

Maud, with whom he had once conspired and whom he had then betrayed in order to save himself. I hoped she had not been lured into trusting him again and for this reason chose not to tell me she had seen him.

Calm reflection might have suggested delaying a visit to the Middleton Tower until I had thought through more carefully the inferences to be drawn from the whirlwind of news I had received: but there have always been occasions when I acted impetuously. My rashness and oversight in this instance were to have significant consequences.

*****

My request to call on Lady Maud was met with an invitation to attend her later that afternoon, as darkness fell, and it was immediately clear that she had taken trouble to prepare herself for the occasion. She was more richly attired than I had seen her previously at Ravensmoor, wearing one of her old court dresses, and the candlelight from the wall-sconces threw flattering shadows over her still beautiful face. I could not fail to be impressed by the improvement in her appearance since I last saw her and she knew it. She waved me graciously to a window seat facing her across the splayed recess while deaf Marian hovered at the far end of the room.

'I take it you are not come as my physician, Harry, but you may observe my health has benefitted from the posset you recommended.'

'I'm glad. But I do have serious concerns to discuss.'

She pursed her lips but seemed to repress an instinct for frivolity. 'Earl Roger's impertinent offer for my daughter's hand?'

She interlaced her fingers at the top of her stomacher so that they rose and fell with her breath. 'I'm relieved you've been told of the proposition.' I needed to sense her mood before raising the issue I had come to pursue.

'Oh, the Dowager took great delight in telling me of the new Earl's designs on my child and the threats which accompany them. The choice of Eleanor's bedfellow may drive the north of the kingdom into armed discord, it seems.'

'Hardly a matter for jest, my Lady.'

'Do you think I don't know it? If you've come to pontificate, Harry, you can save your efforts. My heart is riven in two worrying for Eleanor – and for what callous wretches may do to her. I'm helpless, I, her mother! While a rapacious scoundrel plots to take her inheritance and that pious bitch of a Dowager schemes to cause me the greatest grief! Are you come to help me, Harry? You alone?'

She had not changed. She was still given to exaggerated displays of emotion, in which I did not doubt there was a core of sincerity. 'Calm yourself, Lady Maud. I will do anything I can to safeguard Eleanor but I have little influence. There are circumstances I need to understand better. You can help me.'

She purred contentedly, tilting her chin towards me. 'Sweet Harry.' I set myself to ignore the curl escaping from her headdress which quivered down the line of her throat as she moved.

'I must ask you to answer truly, my Lady, with no embellishment or hypotheses.'

She gurgled with glee. 'Oh, you remind me of when you first interrogated me, years and years ago when you were enquiring into that woman's murder at Humphrey of Gloucester's palace. Do you remember?'

The memory was such that I would much rather forget it. 'I do and this is every bit as serious. When you told me your husband was seeking to become Eleanor's guardian, was that true?'

'Of course it was. Ralph signed a petition to the King supporting Walter's submission. He was confident it would be granted as they both enjoyed the King's favour.'

I took a deep breath. 'How do you know that, my Lady?'

With a rustle of silk and ripple of beads she rose to her feet and glided to sit at my side. 'Why do you persist with this nonsense of "my Lady" this and "my Lady" that? You used to call me Maud.'

My mouth was dry. 'You know very well why. I beg you not to distract me from my questions. I want to help you and your daughter. Did Earl Ralph tell you himself he supported your husband's petition?'

'I was scarcely ever allowed to see Ralph. You know perfectly well who told me.'

'Who?'

'That treacherous bastard who usurps my place at Walter's side.'

'Why didn't you tell me Gaston de la Tour had been here?'

She shrugged and contrived to nestle against me. 'It didn't seem important. He came to see Ralph. He brought me courteous greetings from my husband as an afterthought. There, are you satisfied?' She slid her arm around my neck and stroked my cheek. 'You're trembling, Harry.'

I made a half-hearted attempt to disengage from her but she held tight to my arm. 'You didn't come only to question me, did you? Why pretend?'

Her hand strayed towards my crotch and I glanced round in panic, hoping that Marian's presence would bring Maud to her senses but the far end of the room was deserted.

'We are alone,' she said with complacency and pulled at the laces of her stomacher. 'Do you remember when I was first sent to seduce you, when you were a green boy? I think you've learned much since then and now we

154

shall pleasure each other as we deserve. I don't think you will object and we shall not be interrupted.'

Her lips fastened on mine and this time I made no protest. My resolve crumbled and I lifted her onto the bench beneath the darkened window.

Chapter 13

The next few weeks, while spring gradually softened the bleak landscape around Ravensmoor, were a charmed interlude of indulgence. Grey-green buds, imperceptible at first, formed on the tips of naked, wintery boughs and here and there on the hillsides the low sun picked out the sheen of new growth among the dead bracken. Nature spoke of renewed hope and, although I could not discern any prospect of true joyfulness in my own existence, I clutched at the single wisp of satisfaction which was available.

I had never loved Maud but the power of her physical attractions always threatened to overwhelm me. Although not wholly successfully, I had resisted the temptation she offered, over the years, mindful of her husband's honour and my own integrity. Now these constraints seemed valueless. Lord Fitzvaughan had set her aside and I had lost everything I treasured. I thought myself abandoned in a remote backwater of the kingdom, committed to the practice of medicine and care of my patients but isolated from the enquiring minds of other professional men and the pursuit of new knowledge. The self-respect I had sustained during my sojourn in Winchester had become meaningless and I felt adrift.

The moments of carnal pleasure Maud offered were diversions from my melancholy fixation, but she remained as capricious as she had always been and this was exhausting. Sometimes she would look at me coquettishly as if she possessed information I did not and on one occasion she made great show of covering the seal hanging from a folded letter she claimed to have just received. It looked similar to the Fitzvaughan crest but there had been no messenger from the south for more than two weeks and I concluded she had produced an old communication hoping to goad my curiosity. I knew it amused her to simper and tease me and the sensible response was to ignore the petty pinpricks of her pride. When I made no enquiry about the document she thrust it aside with a glare and I was saved from the need to pretend interest in her tricks.

Too much was uncertain, incapable of resolution. Had the Marquis of Suffolk sent me to Ravensmoor to live out the rest of my days in obscurity? He had spoken of summoning me back to his service when he felt more secure in his own position but did he suspect that day would never come? Was my absence, so far from the royal court, merely a convenience to him? I was even unsure whether my life was still in danger from Stephen Boice's contrivances or whether I had imagined his hand behind the senseless viciousness of a madman. I doubted that Gilbert Iffley's fair words could be trusted but it scarcely mattered; I had heard nothing more from him and a report had reached us that the Duke of York was to pay a preliminary visit to his new jurisdiction in Ireland. It pleased me to think of Iffley and Boice out of the way, on the other side of the Irish Sea.

I was well aware that if Roger Egremont arrived in the north of England, perhaps backed by a score of warlike Nevilles, I should need to rouse myself from my self-absorption but the Dowager had received no further communications from him. It seemed possible that his bluster would not lead to action, if he had succumbed to the distractions of a dissolute life; or maybe the Nevilles saw no advantage in pursuing his cause. Whether he had put his claim for Eleanor's hand to Lord Fitzvaughan, now designated her guardian, we did not know; but neither had Henry Percy received consent for the girl's betrothal to young Cuthbert. Walter Fitzvaughan was rumoured to be in France once again, on the King's business, and might well have deferred consideration of his ward's destiny until he had discharged more weighty duties. Meanwhile the future of Ravensmoor and its residents rested in limbo, subject to the decisions of men far removed from its grave beauties and, until those decisions were made, life on the Stanwick demesne was cocooned from adversity.

My improper association with Maud attracted no derogatory remarks – to my face at any rate – although it could scarcely be a secret. After our first encounter I became a regular visitor to the Middleton Tower and there was little chance that our rendezvous went unnoticed but I did not care. Only on the occasion when Eleanor was leaving the tower as I arrived did I feel embarrassment but she gave me a kindly smile and said I was expected. Whether her smile was innocent or knowing, I was too confused to tell.

The Dowager Countess became reclusive as the months passed, sending out instructions through her Steward and consulting me from time to time about the health of her servitors. She told me that as soon as Eleanor's marriage to Cuthbert Percy had taken place she would leave Ravensmoor to enter a religious house and I realised that she was chafing at the long period of silence from Lord Fitzvaughan. She longed for the peaceful contemplation of the cloister and was already detaching herself from secular distractions. Perhaps for this reason she did not chide me about the frequency of my visits to the Middleton Tower but I felt too awkward to question her about where Maud might find a home in future.

Midsummer's Day was approaching and the customary festivities were planned although the Dowager would not attend them. Eleanor and her companions gathered armfuls of hawthorn blossom, fashioning beribboned garlands to encircle their heads, and there was much giggling about the tradition which said an unmarried girl could see the face of the man she would wed if she bathed in the dewpond at daybreak. Then a messenger arrived and these preparations gained new solemnity. On the festive day Cuthbert Percy and his escort were to visit Ravensmoor and he would pay court openly to his intended bride. Nothing had yet been heard from Lord Fitzvaughan but the bold gallant was not to be discouraged from pressing his suit in person.

On the auspicious day Eleanor blushed prettily as a maiden should when Cuthbert complimented her on her dancing amidst her companions and presented her with a chaplet of lilies. She received his attentions without coyness, not disguising her delight but maintaining a modest demeanour, and I admired her precocious maturity.

Lady Maud had lingered in her rooms earlier in the day but now she sidled to stand beside me as the formalities were concluded and, although her exclusion from any role in the ceremony must have rankled, she looked happy. 'How did my offspring achieve such decorum and good sense?' she whispered in the provoking tone I recognised so well.

I answered in kind. 'The late Earl had ample reserves of both qualities, my Lady. She has her father's legacy in every way.'

'Bastard,' Maud hissed. 'Don't expect me to receive you tonight. I'd sooner take the blacksmith's filthy apprentice to my bed.'

'It's your privilege but you might find the weight of his muscular chest troublesome. Also I recall you are somewhat fastidious about the stench of horses.'

'Bastard,' she repeated and glided away from me while I grinned after her.

Earlier in the year, following Egremont's threats, great care had been taken to ensure Eleanor never journeyed beyond the village at Ravensmoor without an armed escort. This degree of caution had lessened but a squire always attended her, as well as one of her women, and she was generally discouraged from riding too far from the castle. While young Percy and his followers were preparing to leave for Topcliffe, after a sumptuous meal in the hall and the exchange of lavish gifts and loving declarations, I noticed Eleanor's squire leading forward two horses draped in the Stanwick colours and bearing elaborate saddles. I turned to the Steward who was nearby.

'Is Mistress Eleanor to ride with them?'

'Only to the head of the valley. She will ride pillion behind her squire on the big bay horse and her woman will be seated with his attendant on the chestnut. Mistress Eleanor requested the arrangements herself and there is no impropriety. She will wave her admirer goodbye as his party climb the hillside and then return.'

I smiled, thinking no more of it, and was intercepted by deaf Marian, rolling her eyes and pointing to the entrance to her mistress's lodgings. The unvoiced request did not surprise me and I was prepared for the display of extravagant passions which awaited me.

I found Maud writhing on her bed, her hair torn loose from her headdress, her body shaken by loud sobs. I saw her stiffen momentarily as I entered the room before she reverted to her drama, aware I had come.

'My Lady, don't distress yourself. I'm sorry if my jest offended you.'

'Jest? Oh, I've forgotten what you said. Nothing you said could hurt me as does this disregard, this denial of my feelings. I am a mother, Harry, a mother not acknowledged, slighted, forced to watch like a menial while my sweet daughter entertains an suitor whom I should embrace and welcome.'

'Maud, I beg you to control yourself. I understand your grief but the occasion wasn't unexpected and you could have spared yourself pain by staying away. You didn't need to watch.'

She sprang to her feet and hurled herself at me, pummelling my chest. 'Callous, brutal man! Would you deprive me of a mother's joy to see her child so happy? You use my body to satisfy your lust but my anguish means nothing. I am a plaything to you, as I have always been to evil men.'

I held her at arms' length, fighting back annoyance at the injustice of her accusation. 'Maud, you know that isn't true. I respect you and am grateful we can bring each other a little comfort in our lonely situations.'

Her body shook and I wondered if she would strike me for my temerity in comparing our positions. Instead her lips began to tremble and tears flooded down her cheeks. I drew her close to me and kissed her brow. 'Forgive me, Maud, if I can't match your sensitivity. I'm only a clod-footed man, albeit a physician.'

She nestled against me before pulling back to look into my eyes, oblivious of my feeble attempt at humour. 'You mean to be kind, Harry. I appreciate that.' Her tone was lofty, patronising, but I would not let it rile me. The part I had to play was galling but it earned me a portion of ease.

'It's been a difficult day for you,' I said, regretting my pomposity, but her mood was changing.

Her hands cupped my chin. 'Perhaps we could set its difficulties aside. As you have come, physician, perhaps you could administer your inimitable remedy. It's unbecoming for a lady to solicit attentions from a mere artisan but...'

This was an outrageous aspersion which slandered my profession and ignored the pattern of our encounters over many years but I knew she was being provocative and kissed her. Then she pulled me down onto her bed and for a little while we lost ourselves in giving and receiving the simulacrum of love.

*****

We were still lying together and my eyelids had closed when I heard the shout from across the courtyard, followed by thundering hooves and a woman's scream. It was the scream that rallied my senses and caused me to stumble from the bed to the narrow window. Maud was equally alert, dragging the bed-cover with her to cover her nakedness, and we looked down into the inner ward, now teeming with soldiers and attendants.

'Dear God, Harry!'

Her face was ashen and there was nothing artificial in her horror. She knew as I did what the scene implied and we both seized our scattered garments and hurriedly began to dress. Outside the early evening sun glowed on the steaming flanks of the chestnut horse and illumined the darkened stain across the empty saddle as the rider slipped to the ground, clutching a blood-drenched arm. Heedless of my flapping shirt and without my gown, I flung myself down the stairs of the Middleton Tower, into the courtyard, and while others wailed and bellowed questions, I concentrated on binding the lad's upper arm tightly to staunch his bleeding. He was weak and I ordered wine to be brought to strengthen him while I cradled his limp body.

On my knees in a pool of gore, I was aware that the Dowager Countess had joined the group around us. I had already heard the sound of mounted men clattering over the drawbridge but the crescendo of speculation in the crowd was confused and I did not comprehend what had happened. The Dowager quietened her servitors and addressed the injured boy firmly but with compassion.

'Robbie, Doctor Somers has you safe now but we need to understand what has occurred. Where is Mistress Eleanor?'

He twitched and gulped the wine. 'Gone, Lady, gone but not hurt, I swear. They took her. That was what they were after.'

'Do you mean the Percys took her?' Disbelief made her voice falter.

'No, Lady. They'd ridden on. The rogues waited until they were over the hill, out of sight. Mistress Eleanor and her woman had dismounted to watch them go and we held the horses.' A tremor convulsed the lad and I moistened his forehead.

The Countess appreciated he could not hold out much longer. 'Do you know who the attackers were? Where are the others?'

162

He began to sob and I summoned men to carry him indoors. 'They're both dead, Lady, skewered right through, mistress's squire and her woman. I was lucky to get away. They wore no crests. Maybe the Nevilles, I thought.'

His head flopped forward and his eyes closed as the men lifted him onto a hurdle. The Dowager nodded to me to take him indoors as the Steward strode forward. 'The captain of the guard has already set off with an armed troop to pursue the villains,' he said.

'To the gates of Raby Castle, I presume,' I heard her say as I entered the guardhouse with my patient. 'But not, I imagine, beyond.'

*****

When the captain of the guard and his party returned the Dowager summoned me to hear his account of their abortive expedition. They had been refused entry to Raby Castle but were answered civilly by the guards who insisted no Neville underlings had been involved in the abduction. The Earl of Salisbury and his family were not in residence and their chamberlain declined to meet a posse of armed and angry men champing at the gates. The Dowager showed her exasperation.

'Captain,' I said, 'did you happen to note whether there were signs of horsemen arriving at Raby Castle recently?'

'I looked around, of course, Doctor. The ground was dry so it was difficult to tell but there were no obvious indications that a troop of riders had arrived there recently. I'm inclined to believe what I was told.'

'Tush!' The Dowager was not convinced. 'You're a man of action but you're too trusting. Where else would they have taken Eleanor?'

The captain contained his irritation but nothing would be gained by antagonising him. 'My Lady, you're probably right,' I said, 'but perhaps we should send scouts

163

to check other routes from Ravensmoor in case there are traces of riders heading in a different direction.'

She jerked up her chin causing the folds of her widow's wimple to undulate but she did not dismiss my suggestion. 'Captain, you will organise search parties,' she said after a pause and the soldier, looking relieved, bowed and went to carry out her order.

'Doctor Somers.' She spoke to me sharply and her eyes were blazing. 'I do not trust the Nevilles one inch from their firesides. It is too convenient that Salisbury and his kin are absent from Raby. The captain lacks imagination but I accept his warlike appearance would not have encouraged a friendly exchange. In the morning you will take a single guide and go to the castle, in your physician's gown, clearly a man of peace, and you will assess the likelihood that the Nevilles have captured Eleanor. You will see what they know of Roger Egremont and return to advise me without delay. Is that clear?

'Perfectly, my Lady,' I said with scant enthusiasm.

*****

Maud's recriminations against the Dowager, Eleanor's attendants, the Nevilles, the Percys and Roger Egremont were frantic and indiscriminate. I felt bound to stay with her until she was calmer but in consequence I had little sleep before I set out for Raby. I had a tiring ride across open country, a difficult if courteous conversation with the Earl of Salisbury's chamberlain and a still more tiring return journey in blustery rain. I was not looking forward to reporting my conclusions to the Dowager for all my enquiries had drawn a blank and I was persuaded the occupants of the Nevilles' stronghold knew nothing of Eleanor's abduction.

Countess Mary listened to me with obvious impatience and then leaned back in her chair with a satisfied sigh. 'You confirm our conclusions,' she said. 'The men who searched near here, while you were gone, found clear signs that a large troop of riders struck south away from Ravensmoor. It was possible to follow faint tracks before the rain came. The villains were not bound for Raby.'

I must have looked despondent at this news for if the Nevilles were not involved it was difficult to know where to seek the culprits. The Dowager rapped the table.

'We are not defenceless, Doctor Somers,' she said. 'Heaven favours us. The captain apprehended a boy who had guided the scoundrels across the moors to the west. He knew little about them but it's enough to help us. They spoke in strange dialect of making for the coast so their purpose is evident. They are taking Eleanor to Ireland. Richard of York has gone there and Egremont is with him.'

The supposition lacked substance, in my opinion, but it was possible and, if it was true, Eleanor's prospects of escaping Earl Roger's clutches were pitiful. Exhaustion stole over me and I put my hand to my brow.

'I've sent a messenger with an appeal to Richard of York,' the Dowager said. 'He is an honourable man and will not permit a follower of his to shame a virtuous maiden with a vile marriage.'

I nodded sleepily, thinking it should at least elicit a response, but her next words startled me wide awake. 'You will not go to your whore tonight, Doctor Somers. You will carry out your promise to my late husband to defend his daughter. So you will pack your things, take a short rest and at first light you will set out, as my representative, – for Ireland.'

Chapter 14

Of all the journeys I had been compelled to make, the length and breadth of England, this was the most dismal. The damp weather as we crossed the hills did nothing to lift my spirits and I found the idea of visiting Richard of York's household repellent. Gilbert Iffley and Stephen Boice would taunt me and try to cajole me into joining their master's retinue and if I were to encounter Doctor Willison I did not know how I would mask my suspicions that he had murdered Brother Joseph in cold blood.

Beyond my personal disinclination to go to Ireland on the Countess's whim, the expedition seemed doomed to failure. If Roger Egremont was holding Eleanor and his reputation was justified, he would already have violated the poor girl and dragged her to the altar. She could not hope for succour from anyone in Dublin. The mere fact of her kidnapping compromised her honour and, if appeal was made to Richard of York, he would see it his duty to ensure that a follower guilty of such a crime made reparation by marrying the maiden he had shamed. Wealthy heiress she might be but her wealth only made her a more desirable chattel to satisfy men's greed. Her tragedy was all the greater because she had gained a suitor whom she favoured but now her hope of living with a husband in mutual contentment, a prospect all too uncommon for a woman, was lost forever.

Despite the Dowager Countess's command I had managed to see Maud briefly before I set out from Ranvensmoor but I found her in a peculiar mood. Her agitation of the previous day had been replaced by sullen acquiescence in Heaven's decree and the presumption that there was no way of evading it. Her eyes glittered, I thought with assumed piety, when she spoke of the girl's destiny and her own sacrifice, but then she directed her wilful complaints towards me.

'So you have agreed to make this journey, to leave me friendless. You will not return to me, I know it. You are as faithless as any other man.'

'It is your daughter I am sent to find. In the past you have claimed her safety was all you cared for.'

Then she laughed like a woman whose wits have been curdled and the sound froze my blood. 'This time it's too late for that. She is to be martyred. Purity is no match for evil. You should know that.'

I set out with that horrible sentiment rebounding in my head. After two days, as my misery increased, I was tempted to turn tail and abandon my commission but I knew that the three armed men who accompanied me, on the Dowager's instruction, were not there simply to safeguard my person but to make certain I fulfilled my remit. When we reached Chester they conducted me to a vessel ready to cross the Irish Sea, making sure I was immured in a small cabin before they left. It was too late to escape whatever lay in wait for me on the further shore.

*****

It was an uncomfortable crossing with the wind increasing in strength so the small vessel pitched and rolled in a manner my stomach found most disagreeable. By the time we entered the wide estuary of the River Liffey it was all I could do to focus my thoughts on what I must say when I was questioned but my inclination was to hide among the barrels on deck and hope to be taken back across the sea without setting foot on land. This was a ridiculous fantasy but it was proof of my disturbed mind.

We pulled over towards the southern bank of the river and the roofs of tight-packed buildings descending the steep slope from a ridge came into view. I glimpsed a quay in the distance with wooden cranes ready to unload cargo but then I realised we were turning, away from the main course of the river and into a side stream. We made our way between islands and, as we followed the curve of

167

the shore, on the eastern spur of the ridge the towers of Dublin castle were visible. I was being taken directly to the headquarters of the King's Lieutenant in Ireland. Sure enough, we made fast at a jetty, the gangplank was set in place and I was hustled along it to where a liveried attendant was waiting.

'Doctor Somers,' he said, bowing obsequiously, 'you are expected. Please follow me. The postern gate to the castle lies over there.'

My heart was fluttering despite my attempt to reason. The Dowager had sent a messenger ahead of me; they knew I was coming. There was nothing to be concerned about – it all made sense and yet I could not convince myself.

I was taken to a small room in a house jutting into the courtyard of the castle and given water with which to wash. I was told I would be taken to meet the Duke himself when I was refreshed and I tried to persuade myself this was a good sign, that I was being accorded fitting status as the Dowager Countess's representative. Nevertheless when I was conducted through a great hall with trappings worthy of royalty and into a private chamber where a throne-like seat stood upon a dais, I was extremely nervous.

I had seen Richard, Duke of York, only once before and from a distance when, three years previously, I watched the arrival of Queen Margaret in Normandy where he was the King's Lieutenant-General. The fleeting impression I had then of his pride and condescension was reinforced as soon as he entered the room but closer at hand he revealed deep-set eyes which were both penetrating and intelligent. I bowed low.

'Doctor Somers, you are welcome to Dublin. You have done well to track us down when we are here only a short while to gauge the scale of the responsibilities laid on us by his Grace, the King. We esteem greatly the noble Countess Mary who has sent you but regret that your mission is in all probability misconceived.'

Not a man to beat about the bush, I concluded, but as I straightened from my obeisance I noticed among the henchmen who had followed him into the chamber one I did not want to encounter. Stephen Boice smiled thinly and nodded at me.

'You are acquainted with good Master Boice,' the Duke said. 'He will be delighted to show you the castle and the town when you have concluded your business with us.'

I feared the King's Lieutenant designate was ready to sweep out as quickly as he had come and although I had not been invited to speak I needed to question him 'My Lord Duke,' I said, 'I should be grateful to understand why you think my mission is misconceived.'

He fixed me with those probing eyes. 'You served the late Humphrey of Gloucester for many years, did you not?'

The two royal Dukes had been friends and York might hold me guilty of disloyalty in leaving my first master's service for that of his rival, Suffolk. 'I grew up in Gloucester's household,' I said, 'and owe my education to his patronage. I was compelled to take a post elsewhere after my return from exile.'

'I've heard it rumoured you eased Humphrey into the next world when you attended him in Saint Edmundsbury.'

This needed firm rebuttal. 'Your Grace, it is untrue. My physician's skill could not save him in his extremity but I did nothing to hasten his end.'

York continued to look at me and I made myself hold his gaze until he spoke. 'Suffolk would have been glad had you done so.'

'That is surmise, your Grace. Suffolk instructed me only to examine the Duke and form a view as to the severity of his ailment. It is my training to assess the condition of a man's body but I cannot read any other man's heart.'

I heard Boice's intake of breath and two of his companions turned to each other in annoyance for I had

169

spoken out of turn but Richard of York smiled. 'Humphrey told me you were an honest man,' he said, 'and I believe it. I will explain why your journey here is misguided.' He turned to a serving man. 'Admit the Earl of Stanwick.'

I held my breath as the door was opened and a heavily built and richly dressed but slightly scruffy man was ushered through it. I judged him to be about forty years in age although his flushed complexion and the furrows from eyes to mouth might make him look older than he was. He stood rigidly upright and looked indignant but the most remarkable fact which I noted was that his wrists were bound together in front of him.

'Earl Roger,' York said courteously, 'this is Doctor Somers, the Dowager Countess of Stanwick's emissary. He is come to enquire whether you have abducted young Mistress Eleanor, the late Earl's ward.'

'What?' The Earl spluttered in fury. 'Mistress Eleanor abducted? She is to be my bride. I have written to her appointed guardian to seek his blessing.'

The Duke showed his amusement. 'Would you tell Doctor Somers where you have been lodged for the past six weeks and answer his direct enquiry about your responsibility for the young lady's disappearance.'

The Earl had become agitated. 'My Lord Duke, what game is this? I was lodged in the keep of your castle of Fotheringhay for four weeks, at your Grace's pleasure, incarcerated there, unable to leave my quarters, because my behaviour had offended some of your followers. All I did, when in my cups, was draw my sword to chastise an impudent pup. Then I was brought under escort to accompany your visit here to Dublin. I have not been at liberty throughout the whole time.'

'The account of the offence you committed which was put before me described your behaviour in more robust terms.' York stretched back in his chair. 'But Doctor Somers is not concerned with the reasons for your imprisonment, only to know that you have been in no position to arrange the abduction of Mistress Eleanor.

170

Access to your room has been restricted to my own servitors whom I trust absolutely.'

The Earl was only half-listening to Duke Richard and as soon as his superior stopped speaking he erupted. 'How could Mistress Eleanor be abducted? Why was she not more carefully guarded? Where is she? Has she been harmed – compelled to wed another? Who has committed this outrage?'

'These are the questions Doctor Somers has been commissioned to investigate but, for your comfort, I would suggest the circumstances are obvious. The sad young lady is being held to ransom and I would wager that the Dowager has by now received a request to make payment to obtain her release. Some ne'er-do-wells have taken her, probably Scots raiders, in the hope of securing some of her wealth. They are unlikely to have harmed her. It is gold they will be looking for, not her maidenhead.'

I guessed the Duke's speech was aimed at me as well as the Earl and what he said was plausible but I could not dismiss the possibility that the whole scene with Roger Egremont was contrived for my benefit. His imprisonment seemed too convenient. Yet if this was a charade it meant the Duke of York was a willing participant in duping me and that did not ring true. I sensed his contempt for his prisoner. He gestured to a follower.

'Return the Earl of Stanwick to his quarters. He will remain there for one more week and can then be released on his own surety and solemn pledge to cause no more disruption in my household.'

'My Lord Duke, I beg you to take steps to find my bride. Lord Fitzvaughan must be alerted to Eleanor's capture. He will surely grant my request to marry her, uniting the title of Stanwick with its lands and property. My Lord, I implore...'

The Earl's voice faded as he was escorted from the room, along the corridor, while the Duke picked a minute piece of fluff from his mantle and dropped it casually on the floor. My presence now seemed redundant so I bowed and prepared to leave. 'Wait, Doctor Somers. I have something to say to you.' He signalled for all his attendants except Stephen Boice to leave him and rose from his chair. 'I am sorry you have crossed the Irish Sea to no purpose, Harry. I trust I may call you by your first name, as Duke Humphrey did. I know Stephen and Gilbert Iffley have tried to persuade you to join my entourage and I respect the reluctance you have shown to change allegiance. However, it must be apparent to you how little the Marquis of Suffolk values your loyalty when he leaves you to moulder in a remote northern fastness among a bevy of women. I merely wish to assure you that I would welcome your service and would mark your commitment with more generosity than William de la Pole has demonstrated. I bear you only good will and I ask you to consider my offer.'

'Your Grace, you are kind.' It was all I could bring myself to say but he brushed my words aside.

'A ship will be sailing from here for Chester in two days. Stephen will entertain you until then. Your place on the ship is reserved but it is my hope you will decide to stay and accompany us in a week's time to visit my castle of Ludlow in the Welsh Marches.'

*****

I did not object to Boice showing me round the castle after we had dined with threescore others in the hall. It was revealing to see the regal state in which Duke Richard lived, even on a short visit, and the smooth running of his immense household. Swarms of liveried attendants filled the passages and milled about in the courtyard, coming and going from the miscellany of buildings within the walls of the fortress. Everything was on a majestic scale. I was never at ease in Boice's company but amid such bustle I felt secure from his malevolence. We visited bakehouse and buttery, exercise yard and the terrace where cannon were positioned, pointing south. We overheard a merry tune resounding from one of the towers and my guide explained that visiting musicians were to perform for the Duke after supper so we had best not disturb them. Instead he led me into the vestibule of a small outhouse where a voice droned in the background; it was unpleasantly familiar.

I would have liked to turn back but Boice flung open an inner door and there was Gilbert Iffley, Baron Glasbury, standing over a tousled young man seated at a table. 'Philippa, Countess of March,' he said, rapping his knuckles on the board. 'Remember that. The Duke's maternal grandmother.'

He caught sight of me and his scowl was instinctive although speedily controlled and replaced by the glimmer of a smile. 'I rejoice to see you come to Dublin, Doctor Somers. It would be my pleasure to wait upon you presently but I have little time at my disposal. I am occupied with my duties here and have family business to attend to also.'

'Please don't trouble yourself, Baron. My visit will be brief.' I was only too glad there was no need to converse further but I was intrigued and as we crossed the courtyard I questioned Boice. 'Baron Glasbury acts as tutor? Who is his pupil?'

Boice shrugged. 'Some connection of the Duke's on his mother's side, a Mortimer relative. Richard of York has dragged his entire household on this reconnaissance. Come, let us broach a flask of wine before supper is served.'

I was happy enough not to pursue the subject of Gilbert Iffley's activities and welcomed the respite when Boice left me for perhaps half an hour while trestles were set in place for the meal. I was intent on trying to reconcile the Baron's manifest hostility when he first saw me, not just with his assumed politeness a moment later but with the cordial letter he had sent me at Ravensmoor earlier in the year. Could he have sent the letter only because of the Duke's command while never varying in his personal animosity towards me? It seemed entirely possible.

Boice reappeared while York's followers were trooping into the hall, taking their seats on the benches at table. He waved at me from the gallery above the screens while he was ushering the musicians into position. By his side one of their number also raised his hand and with delight I recognised Master Wilby whom I had met at Topcliffe when he and his colleagues were playing for Henry Percy. I was determined that after the meal I would seek him out but I had no need as, when the festivities were concluded, Boice led him directly to my side.

'Master Wilby claims your acquaintance,' he said with a sardonic grin which put me on my guard.

'Certainly, we met at the Earl of Northumberland's house.' I extended my hand which Wilby grasped amicably. 'Have you been long in Ireland?'

'No, only a few days. We were in London a fortnight ago, playing for the Marquis of Suffolk, when we received the Duke's invitation to join his expedition to Dublin and provide entertainment here. We are fortunate our reputation goes before us.'

'Well merited. Here, take some wine.' I held out the flagon at my elbow and wished Boice would leave us to gossip alone but it was clear he had no intention of obliging me. He proffered his own goblet to be filled.

'Master Wilby was telling me how he heard interesting news of your diversions at Ravensmoor while he resided at Topcliffe.'

I did not like Boice's tone of voice but imagined I was to be taunted about running messages for the late Earl of Stanwick.

'We stayed at Topcliffe well into the spring,' the musician said. 'We learned of the Countess's bereavement. She sent messages to Henry Percy on more than one occasion and I always asked the messenger for news of you.' Too late to stop him I realised what he was about to say and held my breath. 'You earned yourself a gallant's reputation, bedding the mysterious lady in the Middleton Tower. The servants were much entertained by the story.'

I gave a rueful smile, hoping this was all there was to a scurrilous tale of an anonymous amour, but Boice punched my shoulder and smirked. 'Another man's wife, you rascal. If I were you I should not want Lord Fitzvaughan to hear of your dalliance with the delightful Lady Maud.'

Wilby glanced quickly from Boice to me and he bit his lip. I was sorry he had been led into this awkward situation and tried to set his mind at rest. 'I've known Lady Maud for many years,' I laughed. 'Lord Fitzvaughan is well aware of it. He has his own preoccupations.'

The issue was not pursued but later, as the company broke up, Boice insisted on accompanying me to my room and he put his arm across the doorway as I went to enter. 'An ambiguous word: "It". I would define the position more crudely, Doctor Somers. Does Walter Fitzvaughan truly know that your prick has been often in his lady's cunt? If I were you I would do all in my power to avoid him finding out. Don't you agree?'

The threat could not have been silkier or more menacing and I was horrified that he knew so much of my most intimate affairs.

*****

Next morning I longed to evade Stephen Boice but I had no option for the Duke had appointed him my guide to explore the town. I surmised that York's underlings were compiling reports for their master describing in detail characteristics of the province he was called on to govern in the King's name, before he formally took up his post. To my relief Boice made no reference to the previous evening's conversation and led me down the steep slope to the River Liffey, along to the quay I had seen from my ship. We stood observing crates being unloaded from small boats, to be carried to Fishamble Street, the one place in Dublin where sales of fish were permitted, and as no one was paying us attention I decided to take the offensive.

175

'Master Boice, there's something I should like to clarify.' He raised an eyebrow and I continued. 'I have reason to believe you sought to have me killed when I arrived in Yorkshire by suborning a wretched ostler and a pathetic madman to contrive my death.'

'My dear Doctor Somers, on what grounds to you link these regrettable circumstances to me?' His tone was honeyed.

I held his eyes. 'Both rogues spoke of a man come from Normandy and I was told you had lately landed at Hull, I presume from the Duchy.'

He did not hesitate in his reply. 'You are too hasty in your conjecture. It's true I did land at Hull and journey on to Raby Castle. I had a commission to deliver a message from the Lady Cicely, Duke Richard's wife, to her brother, the Earl of Salisbury. I even made a call at Topcliffe to give greetings to her sister, who you may know is married to Henry Percy. The Nevilles are everywhere, are they not?'

'These commitments did not preclude you making arrangements of your own.'

He narrowed his eyes. 'No, Harry Somers, they did not but in fact I in this matter I am innocent. Indeed if I had sought your death, I suggest I would have done so with some expertise and we would not be standing here together so pleasantly. I suggest you look elsewhere for a traveller from Normandy, if indeed there is such a fellow bent on your destruction.'

'I'm obliged for your answer,' I said but I had no confidence in what I had been told.

We turned back up the ridge towards the great cathedral of Christchurch and, as I expected, Boice began to badger me about accepting a position in the Duke's household. I was still uncertain whether I had been tricked by the scene with Roger Egremont and was desperate to escape from my companion. All I wanted was to return as quickly as I could to Ravensmoor. If it was true that a ransom demand had been received there, the Dowager would probably send a messenger to inform me but I did not want to linger in Dublin a moment longer than was necessary. Somehow I must live out the hours until I could board the ship bound for Chester in the morning.

Near to the cathedral I observed some grand houses and a number of public buildings but, lost in my thoughts, I ignored these sights until Boice pulled my sleeve and indicated a fine edifice dominating the corner of two thoroughfares. 'The Tholsel,' he said. 'It houses the courthouse and the headquarters for the merchants here. Trade is the lifeblood of the town and its English merchants. Duke Richard is resolved to foster their wellbeing.'

I made an effort to show intelligent interest. 'I've heard only English spoken as we've walked around. Do the native Irish have their homes elsewhere?'

'Not within the town walls, so far as can be enforced. The natives are barbarous creatures to be kept at arms' length. The castle defends Dublin's honest citizens from the threat of harm. The memory is kept fresh of how the villains massacred their English neighbours some years ago but Richard of York will know how to govern these wild men sagely. Among the titles he holds he is Earl of Ulster and Earl of Cork. He's respected here and he's intent on keeping good relations with the chiefs of Desmond and Kildare. He has made approaches to them during this visit and they will support him in his Governorship. It will give him a valuable base outside England.'

Boice was probably hinting at plans or precautions which it might be dangerous to know and I did not want to hear more. I hastened my steps but we had come to a particularly splendid house with a stone portico and upper storeys cantilevered out over the roadway. He looked sideways at me as he rapped on the door.

'I must enquire as to Lady Glasbury's health.'

'Lady Glasbury!' I knew very well it was Gilbert Iffley's wife to whom he referred but I had uncomfortable recollections of her some years earlier when she was the

177

recently widowed Jane Cawfield and I had aspired to court her. That was a futile fantasy on my part and the Prioress had rebuked me for contemplating marriage with one who was kin to the Nevilles. 'The Baron has taken this house while he's in Dublin?'

'My sister's labouring to give birth. It's come too soon and Gilbert's concerned about her. The journey may have been unwise in her condition but he wished her to accompany him. He's been granted leave of absence from the Duke's court today.'

Childbirth was a matter for womenfolk but there had been occasions when difficulties arose and I was summoned as physician to offer advice. I indicated I was ready to be consulted by Lady Glasbury if required so, when invited, I followed the serving maid upstairs, welcoming the prospect of filling my professional role once more. I waited in an antechamber while the girl entered the bedroom, until a moment later a man in a doctor's gown flung open the door and embraced me.

'Great God in Heaven, Somers, have you been sent by His mercy to help me? Come quickly.'

I shuddered, recognising Doctor Willison, but had no chance to escape. He hustled me to the bedside and dismissed all the servants from the room except an elderly matron who I took to be the birthing woman. 'She's had a difficult pregnancy and seems in uncontrollable pain,' he said, 'but the birth is imminent. I fear all is not well.'

I reflected silently that Lady Glasbury had given birth successfully perhaps half a dozen times but she was now approaching an age where she would not conceive again. Her face was grey and damp with sweat but I was glad she seemed not to recognise me, so distracted was she by her suffering. I knelt by the bed and raised the coverlet 'You're right,' I said. 'The head is coming. At least the child presents itself properly.'

The woman lifted her patient's knees and stood to the side with an armful of rags. Her expression was grim. Willison grasped the emerging infant, plainly too small to be viable, easing head and shoulders from the birth channel until a pair of arms twitched feebly and he clasped a slender torso. Abruptly he withdrew his hands and jumped to his feet, staring at me in horror. Then he rushed from the room and I thought he must have been seized with some frightful malady of the gut which required him to seek a close-stool. I took his place and supported the dangling child as a leg became visible, turning the body slightly to help its passage, but at that instant I gagged, forcing the bile back down my throat, for now I understood. The woman also saw what I saw and she started to scream.

I had read of monstrous births but knew they rarely came to term. This one looked fully formed in miniature but was an affront to nature and God's creation. Four little legs protruding at opposite angles from a common body were followed by another pair of arms and, most frighteningly, by a second head. It had no obvious sex. Stubbornly I held on to the chimera as the afterbirth came free, wondering if I imagined a weak pulse of life in the distorted frame. Instantly, in a sweeping movement which took me by surprise, the woman wrenched the double-child from my hands and thrust it into the cauldron of hot water standing ready by the bedside. I fancied a thin cry came from the creature as it was plunged into oblivion and I heard myself give a sob.

'The Devil's work! God save us all.' The woman rounded on me. 'Who are you to put the evil eye on my mistress? Who sent you? Help! Help! Satan is amongst us.'

I staggered to my feet, trembling, my gown bespattered with blood, my hands thick with gore, while the woman screamed again and the door opened. Gilbert Iffley stood for a moment appraising the scene before striding to the tub of crimson water. He stifled a cry at what he saw as I felt his wife's pulse and was ready to reassure him that Lady Glasbury was regaining consciousness. Wild-eyed he moved to my side, his mouth shaking, and with his fist he landed a blow on my jaw which sent me crashing to the floor.

Chapter 15

When I came to myself I lay crumpled on sodden ground. The back of my head was throbbing, my jaw sore, my mind muzzy, and at first I could not make out why I was unable to raise myself. Then I realised that my wrists were shackled to an iron ring only a few inches above ground-level so I was compelled to remain supine. The place smelled musty and I decided I was in a cellar. Recollection had returned to me and I wondered if I had been taken to the castle to await some gruesome trial designed to prove my devilish intentions. The birthmark on my cheek had led me to be jeered at in my youth and called the Devil's spawn. Was I to end my days in uncanny endorsement of that vile allegation?

The chamber was narrow and low ceilinged but there was something strange about it which I puzzled over until my mind cleared sufficiently for me to reason. There was no window in its walls and it should have been pitch-black, yet I could distinguish my surroundings dimly. Clenching my teeth against the pain, I turned my head and saw behind me on the wall, beside the door, a sconce with two rush lights and I had enough comprehension of logic to know that this was odd. Why would my gaoler give me light when darkness would increase my misery and disorder my senses? I shut my eyes to ponder this riddle and I may have dozed but when I awoke I was fully conscious and I peered around my cell with growing apprehension.

I had been supplied with light because I was intended to see and to comprehend what was to happen. A few feet above my head, as I lay on the beaten earth, a clear wavy mark ran round the walls, with here and there a trace of green colouring its outline. On the opposite wall from the one to which I was tethered a grille was visible, impenetrably black beyond the grating but with a pool of water in the dip at its base. This cellar was below the waterline, no doubt beside the river, and at high tide it flooded for half its height. A man able to stand, albeit bending beneath the vault, would succeed in keeping his head dry but a prisoner bound as I was had no chance to avoid the death by drowning which was unquestionably planned for me. Then I presumed my body would be released from its shackles, the grille raised and my bloated corpse would be consigned to the waters of the Liffey. Perhaps it was even some bizarre test, I thought sourly: perhaps as the Devil's agent I was expected to survive, under demonic protection, and so substantiate the charge against me. Perhaps when I sank beneath the tide, like any mortal man, I would be judged innocent.

There would be few to mourn me. It was months since I had news of Rendell, Thomas and Grizel who had become used to living their own lives without me and my long-neglected mother was dead. At Ravensmoor the Dowager would regret my disappearance because I had failed in the assignment she had given me. Perhaps Lady Maud would miss my attentions for a time but she would probably regard my death merely as an affront and inconvenience to her. Two years previously, attached to Suffolk's household and welcomed at the court, I had been a figure of modest significance; even in the constrained life I was obliged to lead in Winchester I found friends. Now I was of no account to anyone.

I speculated how long I had to wait for the tide to rise and engulf me. I said my prayers so my soul would be prepared for its journey from my carcase but the prospect seemed unreal and it was difficult to concentrate on my impending demise. My mind drifted to the women I had loved and I lamented the opportunities for happiness which had been torn from me, especially with Yolande, so nearly my wife and the mother of my tiny dead son. It would have been a doomed match because of the difference in our status and she was fortunate to be spared inevitable ignominy but that was cruel comfort to me. I remembered Beatrice, the Italian courtesan whom I adored, who had loved and betrayed me: I hoped she was content and safe with her violent protector. Then a wave of gentle pleasure stole over me to think of Bess, my first and purest love; through misadventure she had believed me untrue and married a worthy fellow who brought her joy. She at least had been spared the worst consequences of knowing me and the curse I seemed to carry to those I loved.

I could not judge the time which had passed since I came to my senses and there was no discernible change in the darkness outside the grille. A spasm of panic gripped me. Must I lie waiting for the end with my mind as supine as my body? I must occupy my thoughts, no matter how futile the exercise. Surely there was something to contemplate which would divert me? Oblivion would come soon enough.

I drew up my knees to relieve the pressure on my back and made myself think through the scene with Roger Egremont and his denial of responsibility for Eleanor's abduction. I did not trust him but his words rang true, more so because Richard of York accepted them. The Duke had around him scheming villains, like Iffley and Boice, and I did not doubt he might one day assert a claim to his distant cousin's throne but I felt instinctively his natural mode of action would be open and forthright. He chose to personify nobleness of spirit, so surely he would scorn whatever was false and underhand? That left the question of Eleanor's fate unanswered unless the theory of a ransom demand by unknown persons proved correct.

The other mystery concerned the earlier attempts on my life in Yorkshire. It was unlike Boice to shrug off my accusation that he had organised them; in the past he and Iffley had made no secret of their efforts to silence me. Why should he lie now? Could it be that someone else had been involved? Someone else who had links with Normandy? A frightening possibility occurred to me and I so far forgot my situation that I tried to jerk myself upwards and groaned with the pain of the fetters jarring on my wrists. I was so engrossed in my speculation and discomfort that I did not immediately respond to the creaking of the door behind me.

A puff of air made me appreciate what was happening and by then the man had dropped to his knees at my side. 'Good, you're conscious,' he said. 'I feared that crack on the head when you fell might have finished you off.'

'Willison!'

'Don't talk. You'll need all your strength. The back of your head is a nasty mess and the wound may open again. We'll have to take that risk.' He had produced a pair of finely curved tweezers which physicians use to extract deep-set splinters or fragments of bone and was bent over the lock which fixed my fetters to the iron ring. 'This is a skill I learned years ago.'

'Where are you taking me?'

He sat back on his heels. 'I can't take you anywhere, Somers. Even in the turmoil around us I daren't lead you upstairs in case the watchman spots us. I can give you a chance, though, as you did for me: a life for a life. Ah, success!' The lock sprang open, releasing me from the ring on the wall, and with my wrists still chained together I struggled to my feet. 'Now listen to me,' he continued. 'The tide's beginning to come in and I must get back before I'm missed. I'm going to lift the grating. It's where they push inconvenient corpses into the sea but you'll have the opportunity to get away. You'll have to slide out on your belly, onto the muddy foreshore. Turn to your left and keep low on the ground until you've rounded the bend. Try to look like a beached seal. Then you'll see the fellow with the rowing boat. He'll take you to the ship bound for England. He's been well paid.' Willison had worked the grille free from its fastening and lifted it a couple of feet.

'Won't you be caught?'

He pushed me down on my knees. 'Lie flat. We're in a warehouse just outside the castle and the watchman they posted outside is well primed with drink. He's wandered over to talk to the guard by the postern gate.

They're all agog with the news and Richard of York is ranting and raving in fury.' I stared at him blankly and he gave a soft chortle. 'You don't know? Of course. News has come in from London – news of the Duke of Suffolk's elevation.'

'Duke of Suffolk? But Duke's a royal title. William de la Pole has no royal blood.'

'Exactly and Richard of York's spitting blood. There's never been a Duke without royal blood. It won't just be York who's outraged. Now go.'

I lay down on my stomach and felt the water rippling up round me. 'They'll know someone let me out.'

Willison gave me a light kick on my behind. 'The Devil,' he said. 'They'll save face by saying the Devil preserved his own. There's enough credulity among the servants for it to become a legend of Satan's power. The master of the ship will file the fetters off your wrists when you're on-board. Quick now, before the water covers your mouth. God be with you.'

'And with you, Willison,' I gulped as my head emerged through the grille and I breathed fresh air.

*****

I had not realised how weak I was and when they hauled me on board the round cog as she raised her anchor I nearly collapsed. I spent the voyage dozing on a pile of sacks, my wrists unfettered but my mind too full of conflicting emotions to think straight. I never knew how long the crossing took but when land was sighted and I dragged myself to the gunnel I did not recognise the stretch of coast we were passing as we turned towards a port.

'This isn't Chester?' I asked a sailor uncoiling ropes.

'Not on your life, mate,' he said with a wink. 'Bristol, queen of the west coast. Mind your feet there.'

No one had bothered to pick my pocket when Iffley consigned me to the underground cell so I had a little money but no change of clothes or the letter of accreditation from the Dowager. I had no business to be in Bristol and needed to return to the north as soon as I could but my head still ached and I decided a day's rest would fit me better for the long ride. I hoped I could assume that Richard of York's men would not come seeking me and his party was not due to return to England for another week.

I took a bed in a shabby hostelry and tried to push aside my anxieties while I slept but I woke with a realisation which should have come to me before. Willison had undoubtedly saved my life but his action was not altruistic. The moment he had seen the unnatural creature Lady Glasbury bore he rushed from the room. At the time I thought this due to the effect of overwhelming horror but now it came to me that he had taken the opportunity to leave me in charge of the shocking occurrence. Otherwise he might have been held responsible for the deviant birth and suffered punishment: for, however unjustified, physicians were liable to be blamed for the misadventures of their patients. Willison was quick-thinking and unscrupulous and this understanding made me more certain he had tricked me over Brother Joseph's death in Winchester.

Next morning I went to find a hardy but gentle horse for the first stage of my lengthy journey. I was undecided which route to follow and worried that my resources would not stretch to hiring a guide, much less an armed escort. The main thoroughfare, well used by merchants, ran east from Bristol towards London but I hesitated to stray many miles in that direction for fear of arrest by Suffolk's agents if they should discover me so far from Ravensmoor. The alternative was to follow less well frequented roads through Gloucester and Hereford, places I did not know, taking me close to Richard of York's seat of power at Ludlow and the Welsh Marches where I would be more at risk of attack by rogues. I questioned the stableman on the choices before me but our conversation was disturbed by three exuberant fellows bursting into the yard, claiming the man's attention for a lucrative transaction 'A dozen good horses, we need, and we'll pay generously,' said a voice which to my amazement I knew.

I flattened myself against the door of the tack-room, for I feared Master Wilby and his companions would have imbibed the poisonous allegations about me and would haul me before the justices. Perhaps they might even be the advance party of Duke Richard's own return from Ireland, sent on to apprehend me. I held my breath but my attempt to hide was in vain: the musician saw me and gave a shout of elation.

'Harry, you're safe! I prayed you had escaped when there were rumours of your disappearance – and that you were helped by a well-wisher not the Devil. Where are you bound? We are returning to Windsor. Come with us.'

I flung myself into his outstretched arms but shook my head. 'I must go north again, as quickly as I can, to Ravensmoor.'

'Then you shall go with us to Oxford. You'll have a choice of tracks from there. Come, join our company. We shall tell ribald stories while we ride and in the evenings we'll sing for our suppers. You'll enjoy the journey.'

Whether from delicacy or ignorance, Wilby said nothing of the unnatural birth and I needed no further persuasion to join his troop. For two days I set aside all the troubles which beset me and relaxed in the comradeship of the musicians.

At Oxford I was sorry that I must leave them and find my way across country until I could join the great road to the north. I was tempted by the chance to call at Stamford, for I would welcome guidance from the redoubtable Prioress, but I did not like to face her without news of Eleanor and never doubted she would know of the girl's abduction. Master Wilby and his companions were already in the saddle, ready to make their farewells to me, and the ostler had gone to fetch my horse when a clattering of harness and weapons announced the arrival at the inn of a group of soldiers. I shrank back into the shadows, unable to make out whose badge they wore, and my distrust was re-awoken to such an extent that I wondered if one of the musicians had betrayed my whereabouts to Richard of York's allies in the area. Then I made out the dusty outline of the clog and chain on his tunic as a young man jumped from his mount and ran towards me. These were the Duke of Suffolk's men.

'Christ be praised! It's him. Saved us a wasted expedition. Thought we'd have to go on to Bristol, looking for you. Here, Sergeant, he's here. Wake up, Doctor! Don't you recognise me or are you still as bad-tempered as you were when I last saw you?'

'Rendell,' I said weakly. 'Have you come to arrest me?'

The sergeant joined us and took my arm 'We're to escort you to London, sir. The Duke requires your presence at his house in the City.'

'Did you know he was made Duke?' Rendell winked cheerily as I nodded. 'He wants you back in his service. He said so. He's proclaimed the King's principal counsellor now, no one can touch him. You're back in favour, Doctor. Ain't you glad to see us? Turn of the wheel, ain't it? You've got your old position back – physician to his household. Suppose I'd better not cheek you too much. What d'you think of that?'

*****

For the rest of our journey I felt numb, not daring to accept the cheery assurances I was given, my trust in great men's sincerity so undermined that I refused to give credit to their pronouncements. Even when I was taken upstairs in Suffolk's London mansion, the Manor of the Rose, to attend the new-made Duke, the Great Chamberlain of England, in his private study, I dared not believe I was being transported back to the respected position I had held until he cast me off eighteen months previously at Saint Edmundsbury. I bowed nervously as he regarded me through narrowed eyes. 'Your Grace. You summoned me?'

He came towards me as I straightened and put his hands on my shoulders. 'I don't admit as much to many men, Harry, but you've suffered a number of tribulations on my account. I can make recompense now. My place is unassailable at the King's side.'

I caught my breath, troubled by his absolute confidence. 'Your elevation is proof of that, my Lord, but I fancy it will provoke some envious side-glances.'

'Oh, I have missed your honesty. You're speaking of Richard of York?'

'Only a report I was given of him ranting when he heard you were made Duke.'

'He'll not be the only one, I grant you, but if we keep the King's approval for our actions, no one can touch us.'

His use of the supercilious plural was disheartening but I tried to ignore it. 'My Lord, if I can serve your household, I should be overjoyed.'

'So you shall, Harry. The old physician I engaged is contented to slip back into a quiet life and your young Italian protégé is returned from the university to help you.'

'Leone? He can work with me again?' I felt my throat catch as I spoke. 'My Lord, that's gracious but I have obligations to the Dowager Countess of Stanwick which I must discharge.

The Duke looked amused. 'A messenger has set off to tell her I have reclaimed your services.'

'My mission to Dublin was on her behalf. Her late husband's child was abducted from Ravensmoor and I have failed to find the girl.'

'The failure by those involved to send the lady a timely message after that escapade was a luckless omission but it's been rectified. Her mind will be at rest by now and I understand she's likely to seek a peaceful retirement in

189

the cloister. You've been led a merry dance by the carelessness of others but your obligations are discharged.

I stared at the Duke in bewilderment. 'Your Grace, you know what has happened to Mistress Eleanor?'

Suffolk saw my confusion and laughed. 'I mustn't tease you further, Harry. Mistress Eleanor is safe with her guardian, Lord Fitzvaughan, in Normandy. Walter was not happy that the child was abandoned, after her father's death, in a barbarous part of the kingdom. As a known heiress, she could have been at risk from all kinds of scoundrels. He couldn't provide suitably for her on his estate in Norfolk, while he's so often across the sea at the King's behest, so he decided she should join him in Normandy where he's spending the winter. He wrote to the Dowager Countess suggesting that his representative would call to escort the girl on her journey but the old woman refused to cooperate unless Walter went to Ravensmoor in person and showed her the royal mandate appointing him guardian. He had no time for such nonsense so he sent his man to bring the child to him by force if necessary. Unfortunate necessity, he told me in his letter I received last week.'

I seethed with outrage – for Eleanor's mistreatment, the Dowager's deceit in failing to tell me of Lord Fitzvaughan's approach to her and the dangers to which I had been exposed in my futile undertaking. 'Two attendants were killed when Eleanor was abducted,' I said and I did not hide my bitterness.

'Walter mentioned his regrets for that. The girl's squire foolishly resisted armed men and reaped his reward.'

'Eleanor's woman was murdered too.'

The Duke lifted his hands in resignation. 'Walter's man had hired rough fellows to ensure the task was carried out effectively. They lacked finesse.'

'Finesse?' I choked on the word. 'Eleanor must have been terrified.'

'Walter says she quickly recovered. She was content to obey her guardian's wishes. She'd met his man when he went previously to Ravensmoor and she seems to have a liking for him.

'For Gaston de la Tour?'

The Duke raised his eyebrows. 'You're making assumptions. Walter doesn't say who he sent. What he has told me is that he hopes Eleanor's betrothal will take place in the spring.'

'To Cuthbert Percy?'

'I think you can be confident it won't be Roger Egremont.'

I managed a slight grin to show appreciation of that news and Suffolk slapped me on the shoulder. 'Come,' he said, 'I promised Alice I'd take you to her. She's anxious to welcome you back into the household.'

My mind was spinning as I followed him through a door at the back of his study and along private corridors leading to his wife's apartments. I reminded myself that I must learn to call her Duchess Alice. As we approached the solar I heard waves of feminine laughter and when we entered half a dozen ladies of varying ages looked round from their chattering and sank low in curtseys to the Duke. In turn I bowed to their mistress.

'Your Grace.'

She held out her hand and bustled across to me. 'Doctor Somers, I'm so glad you have returned to us. I fear you've been put to many inconveniences since we last saw you and we have missed your ministrations. You will not recognise young John. He's grown so tall.'

She was speaking of John de la Pole, Suffolk's only son. 'He must be, what, six years old now, your Grace?'

'How well you remember! He will be pleased to see you. I think you will recall all your former charges – the household has not changed greatly. I have one new attendant you must meet.' She beckoned and a young woman came forward. 'Mistress Katherine Devereux.'

The maiden's startling green eyes appraised me and I bowed, struggling to keep my composure, to persuade myself that the Devereux family must have many branches and this girl probably knew nothing of the unfortunates in Winchester. She was tiny and delicately made, with a pointed chin and pale creamy cheeks which made those shining irises more unsettling. As she moved back to her stool she lifted them to stare boldly at the Duke and her lips curled into a smile which seemed at odds with her modest grace.

'Come, Harry,' said the Duke who gave no indication that he noticed her interest, 'I shall claim some minutes of your time so you can pummel the muscles of my back and give relief as you used to do. Then you must go and greet Leone, re-establish your consulting room and begin to renew acquaintance with my servitors. In due course no doubt you will find time to give attention to these frivolous damsels and their make-believe ailments.'

The twitter of amusement followed us out of the door and I accompanied the Duke along the corridor, still overwhelmed by what I had learned. Far away, in a corner of my mind, I felt a twinge of sadness for Lady Maud Fitzvaughan, abandoned in an isolated castle, her daughter taken from her where she could not follow, even her convenient paramour apparently faithless, deserting her when his own convenience dictated. I was not a free agent but I felt a qualm of conscience on her account, all the more for the way Walter Fitzvaughan had behaved in arranging Eleanor's abduction. The only welcome news I had heard that day was that his lordship was to remain on the other side of the Narrow Sea for the foreseeable future; I had no stomach to meet him after my renewed dalliance with his wife. I had no ambition now but to carry out my physician's role, serving a large and varied household, and to avoid entanglement in great men's schemes.

Except that, every now and then, a shimmer of light from a pair of inquisitive green eyes came into my mind and distracted my thoughts.

Part III London, Normandy and East Anglia: 1448-1449

Chapter 16

Through the remainder of the summer and the autumn I settled myself back into the usual role of household physician to a large entourage. Those for whom I had a care ranged from kitchen boys to men at arms, laundresses to the Duchess's serving ladies and included William and Alice de la Pole themselves. Scalds, sprains, knife wounds, numerous belly upsets, the ague and the horrors of fevers which drenched the sufferer in sweat: all required my attention and kept me busy. At my side Leone had become newly knowledgeable and I relished learning fresh ideas from him, although Oxford was still a good way behind Padua in the practice of physic so I considered myself fortunate to have experienced the teaching of both establishments.

As the weeks passed and the horrors I encountered in Dublin seemed more remote I gained in confidence that I had finally escaped Iffley's and Boice's designs. Whether they supposed me drowned in the Liffey, I did not know, but sooner or later they would inevitably discover my continued existence. Yet I heard nothing from them and I concluded that if they knew of my willing return to Suffolk's service they must have written me out of their plans. After so many attempts which I had rebutted, if they had abandoned the intention of subverting my allegiance, I was glad. William de la Pole shared flaws of character with many other proud and ambitious noblemen but he was loyal to his King and he displayed a love of culture which many of his peers lacked. I was content to tie my fortunes to his.

I was surprised how assiduously the Duke sought my company, not merely as physician but as someone to whom he could speak with relative freedom; so I was privileged to gain an appreciation of his latent anxieties.

194

With the ardent support of Queen Margaret and the grateful dependence of the King, he gloried in his impregnable position and most of the time this seemed justified. Richard of York might sulk in Ludlow but there was no sign of a serious or immediate threat coming from that direction and Suffolk enjoyed the backing of several lords who saw advantage in seeking his favour. In particular he counted Edmund Beaufort, Duke of Somerset and now King Henry's Lieutenant in Normandy, as his ally. Only sometimes, when a sombre mood took him, he hinted to me his concerns that Somerset might not prove a competent commander if put to the test. The King's new Lieutenant across the Narrow Sea lacked military experience and had already faced problems in securing the surrender to the French of Anjou and Maine, agreed under the terms of the truce Suffolk had negotiated with King Charles three years previously. This was the festering sore beneath the skin, often ignored, but which might at some point erupt with toxic force.

One evening in November it was clear the Duke wanted to gossip when he invited me to sit with him and share a flask of wine. 'The truce runs out next year,' he said, fingering a spillage of liquid on the table-top, 'and it's clear the French may not renew it. Walter Fitzvaughan has already spent many months cajoling King Charles and admonishing the English captains who've been reluctant to obey orders and cede land. If one of them were to do something foolish...' His voice tailed away.

'Would King Charles see advantage in going to war again?' I was appalled by the prospect.

'If he believed he could drive the English out of Normandy altogether. He'll have picked up rumours that King Henry's attempts to raise money for an army have met resistance, even from his own courtiers who might be expected to make him loans.'

'So Lord Fitzvauaghan has a difficult task to win round the French king?'

The Duke seized the opportunity to speak of more cheerful matters. 'Never underestimate Walter. He's skilful and can spring surprises. You may not have heard that he's installed his lady back on his estate in Norfolk.'

I controlled my voice rigorously. 'Lady Maud has returned to Attleborough?'

'Yes. Gaston de la Tour was sent to escort her there. It was hardly appropriate to leave her stranded at Ravensmoor after the Dowager Countess entered a convent. I gather she's confined to the estate and Walter will seldom go there but conjugal appearances are restored. King Henry approves of marital harmony.'

I hoped I glided naturally to my question. 'Have you news of Mistress Eleanor's well-being?'

'She's thriving according to Walter who seems delighted with her.' The Duke stood up and swirled the wine in his goblet. 'There's another issue I need to look into and you can help me, Harry.'

'Your Grace?' I hoped my unease was not evident.

'Naturally I have agents who advise me of activity among Richard of York's associates but there's always a danger that he's infiltrated someone I'd be unwise to trust into my household or bribed one of my men to betray me. I've been warned that he may be trying to foment dissension among my followers or to blacken my reputation because of their misdeeds. I'd be obliged if you'd keep your eyes and ears open for signs of treachery as you move round the house.'

I shivered, remembering that Stephen Boice had taunted me about my association with Lady Maud, and the old fear of being pressurized to act as his spy was revived. If he threatened disclosure of my transgressions to Walter Fitzvaughan I would be in a cleft stick. 'I'll do what I can,' I said.

'Good. Keep it to yourself, Harry. This is not something I'm ready to share with the Reverend Mother in Stamford.' The Duke winked and I felt stupid not to have realised he would know of the correspondence I had revived with the Prioress. 'Don't worry. I've no objection to you writing to the lady. She's firmly committed to her Percy kin and they are my friends. But occasionally I'll ask for your discretion in what you tell her.'

I bowed. The Prioress lived in the secular world, as well as serving God's higher purposes. She would understand.

*****

Most members of Suffolk's household had been in post when I served alongside them formerly and it seemed unlikely one of these established followers would have turned traitor. I knew such a presumption was not watertight as there might be a price that could turn an individual, or Suffolk's imperious grandeur could have disgruntled someone. Nevertheless I decided to concentrate my attention initially on those who had come to the Manor of the Rose while I had been absent. I made sure I met all the new-comers but there was no senior office-holder among them and I did not identify a possible candidate for treachery.

I had not included the womenfolk in my opening discussions but moved on to make their acquaintance. I tried not to become obsessed by a baseless theory, yet I could not rid myself of a suspicion that Mistress Devereux guarded some secret. Her fascination with the Duke seemed to me obvious when I first met her and I wondered if the way she regarded him through her luxuriant eyelashes was intended to attract him into seeking her favours. If this was her aim it did not mean she had been sent by a third party to do him harm; it was a familiar story for an attractive woman to seek advantage by beguiling a great man. In this case I deemed it improbable that she would succeed. The Suffolk marriage was underpinned by affection and respect and I could not imagine William de la Pole disdaining his wife by dallying with one of her own attendants. In any case, as time passed, I observed that Mistress Devereux appeared less fixated on the Duke's person, which might suggest she had come to the same conclusion, but I had still not sought to exercise a physician's privilege of conversation with her. Some imprecise caution held me back.

On a chilly, dank day, I was speaking to the Duchess's page in the gallery overlooking the courtyard when Mistress Devereux summoned him to attend her mistress. I waved him on his way and expected her to follow but, once he had passed through the door, the young woman turned back to me and fixed those luminous green eyes upon my person. 'Have you a moment, Doctor Somers? I should be glad to speak to you.'

'I'm at your service, Mistress Devereux.'

She gave a slight shiver and drew her wrap closer over her shoulders. 'You're well thought of in the household, Doctor. Several of the older attendants have sung your praises for the care you gave them when you were with the Suffolks two years past.'

There was an odd mixture of timidity and condescension in her demeanour and I was surprised a girl some seven or eight years my junior should address me with such a patronising air. 'That's gratifying, Mistress. How may I help you?'

The vivid eyes narrowed but did not shift their gaze and I assumed she was near-sighted and in consequence peered more intently than was usual but without any hidden meaning. 'I don't know the answer to your question,' she said, 'but I should like to explore the possibilities. Have you met my brother?'

'I don't think so. Is it likely?'

'He's a notary in the City, as was my dear father. You see I am not born of gentle stock but my father had many noble clients in the City, until his death more than a year ago. I believe my brother still undertakes commissions for those at court.'

I detected the note of uncertainty in her voice but did not want to deflect her from what she wished to say. 'You came here after your father's death?'

She tossed her head. 'Not at once. It was presumed I would live with my brother but he was not kind to me and I went for a while to Kent, to live in my uncle's house. I've been here only a few months.'

She paused and I was not clear how I should respond. 'You are content here?'

Her smile was loaded with meaning I could not fathom. 'I must await events before I can answer you. A woman is not accorded the luxury of meaningful thought.'

I attempted to give reassurance. 'I've known many women capable of meaningful thought, Mistress Devereux. Don't imagine you are not blessed with intelligence because you lack freedoms men have.'

Her voice became shrill. 'They say I am too excitable and hasty in my emotions. My mind tortures me with foul imaginings. Sometimes I lie on my bed and scream in unremitting misery. A priest once told me I am a lost soul.'

'I can't comment on the state of your soul, Mistress, but as a physician I would recommend you to occupy your vigorous mind with useful or creative tasks.'

'Creative tasks? A woman?' She did not hide her scorn.

'Women have written poetry and many play musical instruments. Don't construct imaginary barriers to what you might do.'

She took a step closer to me. 'You're a curious man, Doctor Somers. You don't dismiss me as a mad woman?'

I gave a tense laugh. 'Certainly not. I've seen poor wretches possessed by demons. They are not like you.'

She turned away and I supposed our dialogue was at an end but then she swivelled back towards me and she spoke in a lower, conversational tone. 'You've been in the north, I understand.'

It was encouraging to see how she could calm herself when she chose. 'I was in Yorkshire for a while before I returned to London.'

'It's rumoured you were complicit in the Duke of Gloucester's death.'

This was an astonishingly direct accusation and it unnerved me. 'The Duke of Suffolk has exonerated me from suspicion and I'd be grateful if you give such rumours no credence.'

'But you had to go and hide in Yorkshire?'

'Not at all. The Duke asked me to go there to attend a friend who was very ill. I'd been staying in Winchester previously.'

Her eyes gleamed with triumph and I realised I had blundered into a trap. 'Winchester? Dear me, were you there when the shameful deaths took place?'

My attempt to look blank failed but I would not give her the satisfaction of showing comprehension. She was not deterred by my silence. 'Devereux,' she said crisply. 'The name I bear. My great-grandfather was a by-blow of the family, got on a serving maid but graciously acknowledged by his noble father and given his name. There are many lawfully begotten branches of the Devereux tree and, whether or not they would prefer to deny it, we are all kin. It seems we are rotten at the core, don't you think? When one of the most honoured limbs proves to be corrupted? A maiden little older than I am serving as her father's whore?

I was startled that the disgrace of her distant relatives should disturb her so acutely and wished I could tell her what I knew, at least to acquit Mistress Isabella of perverted passion, but I dared not break my seal of silence. I was troubled by this blunt and strangely overwrought young woman yet I judged it my physician's duty to help her if I could. 'The episode has no relevance to you, Mistress. You mustn't let it worry you. Try to put it from your mind.'

She ignored my soothing words. 'I overheard mention that you had been in Winchester and wanted to see if it was true. The account of the deaths which came to the City spared few foul details of the incestuous pair. Did you see the bodies, Doctor Somers?'

I drew myself erect and faced her sternly. 'I will not give nourishment to your wild fancies, Mistress. It isn't fitting that you dwell on something so unusual and extreme. It will poison your mind.'

She sank low in an ironic curtsey. 'Your pardon, Doctor Somers, I hadn't intended to burden you with my anxieties. The knowledge of my tainted stock is for me to confront. I shan't inconvenience you again with my wayward thoughts.'

The derision in her voice stung me and I felt bound to protest. 'Mistress, I'm a physician. If I can help you I shall be pleased do what I can but I can only advise as seems best to me.'

She gave me a radiant smile and I felt my heart miss a beat. 'Then I may yet claim your care, physician. I hope you are prepared.'

I stared after her and a cold spasm ran up my spine.

*****

Since my return to London I had already called on my old friends Thomas and Grizel in their house near the Tower, where Thomas had established himself in business as a master carpenter, but as the Feast of the Nativity approached I arranged to go again and Rendell secured leave of absence to go with me. Grizel was now the mother of four healthy children, although Rendell told me she had lost a new-born baby in the previous year, and I expected a merry and boisterous visit. Indeed we had no sooner arrived than three urchins were chasing each other round her skirts, shrieking with glee. Thomas delighted in his sons, reprimanding them for exuberance with such

201

gentleness that they were not in the least intimidated, but his latest infant was a daughter and his paternal pride in this shrivelled scrap of femininity knew no bounds.

'We've called her Margery in honour of old Dame Margery, who was so kind to us when we were young, at Greenwich.'

I remembered the wife to Humphrey of Gloucester's late chamberlain with affection and complimented her namesake's parents on their choice. At that point my own namesake, now four years old and the eldest of the brood, turned his attention from his siblings to pull at my gown. 'Why'd you wear this dull thing then?' he asked.

'It's what physicians wear, Hal. People know what I am when they see it.'

He nodded wisely. 'People know Nuncle Rendie's a soldier, cos' he wears armour. I'd rather wear armour.'

'I ain't wearing armour now,' said Rendell with a wink.

'Nah but you've got two colours on your legs. That's as good.'

'Parti-coloured hose, they call it: fashionable among military men.'

'Stop your boasting. I don't want my sons following you into soldiering.' Grizel landed a hefty clomp on her brother's shoulder. 'They'll be honest craftsmen like their father if I've anything to do with it.'

'You won't have,' Rendell said as he dodged another blow.

While his offspring commandeered their uncle's attention, Thomas drew me aside and I was not sorry to escape the duty of holding his baby daughter. The loss of my own little son had become a raw wound again as soon as I saw the tiny infant.

'You know how pleased we are to see you back with Suffolk's household, in a position that befits your learning, but there's something you should be aware of – if you're not already. Suffolk's reputation in the City has suffered badly in recent weeks.'

I was touched by my friends' concern but also amused. 'Suffolk's never been popular in the City and now he's pre-eminent among the King's counsellors he attracts the envy of other nobles.'

'There's more to it,' Thomas said and I could tell this was not a trivial apprehension on his part. 'Word has it that the King's finances are in dire jeopardy – the treasury empty and even the money-lenders refusing credit. We're all taxed to the hilt as it is and the merchants are complaining about their impositions. Now Suffolk is said to be behind the latest ploy for raising funds and it's not well received.'

'What do you mean?'

'Selling honours to the highest bidder. There's a mean-minded goldsmith in Cheapside said to have bought three baronies and even churchmen have joined the scramble for privileges that are up for sale. I could tell you of a case where a judge was bribed and a jury packed to secure acquittal for a wealthy villain who was prepared to pay for the favour.'

'There've been stories like this before, Tom. Even Cardinal Beaufort was alleged to be guilty of peculation – Humphrey of Gloucester claimed it and tried to get him disgraced.'

Thomas bent close to whisper in my ear. 'The worst rumour has it that Suffolk has held secret meetings with a French noble and passed over papers which should be confidential to the King's Council.'

'That's preposterous!'

The master carpenter had acquired new gravitas since he set up in business alone. He shook his head solemnly. 'I'm afraid there's a head of steam building up which may scald the new-made Duke if it bubbles away for long enough. I don't want to see you scorched in the boiling residue. You've had to put up with enough from the nobility you've served.'

Thomas, the most prosaic of practical men, sounded morbidly poetic and I expressed my gratitude for his warning. I did not believe Suffolk's immediate position was vulnerable but I remembered the Duke's own reservation about the state of affairs in Normandy – if one of King Henry's captains proved recalcitrant and did something foolish. The cost of going to war again would be ruinous and if that were to happen and Suffolk bore the blame, the danger to a man hated and envied by so many might mushroom into an explosive force.

*****

I returned to the Manor of the Rose in reflective mood. Rendell had left me after our visit to his sister's family and I gathered that he had an assignation with a young woman. He was unwilling to be drawn on the subject and I knew I must not trespass on his private pursuits now he was a man but I had not accustomed myself to his new status and felt disconcerted.

I was requested to join the Duke without delay and took with me a jar of my ointment which eased the twinges he suffered from an old wound to his back. When I saw him looking jovial, jumping up with agility from his seat, the Duchess at his side, I realised that was not the purpose of my summons. 'Your Graces.' I bowed.

'We wish you to hear this news from us, Harry,' the Duke said, 'in case it trickles out from other quarters. We have been greatly honoured by Queen Margaret. She has given her support to a proposal that our young John should be betrothed... should be betrothed to the little Beaufort heiress, to a maiden with royal blood, King Henry's own kindred. We are humbled and delighted.'

The Duke's voice gave the lie to his words for he sounded far from humble and my instinct was to cry out against this rash announcement. He exalted in his personal success and viewed the prospective union of these small children as no more than due recognition of his own

204

achievements. He was the first holder of a Dukedom who lacked royal blood but this was to be corrected in the next generation. Did he not realise how English nobles who could trace their unblemished lineage back for hundreds of years would react to news of a jumped-up merchant's grandson wedding a girl descended from royal stock? Was he blinded by pride to the dangers he was courting?

I bowed again and cleared my throat. 'An unparalleled honour indeed, your Grace. My deepest congratulations. May heaven bless the betrothal.'

The Feast of the Nativity was celebrated with the usual combination of solemn Masses and more raucous jollity over the ensuing twelve days. The Duke and Duchess were in attendance on the King and Queen, accompanied only by their closest followers. In their absence the cellarer, who acted as Lord of Misrule at the Manor of the Rose, took advantage of his unsupervised freedom to encourage a degree of licence which his master might have judged unseemly. At the climax of the festivities on Twelfth Night I held back from the frolics of the lesser servants but did not wish to appear aloof so I consented to join the round of dancing, in which most present participated, despite the awkwardness of my gait.

After working my way along the chain of women facing the line of men, setting and bowing to each one, I found myself opposite Mistress Devereux clad in a crimson gown, and I needed to take her hand as we passed beneath the archway of raised arms, to the head of the column. Her hand was in mine for only a few moments but the pressure of her thumb moving across my palm was undeniable. I glanced quickly at her before we turned away from each other to move down the outsides of the formation and encounter different partners for the next part of the dance. Her lips curved into an open smile and she lowered those penetrating eyes in a manner which I concluded must be intentionally provocative. Her conduct disturbed and bemused me but against the background of the Yule revels, I determined to ignore it.

With an aching foot, I left the assembly when the dance finished and sought refreshment beside the Duke's steward, listening to his account of papers mislaid from his desk and then retrieved on a nearby shelf where he was convinced he had never put them. I was hot from my unaccustomed activity and drank from the chalice of wine he gave me with unwise haste, while considering whether his tale was of any significance or merely incidental. Then he was summoned to speak to the Duke's fool, who had upset one of the younger maids with his ribald jests. I took another mouthful of wine and became aware of a crimson skirt brushing my foot and the waft of perfume as the lady bent towards me when she passed.

'I beg you to follow me into the corridor,' she said. 'I have need of your counsel.'

Along the passage outside the great hall, in window niches and other shadowy corners, couples were in conversation or more intimate engagement. I hesitated briefly when I saw Mistress Devereux spreading her skirts as she sat on a bench at the far end of the aisle but I persuaded myself that she might have a legitimate reason to seek my help and I hobbled to her side. She looked up at me and pouted, causing me to think she was disparaging my ability as a dancer.

'My apologies, Mistress, for my clumsiness. I'm not fitted for graceful movement.'

'How did you come by your crooked ankle?'

Once again I was unsettled by her forthright questioning. 'A boyhood accident. I fell from scaffolding which I should not have climbed.'

'You have learned to overcome the inconvenience.'

The statement seemed to imply approval and I inclined my head. 'How may I help you, Mistress Devereux?'

She tapped the seat beside her. 'I wish for your attention as a physician.' I felt a wave of relief and sat down where she indicated but I quickly realised my error when she took my wrist and prevented me rising. 'I have been told I suffer from perturbation of the blood, Doctor Somers, and need to be calmed regularly when the phase of the moon is propitious. I wish you to bleed me so that my unruly emotions may be purged as I feel the heat rising. You have leeches I presume?'

'Certainly, but I'm not a physician who uses them carelessly. You appear to me to be in good health, Mistress. I think your fancy may be overactive but nothing more. I wouldn't wish to set leeches to suck your lifeblood from your arm. It's a painful process and probably unnecessary.'

She did not reply at once but gave a shiver. 'I would have you set them on my breast, physician, not my arm. Unless your lips can serve the purpose and draw the venom from my veins.'

Too late I tried to pull my wrist free but in our feeble tussle she thrust my hand against the top of her low-cut bodice. 'Do you feel how my blood is pounding, Doctor Somers? Won't you soothe me?' Then her mouth fastened on mine and my resistance dissolved. I kissed her with increasing passion, in a state of conscious arousal, until she pushed me away and rose to her feet. 'I shall come to your dispensary tomorrow afternoon after we have dined, physician. Make sure your charming Italian assistant is not there or I may be perplexed which of you should minister to me. I shall satisfy your hungry leeches.'

She swept off along the passageway while I crouched on the bench, hugging myself, seeking to regain my self-control and judge whether her seductive behaviour was expertly contrived or immature.

Next morning, in excruciating sobriety, I was appalled by what had happened and dreaded the possibility that she would come to my dispensary, as she had promised, even while I lusted for her. I knew I was not alone in my remorse for the actions of the previous evening when I noted many pallid faces and was called on to administer several cures for headaches. The Suffolks had returned to the Manor of the Rose and looked benignly on their subdued household as if they expected nothing else after the excesses of Twelfth Night. I wondered if Duchess Alice appreciated the nature of her youngest waiting lady but I was uncertain myself what that nature truly was. Mistress Devereux might be a forward but naïve flirt, a seasoned cock-teaser or a whore, I could not tell, but she fascinated me beyond measure.

At dinner soon after midday I ate little and grew more and more uncomfortable. I had not arranged for

Leone to be otherwise engaged but I turned over in my mind which spurious excuse would serve best to send him on an errand elsewhere. Then I dismissed the idea, unable to credit that Mistress Devereux would persist with her visit to my rooms until, when the ladies rose to leave the hall, a pair of flashing green eyes rested on me for a moment and I had no doubt of her intention.

Shortly after this the Duke stood and to my utmost joy and compounded chagrin he beckoned me to attend him in his chamber. Fate, it seemed, had intervened to save me from whatever misfortune lay in store for me. Leone heard my summons and could be relied on to inform Mistress Devereux of my obligation if she appeared at the pharmacy door. Whether she then turned her wiles upon the young Italian was for her to judge and I was confident he was capable of deciding his rejoinder. I walked to Suffolk's room with a lightness of heart I had not felt since the previous day.

The Duke was standing beside his desk and in his usual chair the Duchess sat with clasped hands and the hint of a frown. Suffolk looked unruffled and waved me to a stool. I was puzzled by the occasion but so grateful for the respite they had given me that I took my seat with nonchalance. To my surprise it was the Duchess who spoke first.

'Doctor Somers, we have a matter to ask you about which you may think presumptuous but we have only your future well-being in mind.' She paused and a jumble of worries raced through my mind. 'Have you given thought to marrying?'

The Duke patted his wife's arm and his expression as he faced me was sympathetic. 'I know you've had disappointments in the past, Harry, but much flotsam has been swept down the Thames since then. You're still a young man and should think of your future comfort with a wife and family.'

My mouth had become dry but their interest was kindly meant and I acknowledged the truth of their words. 'I should like to marry, your Grace, when the time is right.'

'Good, good, then we have a proposition. It's Alice's idea but I approve in every way. Tell him, my love.'

The Duchess gave a becoming smile. 'Doctor Somers, you have made the acquaintance of my young attendant, Katherine Devereux. She is a maiden of good birth. Her father was a respected lawyer in the City. She is now in my charge and I wish to provide for her appropriately. I suggest that she would make you a most fitting wife and satisfy your needs in every way. I believe furthermore that she would not be averse if you were to pay court and ask for her hand. What do you say?'

I felt my knees tremble and fought against the instinct to drop to the floor. Without any doubt the Duchess knew of my fumbling caresses with her attendant and, I surmised, in all likelihood she had been told that I cajoled Katherine into visiting me alone in my pharmacy where I planned to seduce her. I had been trapped. Yet, in spite of my alarm, I remembered those fascinating green eyes and the lips which had opened invitingly beneath mine.

'Your Grace,' I said after breathing deeply, 'I admit my laggard thoughts hadn't moved to such a conclusion. But the lady is very attractive.' I felt the flush warm my cheeks.

'Ha! She pleases you, Harry!' The Duke gave a roar of approval. 'Well done, Alice, your instinct is impeccable. Speak to the girl, Doctor, and conclude your betrothal as soon as you like. You have our blessing and we shall be generous with your wedding gift.'

The Duchess rose and I bowed, speechless with embarrassment. 'She's a bright, full-blooded young woman, Harry, and adept in household duties. She'll serve you well at bed and board.'

From a corner of my memory I heard Mistress Dutton in her widowhood offering me that same combined provision and a wave of nausea gripped me but the Duke had grasped my hand.

'We'll arrange your speedy betrothal so you can enjoy her without a long period of frustration. I deduce she's one who needs a man's prick between her legs and a babe in her belly. You'll know how to captivate her.'

'William!' His wife's disapproval was not serious and she cuffed his cheek with affection. 'Go to my solar, Harry, and I'll send Katherine to you. Our rascally physician will get his reward for audacious impropriety.'

I stumbled from the room with her merriment ringing in my ears and I understood my position very well. I had dallied with the Duchess's gentlewoman in public beyond the limits of good manners. If I wished to remain in Suffolk's service I had no choice but to wed this girl I scarcely knew, whose mind was subject to weird fancies and whose blatantly provocative behaviour was unusual among ladies of her rank. Whatever the truth of the matter, Mistress Devereux's virtue was to be treated as sacrosanct and I could not be allowed to sully her reputation. I had ensnared myself inadvertently yet I could not deny that I felt protective towards this troubled young woman, more than protective. Indeed I longed to soothe away the fretful lines from her brow with my lips and the thought of those extraordinary eyes gazing up into mine as we lay together was undeniably tantalising.

Those eyes were modestly downcast when Katherine entered the solar leaving the door ajar so we were not out of sight of her companions. She curtsied and I bowed while my mind churned with indecision about how to begin.

'The Duchess is aware of our familiarity at the revels yesterday' I blurted.

'Of course, I made confession to her.' She spoke with easy self-assurance. 'A professional man does not trifle with a lady of like or superior station without having the intention of seeking her hand. In such circumstances it was proper to tell the Duchess.'

It was pointless to challenge the assumptions behind her statement. 'You don't find the prospect of my intention distasteful, Mistress Devereux?'

'I think you should be explicit at this juncture, Doctor Somers, so there is no possibility of misunderstanding between us.'

I could not restrain my smile. 'That's most desirable. In that case, Mistress, I shall put my question in the most straightforward way. I am asking you to marry me.'

I dropped to my knees and she put a knuckle to her mouth as if she were considering which piece of fruit to buy on a market stall. 'The Duchess honours me by giving me the luxury of choice but if I declined your proposal my reputation would be tarnished. You have sprung your trap, Doctor Somers.'

I held her eyes with mine. 'I rather think it was you who sprang the trap, Mistress Devereux.'

'But you don't object, I believe. I've told you of my father's lineage. It will not disgrace you and my dowry is worthwhile to one of your estate.'

'My lineage is far inferior to yours but I have risen from it to claim a physician's rank. That is all I can offer.'

'Not all. I've heard ladies' gossip at the court about your prowess as a lover with a tally of notable beauties as your bedfellows.'

I was learning how she enjoyed suggestive repartee and disregarded conventional limits to what was permissible for an unmarried maiden in badinage with a man. I would not give her the satisfaction of seeing the mortification I felt. 'Such stories are much exaggerated, I'm sure.'

'Perhaps. But I need to confirm that you are free to offer me marriage. I have no father to make enquiry on my behalf.'

'I've never married, Mistress Devereux, and have only been formally betrothed once, years ago in Italy, when it was officially revoked. The lady preferred to enter a convent.'

Her peal of laughter echoed against the high ceiling and she stepped forward, taking my arm. 'May the Lord God preserve me from that fate! You are the alternative with which I am presented and I find your offer preferable. I am content to become your wife, Harry Somers.'

The enormity of what was happening enveloped me and I stared at her in disbelief. 'Mistress Devereux, I am...'

'My name is Katherine but my father always called me Kate. I would find it agreeable for you to do so.'

'Kate,' I repeated while she nestled against me very pleasantly and, as if summoned by the sounding of a horn, the Duchess and her attendants swept into the room to offer felicitations.

*****

It was arranged that our betrothal would take place within a few weeks before the Lenten fasts and our marriage would be held during the season of Easter. In the days before the betrothal ceremony I saw little of Kate, as she accompanied the Duchess when the court moved from London to Windsor, but I did prevail on her to meet my friends, Thomas and Grizel. It was not a comfortable occasion. I suspected that in spite of her veneer of bravado Kate was nervous of meeting people I had been close to since childhood and, angry at her own timidity, she acted as if they were beneath her contempt. Her dismissive attitude bordered on rudeness and I was torn between annoyance on behalf of my friends and sadness that Kate found the meeting so difficult. I wanted to enfold her in my arms and tell her that she had no need to withdraw into her shell of superiority: Grizel and Tom would welcome my promised bride readily if she did not distance herself from them.

As it was, Grizel made sure I was under no illusion about her displeasure when she drew me aside. 'She's a

213

stuck-up man-eater, Harry, and she's got her claws into your gizzard. Get rid of her. She'll ruin your life.'

'She's been forced to stand up for herself since her father died and she's disaffected from her brother. I think she's developed a carapace of sophistication but she's troubled by unusual fancies for a young woman. At heart I think she's frightened of the world. You need to know her better to understand.'

'Well, I'm sorry, Harry, but I'm not going out of my way to try. Nor should you. You talk about her as if she was just your patient, an interesting case of a wayward woman possessed by devils. You're proposing to marry her, for heaven's sake! What does Rendell say?'

'He's in attendance on the Duke at court so I haven't seen him.'

'He'll have heard the soldiers' chatter about the match. Can't you imagine what they're saying, what they're calling her? Christ, Harry, you're out of your mind.'

It hurt me to listen to Grizel but I knew her well and was not surprised by her immediate impression of Kate. Nevertheless I had to reject her conclusion. I needed to believe that as my wife, in the security of our marriage, Kate would blossom and deploy her undoubted intelligence positively. Besides, I had grounds for optimism for, in the moments when we were alone together, she seemed calmer, more natural, so my hopes were justified. It was the suddenness with which our relationship had been concluded that required us both to make adjustments to our conduct.

Sure enough, after her meeting with Thomas and Grizel, Kate became contrite and begged my forgiveness for appearing impolite, citing her nervousness as the reason for her incivility. Confirmed in my diagnosis of her discomfort, I did not want her to dwell on the matter so I brushed it aside by asking her something which had puzzled me.

'Is there no relative or friend of yours that I should meet?'

214

She shook her head and her expression was fierce. 'No. There's no one. Such friends as I have are in the Duchess's service. You know them.'

'But you have a brother. Shouldn't he meet me?'

She twisted away from me. 'No. Never. He's a brute. I shall have nothing to do with him.'

Her ferocity made me wonder if her brother's behaviour had worsened the fears which plagued her mind and I decided it would be unwise to pursue the question. 'You mentioned living at your uncle's house. Shouldn't he be told of your betrothal?'

The look she gave me was almost sly before she giggled. 'I did stay for a while at my uncle's house in Kent where his wife and children live, but he's seldom there. He's a merchant who travels widely. I'll write and tell him of our marriage. He may send us a gift – he's wealthy – but he won't be concerned to attend the ceremony. I expect you'll meet him in due course.'

Then she pressed herself against me fondly before slipping away to join her mistress and I gazed after her with yearning and fiercely burgeoning love.

*****

In common with many another man I have no very clear remembrance of the solemn Mass of our betrothal, only of Kate taking my hand in front of all the household at the Manor of the Rose as we were conducted from the chapel. Then our companions, led by the Duke and Duchess, joined us in feasting and drank our health until Kate was taken off by the sniggering women and I was primed generously with wine. It was accepted that the bodily consummation of our union need not await the marriage ceremony, for our contract already had the blessing of Holy Church, so after darkness fell I was conducted to the chamber where my pledged wife had been put to bed with all the proper ritual.

With thumping in my chest I waited until the door opened and the chaperone assigned to sleep at Kate's side and guard her virtue slipped from the room, as was the convention. I took the empty place and our coupling was joyful, our mutual pleasure free from pretence, so that at dawn I reeled from the bedchamber confident our hastily procured bond was a gift from Heaven sent to redeem the past. The melancholy coiled in my entrails for the last two years, since I lost Yolande and our infant son, was finally moderated and replaced by hope. I had not thought I should love again but Kate had won my heart and I prayed with humility that I could win hers.

Chapter 18

After the joys of our betrothal night I did not relish the need to wait until Eastertide before I could bed my wife a second time and she was often absent from the Manor of the Rose in attendance on the Duchess, the Queen's Mistress of the Robes. In consequence, when the Duke asked me to make a brief visit to Normandy to convey a private message he was unwilling to commit to an ordinary courier, I welcomed the opportunity to fill the void confronting me until April but also had reservations. Suffolk read my mind and laughed.

'Don't worry, I shan't prolong your commission and delay your marriage. I've received tiresome news that some of our English captains in Normandy are still restless, despite all our efforts to bring them to heel. Renewing the truce will be difficult enough without some hothead acting rashly and I want Walter Fitzvaughan to travel round our garrisons and ensure they understand their duty.'

'Lord Fitzvaughan?' My voice sounded reedy as I tried to keep it from shaking. I had no wish to see the man whose good faith I had betrayed and who might have learned of my liaison with his wife at Ravensmoor.

'He's wintering in Normandy before he meets the French King for further discussions. He's well placed to quieten down the least reliable commanders.'

A happier recollection came to me. 'Is his ward, young Mistress Eleanor, still with him?'

'I think she is. Walter mentioned her in his last letter – something about her betrothal. Fashionable event, betrothal!'

'She's a charming girl and her betrothal to a kinsman of Henry Percy is expected to please many.'

'Good. Convey my compliments. A ship leaves Deptford tomorrow morning. I wish you a calm crossing.'

*****

The sea was choppy but we made reasonable time across the Narrow Sea to land at Harfleur and I found the abusive gossip of the sailors more disturbing than the motion of the ship. Hearing how they castigated the Duke of Suffolk and his influence with the King, I kept silent about my service in his household, glad that I wore no livery, and presented myself merely as a physician sent to help colleagues in Rouen. I noted that their badmouthing repeated the allegations Thomas had quoted, adding rumours of peculation from the Treasury, and revived the old slander that Suffolk was the Queen's lover. Powerful men always acquired adversaries but William de la Pole was gaining a range of enemies from the greatest to the meanest in the land and such universal opprobrium did not bode well.

I was given unexpected news on landing in Normandy for Walter Fitzvaughan was not staying in King Henry's fortress at Rouen, as Suffolk had believed, but in a castle some miles to the west, the patrimony of his beloved minion, Gaston de la Tour. I told myself this was of no significance but felt a wave of regret that we would not meet on neutral territory. I spent a day renewing old acquaintances in Rouen and then rode on to the appointment I viewed with considerable ambivalence.

My reception on arrival at Gaston de la Tour's castellated home was cordial, with no sign of my nominal host, and after I had refreshed myself I was conducted to see Lord Fitzvaughan. To my immense relief he greeted me amicably and expressed his delight that I was restored to my position at the Manor of the Rose. This made it easy for me to deliver Suffolk's message and to answer shrewd questions about the Duke's standing in England. I did not disguise my misgivings on his behalf.

Lord Fitzvaughan rested his elbow on the arm of his chair and his chin on his fist, pausing before he spoke. 'You confirm whispers I've heard. I've always respected William de la Pole and I'll do what I can to guarantee that events this aside of the Narrow Sea don't threaten his position. There are some complications because the Duke of Brittany, King Henry's vassal, has become reconciled with the French King, creating a new source of tension, while the Duke of Somerset who now represents our King here lacks experience. I'll try to calm antagonisms and dissuade any of our madcap captains from taking precipitate action. I find myself well favoured by fortune at the present time and I'm loath to think my friend, William, runs the gauntlet of adversity. I'll write a letter you can deliver to him.'

I murmured my support, wondering what particular cause of pleasure had come his way and whether I could enquire discreetly as to Mistress Eleanor's welfare without provoking thoughts of her problematic mother. Fortunately Walter Fitzvaughan was ready to share the news which gave him satisfaction.

'There's someone here who will be overjoyed to meet you again, a young lady you met at Ravensmoor.'

'Mistress Eleanor!'

'Now we have concluded our business I'll signal for her to join us.' Lord Fitzvaughan gave a thin smile and lifted a silver handbell.

It was quickly answered and I subdued a tremor of disappointment when she was led into the chamber by Gaston de la Tour, concentrating instead on the fact that she looked radiantly happy. I bowed to them both.

'Welcome to my home, Doctor Somers,' Gaston said with a curl of his lip. 'I am honoured to offer you hospitality. May I present to you my esteemed wife, La Dame de la Tour.'

To record that I was dumbfounded is to minimise my astonishment a hundredfold. My blood ran cold and my mouth fell open. 'My pardon, I didn't know.'

'It's but a fortnight since we stood in God's house and spoke our marriage vows,' Gaston sneered. 'Since my dear lady came to Normandy it has been all my ambition to win her hand.'

Eleanor's eyes were modestly lowered but she could not hide her smile. Whatever artifice the Norman had used to win her, I did not doubt she found this extraordinary union to her liking – at least as she perceived it. Then Lord Fitzvaughan spoke and the full implications of the match which I had been slow to grasp became apparent.

'You will appreciate my profound joy at this development, Harry. My ward's Stanwick inheritance has now passed to her husband, my dearest friend, and my own lands are settled upon her so they too will be Gaston's and his heirs' in due course. I have already sent my petition to the King begging that when Eleanor inherits, on my death, Gaston may assume the Fitzvaughan title. He will then have fitting estates in England as well as Normandy.'

Enormous and far-flung estates! I saw the triumphant glance that passed between the two men and I shuddered. Did Eleanor understand the nature of the triangle she had joined? It would fit the deviousness of their plan that Gaston should try to get his wife with child, and so provide an heir, but it could be presumed he had every intention of sharing Walter Fitzvaughan's bed at least as often as his wife's. I felt physically sick to realise how the innocent young woman had been charmed and tricked to serve their purposes.

'My lady wishes to ask you something, Doctor Somers,' Gaston said with an ingratiating nod to his wife, public acknowledgement that he granted permission for her to speak.

'I'm truly glad to see you, Doctor.' Eleanor sounded unusually bashful. 'One thing has troubled me since I left Ravensmoor and you can set my heart at rest. Was Lady Stanwick very angry?'

I noted she did not refer to the Dowager as "mother" and I responded carefully. 'She was inevitably distressed while she didn't know what had happened to you. A message went astray, I understand. Later when she learned you were safe and with your guardian, she was free to follow her own desire to enter a convent.'

Eleanor smiled guilelessly. 'Thank you. I'm grateful.'

I should not have said more but I could not stop myself. 'The Dowager Countess understood your betrothal was to proceed, as your father had planned.'

Gaston exclaimed in exasperation but Lord Fitzvaughan smoothly intervened. 'Dame Eleanor did indeed have a girlish fancy for the Percy boy when she first came to Normandy but, as is the nature of these things, she found herself swept into a womanly passion for my sweet friend.'

It pained me to see Eleanor simpering as she concurred with her former guardian's words, for at that moment she looked more like her natural mother than I had ever recognised. Maud had been men's plaything since her youth, humiliated and treated cruelly, but she had discerned how to profit from the situation. In the interests of self-preservation she had cloaked herself with the fabric of inhumanity towards others. God forbid her daughter must suffer a similar life of disillusionment.

While I stood horror-stricken, Gaston stroked his wife's cheek with patronising authority and summoned her attendant to escort her from the room. Then, with a wink, he suggested to Walter Fitvaughan that he would like a word alone with me and his lordship obliged by following his erstwhile ward through the door. Gaston held out a cup of wine.

'Would you like me to sip from the same goblet, Harry, just to show it's unadulterated?'

If this was a jest, it was in poor taste because Gaston had sought my death once, years before. 'I'll trust that you observe the laws of hospitality.' I attempted a dry laugh.

'Unwise; but perhaps you aren't aware how I tried to encompass your demise in Yorkshire.'

'You?' My gasp was audible.

After Stephen Boice roundly denied he was responsible, the possibility that it was Gaston who suborned my attackers had occurred to me fleetingly, while I lay manacled in my Dublin cell. Willison's arrival and my escape pushed the idea to the back of my mind and I dismissed it as a motiveless fancy. How could I have been such a fool? Faced with my stupidity I became angry.

'Your assassins were not the most proficient. Why did you go to such trouble but fail to find efficient vagabonds?'

He raised his hands and spread his elegant fingers wide. 'I had aspirations towards that appealing little heiress as soon as I heard of her and Walter was most supportive of my design. I journeyed to Ravensmoor to test the water and realised I could achieve nothing while Earl Stanwick lived but I found Lady Maud more complaisant. However, I also learned that you were shortly to arrive there and that I did not welcome. I've encountered your interfering persistence in the past, so I concluded you should be eliminated. Unfortunately my hastily bribed agents were inadequate and you thwarted them. In the end it didn't matter because I achieved my ends without soiling my marriage bed with your blood.'

It was wholly credible and I had been blinkered but one word he had used echoed in my mind. Maud had been "complaisant". Suddenly the detail which had puzzled me became clear and I remembered her covering the Fitzvaughan seal on a letter she had received. 'You kept in touch with Lady Maud after your first visit to Ravensmoor?'

'Oh, certainly. How do you think I knew of Cuthbert Percy's plans on Midsummer's Day? Lady Maud made sure I had the opportunity I craved to waylay her daughter and dear little Eleanor came willingly enough when she saw me because I'd already charmed her when I visited Ravensmoor before you arrived. The sweet child trusted me – still does. Walter agreed to recompense his wife for her co-operation by restoring her to his Norfolk estate where she can live in honour for her wifely obedience.'

So that was the truth. Maud had betrayed her daughter. She had carolled her love for the girl with extravagant declarations but they were worthless. She knew full well what lay in store for Eleanor and she facilitated it. She assumed the guise of a woman distracted by grief after the child vanished but it was all simulation. Bile rose in my throat and I retched, clutching my stomach. I would have spewed on Gaston de la Tour's immaculate tiled floor without compunction but he propelled me to the door and pushed me into the passageway.

'Walter is so jubilant at the outcome he is even willing to overlook the way you used his lady as your whore while you were both immured in Ravensmoor Castle but I'm to warn you that if you go within five miles of her in Attleborough he will have you eviscerated.'

Rallying what fragments of self-respect I still possessed, I dragged myself into the open air and leaned against a wall, taking deep breaths, subduing my churning guts. I would not give Gaston the satisfaction of seeing me vomit however distraught I felt. I resolved to collect Walter Fitzvaughan's reply to Suffolk and return to Rouen at once. I had always revered his lordship's integrity, which in public affairs was unquestionable, and his involvement in the shameful treatment of his ward pained me acutely. His love for Gaston and his wish for an heir had subverted his usual scruples. I could not bear to sleep under the same roof as these devious fiends.

*****

While I journeyed slowly northwards I reflected on Eleanor's fate, trying to convince myself that her position might prove no worse than that of other maidens who were required to enter loveless marriages. I had no doubt Eleanor was entranced by Gaston de la Tour and, provided

223

he treated her with respect and courtesy, she might find it a tolerable union. Indeed his faithful commitment to Walter Fitzvaughan could be judged preferable to the promiscuity of husbands who consorted with a miscellany of mistresses. It was a realistic but doleful philosophy and it failed to cheer me. I was perhaps unusually sensitive to the unknown risks the partners in a marriage contract faced.

It took me more than two weeks to return to London because of adverse winds and water-logged roads and each delay compounded my frustration while I hankered to hold Kate in my arms again. When I did at last arrive there, to my disappointment the Duke and Duchess with their entourages were still absent from the Manor of the Rose in attendance at court. I had no time to indulge my regrets, however, as my services were in demand. I was told the steward was anxious to consult me about some missing papers and Leone clamoured for my attention as he was alarmed by the condition of a potman's child with the falling sickness. He asked me to examine the little boy without delay and I agreed.

'It was yesterday he fell down. His mouth foamed and was set awry while his body twitched uncontrollably. I kept him quiet and put a stick in his mouth for him to bite on and hold his tongue down. I remember the professors said such attacks are governed by the phases of the moon.'

'Perhaps; but you did right to stop the child swallowing his tongue. I recommend keeping the patient calm, avoid overeating and ensure regular bowel movements. Some leech-books suggest drinking hare's urine to dissolve the humours affecting the brain but I've never tried that.'

The child was showing signs of recovery when I saw him and his parents were full of praise for Leone's care so I went to my room pleased with my assistant and relieved to be once more treating ailments rather than running messages for the nobility. A letter was waiting, addressed to me in the familiar writing of the Prioress of St. Michael's in Stamford. I was always happy to read her incisive comments but I had mentioned my betrothal when I last wrote to her and feared she might not approve of my hasty contract. In fact it merited only a passing reference.

Doctor Somers, I would welcome your comments on affairs of state. I have heard little from you since you returned to London and I am alarmed by rumours of growing antagonisms among the nobility and increasing hostility towards the Duke of Suffolk. News comes to me of unrest in the south of Norfolk, near to William de la Pole's own estates, and it is said that common folk are being roused to violent action by disaffected rogues. What do you know of this? I understand Richard of York is at last due to remove himself permanently to Ireland but I fear his agents have been stirring up dissent this side of the Irish Sea and will continue to create havoc. I foresee great danger.

I welcome news of your betrothal if the girl is modest and seemly. I have not heard of Mistress Devereux but it seems her father was a respected notary. It is a more fitting alliance for you than the one to which you rashly aspired two years ago.

Pray oblige me with an early reply and give as much information as possible about the matters which concern me.

I frowned while reading the letter because the Prioress was normally unperturbable and I had not heard previously of any insurrection in East Anglia. I also dreaded having to tell her, in my next letter, of Lord Fitzvaughan's perfidious behaviour towards Eleanor, whom she had nurtured as a child at St. Michael's. I was not allowed to dwell on these worries however, as almost immediately the Duke's steward thumped on the door and erupted into my room with an ashen face. He was a man I had come to like and I was sorry to see him so disconsolate and agitated.

'Doctor Somers, I beg you to counsel me. You have experience of investigating misdeeds, I understand.'

Suffolk must have mentioned commissions he had given me in the past. 'What's happened?'

'Papers have been taken from the Duke's study. I'd gone in there to leave some correspondence for his secretary to deal with when they return to the house. I set the letters on the table beside other confidential documents I'd left there a few days ago. I was summoned from the room for a moment or two and when I returned the earlier pile of papers had gone. I shall be much blamed for not locking the door but I was away only an instant.'

'Master Steward, do you know what the documents were that have been taken?' I made him sit down as I was speaking.

'Not precisely but they were records of financial transactions. Columns of figures.'

'Who summoned you from the study?' I poured him some wine.

'One of the pages. The cellarer wanted a word – he was waiting round the corner. It was quickly dealt with.'

'Did the page accompany you when you saw the cellarer?'

'Yes. He stayed with me all the time. He couldn't have taken the papers.'

'So someone else was skulking in the corridor on the chance the door would be left open? It doesn't sound very probable. Do you regularly go into the Duke's study?'

'Most days, I suppose, after the messenger has brought letters from the court.'

'And people in the household would know your habit. Did the cellarer have a proper reason to consult you? Is he trustworthy?'

'He'd received an unusual note about a delivery of ale. It was entirely reasonable that he wanted to check details with me. He's one of the Duke's longest serving followers.'

'Did you ask him who sent the note and how he was given it?' The steward shook his head. 'Would you like me to question him?'

'I'd be grateful, Doctor Somers. I thought papers had been moved once before in my own office. I should have followed up that incident but I assumed I was mistaken.'

'Send the cellarer to me and also the page who brought you his message. I'll see what I can find out.'

The steward stumbled out of my room expressing his thanks and still holding the goblet of wine I had given him. Until that point I had found nothing to substantiate Suffolk's fear that there might be a spy within his household. Now I was not so sure and knew I must probe the circumstances with caution.

The elderly cellarer confirmed everything the steward had said. He stated he had been puzzled to be given the note listing the kegs which were expected as he had already agreed the schedule with the brewery-man. 'It was a lad I didn't know who brought the list,' he said rubbing his stubbly chin. 'Rather a scruffy urchin. I was surprised the brewer made use of him.'

'I suspect he didn't. It may have been part of an elaborate trick but you couldn't know that. You did nothing wrong.' The man grunted his endorsement of this statement.

While I waited for the page to come to my room I went over what I had learned and was clear that someone within the household must have played a part in setting events in motion as well as in taking the papers. I soon confirmed it could not have been the jittery boy in front of me who had stayed at the steward's side when he spoke to the cellarer and I tried not to sound intimidating.

'How did you know where to find the steward when the cellarer came asking for him?'

'Barty told me. He'd seen him go in the Duke's study.'

'Who's Barty?'

'He's only been here a few weeks but he's older than me. I think he came from one of the Duke's other houses. We were together when the cellarer found us, looking out of the window. We'd been watching a tussle in the street between two drovers. Barty was cheering them on, waving his arms about. He told me to take the cellarer to the study.'

I could not repress a sigh as events fell into place. 'Thank you. That's very helpful. Would you ask Barty to come and see me, please, and let the steward know I've asked to see him?'

The boy nodded and ran off but an hour or more passed before anyone came to my room and then it was not Barty but the steward, red in the face and panting. I was unsurprised by his news.

'The page you wanted to see, he's not to be found. It appears he's left the house. His bundle of clothes has gone. I've sent men to look for him. His behaviour proclaims his guilt.'

'I gather he hadn't been here long. Do you know who arranged for him to come to the Manor of the Rose?'

'He'd been sent to serve the Duchess; recommended by one of her connections. He'd been a page in some other house but illness made it inconvenient for him to stay there. I know no more and there's no one else to vouch for him although Duchess Alice will have more information.'

'Exactly.' I took the steward's arm in comradely fashion. 'Don't blame yourself but the Duke needs to be informed. This is a craftily contrived trick and I fear it's intended to do him harm. It's imperative we find out where that boy has gone. Get your men to make a methodical search and check at all the City gates. I suspect he won't be alone. His accomplices may have whisked him out of London but we must trace them.'

The Duke returned to the Manor of the Rose five days later, having ridden from Leicester, where the court was assembled, after receiving our cautiously worded message. As soon as he had refreshed himself I gave him an account of my conjectures, urging him not to judge the steward's negligence harshly, and was re-assured to find he was in a benign mood.

He stretched his back as he eased himself into his chair. 'I've no doubt of my steward's reliability, Harry, and I'd issued no instructions to the household to beware of traitors in our midst and lock all doors. Perhaps I should have done. You think this page of Alice's was incited – bribed, I suppose – to steal my papers?'

'Bribed or intentionally sent here for the purpose. I suspect he signalled from the window to a colleague in the street when he was sure he could get access to your study. The Duchess may know more about how the boy came to join the household.'

'She'll be here in a day or two. How would a page be aware what to look for?'

'He'll have been able to read and told the kind of thing that would be of interest. We can't be certain he was looking for specific documents. Forgive me, your Grace, but I presume the missing papers contain particulars you wouldn't want made public?'

William de la Pole snorted. 'They could be misconstrued, misrepresented. Damn it, why haven't my men found any trace of where the boy went?'

'I'd guess a horseman was waiting to carry him off as soon as he left the house. Enquiries have been made at the City gates but nothing definite has been found. There've been innumerable sightings of horsemen with young lads riding pillion, well wrapped up against the wind. It's impossible to link any of them to the Manor of the Rose.'

Suffolk shrugged. 'If all goes well in Normandy my enemies won't dare act against me. Was Walter Fitzvaughan optimistic?'

I was about to give a cautious reply when a knock at the door distracted us and the steward hurried in, pulling his gown around him, his face drained of colour. 'Pardon, your Grace, there's news. The page Barty has been found.'

'Where?'

The steward gulped. 'In the marshes to the north east of the City, face down in a pool. His throat had been cut.'

I shut my eyes. 'God rest the poor lad's soul. His employers were taking no risk that he might be found and forced to confess who paid him.'

The Duke held my gaze but addressed the steward. 'How was he identified?'

'He still wore your livery, your Grace, under a cloak. A fellow on his way to fish in the River Lea came upon the body as he crossed the marsh and the local priest recognised your crest. The corpse has been brought here.'

I stood and bowed to Suffolk. 'I'll go to inspect it. Would that it could tell us who ordered the deed.'

'We have but to wait for the papers to be produced and accusations made against me, if they dare,' the Duke said. 'York and his henchmen are now ensconced far from here across the Irish Sea so we know the direction from which trouble will come.'

*****

For me the return of the Duchess and her ladies to the Manor of the Rose was a bitter-sweet occasion. Outside the solar, where I had been summoned to attend, I briefly held Kate in my arms, rejoicing at her willingness to embrace me in front of her companions with a fervent kiss. Then I was admitted to her mistress's presence and Alice de la Pole faced me with uneasiness etched across her face.

'Oh, Harry, that poor boy, the page, Barty. Who can have abused his trust? He seemed a gentle child although I'd seen little of him since he came here.'

'Would you tell me how he joined the household, your Grace?'

'I received a letter from the widow of a man who served the Duke for years. She had recommended attendants to me previously. She said the boy was well trained – in her own household, I imagine – but she could no longer keep him as she had been very ill and needed to change her domestic dispositions. I accepted the request at face value and agreed to take Barty. I had no reason to question Jane's good faith.'

I froze, filled with foreboding. 'Jane?'

'Jane Cawfield. Her late husband was William's secretary until he died. You probably met him when you were in France for the truce negotiations years back.'

I had certainly known Andrew Cawfield and I attended his deathbed after, as I suspected, he had been poisoned. 'You didn't know that Jane Cawfield had remarried, your Grace?'

The Duchess raised her eyebrows in surprise. 'Why, no, she wrote to me as Jane Cawfield. Those she had recommended in the past have always served me well. She...' Alice de la Pole paused and seemed momentarily confused before adjusting her necklace. 'She said she was resting with her Neville relations in the north of the country.'

'That at least could have been true but her name now is Lady Glasbury, wife to Gilbert Iffley who serves Richard of York. She is sister to another of his followers, Stephen Boice. I regret she has deceived you grossly.'

Alice de la Pole winced and crossed herself. 'Merciful Heaven: that is base infamy. I pray William will not suffer as a result of my innocent sincerity. How could the woman be so deceitful?'

'She is her husband's catspaw,' I said but I did not add that she would be more than ever beholden to do his

231

bidding after the shame of bearing their monstrous double-headed infant.

The Duchess sighed 'Leave me now, Harry. I wish to pray for the Blessed Virgin's help in this dilemma. Take Kate to your chamber and make her welcome. She's served me well but she has longed to return to you.'

Despite the turmoil in my heart at what I had learned about the machinations of the Duke's enemies, I had no difficulty in obeying the Duchess's compassionate command to welcome my betrothed wife. I found her weeping for the murdered page and I loved her all the more for her soft-heartedness. My mission must be to comfort and protect her.

*****

The next week or two passed peacefully with no disclosure of private papers threatening Suffolk's reputation but then news was brought from Normandy which pushed that putative danger from our thoughts, replacing it with a real and horrifying menace. On the Eve of the Feast of the Annunciation one of King Henry's captains had mounted an unprovoked and unauthorised attack upon the town and fortress of Fougères which owed allegiance to the Duke of Brittany. This Duke, a vassal of the English King, was now cheek by jowl with his overlord's French counterpart and it was to King Charles the aggrieved noble appealed, claiming that the English had broken the terms of the truce with France – the truce which Suffolk was desperate to renew.

Messengers were sent scurrying back and forth across the Narrow Sea and Suffolk directed Walter Fitzvaughan to open negotiations with the Bretons and the French, to soothe ruffled feathers and re-establish harmony. To my relief there was no suggestion that I might journey to Rouen on this occasion but I followed developments from a distance with disquiet. I was encouraged when I heard that the Duke of Somerset, as the

King's Lieutenant in Normandy, had been personally charged to join Lord Fitzvaughan in restoring peaceful relations and while the deluge of communications to the Manor of the Rose subsided I ceased fretting over events I could not influence.

I had my own obligations to discharge.

*****

At Eastertide in the year of Our Lord 1449 I finally fulfilled the wish my mother had often expressed and friends had recommended by entering into the estate of Holy Matrimony. The circumstances which compelled me to this change of status had occurred so rapidly that I still found the outcome bewildering, implausible, but there was no dishonesty in my bonding with Kate who gave herself with a readiness and passion equal to mine. The Duke and Duchess attended the marriage ceremony in the chapel at their house and Thomas stood by my side as groom's man. Grizel pleaded maternal duties as her excuse for shunning the event and although I regretted her absence it avoided awkwardness with my wife. Time, I hoped, would reconcile these two properly opinionated women but any attempt to compel mutual toleration would be ill-advised.

Rendell was a member of the guard of honour the Duke provided but he was careful not to catch my eye and I sensed he shared his sister's disapproval of the match. Knowing how he had revered Countess Yolande, I found it easier to forgive his truculence at seeing me yoked with a woman he scarcely knew. Once again, in my elated optimism, I relied on the passage of time to remedy this deficiency.

One incident a few days before my marriage had distressed me but I said nothing of it to Kate in order not to agitate her when she must already be in a state of heightened emotion. On Maundy Thursday the Duke and Duchess were absent from the Manor of the Rose, in attendance on the King as he disbursed the traditional gifts to the poor, and Kate was among the ladies accompanying them. I walked out to visit the City apothecary who had supplied me with goods for several years and, near to his premises by Newgate, I was accosted by a thin-faced, surly looking man who wore a notary's robe.

'Doctor Somers? Am I right to address you as Doctor Harry Somers?'

'Yes, that's my name but you have the advantage of me. I don't think we've met.'

He had a penetrating stare and his eyes were curiously flecked with amber lights. 'My name is Edward Devereux.'

'You are Kate's brother?'

He moistened his lips. 'Katherine is my sister. Is it true you plan to wed her?'

'It is. We are formally betrothed. You may know I am physician to the Duke of Suffolk.'

He smiled in an unfriendly fashion. 'You don't need to convince me of your credentials, Doctor. I'm aware you are a perfectly suitable husband for my sister but I would advise you not to proceed with the binding contract of your marriage vows. You cannot know her very well and may not understand how unstable her nature is, how volatile her caprices.'

'I'm a physician, Master Devereux. I appreciate Kate is prone to excitable moods but I trust she'll find comfort in our marriage. She is intelligent and full of curiosity. I welcome that in woman as well as man.'

The notary drew himself up to his full height. 'She is possessed of the Devil, Doctor Somers. I hesitate to speak ill of my only sibling but it's the truth. I've made enquiry and heard good reports of you and your expertise. Don't hazard your future peace of mind and advancement for the sake of bedding a brazen trouble-maker. Believe me, I've hesitated to advise you but I feel it is my duty.'

I controlled my fury despite the temptation to punch his narrow, self-satisfied face. 'I'm sure you mean well, Master Devereux, and I recognise you are estranged from your sister. She's told me there have been disagreements between you. But I must be judge of where happiness lies for myself and for Kate. I love your sister and will seek to protect and care for her as my wife. If we meet again I hope it will be in her company and you will see that our union brings us both joy. Good-day to you, Master Devereux.'

He bowed. 'I regret I've wasted my breath but it was incumbent on me to make the attempt. I see she has bewitched you with her evil enchantments. I pray you will be justified in your hopes.'

'Amen.' I turned on my heel and strode away in anger. It seemed all too likely that Edward Devereux's pitiless hostility towards his sister had jarred with her sensitive nature and aggravated her nervous condition.

*****

William de la Pole was as good as his word in providing generously for our marriage and more commodious rooms were provided within the London house for a married physician and his wife. More surprisingly, a month after our nuptials, the Duke insisted on restoring to me the manor of Worthwaite, near to his lands at Wingfield in the county of Suffolk, which I had held from him before the accusations against me following Humphrey of Gloucester's death. I demurred when he announced his intention but my unwillingness to accept the gift owed nothing to modesty and he understood my reluctance.

'You need never visit Worthwaite, Harry, if its bitter memories still pain you. The income from the manor is yours and your dependable steward will serve you as faithfully as he did previously. The arrangement gives you land which your Devereux bride will not disdain. She has brought you a significant dowry and in time you may wish to acquire your own house in the City but possession of a small country estate adds prestige to your position.'

I shook my head in confusion at his liberality and unexpected compassion. 'Your Grace, I'm overwhelmed. I will do you homage for Worthwaite, if it is your wish to endow me with the manor, and I swear to serve you faithfully.'

'That's what I ask, Harry. I rely on your loyalty and trust your honesty. Difficulties lie ahead and I may welcome your good sense to counsel me as well as benefitting from the embrocation you apply to the tiresome muscles of my back.'

I realised then the Duke's largesse was part of a more complex picture. 'Is there fresh news from Normandy, your Grace?'

'Acute as ever. Yes, Harry, and to you I will admit I'm worried. I always knew Somerset was no great warrior, nor indeed a man of the highest intellect, but I thought him prudent and sensible. I was wrong. The fool has asserted that he sanctioned the sacking of Fougères and he's refusing to negotiate with the French about it because the Duke of Brittany owes allegiance to King Henry not King Charles. This is a dangerous situation and the lasting peace for which I've striven these last six years is in jeopardy. I mourn any return to warfare but I also foresee peril for myself. My enemies will trumpet the failure of my policy and seek my downfall.'

He did not need to remind me that those enemies almost certainly had within their possession papers inculpating the Duke with serious misdemeanours which it might be difficult to disprove.

*****

Those first three months of our marriage were a joyful time despite the cloud of state affairs which shadowed the Manor of the Rose. Kate continued to serve the Duchess when required and I was glad she had activities to fill her time while I was absorbed by my physician's duties. It would take me a while to accustom myself to married life and it seemed reasonable to assume Kate had to make a similar transition. She seemed content and I was hopeful that, at my side, she would gain in confidence and serenity.

I needed to give particular attention to the boy who suffered from the falling sickness, who had caused concern earlier in the year, and whose condition had worsened. Leone and I shared his care but the attacks became more frequent and severe. I was sadly aware that we had little understanding of how to treat this illness, when the humours were out of equilibrium and the brain could not control the body. Fortunately the lad himself commonly experienced an aura before an attack and was able to alert us so we could safeguard him from the worst effects of gnashing teeth and uncontrolled excretions. All the same I felt inadequate before the violence of his writhing and wished we could comprehend more about the physical perversion gripping him. This was an experience which demonstrated the paucity of a physician's knowledge and made me wish that we might learn more about God's creation and its natural laws.

One evening I returned to our quarters after quieting our patient, going directly to the storeroom where my remedies were kept in order to return a potion I had not used. I was surprised to find Kate standing between the shelves, peering at the jars and boxes, and she gave a guilty start when I opened the door.

'Forgive me, Harry. I shouldn't have come here without your permission. I haven't touched anything.' Her blush brought unaccustomed colour to her cheeks.

'It's all right. Have you a headache? Do you need physic?'

She lowered her eyes. 'No, I didn't come to find medication for myself – I wouldn't know what to look for. That's what intrigued me. I wondered what was kept here and what purposes it was put to. I've seen that the herbs are all labelled but I don't know their uses. You'll think me too inquisitive.'

'Would you like to learn about the herbs?'

She looked up and her lip trembled. 'You'll think me impudent.'

'Not at all. I'd be delighted if you wanted to learn about our preparations and the plants we use. It's most appropriate for a physician's wife, if she's interested.'

'You would teach a woman?'

I put my arms round her and kissed her. 'Kate Somers, you're a goose. You must know of the wise women who live in every village and many a great household. Old Syb who works in the kitchen here is one of them. They depend on their knowledge of herbs and simples to dispense remedies and uphold their reputations. Mind you, their knowledge is often garbled and haphazard. A physician's wife should have accurate information based on sound learning. You're more than competent to do that.'

She smiled and in the subdued light her eyes were dark as green olives. 'You are good to me, my husband. Teach me my first lesson.' She reached out and pointed to a phial on the shelf beside her. 'Oil of camomile,' she read. 'What do you do with this?'

'It is a well-trusted remedy for various pains and cramps. Leaves of the plant are used in tisanes for inflammation of the bowels.'

She giggled. 'I see I shall need to become acquainted with the vilest bodily functions.'

'Indeed you will, Mistress Somers, if we're to make an apothecary of you. Come, my love, I'm weary now. If you've a mind to it, we'll start your instruction proper tomorrow. Let's go to bed.' She pursed her lips and I guessed what she was thinking. 'I'm not so weary that I shall fall asleep on the instant.'

After I had amply demonstrated the truth of my words and Kate lay tucked against me, her smile illuminated by a beam of moonlight, I thanked Heaven for my happiness and the blessing of a clever and devoted wife.

238

Our calm contentment was interrupted early in the month of August when news which he had dreaded was brought to the Duke. He summoned me at once and held out the message from the palace of Westminster bearing the royal seal. His face was grey with worry.

'The truce is over. The French have declared war. Somerset gave them the opportunity they were looking for when he refused to negotiate with King Charles. He seems unconcerned that the French have been building up their strength. They have new alliances with both Brittany and Burgundy. Normandy will be clenched in a vice between three armies and I doubt Somerset possesses the military skill to withstand their assaults. I grieve for our friends across the Narrow Sea. I'll endeavour to send them reinforcements but I must also take heed for myself. My enemies have been waiting for this fuse to be laid; they will bring torches to light it to wreak destruction not just in Normandy but to the bastions of my power in England.'

'We must hope Somerset is more astute than you imagine, your Grace, and can drive a wedge between the French and their allies.' It was the only encouragement I could give. 'Surely three armies could be a weakness, as well as a strength, if their movements are not well attuned?'

'You're right but I fear Somerset won't succeed. York must be relishing my discomfort. His supporters are already flexing their muscles. There are reports of fresh rioting in Norfolk. Walter Fitzvaughan's estates have been attacked.'

I shuddered, remembering that duplicitous woman, who had been my mistress, whose actions I abhorred but whose safety troubled me. 'His lady is there.'

'She's unharmed. The attack on the castle was a half-hearted affair and Walter's bailiff led a sortie which drove them away – for the moment.'

Walter's bailiff: Robin Willoughby, the man my first love, Bess, had married. 'Were there casualties?' I asked.

'None of significance, I gather. But this may be the opening salvo of a longer campaign. The news has set my old battle wounds throbbing. Fetch your poultices, Harry. I shall have need of them'

I bowed and did as I was bidden, struggling to hold at bay the gloominess which shrouded me, conscious that the interlude of uncomplicated joy I had experienced was already at an end.

Chapter 20

Leone stood in front of me twisting his cap in his hands, fumbling for words as he rarely did since becoming fluent in English, while the flush on his cheeks darkened.

'Perhaps I could be spared... my presence now is not es... es... essential. I think you manage well without me. It will adv...advan... advantage me to gain knowledge of medicine on the battlefield. The dressing of wounds... caring for those with sev...severed limbs will be useful to me.'

I sighed as I pointed him to sit on the bench, thinking he was disgruntled by Kate's access to the storeroom. She had been making out new labels for our supplies, carefully written in her clear round hand, and I regretted that I had not told Leone in advance what I had asked her to do.

'Mistress Somers will in no way intrude on your duties, Leone,' I said by way of an apology. 'There's no harm in her learning about our common remedies. It's quite fitting for a physician's wife. But she won't suddenly acquire a physician's skills and trespass on your role.'

Leone appeared even more uncomfortable. 'No, no, Doctor. It is not Mistress Somers. She is most charming. I have no problem... I want to go to Normandy to learn, to enhance...'

'Yes, I understand that but I don't like to think you feel you've been driven away.'

He clutched his cap more tightly, ruining its shape as he screwed it into a ball. 'Only the maidservant Joanna drives me away. For months she has let me court her. Now she dismisses me in favour of the sergeant-at-arms. I am desolate and have nothing here to live for.'

'Oh dear.' I forbade myself to smile at this display of Italian temperament, recollecting his dejection when our landlord's daughter in Tours, five years previously, had spurned him. 'That's different. If you're looking to mend a broken heart a change of scene might be beneficial.'

At once he brightened. 'You let me go then? You will ask the Duke that I go with his soldiers when they sail for Normandy?'

'Yes, if that's what you want. But it's only leave of absence. You're to come back safely and then we can decide whether you return to the Manor of the Rose or find your own position as a physician in some other household. You'll be ready to do that.'

I waved aside Leone's protestations of gratitude and made the necessary arrangements.

Only a small troop of soldiers was ready to cross the Narrow Sea and I understood from the Duke that financing a larger band of reinforcements would present difficulties as funds in the King's Treasury were depleted. Partly for that reason Suffolk was unwilling to allow any of his own guards to join the expedition and this decision caused outrage for my other young friend in his service.

Rendell stamped up and down the guardroom thumping the table with his fist whenever he passed it.

'Fucking stupid, that's what it is. Trained to fucking fight, we are. We're not ploughboys with pitchforks, we're men-at-arms. If anyone can beat the Frenchies, it'll be us. Put them to flight in no time, we would. Christ, the man's an idiot.'

'Don't speak of the Duke so disrespectfully. He'll have reasons for his decision.'

My mild rejoinder only provoked more vehemence. 'Fucking desert him, I will. Go to Dover and make me own way to Normandy. Trained by the best instructors to use sword and mace and now expected to ponce around as escort when the Duke goes to court. What life's that for a bloody soldier?'

'It's possible one day you'll need to fight in earnest here in England, to defend Suffolk and the Manor of the Rose.'

'D'you reckon?' Rendell stood still and sniffed the air. 'I've heard gossip. Is it true his enemies are out to get him?'

'If they're given the chance. Suffolk needs his best fighters right beside him – just in case.'

Rendell tapped his nose and winked. 'That's different then. Just let them fucking try! Roll on the day.'

*****

The breakdown of the truce had upset Kate and when Leone set off for Normandy she was tearful. The Duke and Duchess were often absent from their house during the next two months, in attendance on the King and Queen, and Kate was usually one of the ladies who accompanied her mistress to court. I missed her terribly but I also found the times when she returned to the Manor of the Rose difficult because she became increasingly distraught as news came in of French forces threatening the towns of Coutances and Saint Lô and fighting already on the Cotentin peninsula. I suggested cautiously that she might beg the Duchess's permission to be excused from presence at the court where scaremongering rumours circulated but she would not hear of it. She insisted she must fulfil her obligations to her mistress and, although her condition worried me, I did not attempt to curtail her freedom.

By early October she seemed calmer and, although I now thought it might be better for her to give up her duties to the Countess, I felt more optimistic. Secretly I hoped that before long we would be blessed with a child but I never mentioned it to Kate as I did not want her to think I was in any way disappointed with our marriage. I was not. My love for my wife deepened, even as my concern for the balance of her mind wavered between apprehension and re-assurance. I wanted to create a home for her where she could be safe and peaceful but it was not within my power to order the affairs of the world to provide the necessary setting.

It was not long before the military setbacks which the Duke feared were reported and it was Kate, newly

243

returned from court, who brought me the disconcerting news. The English defence in Normandy had begun to crumble because the inhabitants of towns under siege were expelling their garrisons and yielding voluntarily to the French. Kate's despondency was understandable but I tried to comfort and divert her, suggesting that we spend an hour rehearsing the properties of various herbs which she generally found of absorbing interest. She duly recited the names and uses of half a dozen plants and began to sound more cheerful when, abruptly, she screamed and hurled herself into my arms, sobbing wildly while I caressed and tried to soothe her.

'You must not let these events tear you apart, Kate. We can but pray for the poor folk facing cannon and bombards. Don't let yourself dwell on the horrors they face.'

Her expression was fierce as she looked up at me.

'It isn't that. Not only that. Oh dear God, help me. Harry, don't let me go. The sweet Virgin knows you are a good man. I never thought... God forgive me, I never thought... Why must we all suffer?'

Bemused by her wild words and agonisingly grief-stricken to see her misery, I held her close until the tumult in her mind subsided. I wished I could take her away from the City and the court, thinking poignantly of somewhere like Winchester where a physician might build up a practice in tranquillity and his wife need not be troubled by the battle-cries of wars across the Narrow Sea.

It was only a few days after this painful incident that Rendell joined me for a jug of ale before dinner. Kate had insisted on travelling to Westminster with the Duchess, saying she was much recovered, and I was not too burdened with the care of my patients, so I welcomed his company. When my young friend was unusually quiet, swirling his ale in his beaker without drinking, I concluded that he was still morose about remaining in London while the fighting was going so badly in Normandy and I said as much.

'No, it ain't that, Doctor, though I am pissed off about it. It's more – more delicate.'

'What do you mean?' It crossed my mind that he had got some unfortunate girl into trouble and readied myself to give unpalatable advice.

'I go to court sometimes as part of the Duke's bodyguard.' He paused and I nodded for him to continue. 'We stand around waiting and I see things. I dunno how to say it but you ought to know.'

His tone made the hairs on the back of my neck tingle and I blinked. 'What?'

'It's Mistress Somers, Doctor, the way she behaves sometimes.'

It had not occurred to me that Kate might give way to her turmoil of mind in public. I had supposed that her outbursts in the privacy of our rooms gave her relief from the tension she was under with other people. 'What has she done?' I asked softly.

'She's a deal too friendly with some foppish courtier, some noble bugger who chats to her whenever she's passing and paws her arm as if he'd a right to maul her.'

'Court ways are full of play-acting and affectation.' I forced myself to appear unruffled.

'Don't think you should dismiss it, Doctor.' Rendell sounded remarkably mature and this made his advice more chilling. 'I've never taken to her, it's true, but I ain't had nothing specific against her. But the way she fixes those great eyes of hers on this bloke and he leers at her, it ain't right for a respectable married woman.'

'I expect you're exaggerating,' I said lamely.

'Come to court and have a gander yourself, without her knowing. Make your own mind up.'

I swallowed hard. 'I haven't been to court for around three years. The Queen would have me thrown in the Thames if she saw me there.'

'She won't. She's always closeted with the King and his advisers. The ladies all hang around in the long gallery

245

while their mistresses are busy. Mistress Somers stands near the great double doors. That's when the lovey-dovey stuff happens.'

'Don't call it that!' Rendell raised an eyebrow and I felt deeply uncomfortable. 'I don't want to spy on my wife but she's troubled in her mind and I'd hate her to be inveigled into behaviour she'd regret. I'll see what I can do.'

Rendell nodded sagely. 'Be for the best,' he said.

*****

In the year following Queen Margaret's arrival in England I had enjoyed free entrance to the court and her lodgings, an esteemed physician whose services were sought after and valued by her and her entourage. This was all lost to me after I was brazen enough to pay court to the Countess Yolande and arranged her flight from Westminster. In consequence I had mixed memories when I disembarked from the waterman's boat at the river steps to the palace. A guard stepped forward and squinted at me with uncertainty half-remembering my face, but he satisfied himself and beckoned me to enter the courtyard. From there I would know my way in darkness to the long gallery and the convenient curtained balcony at a higher level which overlooked the double doors. The only risk was that someone else might have sneaked onto the balcony to spy on the activity below. Fortunately it was unoccupied but thinking in those crude terms made me deeply unhappy and I felt guilt at my subterfuge.

I waited while a host of courtiers and hangers-on bustled up and down the gallery. Flurries of laughing girls, solemnly pacing functionaries and self-important lackeys made their way between the knots of dignitaries intent on their whispered conversations. From time to time the doors were opened and a name called for a petitioner to enter the royal apartments or more often supplicants were disgorged from the inner rooms with the success or failure of their quests marked on their features. I began to despair of seeing Kate at all but I noted an elegant young nobleman hovering near the doors. He was ostentatiously dressed in a blue silk tunic with broad padded shoulders, the narrowest of waists and cut so short below his belt that his neatly rounded buttocks were visible. Although there were many richly clad men in the gallery I had no doubt this was the fellow Rendell had observed.

Eventually the doors were flung back by attendants and half a dozen ladies drifted from the interior sanctum, chattering and smiling, unhurried and utterly at ease. At the rear came Kate, alone, frowning, and as soon as she appeared the silken popinjay made her an elaborate bow; then he reached out his hand to take her wrist, speaking to her in an undertone I could not hear. All of a sudden my underhanded ploy became unbearable and I hurtled from the balcony, stumbling down the turnpike as best I could, emerging into the gallery directly opposite my wife so I saw with perfect clarity how she blanched and leaned sideways as if to steady herself against the wall.

'My pardon for startling you, my love, when you had no notion I'd been summoned to Westminster. An old acquaintance who is ailing wished to see me. I hoped I might encounter you before I left.'

The lies came with disgraceful smoothness and I cursed my double-dealing. I gave a polite but casual acknowledgement to her companion.

'Indeed, you did startle me, husband.' To my relief Kate sounded composed despite her shivering. 'May I present my kinsman, Philip Neville, Baron Thornton. Philip, this is Doctor Somers.'

Her kinsman? A Neville? I was thunderstruck but dared not show surprise for fear of offending her. No further explanation was given and we exchanged pleasantries with the utmost courtesy before I made my excuses, asserting my obligation to attend patients at the Manor of the Rose. Baron Thornton inclined his head with an unconcealed sneer but Kate's face was blank as I left them and I could sense her hostility.

I have no recollection of my boat ride downstream to the City, only of the agitation in my mind and heart. How could I have been so underhand? What had I gained? Which of us had betrayed the other more seriously? Had she guessed my presence at Westminster was no coincidence? Did she believe that I suspected her honesty? Were there grounds for such suspicion? Was her conversation with a *kinsman* innocent? Why had she never mentioned his existence to me? Was she ashamed to admit to him that her husband was a humble physician, unequal to him in status, wealth and appearance? Had I humiliated her by making myself known? How was she related to the ubiquitous Nevilles? Could there possibly be cause for concern in this relationship?

I saw no patients on my return to the Manor of the Rose but sat miserably in our room, unwisely placing a flagon of ale at my elbow and even more unwisely resorting to its contents as the hours dragged on while I waited for Kate's return. When, late in the evening, the Duchess and her ladies re-entered the house, my wife found me slumped forward onto the table with a mere dribble of liquid remaining in my cup. I quickly rallied my senses and stood to embrace her but she stepped out of my reach as she flung off her cloak. I was determined to be conciliatory.

'Kate, I'm so sorry if I embarrassed you.'

She spat her response. 'How dare you? How dare you spy on me? You had no business at the court. You told a pack of lies.' Her voice was shrill and faced with her anger my good intentions evaporated into a drunken rant.

'Why are you attacking me? Have you something to hide? Is that bumptious fop your lover? Is he truly your kinsman? For how long have you deceived me?'

My speech must have been blurred and my intoxication infuriated her. Her eyes blazed and she whirled towards me, striking my face a stinging blow with her palm. I rocked on my feet, shocked into sobriety.

'Kate, forgive me. I shouldn't have gone to court but I was worried for you. You are sometimes restless and strained... I thought perhaps...you were unhappy with me... I thought perhaps...' I stammered to a halt, unwilling to say I was nervous her state of mind might lead to unbecoming behaviour. 'I made a mistake.'

'You believed I'm unfaithful to you.'

'No, not believed... feared... dreaded. Seeing you with a man I'd never heard of... Baron Thornton seemed most attentive... you'd never mentioned him...' I was overcome with contrition.

There was no colour in her cheeks but she stood erect and narrowed her lips, grandeur in her bearing. 'Manners at the court – even King Henry's court – among the nobility, are a mixture of elaborate etiquette and excessive familiarity. But I give you my oath before Our Blessed Lord that I have not betrayed our marriage. Will that satisfy you?'

I sank onto a stool, my face in my hands and sobbed silently. 'I should not have compelled you to give me your oath. I love you, Kate...'

'You did not compel me. I chose to give my word. Trust between us is something to be learned, it seems. I did not realise I was marrying a jealous man.'

'I didn't mean to be. Why have you never mentioned Philip Neville? I thought you had no contact with your wider family.'

Her mouth twisted into a contemptuous smile. 'The Duke of Suffolk has little love for the Nevilles. The Duchess is aware that my grandam bore that name but I have not trumpeted the information. I assumed you would share William de la Pole's prejudices. It seemed unnecessary to burden you with unwelcome details of my distant kindred. It was unavoidable you should know I am related to the notorious Devereux family of Winchester. I wanted to spare you the shame, as you would see it, of my maternal grandmother being a Neville.'

Her belligerence had faded into hurt pride and I felt sorry for my misgivings. 'We've both acted as we saw best but it's led to torment. Can we truly learn to share trust and keep no secrets from each other?'

She let me take her hand and sighed. 'If God wills it,' she said. 'I know the duty I owe to you and others with claims upon me but I hadn't bargained for a husband who loves me. It creates new pressures in my mind, an unfamiliar tumult of feelings.' She withdrew her hand and was convulsed by a paroxysm of trembling. Then she became still and she tilted her chin towards me. 'Still less had I bargained for a husband whom I should love.'

'Oh, Kate.' I held her, unable to say more, glorying in her admission – the first time she had spoken to me of her love. It was a precious moment and because I recognised how costly it was for her to confess her neediness I sought no other explanation for the grief in her brimming eyes.

*****

It was obvious Suffolk was in a rage when I entered his room. He had summoned me with the explicit message that I was to come immediately, leaving whatever task I had in hand. I was concerned that he felt unwell but quickly realised it was not physic he required. He stood tensely by the window, with clenched fists.

'Walter Fitzvaughan has sent alarming news. There's unrest in Rouen itself. The populace is turning against the garrison, as has happened elsewhere. Walter's not confident Somerset can hold the situation. If Rouen were to be lost to the French, the rest of Normandy will follow. I fought across the Narrow Sea to hold the land King Henry's father won before you were born. Now we risk ignominious defeat and the loss of all we gained.' He reached out his hands to grasp the mullions of the window, supporting himself while he was shaken by tremors.

'Your Grace, sit down. You must rest.'

He ceased shuddering and turned, holding the small of his back. His face was haggard. 'It will give my enemies what they hope for – they will move against me.'

'You have King Henry's trust and Queen Margaret's too. Won't that be enough to protect you?'

'It might not be.' His voice was bleak. 'Remember Richard of York is thought by some to have a claim to the throne. The King is bound to abandon even his most loyal servant if his right to the crown is called in question and prudence dictates he protect himself.'

I opened my mouth to protest but I knew he spoke the truth. He clapped me on the shoulder. 'Don't fear, no one but you will see my weakness. Even with my confessor I maintain a calm demeanour. You're privileged, Harry, and I owe you this sincerity but I didn't summon you to observe my fallibility. I have a task I need you to undertake. Walter Fitzvaughan asks for my help. As you know his ward has married that fellow, Gaston de la Tour. They are both concerned for her safety in view of the uproar in Normandy and they're sending her across the Narrow Sea. I want you to go to Southampton to await her arrival and conduct her here. You can have an armed escort and my authority to require hospitality wherever you need it. The young lady has not been well and may need your attention but she can recover her strength at the Manor of the Rose before travelling on to Attleborough.'

I must have stared stupidly at the Duke. 'She will go to Attleborough?'

'Of course, that is his lordship's estate and she is heiress to it. Lady Fitzvaughan will be able to care for her.'

Suffolk knew nothing of Eleanor's birth mother, nor how Lady Maud had betrayed her. It was useless to make difficulties. 'I'll explain to my wife and set out at dawn.'

'Mistress Somers will have her own duties to attend to while you're away. The Countess and I are to join the court at Windsor and your lady will accompany us. She won't sit here pining, never fret. We won't return before the beginning of November and you may well be back before us.'

I did not comment but failed to find these arrangements entirely reassuring.

Chapter 21

We reached Southampton in two days after riding much faster than I liked but our speed was justified because Lady Eleanor's ship arrived in port that same day. I hurried to the dockside in time to see mariners making the vessel fast and the gangway lowered to the shore. The mood among the watching crowd was sullen and I heard muttering about the dangerous situation in Normandy. It was known that the new arrivals included families of prominent men based in the Duchy and there were vulgar comments about the well-to-do safeguarding their own while ordinary folk were exposed to starvation and the sword at the hands of the French. There were dark murmurs about English soldiers left unpaid. Suffolk's name was frequently spoken, accompanied by spitting and curses, and I advised my escort to draw their cloaks across the crests they wore on their liveried chests.

After a handful of passengers had disembarked a short squat figure, well wrapped and hooded against the cold sea breeze, stepped onto the sloping planks, with the ship's master holding her elbow. The sight jolted me and I peered closely while a female attendant followed her mistress with two seamen carrying baggage. My concern grew as the young Dame de la Tour tottered and I held out my hand to steady her as her foot touched land. Her pale face was drawn and she gazed up at me with tears in her eyes but she spoke bravely.

'Oh, Doctor Somers, I didn't know you would be here! I feel restored already to see a friendly face. I have been so unwell.'

I thrust aside my distress. 'When Queen Margaret arrived in England to marry King Henry she suffered a fearful crossing and was quite ill on arrival. It's not unusual. You need quiet respite to recover.'

The young woman smiled weakly, closing her eyes, while her attendant knitted her brows and inclined her head. 'I think you understand, Doctor,' she said. 'My mistress will benefit from several days' rest. Is there a suitable place for us to stay?'

It came to me on the instant with an enveloping wave of relief as if I had always known it was what I wanted. 'If Dame Eleanor could stomach a half-day's journey by litter we could be accommodated in the royal castle at Winchester. It is well appointed and we could stay there as long as necessary. When we get there I'll see what physic might help her.'

Eleanor nodded and took my arm. 'Take me to the litter please.' As she moved the wind caught her mantle, whipping it back to reveal the marked swelling of her belly; it was all too evident the little matron was with child.

*****

It gave me considerable satisfaction to use Suffolk's authority and commandeer the best rooms in the castle where a year and a half previously I had quaked, fearing for my life. I made sure my charge and her attendant were comfortably installed and the resident retainers appreciated how noble a lady they were to serve during her visit. Then I sent out to an apothecary for herbs and prepared a tincture for Eleanor to ease her sickness. I confirmed that she was suffering no abnormal symptoms at this stage in her pregnancy and I was pleased that her woman, Maria, was sensible and considerate in caring for her mistress. This meant I need have no qualms about leaving the precincts of the castle for a few hours but I hesitated to venture into the town and instead sent a note to St. Swithun's Abbey for the attention of the Reverend Robert Bygbroke. While awaiting a reply I contemplated Eleanor's plight as such a youthful prospective mother – and speculated whether Maud, not yet thirty years old, would relish becoming a grandmother.

Next morning I had scarcely broken my fast when I heard footsteps approaching my room and the carolling voice I had missed since I left the town.

'Is it true, this tittle-tattle? Are you really here, you harum-scarum quack? Are you returned to delight your friends or is it all a rag-tag fantasy?'

'Robert!' I jumped to my feet and embraced the organist, dressed for once in his priestly cassock, and we proceeded to chatter for an hour exchanging news and gossip.

'You've met a musician I admire. George Wilby came to Winchester when Bishop Waynflete was here a few months ago. He told me you'd crossed paths more than once. He thought you'd been in some sort of trouble when he last saw you, trouble in Ireland he said.'

I managed to grin. 'You could say that but all's well now. I've enjoyed his music. He's widely travelled.'

'A fount of knowledge with wide contacts.' Robert winked. 'I picked up a lot of information from him, no mistake. Like your master Suffolk's unpopularity, dingle-dangling over the chasm of disaster.'

'Not quite so hazardous, I hope.' I hadn't come to the town to discuss William de la Pole but he seemed to be a subject for banter and opprobrium everywhere. 'What's the news at the abbey? How are they all?

Robert sighed. 'Prior Aulton is very poorly. I worry for his health. You'd best go to see him. The other brothers seem well. With Bishop Waynflete's blessing work has started on Brother Simon's pet plans for the retro-choir, although it'll be years before they are complete. Brother Lambert has some extra beds in the Infirmary too.'

'He yielded to persuasion and accepted some of the Devereux money?'

'He yielded to a direction from his Abbot, the Lord Bishop.'

We both laughed. 'Do you have news of the townsfolk I met? I confess I'm nervous of encountering Mistress Dutton if I venture to the marketplace.'

'Oh, thoughts of guilt beneath the quilt! You're too late to take up with her again. She's wedded more than a year ago. A worthy miller, ten miles downstream, has carried her away, to nourish his lust and give her inordinate joy.'

'You mean it? She isn't in Winchester! I hope the miller treats her well but I'll be happier walking through the town to know I won't be challenged by shrill assertions that I have obligations to her.'

'You're safe, Harry Somers. Come with me now and renew your acquaintances at the abbey and Wolvesey Castle. Doctor Chauntley will welcome seeing you too. He never ceases to sing your praises. He claims he became the Bishop's physician through your good offices.'

I did as Robert suggested and spent an agreeable afternoon meeting my old friends although I was sorrowful to see Prior Aulton's condition. It was clear to me his illness was mortal and he knew this too but he would permit no discussion of his health. He was still interested in affairs of state and gave me the troubling news, just received, that Rouen was now firmly under siege by the French army. Eleanor had escaped in time but I wondered how Walter Fitzvaughan and Gaston would fare since they had joined the garrison inside the fort.

The Warden of the Works and the Infirmarian were still arguing with each other when I met them but both were animated when speaking of the changes which had enlarged their duties. In accordance with their vows their whole existence was focussed on life inside the monastery and I reflected that, alongside my pleasure at seeing its denizens once more, I felt irritation at the constrictions placed on the conventuals in St. Swithun's Abbey. I was conscious in a way I had not been when I lived with them how ill-suited I would be to adopt their enclosed way of life permanently.

When I was leaving the abbey gate in order to walk to the Bishop's Palace I glimpsed Master Ranken with a group of workmen and I waved enthusiastically, anxious to chat and share a jug of ale with him. He gave a start of surprise to see me, which was understandable, but then he hurried off towards the Sustern Spital without stopping to speak, leaving me disappointed and a little hurt.

Instead I went on my way to Wolvesey Castle where Chauntley made me warmly welcome and my irritation was quickly replaced by conviviality. Only to him did I disclose the fact that I was now married. He teased me with ribald anecdotes about marital disharmony and told me more than I wished to hear of his continuing relationship with the woman in St. Peter's Street. My foray into town, revisiting places and people who had been important to me at a difficult time, evoked mixed emotions but I returned to the royal castle in a contented humour.

Next morning Maria announced that Dame Eleanor was much rested and she believed that in two days' time it would be possible to commence a slow progress to London. This was encouraging and I began to hope that my return to the Manor of the Rose need not be long delayed. The beginning of November was fast approaching and I wanted to be home to greet Kate. In absence I realised how much I treasured her and I was resolved to rebuild the trust and love which my foolishness had damaged.

I walked on the castle ramparts above the town looking towards the ridge where the former Devereux lands lay – now actively managed by the abbey's bailiff. I was glad I had returned to Winchester but was ready to move back into the life to which I was more fitted. I stretched and breathed deeply of the clear cold air when a serving man approached me to ask if I would receive a visitor: 'one Master Ranken,' he said loftily.

I ran forward to greet the familiar nut-brown figure who emerged from the twisting stairs, pulling his cap from his head.

'I was afraid I'd never set eyes on you again, Doctor. I thought you'd gone for good and I've been that bothered what to do. When you appeared yesterday I couldn't credit it.

'I thought you'd turned your back on me. I was looking forward to drinking your health. Come downstairs with me and we'll do just that.'

He restrained me as I moved to the stairs. 'Better to speak up here first. What I've got to say is not for other ears. I've been holding it for a month now. I'll be that glad to pass it over.' His expression was remarkably solemn.

'What is it?'

He came close and lowered his voice. 'We're making alterations to the old Devereux house. Started about five weeks ago. My boys are stripping out some of the worn woodwork and putting in new floorboards. As luck would have it, I tackled Sir William's bedroom myself – bit of good fortune because if one of my men had found it he'd likely have thrown it away. Probably couldn't have read it. I've struggled with it myself, can't manage all the words. But you ought to see it. I reckon it may be relevant.'

He slid his hand inside his jerkin and extracted a folded paper with a broken seal attached. 'It was under a floorboard beside the bed, hidden by the rushes. There were some old accounts and a box of coins there as well but nothing else interesting. I handed the coins to the Almoner. But I knew you should see the letter and I'd no idea how to get it to you safely.'

I unfolded the paper and began to read, then when I had finished I began again, working through the significance of the appalling truths it revealed. It bore a date soon after my own arrival in Winchester more than eighteen months previously.

Sir William Devereux, most honoured sir, I beg you to give careful attention to my letter. When I saw you the other day you were brusque in your rejection of my proposition but I am full of hope that after calm reflection you will reconsider where your advantage best lies.

As I explained we are preparing for the day when we can move with security to bring about the changes we believe necessary. In all our plans our object is to enhance the counsel given to our most gracious King Henry and ensure that those advising him are men of integrity, free from corruption and self-interest. In order that we can move effectively when the time is right to challenge evil counsellors, we are seeking to establish where our friends are to be found, throughout the land. We hope to identify supporters in every county and you, Sir William, are perfectly placed to provide a bastion in Hampshire.

Consider well, Sir William: Y already thinks highly of your qualities and would embrace you in person, were he able to travel to your estate. You know him as a virtuous man of the highest lineage in the land. His approbation would benefit you. Besides, your old acquaintance, I, appeals to you with sincere concern for your well-being. He is anxious to see you part of our most noble enterprise and would not wish you harmed by an obstinate refusal to contemplate the changes we seek.

I beg you to think hard and long, Sir William, and lend us your wholehearted backing. I send this letter by the hand of my old friend, Bertrand Willison, and ask that you will be good enough to give him your reply so that he may pass it to me by a secure means.

Your devoted and deferential friend, Stephen Boice.

I leaned against the parapet, pretending still to read the letter long after I had absorbed its contents. The implications were devastating and required me to re-evaluate so much I had thought concluded. Sir William's letter which Willison had shown me outside Holy Cross must have been his response to Boice's communication, not a rejection of the doctor's personal plea. Its subject matter concerned an attempt to win Devereux's allegiance for York, not the question of his daughter's marriage. 'Y'; clearly stood for York and it followed that 'I' was Iffley, Baron Glasbury, not the unfortunate Isabella.

Clearly Stephen Boice was already acquainted with Willison at the time he called on me at Wolvesey Castle and his clandestine business in Winchester was to win support not just from me but from the far more influential landowner across the river from the town. When he went on his way to Normandy he left Willison to deliver this letter I now held in my hand and to chivvy up a positive response. It was even possible that Sir William's death owed as much to his refusal to accede to Boice's entreaty as to his daughter's murder.

The duplicity was astounding. Willison knew exactly what he was doing when he handed me Sir William's letter, pretending it was addressed to him, not a message meant for Boice and Iffley. He had worked out precisely how he could use it to hoodwink me, if he failed to kill me, and he had dared to speak of himself as a martyr, alongside Isabella. To my shame, I had humoured him. He had duped me comprehensively and I had played the part he contrived for me with consummate idiocy.

'This is invaluable to me, Master Ranken,' I said at length. 'It clarifies things which were obscure. I will gladly take the paper and relieve you of any responsibility for it.' Ranken beamed with gratitude and I took his arm. 'Come down with me now. I have an inappropriate wish, so early in the day, to get extremely drunk and I'd be pleased if you'd keep me company.'

Ranken rolled his eyes and led me down the stairs with genial compliance. I wondered how much of the letter he had actually understood but determined not to enquire.

*****

During our ponderous journey while I rode slowly beside the litter conveying Eleanor and Maria to London I went over in my mind a dozen times the enormity of what I had discovered: how I had gravely underestimated both Willison's connections to Richard of York's cause and his cunning. In the past I had enjoyed notable successes in ferreting out wrongdoers and my failure in this case was painful. I tried to concentrate on merrier thoughts but they would not come and even my longing to be reunited with Kate was tinged with anxiety as to how she would receive me. At each nightly resting place the latest news from Normandy intensified my gloom.

It was the sixth day of November when I escorted Dame Eleanor de la Tour into the Manor of the Rose and delivered her to the care of Suffolk's wife. Duchess Alice looked startled when she saw her young guest's condition but she rapidly hid her apprehension and took charge of arrangements to accommodate the expectant mother and her companion. The Duchess and her ladies had returned from court two days earlier and the Duke was expected to arrive imminently but for the moment I was released from my commitments and free to pursue private pleasures. I hurried to my rooms.

Kate was not there so I occupied myself checking the provisions on the shelves of the pharmacy. The steward had told me that, now Leone was across the Narrow Sea, they called in the elderly physician, who had served in the household when I was in disgrace, to deal with ailments while I was away. The old doctor was meticulous in his work and I was sure he would have noted down any ingredients he used from my stock. I glanced at his detailed list with approval and was momentarily puzzled by one apparent inconsistency when the door flew back and Kate ran towards me glowing with delight.

'Harry, oh my sweet, I only heard you had arrived when I went to collect the Duchess's new gown from the seamstress.'

I clasped her in my arms and kissed her until she giggled and pulled me out of the pharmacy into our bedchamber. 'Has the little lady you escorted arrived safely? How is she?'

'Pregnant,' I laughed and then regretted my misjudgement as Kate froze and the colour left her cheeks.

'She's only a child herself, isn't she?'

'She's fifteen. I would not recommend such juvenile motherhood but she's healthy and younger girls have given birth without difficulty.'

I swung Kate into my arms and kissed her again, fearing that she was troubled by Eleanor's fertility because our own union had not yet proved fruitful. 'Our journey took twice as long as if I'd ridden the distance alone. I yearned to be home every mile of the way. Are you willing to celebrate your husband's homecoming as a married couple should?'

'In the middle of the afternoon?' she chuckled, loosening my points. 'Devilish physician, shall we see?'

After our most joyful celebration we lay quietly with Kate snuggled at my side while I told her how I had been able to revisit Winchester and meet old friends. At once she became animated, lifting her head and gripping my shoulders, her eyes aglow.

'I think of Winchester as a place of gross perversion. Are there more tales of heinous couplings and gory deaths?'

I tried to laugh off instinctive disquiet at her change of mood, convinced I must never worry her with the dangers posed by Willison, Boice and Iffley. 'Not at all. The town appeared decorously peaceful.'

She nestled back against me and ran her fingers across my chest. 'I was so innocent a girl I had never heard of incest until that libidinous story began to circulate. I found it fascinating.'

'Then you were not so innocent at heart,' I said and kissed her lazily.

'Perhaps not but I was still naïve. I did not realise how solemnly my brother would take a jest.'

'Your brother?'

'I asked him to lie with me and take my maidenhood.'

'Good God!' I sat bolt upright.

'It was only in jest but Edward never appreciated such humour. He took a strap and beat me until I bled. Then he declared I could not remain under his roof and sent me to my uncle's. Hah! And I was glad. My brother is a loathsome rat. You haven't met him.'

262

I held her close, smoothing her tangled hair. 'I have. He accosted me in the street, nearly a year ago, after our betrothal.'

'What did he say?' She had begun to tremble.

'He told me not to marry you but I found him tedious and took no notice of his advice. Did I do wrong?'

I hoped to divert her from her bitter reminiscence and it seemed I had succeeded when she wriggled on top of me. 'I have learned,' she said, 'what I did not know when I teased my brother. I believe Edward lusted for me in good earnest but was repelled by the temptation. That is how men are, isn't it? When Adam ate the apple he experienced carnal desire and lay with Eve, who had come from his own body. That is incest, isn't it? All mankind are the seed of incest.'

My mind told me to refute this blasphemous logic but Kate's hands were busy and I yielded to their urging. Only later did I ponder the breadth of my wife's distorted imagination and the dangers into which it might lead her.

Chapter 22

When Suffolk arrived home, late that evening, the whole household was thrown into tumult by his demands. Half-clad pages and serving men scurried to and fro with guttering candles and a succession of officials in their nightgowns entered the Duke's study to emerge with beetled brows and lists of duties to perform. The Duchess summoned her ladies and Kate hurried to do her bidding while I dressed in case William de la Pole required my services, as seemed probable. It was after midnight when the call came and I saw that no other acolyte was waiting to be admitted to the study, so I guessed I was required to listen to ducal confidences as well as administer my liniment. I was not mistaken.

'The hour has come, Harry.' Suffolk's face was haggard, his complexion grey. 'Rouen has fallen. No, that's false. Rouen has capitulated. The inhabitants rebelled and opened the gates. That coward Somerset yielded to their persuasion. He has withdrawn to a castle beyond Caen. Normandy lies open to the French and my fortunes are scattered in the dust.' He paused and sipped from a goblet of wine. 'Parliament has ordered my imprisonment and instituted proceedings to impeach me.'

'What will you do, your Grace?'

He brushed his sleeve across his mouth. 'Try to outwit them. I've ordered a new fighting force to be assembled in an attempt to strengthen King Henry's men in Normandy. It may be too late but the effort must be made. I need to buy time to see if victory can yet be snatched on the battlefield. That would be the most reliable way to safeguard my position. Meanwhile the Duchess will appeal to Queen Margaret to put iron in her husband's soul and stand by his staunchest ally while I will throw myself at the King's feet and beg royal protection. The devil of it is that men whose careers I have nurtured are already deserting me. Bishop Lumley, the Lord Treasurer, has resigned rather than back my cause and even Bishop Moleyns of Chichester, who owes his elevation to me alone, has surrendered the Privy Seal. Cowards, the lot of them! Richard of York must be rubbing his hands with glee in Dublin Castle, safe from soiling them directly in my downfall.'

'He has followers enough to do his underhand work.'

'Certainly. Iffley and Boice have already crossed the Irish Sea and are in Ludlow. We may look for their fingers poking in the filth which will be thrown at me. The City is restless and in the morning news of Rouen's fall and Parliament's move against me will spread like flame on kindling. I'm not blind. The greatest danger may yet come from the London mob.'

'Will you go to Wingfield?'

He shook his head. 'If only I could. There's nowhere I would rather be but this isn't the time to flee. It may come to that but I won't give them the satisfaction of seeing me panicked into flight. I must hold fast as I did all those years ago when I fought in France and stood my ground despite the blows I took. I survived a multitude of physical wounds and I trust I shall survive these pernicious allegations against me.'

There was nobility in his defiance and my heart warmed towards the Duke in a way it seldom had during the time of his ascendancy.

'Is there something you wish me to do, your Grace?'

He sipped his wine again. 'I must ask you to take Dame Eleanor de la Tour on to Attleborough. You can keep the same escort who went with you to Southampton. I can't spare other followers to take over from you and conduct her home, as I'd planned. Get her there as soon as you can and come back to me. I may have need of your cool head. What is it?'

He had noticed how I bit my lip while he was speaking. 'Your Grace, this places me in a difficulty. Lord Fitzvaughan has forbidden me to go to Attleborough.'

265

'Forbidden you to go there? For God's sake, why? Oh! Because his wife is there?' Despite his troubles he laughed. 'Sweet heaven, what a rogue you are, Harry. Well, I shall have to override Walter's decree. He's hardly in a position to do anything about it while he's embroiled in Normandy and if we all escape the mantraps set for us I'll happily explain that I ordered you to go. Don't bed his wife though, I implore you.'

I joined in his mirth, glad to have afforded him some light relief although the subject was not of my choosing. 'I have a beloved wife of my own now, your Grace,' I said meekly.

'That rarely stops a full-blooded man but you and I are alike in being blessed with spouses with whom we are happily uxorious. If Mistress Kate has a mind to ride with you, I'll excuse her absence to the Duchess.'

'That's very kind, your Grace.'

'Go now.' He caught my arm as I bowed. 'Remember what I asked and come back quickly.'

Kate was asleep when I returned to our chamber and I did not wake her but waited until morning to tell her what Suffolk had said. She smiled and stroked my cheek but shook her head.

'I have my own tasks to attend to,' she said. 'The Duchess has need of all her women at such a time. Besides, I have limited competence as a horsewoman. You will return all the more speedily without me. That will please the Duke.'

'God keep you then, my love, while we endure another separation. I wish it could be our last.'

She smoothed my brow with her cool fingers. 'At such a time? We must be realistic, Harry. But my love goes with you.'

Despite her words I shivered. 'And mine with you, always.'

*****

266

Dame Eleanor's sickness was easing and we made reasonable progress as we took the highway towards East Anglia. On the third day, after our mid-day meal, she said she would like to ride pillion for half an hour to escape the monotony and discomfort of travelling in the juddering litter. This would mean setting a gentler pace but I welcomed evidence of her good spirits and my horse was steady and reliable. A suitable saddle was procured from the hostelry where we had rested and we set off with the young lady firmly seated behind me exclaiming with pleasure as we passed through the countryside and taking deep breaths of the fresh air.

'Lady Maud is at her husband's home, isn't she?'

I slowed the horse's measured pace and confirmed her statement without comment.

'I always liked Lady Maud at Ravensmoor. She was kind to me. Countess Mary didn't encourage me to speak of her but I slipped to the Middleton Tower whenever I could, to talk to her. I'm glad I shall see her again – in her own home. Is she quite reconciled with her husband now?'

'I think they may continue to live apart but their relationship seems to be more cordial.' I did not relish discussing the subject with Eleanor, sworn to secrecy about her mother's identity and conscious that this same disreputable mother had betrayed her daughter in order to win benefits for herself.

'She helped me win my darling husband.'

The assured young voice cut across my thoughts and I clutched the reins tighter. 'How so, my lady?'

Eleanor trilled with merriment whenever I addressed her so formally but it did not divert her from her purpose. 'Lady Maud arranged my escape from Ravensmoor. She planned it all with Gaston. I'd liked him when he first visited my father but I never supposed such a sophisticated gentleman would be interested in me. When Lady Maud told me I'd charmed him and he wanted to carry me off, in spite of the Countess's disapproval, I could scarcely believe it. Poor Cuthbert Percy couldn't match

Gaston for elegance and learning although I thought him nice enough. Do you think it was very naughty, what we did to deceive Countess Mary?'

I grunted and put the horse into a vigorous trot making it more difficult for us to converse but my mind was racing faster still as I considered the implications of what Eleanor had told me. She had become much closer to Maud than I realised and the pair of them had been complicit in the girl's departure from Ravensmoor – leading to her effective elopement with Gaston de la Tour. It was dastardly, deceitful, reprehensible, but it was what Eleanor wanted, not simply in Maud's interests. Perhaps I had been too hasty to blame Maud for all that happened. Mother and daughter were more alike than I was ready to admit.

That night we rested at Suffolk's castle of Wingfield and I renewed old acquaintances, especially with Father Wilfred, the chaplain, who had proved a good friend when I was last in the district and suffered such personal anguish. The expression in his eyes told me he remembered my desolation but he was sensitive enough not to refer directly to the circumstances and I was grateful. I did not burden him by seeking priestly guidance on what I had decided to do, for the breaking of a solemn oath was not something he could condone. The decision was mine and I must bear the consequences.

After our evening meal I asked for a few moments of Dame Eleanor's time and sat with her in a window bay, looking out across Suffolk's wide acres of pasture and woodland. For an instant I held back, uncertain why I was putting myself at risk of retribution or whether it was wise. Then I sat upright and faced her.

'My lady, you told me once how your father had spoken to you of your true mother, the woman he had loved but was prevented from marrying. I remember your words. You said he called her glorious in her fortitude.'

Eleanor gasped. 'I'm astonished you can quote him, Doctor Somers.'

'There is a reason. It struck me then that it was cruel to mislead you but it was not for me to speak when your father had forbidden it. He had only your welfare at heart but, as things have transpired, I think continued silence is wrong. I believe the Earl would have judged as I do.'

The young matron had turned pale and she clasped her hands rigidly together on her rounded lap. 'What is it? Did you know my mother?'

I nodded. 'And she still lives, my lady. You know her too.'

'What? She rose to her feet, fingers splayed on the transom of the window. 'What are you saying? Do you mean...?'

'Lady Maud Fitzvaughan is your mother. As a young woman she was treated unkindly by those who should have cared for her and her betrothal to your father was disputed. When she bore you out of wedlock she was forced to send you to the convent in Stamford and to swear never to disclose her relationship. She has had a difficult life, wiped from your memory as if she were dead, and often subject to the whims of evil men, but she has always nurtured regret for losing you. While you were at Stamford she regularly received news of your progress from the Prioress and when your father took you away from there, she grieved until she learned you were safe at Ravensmoor. It was no coincidence that she moved there after her estrangement from Lord Fitzvaughan. She would be overjoyed if you were willing to acknowledge her.'

Eleanor did not speak immediately and I let her muse on the information I had given, wondering if she would round on me and deny its truth. Then she turned and her face was radiant as she reached out to touch my arm. 'You've brought me new life, Doctor Somers. You've filled the gap that has yawned before me throughout the years. And I can bring my mother the new life which I carry. Will she be pleased?'

269

I answered as truly as I could. 'She will find delight in your child – but not maybe at once. She's a vibrant, beautiful woman and her new seniority may startle her. But she facilitated your marriage so it should not be a great shock.'

Eleanor laughed. 'How well you understand her.' Then she turned to face me. 'Do you love her?'

I swallowed but would not dissemble. 'Not in the way I love my wife. But she is a dear and well-esteemed friend.'

'God bless you, Doctor,' she said and the maturity in her voice and comportment surpassed anything her much-abused mother would ever achieve.

Foresworn and faithless I might be but I was confident I had done what was right.

*****

I sent a messenger from Wingfield to notify Lady Maud of Eleanor's impending arrival but I begged to be excused from accompanying her to Attleborough. Suffolk had overridden the ban Walter Fitzvaughan imposed on me approaching his wife but I did not wish to break another promise. I therefore explained that I would escort the young lady to the crossroads some five miles south of Attleborough and asked that Maud provide a trustworthy band of men to meet me there and convey Eleanor safely for the rest of her journey. Maud was acute enough to grasp why I was doing this but in my note I referred only to my marriage as a circumstance which had changed since we last met. I said nothing of the disclosure I had made to her daughter but suggested that she might regard Eleanor's arrival as my parting gift to her. If Eleanor subsequently chose to reveal what she had learned, Maud would appreciate the full significance of that attribution.

Once we had left Wingfield and crossed the River Waveney into the County of Norfolk I became aware of sullen faces watching our headway through fields and across rough pastureland. Labourers and woodmen lifted their heads and stared with unconcealed hostility as we advanced and I was glad our armed escort looked professional and intimidating. I remembered that the Prioress had told me of disturbances in the neighbourhood of Attleborough and, at that turbulent time, the absence of a lord from his demesne encouraged lawless men to give vent to their grievances in violence. I threw back my gown so I could more easily reach my own dagger and was relieved that Eleanor and her woman were hidden in the curtained litter.

I was disconcerted when we arrived at the deserted crossroads, reluctant to wait there in an exposed position, but then I caught the jingle of harness and a troop of riders rounded the edge of a copse. They carried a banner with the Fitzvaughan coat of arms, which was welcome, but in their midst rode a richly dressed lady, which was not. I groaned aloud, hoping the sounds of creaking leather and snorting horses would disguise my rudeness.

Maud urged her grey mare forward to draw beside the leader of her escort and greeted me in peremptory fashion. 'I am offended that you seek to avoid me, Harry Somers, and that you take refuge in your married status. Parting gift indeed! You can scarcely claim credit for bringing me the Lady Eleanor whom my own husband has committed to my charge.'

'Lady Maud, you misunderstand,' I began, conscious of a dozen pairs of eyes fixed on us and two dozen eyebrows raised in anticipation of a stimulating exchange between their principals.

'No, physician, I do not. I comprehend very well that you have cast aside my friendship and jettisoned all care for my interests. You slough me off as a snake in the grass sheds its skin.'

Deeply embarrassed, I dismounted and bowed, searching for a response which might moderate this public display of temperament. I heard the curtain around Eleanor's litter drawn back and regretted that she too

271

would be a witness to whatever indiscretions Maud chose to voice. I was not prepared for her intervention.

'My lady mother, I entreat you not to be displeased with Doctor Somers. He has not only delivered me safely to your home but I come with new understanding he has shared with me and which I am thrilled to acknowledge.'

Eleanor beckoned the soldier attending the litter and he lifted her to the ground. Then she walked towards the grey mare where Maud sat as if turned to stone, all colour drained from her cheeks.

'I may call you mother, may I not?'

Maud slipped from her saddle unassisted and, moving with ineffable grace, enfolded her daughter in her arms, unprecedentedly lost for words. When at length she turned to look up at me she was in tears. 'Harry? You have broken a solemn oath? For my sake?'

'For both your sakes, my lady. I believe the late Earl of Stanwick would forgive me and now the Countess has taken the veil, it can do her no harm. Lord Fitzvaughan may hold me blameworthy.'

Lady Maud dabbed at her face with her sleeve but she paid me no further heed. All her consideration, all her devotion was, for the moment at least, centred on the daughter she had been compelled to repudiate.

We had dallied too long with this emotional reunion and the sound of ribald jeering from the fringe of the wood drew our attention to a group of ne'er-do-wells gawping at us. The leader of Suffolk's men unsheathed his sword and brandished it, whereupon our audience began to disperse, but I judged it desirable for my party to accompany the ladies and the Attleborough attendants into their fortified manor. I gave the signal to move on and rode forward to join the fine-looking fellow at the head of Maud's followers.

'Master Robin Willoughby, isn't it?'

Lord Fitzvaughan's bailiff dipped his head. 'I'm honoured you remember me, sir.'

'I enjoyed hospitality at your house once and of course I had met Mistress Willoughby years earlier when we served together at Greenwich. Is she in good health?'

Master Willoughby beamed at me. 'I thank God both she and our little daughter are well. You did us a great kindness before the child was born and I've never been able to give you thanks until now. You saved me from false imprisonment and my family from the vilest cruelty.'

'You were threatened with dreadful injustice. I was pleased to help.'

He gave me another broad, open smile. 'Bess is with child again.'

I reached across to pat his arm. 'I'm delighted. I'd like to think that all at Attleborough may now share your contentment.'

'Amen,' he said and we rode together serenely: I and the well-chosen husband of the first woman I had loved and lost.

Later, at the manor-house, I met Mistress Willoughby and her daughter, Anne, named for the lady Bess had served when I first met her, more than eight years previously, in Duke Humphrey's household. She was still beautiful and I could tell she had not lost the placid resourcefulness which had once helped save my life. I dismissed the temptation to speculate how different my history might have been if I had not been forced to flee into exile and we had been able to marry. It would be unfair to Bess to imagine her with anyone but Robin Willoughby as her husband. They were well matched and contented and, after several unsuitable liaisons, I now had Kate. Such were the rotations of the wheel of fortune.

I spent the night at Attleborough before bidding my friends adieu and leaving them, I hoped, in security and happiness: the Willoughby family, together and at ease, and Maud with her acknowledged daughter. It seemed to me a phase of my life had been completed and I could progress from involvement in the troubles of others, to

273

build a comfortable domestic life with my wife, shielded from the worst vagaries of fate.

I could not have been more mistaken.

<u>Chapter 23</u>

I dispatched Suffolk's men to return to London with assurances that I would be safe, making my way across country as an unassuming physician, and when I joined the main highway to the south I would find a band of merchants and join their company as I had done many times in the past. Then I rode southwards a few miles to the small town of Diss, scene of so much I would rather forget and occurrences etched on my heart forever. I avoided the area beyond the sombre mere where, for all I knew, the body of the man I killed still mouldered in its reputed bottomless depths. Instead I climbed to the church on the hill, tethered my horse and stood in silent prayer in the graveyard while the wind tore at my gown and lifted the cap from my head.

Somewhere, in a tiny unmarked grave among the heaped earth and featureless plots, my little son's bones had been consigned to rest. Neither I nor his mother, in peril of our lives, had been present when Father Wilfred, Suffolk's chaplain from Wingfield, performed the burial rites. Now I had come to make amends, asking God to sanctify my lost child and take his soul into the eternal realm of the blessed and blameless. It seemed to me a sacred moment and when I remounted and turned to the west, away from Diss, I felt I had been purified in some way no priest would accept as proof of divine compassion.

Another sequence closed, I thought, and although I would not admit it to myself perhaps I was hoping its conclusion would permit us to have the children Kate and I had so far been denied. Maybe already, life was implanted in my wife's womb and she would tell me of her quickening when we were reunited. The idea filled me with warmth as I travelled on with the bitter wind at my back.

I had one more obligation to fulfil. Once before, coming from the west, I had made the journey by navigable waterways and across drained fens so now I confidently hired a guide to take me in the opposite direction. Much as I longed to return to London and re-join my wife, some instinct compelled me to make this further journey, to complete another stanza in the continuing narrative of my life, perhaps to break another link which bound me to my previous existence. And so I came again to Stamford and the Convent of St. Michael's.

It was two years since I had been there but the gatekeeper remembered me and was apologetic when I asked to see the Prioress. She told me to call the following morning and, although she did not say so, I sensed that her superior might be disinclined to receive visitors. That would pose a problem for me and a wasted expedition but I did not object to spending a night at the Raven Inn where I had been hospitably entertained on previous occasions.

Next morning I waited until the office of Tierce had been celebrated within St. Michael's walls before I presented myself again at the gatehouse and this time I was admitted. I judged from the gatekeeper's pinched expression that she had reservations about the wisdom of permitting me to see the Prioress and when the reverend lady entered the parlour where I waited, I understood the reason. The Prioress moved slowly, not with her usual vigorous stride, and she leaned upon a heavy stick but it was her face which bore clearest evidence to the illness she had suffered. Flesh had fallen away from her cheeks and dark grooves ran from her eyes to mouth, throwing into sharp relief the bony prominence of her nose. She paused on the threshold, panting a little before advancing to sit on the window bench.

'Reverend Mother, I did not know you'd been ill.'

She gave an impatient shrug. 'The Lord God has chosen to reprieve me on this occasion and I must believe He has more work for me to undertake on earth. My fever has not proved mortal and I am recovering. It is a further

276

demonstration of His will that you have come to Stamford unbidden. You are welcome, Doctor Somers.'

'If there's anything I can do... perhaps to prescribe a mixture to improve your appetite...'

She waved a dismissive hand and laughed. 'The good sister Infirmarian would be offended if I cajoled you for medicine. She has my treatment in hand. The reason I rejoice to see you is that I was about to write a letter and send it to the Manor of the Rose. I would have needed to await your reply but now I can simply pose my question and you can answer me.'

I bowed my head and she indicated that I might sit on a stool by the hatch into the gatehouse but she did not ask her question immediately. 'Your last letter explained your mission to deliver young Eleanor to Lord Fitzvaughan's manor. I'm glad she is safe in England although I would have wished a different marriage for her.'

'She's delighted with her husband, Reverend Mother. I trust this may continue.'

The Prioress sighed. 'These are profoundly troubling times, Doctor Somers. You know that England's hold on Normandy is in jeopardy?'

'When I left London Suffolk was assembling another force to cross the Narrow Sea and attempt to win back what has been lost.'

'They're likely to be too late. My prediction is that they will fail and Suffolk will fall. Does he realise this?'

'He recognises the danger but hopes to avert it. He believes the King and Queen will defend him.'

'Fool! If Parliament impeaches him, King Henry will be well advised to throw him to the dogs. The accusations against the Duke touch too nearly on the persons of our Sovereign Lord and the Queen. If they act unwisely it will give Richard of York the opportunity he awaits. Mischief is being planned, Doctor.' She paused and tilted her head so that her wimple shaded her face. 'News reaches me from many sources, as you know. There is rumour of a fellow in York's household claiming to be of Mortimer descent.'

'Mortimer?' A flicker of memory came to me but I could not pin it down.

'The second son of England's great King Edward, third of that name, fathered only a daughter. She married Edmund Mortimer, a great Marcher baron. Richard of York's mother is their grandchild. If it were held that the crown could pass twice through a woman, Richard of York would have a stronger claim to the throne than King Henry. Any Mortimer must be regarded with suspicion. Even a by-blow might stir contention where discontent is brewing. It may be idle chatter but I conjecture that York is shrewd enough to let another sound out the extent of opposition to the King before he decides whether to venture forth in open treachery. Your old acquaintance Gilbert Iffley has the Duke's ear. Is this the type of ploy he might devise?'

I shot to my feet as the recollection came to me. 'When I was in Dublin last year Iffley was tutoring a young man said to be a Mortimer relative. What was it I heard him saying – somebody's name, was it Philippa?'

'Philippa, Countess of March?' The Prioress smoothed her skirts and ran her fingers over her rosary. 'The daughter to King Edward's second son: who married Edmund Mortimer. How interesting that Iffley should be instructing a so-called Mortimer on that subject. It is God's will that you should come to tell me this.' She folded her hands in her lap and fixed her eyes on me. 'Beware, Doctor, if you ever hear rumour of a Mortimer stirring up dissent. Remember what I have told you.'

The Prioress shifted position and I thought she was probably in pain but when she saw my look of concern she frowned. 'That is not what I wished to ask you, fascinating though it is. My question is concerned with one of King Henry's humbler subjects. When you were in Winchester did you encounter a fellow physician, a Doctor Willison?'

She must have seen the frisson which passed through me for I felt myself tremble although I steadied my voice. 'I did. He served the late Cardinal but he is now with Richard of York. I encountered him a second time in Dublin.'

'Ah! You are an astute judge of character, I think. Do you consider he is a man capable of murder?'

I cleared my throat before replying. 'He confessed as much to me on one occasion. I do believe him capable of murder – in certain circumstances.'

Her eyes twinkled with amusement. 'Do those circumstances include administering poison to a victim, perhaps in a goblet of tainted hippocras?'

I shut my eyes in horror. Surely the Prioress had not learned of Brother Joseph's death and connected it to Willison?

She noted my confusion and continued. 'One of my most reliable correspondents visited Ludlow Castle recently where I know he encountered Willison. Sadly he was seized suddenly with convulsions in his belly and died soon afterwards. It is fortunate for me that another agent was able to report that he had been entertained by Willison and offered hippocras shortly before his demise. What should I conclude from this?'

I moistened my lips which had become quite dry. 'I believe Willison is capable of murder whether with a dagger in the heat of the moment or by crafty calculation in preparing poisoned hippocras.' My hands were icy cold.

The Prioress rose and as I also stood I noticed colour had come into her cheeks. She smiled. 'Thank you, Doctor. So Iffley has a soulmate in this villainous physician. We must be on our guard.'

I bowed, thinking myself dismissed, but she held up her hand. 'I trust you are contented with your marriage, Doctor Somers.'

'Indeed, I am.'

'Then I advise you to take your wife and leave the service of the Suffolks as soon as you return to London.

Establish yourself as a physician in the City or elsewhere. Be your own man. William de la Pole will only bring you grief if you remain at his side. And your wife would do well to be free of her connections at the court. Don't look surprised. If I had known when you informed me of your betrothal that Katherine Devereux was related to the Nevilles I would have cautioned you against the match. I warned you once before not to tangle with a woman who was kin to the Nevilles.'

The Prioress had regained some of her normal astringency and, directed at my wife, I found it irritating. 'You're referring to a time when I had a fancy to court the widowed Jane Cawfield who went on to marry Gilbert Iffley and is sister to a man I had not then met but whom I now know as Stephen Boice and whom I account my enemy. I accept that was a foolish notion. There is no comparison with Kate's distant kinship to Philip Neville, Baron Thornton.'

The Prioress lowered her gaze. 'I trust you are right, Doctor Somers. I have traced her family association with Baron Thornton but I've learned nothing to her discredit although she is reported to be high-spirited. That is why I recommend you should take her away from the court to live quietly as your wife. Do not expose her to the wiles of evil men who may seek to influence her.'

I stifled my annoyance, appreciating that she meant no harm. 'I'd be happy to follow your advice, Reverend Mother, but to leave Suffolk when his future is under threat smacks of betrayal. Besides, if I leave his service I will no longer be the recipient of information of interest to you.'

She smiled, rather grimly I thought. 'You've been very helpful to me but times change. You would be wise to look to your own future. I wish you well, Doctor, and even in an altered setting you may yet find matter to interest me. I hope we shall still correspond. I shan't bid you farewell and you will not forget me.'

Her final words were an instruction which I accepted wordlessly as she swept through the door to the cloister, leaving me troubled by several aspects of our conversation. I resolved to make all haste to London.

*****

Kate ran down into the courtyard when I rode through the gateway to the Manor of the Rose and in a moment I had dismounted and she was in my arms. It was as happy a homecoming as I could wish for and I vowed to myself that we would seldom be parted in future. The Prioress had strengthened my determination to break away from Suffolk's service and free myself from the intrigues of great men. In a few days I would tell Kate what I planned, the enquiries I must make to establish possibilities, but in the meantime there was our reunion to enjoy.

Once in our rooms I stood in a tub and bathed the dirt of the highway from my body while Kate poured jugs of water over my head, giggling outrageously. It was as well that Leone was not sharing our accommodation and my elderly locum had gone home. We behaved like children, perhaps rather precocious and lewd children, unconstrained and joyful. It seemed a harbinger of the guileless life we might have together.

Later in the afternoon Kate needed to attend Duchess Alice and help her dress for the Duke's return from Westminster where he had been present at the King's Council. I spent the time of her absence checking my medicinal supplies and noting which items needed to be replenished. The odd discrepancy I discovered when I returned from Southampton had slipped my mind but when I realised the stock of pennyroyal was once again depleted and a few dried leaves of tansy lay loose on the shelf, I was puzzled. An infusion of pennyroyal or tansy might well have been given to one of the household with the bellyache but more had been taken than seemed

281

necessary and the list of usages did not accord with what was left. It might be the case that the elderly physician who took my place prescribed his own concoction to maid-servants for dubious purposes but did not care to register the fact. Perhaps he had been badgered by old Syb in the kitchens who I was certain also counselled her workmates on women's ills. Yet I doubted the doctor would let a spillage remain untidied.

When Kate returned I mentioned the mystery to her and she blushed, looking down in embarrassment. 'Oh, I'm so sorry, Harry, I should have made sure the shelves were clean. The old doctor is sometimes forgetful and doesn't put things back neatly. I hadn't wanted to bother you. I've often cleared up after him. Forgive me.'

'I don't expect you to skivvy for me, sweeting. I'm just surprised the old chap has used so much pennyroyal and tansy.'

She put her hands to my cheeks and spoke in a whisper. 'I shouldn't speak out of turn but the housemaid, Joanna, came several times to see the doctor while you were away. She's a flighty girl by all accounts and I wonder if she's in difficulties. I think you told me pennyroyal and tansy are sometimes used to rid a woman of what she does not want.'

'Those attempts are hazardous and the church proclaims them against God's law but perhaps Joanna charmed my substitute physician to try and help her. The strength of the mixture and the dosage would be critical: too much could prove mortal.'

Kate looked serious but gave a faint smile. 'Joanna does not appear to have suffered any ill effects.'

I remembered Leone telling me how he had paid court to Joanna before she turned from him in favour of the sergeant-at-arms and I wondered who was responsible for her difficulties and whether or not they had been resolved. I had no wish to pursue the matter.

Within the hour I was summoned to wait on the Duke and found him in good spirits. He told me Sir

Thomas Kyriel was assembling a new and larger force of soldiers to cross to Normandy and beat back the French troops.

'There'll be no fighting until the spring now so our men can be well armed and battle-ready before they take the field. Moreover the King has allowed me to stay at liberty until Parliament has considered the Bill for my impeachment in more detail – that won't be before the Feast of Yule. It gives me time to prepare my defence. I begin to hope I may yet hold my enemies at bay.'

I thought of the resentful crowd on the quayside at Southampton. 'I hope Sir Thomas will be in funds to pay his men.'

Suffolk shrugged, pulling up his shirt for me to apply the salve to his back. 'Parliament needs to vote more supplies but we have levied new impositions. I'm sure we can rely upon the loyalty of our English soldiers.'

Not if their families are starving, I speculated silently, and I did not care for his offhand reliance on men's loyalty. Doubtless he would call my loyalty in question when I quitted his service but his lack of compassion for his fellow men only reinforced my intention.

*****

Later that week I told Kate that I had in mind leaving the Duke's household and setting up as a physician in the City. I did not mention the dangers threatening Suffolk's future. I was unsure how much she had gleaned of these dire prospects and did not want to frighten her. So I explained that we had sufficient resources to lease a house offering suitable space for a home and consulting room and I was confident I could secure an adequate income from my patients to keep us in reasonable comfort. There was no need for her to continue in the Duchess's service but if she wished to attend the lady from time to time, I had no doubt that could be arranged.

283

'One of the greatest benefits would be that we need not be apart as much as we have been.' I did not disguise my excitement.

Kate stared at me without speaking and I could not read her thoughts. My announcement was unexpected and she would need to reflect on the changes it would bring. I did not want to put her under pressure.

'I propose to visit Grizel and Thomas. They'll be able to advise me where in the City I might seek to launch myself. They may even know of possible premises.'

Kate's expression froze me to the core. 'You will use my dowry to fund this escapade?'

'Only part of it. I have money saved from Suffolk's gifts and it seems a proper use of your dowry to help create our own home.'

'The home of a tradesman touting for business from his wretched neighbours! Is this what you think fitting to offer me?'

Her voice rose to a shriek and I recoiled in horror, stung by her scornful description of my profession. 'A physician is not a tradesman whoever his patients may be. It's a noble calling and I have the highest qualifications.'

'Which is why you rightly serve one of the greatest families in the land. And you propose to throw this aside and drag me with you into the squalor of commerce? Have you forgotten there is Devereux and Neville blood in my veins? How can you demean me so cruelly?'

'Your father was a notary in the City, as is your brother. Their status is akin to a physician's. Please consider this more calmly. I never wanted to upset you, sweet. I believed you would be happy to be free from the constraints of serving the Suffolks.'

'You presumptuous fool! I refuse to leave the Manor of the Rose. Do you hear? I refuse.'

I was appalled by her distress but also by her derision and it made me stubborn. 'I shan't press you now, Kate. It's been a shock. But I beg you to reflect. The way of life I'm suggesting isn't a slight on your family; it's perfectly honourable. We'll discuss it again in a few days.'

She grasped my sleeve. 'You still intend to consult those friends of yours: the carpenter and his wife?'

I bridled anew at her insult. 'Thomas is a master carpenter, who once served the Duke of Gloucester and is now a respected independent craftsman. I'm proud to have him as my friend and, yes, I will visit him. I shall write at once to see if I can call at his house two days hence.'

'So be it. And you too would do well to reflect what the consequences of your proposition may be.'

I hated the arrogance in her words and sank onto a stool with my head in my hands as she slammed the door. Later I rallied myself and wrote my note to Thomas, summoning a page to arrange its delivery. When Kate returned, alongside the lad who took my missive, she seemed altogether different from the virago who had stormed at me earlier and I was cheered by the hope that we would resolve our differences amicably. The rapid switches in her moods were wearing but they buttressed my faith that a more tranquil way of life would be beneficial for her health.

*****

By tacit agreement we did not revert to the reason for my visit to the Chope family and the matter at issue between us was deferred until my return. In fact Kate was pleasingly attentive to my welfare during the intervening day and helped me mix potions which were required for colleagues in the household suffering from the rheum. She accepted without protest that my visit would take place and asked if I would ride through the City. I said I had spent time enough in the saddle recently and preferred to walk, despite the chill wind from the east, so when I prepared to set off she bundled an extra cloak over my shoulders and told me to walk briskly. My relief was enormous and I was smiling as I struck out along

285

Candlewick Street, ready to tolerate her temper if I could be so cossetted.

Although it might be tempting fate, I looked closely at premises on my route which seemed unoccupied and might meet my requirements. I knew the streets well and took for granted the ordure clogging the runnels and the smell of rotting garbage, sweat and excrement, but some locations offered more favourable outlooks and entrance steps swept clean. I was in no doubt that to win Kate's approval I must find a superior house with respectable neighbours and I paid close attention to the quality of each area through which I passed. I had been out of London often enough in recent months to find the crowds swarming along the roadway more oppressive than the filth and stink but I noted how many, even prosperous, citizens appeared unwell and might benefit from the ministrations of a doctor. This gave me encouragement.

I was near to my destination, not far from the Tower of London, when I turned towards a quiet alleyway which gave a shortcut to Thomas's house. My head was filled with calculations of what charges patients would need to pay if I was to make a reasonable living. I edged round a mounted serving man holding the reins of a riderless horse at the entrance to the narrow alley and noticed someone step from a doorway in front of me but thought nothing of it. Then a jarring voice cut across my contemplation and brought me to a standstill.

'Well, well, Doctor Somers, what an agreeable surprise.' Stephen Boice stood before me, elegantly gowned, and gave a scornful bow. 'I proposed to call on you while in the City and this felicitous encounter saves me from the awkwardness of visiting the Duke of Suffolk's residence.'

The coincidence was preposterous. 'Master Boice, I can't pretend the meeting pleases me. In Dublin you and your good-brother, Iffley, had me flung, chained, into a cell and left to drown.'

'A grievous misunderstanding led to your discomfort, I fear. I rejoiced to hear you had evaded the snare.'

'I've no wish to listen to this nonsense. I have an appointment, excuse me.'

He stepped in front of me blocking my passage and from a corner of my eye I saw a fellow at the far end of the alley deterring passers-by from entering it. The horseman behind me was undoubtedly serving the same purpose.

'One moment only. You are intelligent enough to know that Suffolk's time is running out. York would still welcome your adherence to his cause and if you join him now your previous mulishness will not be held against you. You're in a position to help resolve all the woes which threaten the kingdom. Think of that, Doctor Somers. You could foreshorten the otherwise inevitable time lag while Suffolk is impeached and taken to the block. How much unpleasantness could be prevented, do you think, if the Duke were simply eased on his way to face his just desserts in God's final judgement? Without the need for his Grace the King to suffer the agony of ordering his dear friend's execution? You are a faithful subject, are you not? Serve King Henry and the whole kingdom by taking action. A physician has a hundred opportunities to lighten the realm of an acquisitive tyrant. Your reward will be great.'

'Are you mad? Let me pass.'

'Not without your answer.' He had his hand on the hilt of his sword.

'You think you can coerce me into committing murder? I'm a physician, not an assassin. In any case, what value would my word be? I could simply agree and then denounce you to the magistrates.'

'But you won't, Doctor Somers, you won't. Because if you did, or indeed if you refuse to help us, you will rue the consequences. You have a charming wife now, remember.'

I took a step back. 'What do you mean?'

'Mistress Katherine Somers, lately Kate Devereux. A pretty but nervously inclined young woman, prone to alarming fancies. Think what might befall her if you were recalcitrant. Could you live with that?'

Against all common sense I whipped my dagger from inside my gown but he anticipated my move and pushed me backwards with all his sinewy strength. I hit my head on the wall and slid down onto the slimy ground, momentarily dazed, while he ran past me. I saw him bound onto his waiting horse and ride off, with his attendant, beating a way through the bustling crowds, provoking shouts of anger and complaint.

I dragged myself upright but my mind was in turmoil. This was no fortuitous encounter. It had been carefully planned. Boice had known of my visit to Thomas and Grizel and sprung the trap. How could he have known? It was no mystery. I had sent an open note and Thomas had replied by word of mouth. A messenger, perhaps the page in Suffolk's house, must have been in Boice's pay. It had happened before. But the implications were appalling. It meant my every action could be under scrutiny, ready to be betrayed, and they knew how to skewer me in my weakest spot. Kate... Kate... I heard myself sob her name. Boice and Iffley did not make idle threats. They were fully capable of carrying them out. How could I refuse their evil bargain and risk Kate's safety? How could I contemplate what they might do to her? It was inconceivable that I should comply with their demands but I was their prisoner as effectively as if I was chained to that prison wall below the rising tide of the River Liffey.

Chapter 24

'I must protect her, Tom, but I daren't explain to her why. If she knew they'd threatened her, her wild imaginings could tear her to pieces.'

After I stumbled into their house, grey-faced and with a bump on my head, I told my friends the whole story. Grizel muttered something about gentlewomen's pathetic, self-regarding frailty but I ignored her, looking to Thomas for practical advice. He lifted his youngest son from his lap to scramble on the floor and rubbed his chin.

'Suffolk has few friends among the common people,' he said slowly. 'The word is he will fall.'

'Are you suggesting Harry would really be performing a public service if he gave the Duke a lethal potion?' Grizel was being provocative.

'No, of course not.' He turned to me. Do you trust him? He played you false over Gloucester's death. Can you trust him now?'

'I think I can. In an odd way he seems to need me, as someone he can talk to freely.'

'Then tell him what's happened. The Manor of the Rose is as strongly defended as anywhere. Boice can't carry your wife off from there. Get the Duke to give her a bodyguard if she goes outside its walls.'

'How am I going to explain that?

'Tell her it's because of the hostility to Suffolk and it spills onto you and Kate because you're known to be close to him. It's half-true.'

'That's what you tell wives, is it, half-truths?' Grizel stood and forcibly separated her two elder boys who were squaring up for a fight.

'You may be right. At any rate I can't go on with my plan to leave Suffolk and set up my own physician's practice. That's ironic, isn't it! Boice's threats will actually keep me serving the Duke longer than I intended.'

'Only for a while, Harry.' Thomas patted my shoulder. 'If Suffolk's impeached and imprisoned you'll be free. You'll have no longer to wait than a few months. I'll keep my eyes open for premises which might suit you in the meantime. Cheer up, just keep Kate safe indoors and let affairs of state do the rest.'

It was uncomfortable advice but I could think of nothing better.

*****

Tom sent me back to Suffolk's house escorted by a burly apprentice with a bludgeon which was an unnecessary but kindly precaution. On arrival I asked to see the Duke and within a few minutes I had been admitted to his study and was telling him what Boice had proposed. I was ready for him to express fury so his reaction surprised me.

'By all the saints, Harry, they're not certain they can pull it off – the impeachment! They're worried. Why else should they try to incite my physician to commit murder? Surely what York wants is to see me publicly shamed, judged culpable by judicial process, my head struck off in front of the baying populace by the royal executioner! Despatching me behind doors with a cup of poison might get rid of me but it would attract rumours of double-dealing. York aspires to be the honest broom of rectitude, brushing me aside with all my alleged misdeeds. Iffley and Boice may want to hurry things along but I don't believe they have York's sanction. They're at sixes and sevens. Your story gives me reassurance. By God, if we hold our nerve, we'll beat them yet.'

'You may be right, your Grace, but I'm afraid for my wife. She knows none of this. I don't want to frighten her but she may be in danger when they realise I'm not going to kill you. York's agents have infiltrated your household before and someone has been monitoring my movements and reporting them to Boice.'

'You'd better question the page who took your note. See if you can track what happened to it. Don't worry

290

about Kate. It sounds to me like bluster on Boice's part, not a serious threat. But we could smuggle her out of the City and send her to Wingfield or one of my other houses. I'll talk to Alice. After all Kate is one of her women. In any case we've got a few weeks before we need to act. York's cronies will soon find out you won't have the opportunity to doctor my drink. I shan't be here: I'm leaving for Windsor in the morning and I'll be away until the Feast of the Nativity. That's when they'll expect you to lace my wine with venom. A seasonal sacrifice!'

He gave a low chuckle and, although it was scarcely appropriate, I admired his nonchalance.

I did not relish another parting from Kate but I saw the sense in what Suffolk proposed. If she could be spirited away from London, perhaps when the Duchess and her ladies were moving elsewhere, she could remain hidden until anger at my failure to act had been overtaken by events, one way or the other. The drawback to such a scheme would be the need to explain the circumstances to Kate without terrifying her. I did not welcome the prospect.

I duly questioned the page to whom I had given the note suggesting my visit to Thomas. He seemed a timid lad but I could not rule out the possibility he had been paid to intercept any communication I sent. Nevertheless there was little likelihood of proving his involvement and he explained that a messenger had taken my missive with other letters from the Manor of the Rose for recipients in the City. Among less well remembered items there had been bills of fare to be ordered from butchers and fishmongers, demands for ribbons to a draper near London Bridge and for candles to a chandler by Dowgate Steps, together with a request to a goldsmith in Cheapside to call on the Duchess. The messenger was traced and described his route weaving about the City streets to make his deliveries. None of his consignment was confidential and my note was unsealed: it could have been read by half a dozen tradesmen as they picked out what was addressed

291

to them. Boice might have spies throughout London and, whether he had obtained information about my intentions by chance or design, I concluded it was a waste of time to pursue the matter.

*****

As the Duke predicted, all remained quiet while he was absent from the City before the Mass of the Nativity and I ensured Kate stayed ignorant of the threat to her safety. She appeared happy we were together and I let her conclude I had abandoned my plan to leave Suffolk's service – as indeed I had, temporarily. My reward was that she seemed less troubled by idle fancies than she had been in the past and our life was harmonious. I bought her a new gown for the festivities, in rusty-red silk with deep hanging sleeves lined with fur, which delighted her, but she shone among her companions for the brilliance of her eyes as much as the elegance of her dress.

When the Duke returned to the Manor of the Rose he brought with him many guests, along with tumblers, clowns and musicians he had hired to entertain us. I observed them pour into the great hall as the serving men struggled past with their urns of sturgeon in broth, salvers of boiled goose and platters of pork in almond cream. My nose informed my taste buds and I hurriedly escorted Kate to our places, only then recognising, among the company further along the table, my old and valued acquaintance, George Wilby.

He and his troupe were in fine fettle, playing and singing with vigour and sentiment; the acrobats performed amazing feats of contortion and flexibility; while the clowns lived up to expectations with their bawdiness and humour. Throughout the hall there were cheers and raucous catcalls as the evening progressed and there was general acclamation of our host's magnanimity.

In due course, when the ladies had retired after the celebrations, Wilby came to sit at my side and share a jug of wine. He told me slanderous stories from his recent sojourn at the court and I related how I had met Robert Bygbroke again during my short stop in Winchester. We exchanged amused reminiscences of our alliterative friend, traded gossip about the misdoings of our betters and, with a wink, the musician complimented me on my marriage.

'Just a year ago we were promised and wed at Easter. I'm a lucky man.' I was more than a little tipsy and may have slurred my words.

'Indeed!' He slapped me on the back and poured more wine into my goblet. 'What remarkable eyes! I've seen her once before, must have been around four years ago. She was quite young then but those glorious eyes entranced me.'

'You rogue! Where was this?'

'Rouen,' he said, ignoring my raised eyebrows. 'Richard of York was the King's Lieutenant in Normandy and we were engaged to play at revels in honour of some family event – I can't recall what. Your lady was there, with York's wife and other gentlewomen. She watched and listened with such concentration and those wonderful green eyes flashed with excitement as I sang the old songs the troubadours have left us. We've played to hundreds of audiences since then and I can only picture a handful of our spectators in my mind – but your lovely Mistress Somers is one of them.'

'You rogue,' I repeated weakly, bemused why Kate should have been in Normandy, with Richard of York's adherents and why she had never mentioned it to me. Then I remembered her Neville relations and guessed she had chosen not to tell me of occasions I might misconstrue. My heavy-handedness over the encounter with Philip Neville, Baron Thornton, had damaged her confidence in me and it made me hesitant about appearing over-inquisitive concerning her past. The process of learning mutual trust was likely to be a lengthy one.

*****

The revels of Twelfth Night brought the joyful season to an end when our guests and entertainers left the Manor of the Rose. Kate and I fondly remembered the episode the year before which had led to our betrothal and I was encouraged by the open, merry way in which she spoke of it, as if she had no regrets, which I never could be sure was true. I was still unwilling to tell her of my encounter with Boice and the threat he made but Suffolk's suggestion of moving her to a place of safety away from London was sensible. Yet if this was to be arranged, she must be given a reason. The Duke himself remained publicly visible and in good health so my defiance of Boice's menaces would be evident to any observer. My hope was still that events would move on and render those menaces ineffectual.

Events did move on but not in an encouraging way. Suffolk had bowed at last to the unrest among sailors and soldiers assembled for transport to Normandy by sending his supporter, Bishop Adam Moleyns of Chichester, to Portsmouth with money to cover their unpaid wages: a move I welcomed as prudent although overdue. Consequently I was as horrified as any at the court when news was brought by an exhausted rider that the rebellious recipients of Suffolk's bounty had seized his episcopal agent and hacked the poor man to death. The Duke's face was pasty white when he summoned me to relieve his recurring back-pain, which flared anew at the impact of these dreadful tidings, and I could appreciate he saw in Moleyns' murder a premonition of his own demise.

'Moleyns and Richard of York were known enemies. A few years back they exchanged bitter accusations of each other's misdeeds. The Bishop owed his position to my favour.' Suffolk's voice dropped to a whisper. 'Yet as he lay dying he blamed me publicly for the loss of Anjou and Maine and claimed this was the cause of all our subsequent misfortunes. May God absolve him from his sins.'

I crossed myself and silently prayed for the Bishop's soul. His dying words would give credence to the hostile rumours about Suffolk which the men who slaughtered Moleyns already believed. York's enmity added an extra dimension of unease. The shadow of disaster had fallen over the Duke and I shivered.

There was no hope that news of Moleyns' murder could be kept from Kate so I told her myself, as gently as I could. Although she was always unpredictable, I found her reaction chilling. She stared at me, her eyes growing wider.

'He owed his preferment as Bishop to Suffolk; now he has died in place of him. Shouldn't those wretched men who were denied their wages tear Suffolk to pieces, not his henchman?'

I put my finger to her lips. 'Hush. Be careful who hears you say such things. Suffolk's fate lies in the hands of the King and Parliament. He knows the rabble might rip him apart if they have the chance so he's always well-guarded when he leaves the house.'

'And in the house? Is he safe here? His enemies infiltrated the page, Barty, to steal his papers. Couldn't they find a serving man willing to slip poison in his wine?' Her intelligence was daunting and it led her onto precarious ground.

'The Duke is served by faithful followers,' I said pompously. 'Besides, his enemies have embarked on the process of impeachment. That's the lawful way to remove one of the King's counsellors. Why should they resort to violence before Parliament has given its decision?'

'Perhaps because they do not trust the King to accept the will of Parliament.'

'For God's sake, don't speak like that to anyone but me.'

'You believe Suffolk will fall?'

'He'll resist the accusations brought against him but he knows the risks. This is why I suggested we might seek a future away from his service before we're forced to make difficult choices.'

'Ah! You admit your cowardice?'

'Cowardice?

'Running away is cowardly. Taking action is bold.'

'I proposed taking action but you didn't approve.'

She tossed her head and ignored my logic. 'If there's uncertainty about the outcome of the lawful process his enemies might deem it wise to take swifter measures. And they may cover their tracks. You have been blamed before for the death of a Duke.'

I shuddered and my voice was weak. 'Why should I be blamed?'

'Who better than a physician to administer poison? That's what will be said, as it was when Gloucester died. And if you have no other patronage, who will protect you? You would be martyred this time, Harry. But I refuse to share your martyrdom. I scorn your cowardly scruples. Let me pass. I am going to the Duchess.'

She strutted out of the room leaving me perplexed by her reasoning and distressed by her lack of reasonableness. Her disdain cut me the more acutely because her imagination had led her so close to the crux of Boice's bullying, while she remained ignorant of his threat to harm her. Worse still: she had realised I might be accused of murder even if someone else was guilty and that was a shocking idea because I knew it could be true. However honourably I acted, refusing to yield to menaces, it could avail me nothing if others were determined to hold me culpable.

*****

After our corrosive exchange Kate and I became politely distant from each other and avoided further conversation on tendentious issues. It helped that we were both busily occupied as affairs of state meant that the Duke and Duchess needed the backing and solace of their attendants but it tore my heart to see my wife looking more drawn and miserable as the days passed. On the one occasion when I asked if she felt unwell she repulsed me with mockery and I dared not question her again.

King Henry summoned Parliament to meet in Leicester, a centre of royal support, and Suffolk was heartened by the prospect. Within a few days, however, members of the Commons had refused to bow to this decree, insisting they would meet in Westminster and come forward with their detailed bill of impeachment, free from intimidation. They published the first draft of their case and Suffolk spent hours closeted with his secretary preparing his defence. Then, while clerks went scuttling from his study to make fair copies of his submission, he sent for me. I found him sitting at his table with clenched fists in his lap, his appearance that of a man ten years older than he was.

'Well, Harry, we have the first inkling of the charges against me and I'm told there are more to come. Some are absurd. They suggest I've conspired with the French to murder King Henry and taken bribes from them to surrender Normandy. I'm supposed to be plotting to get my son on the throne, no less, by betrothing him to the Beaufort heiress. There's utterly no proof, of course, but that won't stop invention.'

'They're the kind of allegations that get added to a weak indictment – wishful thinking. Isn't there anything more substantial?'

Suffolk sighed and I saw I had touched a raw spot. 'There's a list of so-called corrupt practices, filtering money from the Treasury, misuse of funds, they call it. I'm said to have impoverished the King, siphoned off revenue and possessions from his Duchy of Lancaster.'

'Have they evidence for these assertions?' I already knew the answer.

The Duke spread his fingers wide on the table-top and stared at them. 'The papers that were stolen by that wretched page have provided some material. They can be construed as giving a basis for their contention. It's not irrefutable proof and I shall deny what they allege but they

297

will claim there is a case to answer. There are other charges being framed but meanwhile I'm to answer to the Commons tomorrow. I should like you to attend me.'

I must have looked startled and he gave a wry smile. "It's not unreasonable for a man facing impeachment to have his physician at his side when he appears before the court of Parliament. Listen carefully to all that is said and study their expressions. I can rely on you to peer into their minds and advise me with impartiality.'

So it was that I witnessed the assembled Commons when they arraigned the King's chief adviser. I stood with other attendants in a cluster at the back of the hall as the indictment was read out and Suffolk confronted his accusers with a straight back, well poulticed with lubrication, and his head held high. The atmosphere was heavy with tension, the air we breathed infused with aggression, and the upturned faces of the Commons members, row upon row of them, displayed their hunger for vengeance, long suppressed and now released to savour its reward. They were like ferocious animals freed from restraint with the aroma of fresh meat titillating their snouts. They would glory in the kill.

William de la Pole gave as good an account of himself as any man could in the face of such formidable opponents. He spoke with confidence and apt, if assumed, humility. He specified his past services to King and country, the wounds he had suffered fighting across the Narrow Sea, the peace he had brought the kingdom, the loyalty he had always shown to his liege lord. His performance was impressive and what he said was true but it was not the whole story. His audience were aware of the self-serving acquisition, the sale of offices, the arrogant dismissal of criticism, which had gone hand in hand with his undoubted achievements. He would never sway them and he could not refute every charge.

I rode at his side on our return to the Manor of the Rose and he spoke only once as we galloped along the

Strand in the midst of an armed escort. 'I have ordered the Duchess and her ladies must leave for Wingfield in the morning with my son. They must be safely away from the City before I am arrested. Mistress Somers should go with them.'

He was a practical man and after facing the Commons he did not entertain false hopes. He deserved a matter-of-fact reply although my heart ached.

'That's prudent, your Grace,' I said. 'I am grateful'.

*****

I expected consternation and turmoil at the Manor of the Rose and was not surprised to see wagons in the courtyard ready to be loaded with the ladies' baggage. Already travelling chests and bales of wall hangings were being stacked beside the carts while retainers were staggering down the stairs with the Countess's favourite chairs and footstools. I hurried to my quarters to help Kate get ready for her departure but she was not there and I saw no sign anything had been packed. I imagined she must be assisting her mistress before making her own preparations and sat down to pull off my boots. A loud thump on the door brought me to my feet again as a white-faced maid servant ran into the room without waiting to be called.

'It's Mistress Somers, sir. She's taken awful bad. They've laid her on cushions in the Duchess's solar. That's where she was when it happened. Please come, sir.'

In stockinged feet I shot out of the door behind the girl. 'What happened? What's wrong with her? Was there an accident?'

My messenger gave a quick glance over her shoulder. 'Old Syb says it's a miscarriage, sir. She knows about these things. There's an awful lot of blood.'

I thundered past the maid to reach the solar. Why had Kate not told me she was pregnant? Was she not certain or did she sense all was not right? She must be frightened and distressed. I wanted to hold her in my arms and re-assure her. Such things were not uncommon when a woman conceived for the first time. She must not let grief overwhelm her. I dashed into the Countess's rooms and staggered to a halt.

Kate was enveloped in a blanket but blood was still oozing through the thick folds of material. Her face was deathly pale. A clutch of attendants were at her side, mopping her brow, offering her small beer and scrubbing the floor nearby from which the tiny residue of her disaster had already been removed. I dropped to my knees, grasping her hand, petrified by the sight of her haemorrhage.

'Kate, my sweet. I'm here. We'll do what we can to staunch your bleeding. Don't be afraid.' She shut her eyes and turned her head away as I stood up and the elderly attendant I recognised as Syb whispered in my ear.

'I've given her an infusion of the root of lady's mantle, doctor. It's what we do in such cases but the loss is very heavy, more than is natural. She mustn't be moved.'

'You're quite right. Do you need anything from my pharmacy?'

The old woman lowered her eyes with a crafty expression. 'I've my own stock, Doctor Somers. Just things for women's use, you understand.'

I nodded, in no mood to remonstrate with one who usurped my physician's role but probably knew as much as any university-trained man about female troubles. I sank back beside my wife, smoothing her hair from her face and stayed with her as she slipped into restless sleep, moaning and muttering indistinctly. Syb brought more of the infusion she recommended for her patient to sip and as the evening wore on the horrific bleeding lessened and Kate's slumber became peaceful. Maid servants brought more cushions and blankets so I could lie comfortably beside my wife and bring warmth to her frigid limbs.

In the morning the Duchess came to check on Kate's condition before setting out on the journey to Wingfield and I was touched by her genuine concern.

'It's too early to be confident but I think she will recover, your Grace. Old Syb thinks so too if we can build up her strength with broths and pottage. She's lost a great deal of blood.'

'Poor girl. She has a delicate frame and it's always sad to lose a first baby. I shall pray for her health. When she's strong enough she must join us at Wingfield.' Duchess Alice drew her mantle tighter over her shoulders. 'By then you may be free to come to us yourself, with or without my husband.'

The look she gave conveyed her meaning and I realised she was under no illusions as to the Duke's chance of escaping with his life from his enemies. 'God keep you, your Grace,' I said. 'I wish it may be that I can serve you in happier times.'

The house was quieter after the ladies had gone and Kate slept undisturbed. Syb was released from the kitchen to sit with her while I attended to my duties and we agreed that, if her condition had stabilised, she could be carried to her own bed later in the day. Meanwhile I returned to our rooms and snatched a little sleep to revive myself before Suffolk was ready for me to pummel his back and loosen his taut muscles. Then I went into the pharmacy to mix more of his embrocation.

It could not be accidental. There was no attempt to hide what had occurred. The lids of the boxes were open and leaves of pennyroyal and tansy were scattered by a flask which still contained the dregs of a mixture. I sniffed it and confirmed that the two herbs had been used in a powerful concentration, dangerously powerful. I stood for a moment as if paralysed and old Syb's cautious voice echoed in my head, speaking of my wife's loss of blood – 'more than is natural'.

I groaned and leaned my arms on the shelf, bowing my head, fighting back nausea before I began to sob. It was all clear to me. It had not been the maid, Joanna, who obtained illicit supplies from my store, but my own wife. By popular tradition, small amounts of pennyroyal were

301

said to hinder conception and I suspected now that Kate had been dosing herself with it for many months, although ultimately it had not been successful. Tansy was valuable for treating digestive problems but high doses were used by the unscrupulous to abort an unwanted child, despite its perilous toxicity. Tansy and pennyroyal in combination might have a devastating effect. It was difficult to believe Kate knew how to prepare the requisite mixture but I had no doubt she had brought about her miscarriage. She had nearly killed herself because she did not want our child – the child I longed for us to nurture – and she might still die from her own ministrations.

I slumped in a chair trying to compose myself before joining the Duke, determined to show no sign of my heartache, but rather than soothing thoughts vile questions formed in my mind. Was it possible the child was not mine? Had she lied to me about her fidelity? Was that why Kate had taken such desperate steps? How could this rift between us ever be repaired?

*****

For the next few days Kate hovered between life and death and I was torn by love akin to hatred and an agony of spirit I could barely contain. Then gradually she grew stronger and my confidence increased that she would recover. I knew that when she was well enough I must speak openly of all I suspected and feared, for we could not sustain our marriage on the foundation of deceit and mistrust she had created. I dreaded the prospect of hearing her confirm my nightmarish suppositions but neither could I bear the continuing uncertainty. The only relief I found came from concentrating on the dreadful fate which loomed over the Duke and giving him what succour I could as his physician. I was trapped between two disasters.

As the season of Lent approached the pace of events accelerated. The full Bill of Impeachment was produced, with its mishmash of serious, trivial and false accusations, and the Commons asked the Lords to commit Suffolk to the Tower of London while the process was completed. The order for his arrest was not forthcoming immediately but his hope of evading imprisonment now rested entirely with his royal patrons, although I identified a hazard closer at hand.

'I shall go to Westminster today,' he told me when I entered his room overlooking the inner court and found him formally arrayed in his court gown, wearing his chains of office. 'The Lords will not hesitate for long and I need to forestall their action. I shall throw myself at King Henry's feet to beg protection.'

'Your Grace, I don't advise leaving the house. Have you spoken to the captain of your guard? The rabble collected in front of your gates will tear you to pieces if you set foot outside. Even your bodyguard won't be able to guarantee your safety; there's a horde of angry citizens gathered and many of them are well armed. There are pikes and halberds, as well as swords and daggers. They're not just apprentices with their cudgels.'

He frowned at me with knitted brows. 'I can't cower indoors forever.'

'If you sent a messenger to the palace, your Grace, a humble fellow, not in livery, who could slink out of the postern without attracting attention, he could ask for a strong royal escort to be sent to fetch you. If the mob sees the King's colours and believes they've come to arrest you, they'll cheer them on their way and you'll only suffer their jeering.'

'A cheerful scene you offer me. Send the captain of my bodyguard in and I'll see what he says.'

As I expected the captain endorsed my suggestion and later that day the unobtrusive messenger returned with the assurance that a royal troop would be sent the following morning to convey the Duke to Westminster. In the midst of his troubles Suffolk was generous enough to thank me for the plan and he asked me to be in attendance when he went to the palace. Then he dismissed his

303

followers and retired to his chamber to write to Duchess Alice.

I walked, deep in thought, to the room where Kate was lodged so my comings and goings would not disturb her. Who could tell what would happen to Suffolk when he appeared before the King? The atmosphere was so febrile, he could be arraigned, imprisoned, summarily executed. The least likely outcome was escape. He would of course be well attended when he went to Westminster, but what would befall his coterie of gentlemen and guards thereafter was difficult to assess. If he was held in honourable confinement, as his status merited, he would require his personal retainers to be on hand to serve him – and that would include his physician who strove to prevent the muscles of his back from becoming rigid. It was impossible to tell when I might return to the Manor of the Rose and I was unwilling to leave my wife with so much unresolved between us. Full of foreboding, I had to speak to her.

I was encouraged to find Kate sitting beside her bed on a low chair and there was a faint tinge of colour in her cheeks although dark rings framed her extraordinary eyes. She gave a start when I opened the door but she had become used to my silence in her presence and quickly gazed down at her lap. I stood still until she realised I was not going to ignore her and looked me in the face.

'I'm glad to see you regaining strength. In two weeks or so you should be well enough to travel by litter to Wingfield and join your companions. I'll ask the steward to arrange this but I have to accompany the Duke to Westminster tomorrow and I cannot tell when I will be free to return here.'

She stared at me blankly. 'You fear imprisonment?'

'Not for myself, I trust, but perhaps for the Duke. He wishes me to attend him.'

She leaned her head against the chair back. 'I see.' She closed her eyes as if dismissing me but I could not let the moment pass.

304

'Kate, I don't know when I shall see you again and there are things I must say. We cannot leave this void between us. I need to understand. I know what you did, what you had been doing in the hope of preventing your pregnancy. But I don't understand why. I beg you to tell me the truth.'

Her mouth twisted into an ugly sneer. 'You think you've been cuckolded? That the child was not yours?' Perhaps it would have been better if that was true.'

I controlled my breathing. 'What do you mean?'

'Poor dishonoured man! It's beyond your comprehension that your wife did not want your child. Your child: it was no one else's.'

I bowed my head, acknowledging her admission. 'Why didn't you tell me you were afraid of childbirth?'

'What good would it have done? I'd heard tales that it could be averted and with your store of herbs I hoped for success so that I never became with child. When that failed I took more extreme steps. I knew miscarrying by my own hand might kill me. It seemed preferable.'

'Preferable to becoming a mother? I don't understand.'

Kate's voice became shrill and she flapped her arms, knocking a dish from the bedside table. As it shattered on the floor she picked up a goblet and hurled it across the room with a hideous laugh. 'You know I come of tainted stock. Not just the Devereux with their incestuous lust. I have Neville blood too. You more than anyone should know what that might mean. Neville women can bear monsters, two-headed distortions, horrible unnatural creatures with four arms and four legs but one belly. Is that what you want from me? That's why I had to kill the thing inside me. It might have been a devilish perversion and I refused to give it birth.'

I rocked on my heels. I should have been sympathetic, comforting, re-assuring to a young woman in deep torment but I could only register one incomprehensible fact. 'How do you know of that abnormal birth?'

She gave me a withering look. 'You think such a freak can be kept secret, to save the reputation of the quack who brought the thing to birth? News travels, husband. It takes its time but news travels to the court and when the story spread to Westminster Baron Thornton told me with some relish of your involvement. He was not impressed when he met you and delighted to demean your reputation. Once I knew what had happened to Lady Iffley I swore an oath before the Holy Mother of God that I would never give birth to an aberration which defies His Blessed will.'

I sank down on my haunches beside her. I was pained to realise the extent of her ignorance and fear, filled with guilt that I had assumed her more sophisticated than she was and underestimated her susceptibility to alarming folktales. 'Weirdly abnormal births are very rare, Kate. Most midwives go their whole lives without encountering even the smallest deformity in a baby they've delivered. We have no understanding why the occasional quirk of nature occurs. Some clerics claim it is God's punishment for sin and that is not for a mere physician to judge but I know nothing to suggest a woman is more vulnerable because some distant relative bore a malformed child.'

Kate stared at me and bit her lip. 'So you say. And it was coincidence that you delivered the monster?'

'Completely. It was fortuitous I was in Dublin at all and a physician I had met before asked me to assist at a difficult birth. A physician or midwife cannot affect the shape of a new-born babe. Oh, I wish you had told me of your anxiety. I could have brought you re-assurance and comfort.'

She struggled to her feet, pressing hard on the arms of her chair. The colour had vanished from her cheeks. 'I would not have believed you, husband. What you have told me is too favourable to your interests to be credible.'

I stayed on my knees, looking up at her, fighting back the instinct to contradict her scepticism. 'Perhaps it is best that we shall be parted for a while. I pray that when we are reunited we may find a way forward together which pleases us both. Go to Wingfield as soon as you feel strong enough and rest there. God soothe your mind and keep you safe until we meet again.'

She inclined her head. 'I will leave the Duke's house as you suggest. God keep you too, Harry. I never expected to find the love in my heart that you have prompted. Take that admission as your due, if it brings you contentment. I conjecture that we may not meet again.'

She threw open the door for me to depart and although my lips parted to dispute her melancholy assertion I could not find the words to protest.

Chapter 25

I had little sleep that night as I tossed to and fro repeating in my head all that Kate and I had said to each other. Her state of mind was far more precarious than I had let myself acknowledge, her fancies wilder than could be explained by her combination of naiveté and panicky imagination. And I had failed her. I had not gained her confidence sufficiently to allay her fears or enable her to share them with me. I had always wanted to protect her and credited myself with the skill to calm her but I was wrong. I was lacking in ability, professional ability and loving, husbandly ability to safeguard the woman I had married from herself.

Bleary-eyed and dozy, I found it a relief to ride out of the Manor of the Rose with the substantial body of retainers who accompanied the Duke of Suffolk to Westminster. As I had foreseen the presence of the royal guard proved essential to secure our safe passage through the streets of the City to the palace. Crowds jeered and spat as we passed and as we approached Temple Church it was necessary for a cudgel-waving apprentice to be knocked to the ground by a soldier before the belligerent crowd quietened. Through the baying multitude William de la Pole rode with self-assurance and his followers felt bound to emulate his demeanour. Despite all I knew of his weaknesses I was proud to serve Suffolk that day and willed him to sustain his noble poise.

When we arrived at Westminster Palace Suffolk gave instructions to his followers, some to await him in the gatehouse and some to go with him into the King's presence. To my surprise he asked me to attend him and I made my way to his side through the ranks of liveried followers. His men at arms removed their helmets, becoming recognisable, and as I greeted him, Rendell winked.

'Good luck, Doctor,' he said. 'Mind you ain't sent to the Tower. Been there once as I remember.'

I was not grateful to be reminded how I had once been incarcerated in the Tower of London, threatened with execution, and I sincerely hoped I would never set foot there again. I scowled at my rascally young friend in mock annoyance. Nevertheless I did experience trepidation as I followed Suffolk into the royal apartments because I had offended Queen Margaret in the past and she would not forget my transgression.

Seven of us stood in a semi-circle behind the Duke as he faced the dais, waiting for King Henry, and my fears were realised when the Queen and two of her ladies entered first and took their positions to the right of the throne. We all bowed and lifted our heads to see Margaret of Anjou appraising us with narrowed eyes, her luxuriant auburn hair partly hidden by the diaphanous veil beneath her crown. She peered at me and addressed Suffolk.

'Doctor Somers is your physician, my lord Duke?'

'Your Grace, he is my physician and my valued friend. He has served me loyally.'

The Queen raised her eyebrows and gave a deprecating smile. 'Then he is welcome to our court as your faithful devotee.'

I bowed again, full of gratitude to Suffolk for his endorsement and hope that the Queen, who clearly esteemed him, would support his cause against unjustified slurs. Then the door behind the throne was flung open and King Henry took his place. It was several years since I had seen him at close quarters and I could be confident he would not remember me. He did not look in good health, his cheeks gaunt and his complexion sallow, but the blankness in his eyes worried me most. He was reputed to be pious by nature, a gentle soul who would never ride boldly into battle as his martial father had done, but one who gained pleasure from founding schools and colleges, places of learning and divinity. He was known to adore his vivacious wife and I did not doubt she was able to influence his actions with a flick of her fingers.

We made our obeisance and Suffolk fell to his knees.

'Your Highness, my sovereign and puissant prince, I humbly come before you as your most true and dedicated servant, to beg your assistance. Parliament has formulated this Bill against me, peppered with allegations of little substance, and it's clear that my enemies are intent on my destruction. I have ever been your loyal follower, serving to the utmost of my ability, whether on the battlefield or in the council chamber, and I crave your aid to thwart those who would crush me like a beetle underfoot.'

The King looked uncomfortable but Queen Margaret lifted her chin and beamed triumphantly at the assembly during an awkward pause before her husband spoke.

'My lord Duke,' he said in a tremulous voice, 'we regret the circumstances which have led us here. The charges raised against you have been read over to me and they are weighty, albeit perhaps inflated by the resentment and envy of lesser men. It had seemed appropriate to reserve the case for my own judgement as your overlord and King...' He wavered and in the hiatus I glimpsed the flush on Suffolk's cheek as the possibility of a royal pardon occurred to him.

'It cannot be, however,' the King continued with a sideways glance at his wife. 'My faithful Lords will not have it and have ruled that the impeachment sought by the Commons must proceed. I am advised it would be wholly improper for me to intervene in the way I had considered.'

'Highness,' the Duke spoke into the silence which followed the King's words, 'may I know who has advised you in these terms on behalf of the Lords?'

'My dear and steadfast cousin, Richard of York: who loves me well and has sent me word from Ireland through one of his closest adherents.'

Queen Margaret could contain her decorous serenity no longer and she sniffed. 'I pray God your

310

Grace's trust is not misplaced. Richard of York has his own devious aspirations and he is served by villains.'

I knew to my cost it did not do to cross the Queen but I admired her decisiveness. She was no fool.

The King did not contradict his wife but continued with his prepared speech. 'I wish to deliberate further and to take advice from the widest number of my advisers but I am informed that while no action is taken to implement the Bill, which the Commons have promoted, there is unrest in the country and especially in the City of London. You yourself, my lord Duke, are at risk from the vicious mob and we need look no further than the appalling death of our beloved Bishop of Chichester to see what might befall you. For your own safety therefore, during my consideration of the case against you, I decree that you be lodged in the Tower in honourable confinement, not as prisoner found guilty of crimes alleged against him but as a guest, who for his own security needs the protection of stout walls and armed guards.'

Suffolk gulped but otherwise showed no emotion. 'Your Grace is most considerate. May I be accompanied by my closest retainers?'

The King sighed with relief and I guessed he had feared the Duke would dispute his ordinance. 'Certainly, certainly. Make your arrangements with the Constable of the Tower. He will provide accommodation fitting for your rank. I trust your stay there will be short and a resolution of this most unfortunate contretemps can be found.' His gloomy tone suggested he lacked confidence in this outcome.

The King rose and we bowed as he left the room. Queen Margaret followed but as she crossed the dais she smiled down at Suffolk. 'Courage, mon ami,' she said. 'We will thwart those who wish you ill. Bâtards!'

We were still chuckling at her imprecation when a captain of the royal guard stepped forward. 'My lord Duke', he said 'my instructions are to take you under heavy guard by river to the Tower so that the populace believe you are under arrest. Your retainers can follow in your train.'

'I understand. Please ask my sergeant to lead my bodyguard back to my house. They are waiting in the gatehouse. My body servants should accompany me to the Tower, along with these gentlemen beside me.'

The captain saluted and sent a soldier to do the Duke's bidding while Suffolk turned to me.

'I'm a physician, not a gentleman,' I said, trying to lighten the tension in the chamber.

'You forget,' the Duke replied, 'you hold the manor of Worthwaite from me. That confers something akin to gentlemanly status. In any case I claim your allegiance, Harry, whatever may transpire.'

'You have it, your Grace.' I spoke wholeheartedly, not simply for Suffolk's sake but because it suited my convenience to be absolved from the need to return to the Manor of the Rose, at least until Kate had safely left for Wingfield.

*****

Disembarking at the Watergate and making our way across the wide courtyards inside the walls of the Tower brought back grim memories for me and I shivered. Those with whom I had allegedly been associated in treasonous necromancy nine years earlier died at the stake or on the executioner's block; I would have been throttled at the end of a rope had I not been saved. Fortunately it soon became clear that Suffolk was to be lodged in airy, well-furnished quarters, very different from the noisome cell in which I had awaited my fate. The Constable of the Tower was in attendance to ensure the rooms were adequately fitted out for such a distinguished guest and each of the Duke's followers was given a clean pallet fragrant with dried herbs. My sleep should be undisturbed by spectres from the past.

For the first two weeks of Suffolk's confinement I did not venture outside the confines of the Tower but there was no prohibition on his followers coming and going, subject to a search for hidden weapons on re-entry, so I arranged to call on Thomas and Grizel who lived nearby. I left by the land gate to make my way towards St. Olave's Church but I had no sooner reached the row of houses facing the fortress on Tower Hill when a man stepped from a side-door directly into my path.

'We are destined to meet in the shadow of the Tower, it seems, Doctor Somers. Once again I have been waiting for you to give you greetings and convey a message.'

I looked around quickly, glad to see other folk were in the street nearby. 'Master Boice, you cannot expect me to reciprocate or welcome your ambush.'

'Ambush? Ah, you are so lacking in trust. I admit it is not by chance that we are encountering each other. My message for William de la Pole is that all gates to the Tower, including the Watergate, are being watched day and night. If he should imagine at any time that he could engineer his escape, he will be detected and accosted – none too peaceably. For his own welfare and to uphold the rule of justice in the realm, Suffolk will remain confined until sentence is passed on him.'

'As decreed by Richard of York's vigilantes, I presume.'

'The Duke of York is King Henry's most loyal servant and we who are privileged to serve him are committed to the best interests of the kingdom. You really are extraordinarily blinkered, Harry, not to join us.'

'I've given you my answer and it hasn't changed, despite your threats and physical assault. I shall inform the Duke of your message. Excuse me.'

I took a step to my side but he moved in parallel with me. 'When we met before you spurned my suggestion that you could contrive a speedy resolution of the King's dilemma by easing Suffolk on his way to God's judgement.

313

Think how much more cogent my argument has become now our sainted King has his esteemed adviser locked in his bastion with the Commons baying for blood. Any display of leniency on Henry's part will rebound against his Highness, even threaten his hold on the crown. Assuredly it would be a gracious act to release us all from further anguish by expediting the conclusion which must be inevitable.'

'No!' I turned my back on him but he pulled my sleeve.

'Permit me to enquire as to the well-being of the delightful Mistress Somers. I heard she has been in indifferent health.'

I cursed under my breath. How the devil did he know that? 'She has suffered a woman's complaint but will soon be restored to health.'

'I'm relieved to hear it. You will recall I did suggest she might suffer if you were foolishly recalcitrant and disobliging.'

'So you did and I abominated your gross intimidation. Fortunately, although my wife has faced difficulties they are in no way attributable to your evil intentions. Good day to you.'

This time he did not attempt to hinder my progress but his sneering chortle followed me as I hurried on my way.

*****

By coincidence Rendell was visiting Grizel and Thomas when I arrived and I learned he was spending a good deal of time with his sister's family while there was little to occupy the Duke's bodyguard at the Manor of the Rose. He started to tease me about my second period of residence at the Tower but Grizel caught my frown and sent him off with Thomas to inspect some wood-carving in the carpenter's workshop. Her sons were playing in the yard but her infant daughter was toddling at her feet,

314

pulling at her skirt and tumbling over in a fit of giggles. I had interrupted her in stowing some pots on a shelf and she handed me the largest to hold while she made room for it.

'If the City has anything to do with it, Suffolk's head'll be parted from his shoulders before he leaves the Tower. The King won't try to save him surely?'

'He looked distraught at the allegations against Suffolk.'

'You've seen the King! My, you are flying high with the Duke. Don't get dragged down with him. Oops! Up you come, Margery. There, there, you're not hurt.' She cuddled her daughter and observed me over a tangle of baby curls. 'Why haven't you left his service? Was it Kate?'

'She wasn't pleased at the idea but in any case I can't abandon him now.'

Grizel gave a snort. 'Are you happy with her?'

I had known Grizel for a long time and she was entitled to ask me a personal question but I was unable to give her an adequate answer. 'I love her but her moods are difficult to cope with – she's so fanciful.'

'Why hasn't she gone to Wingfield with the Duchess? Rendell said she was still at Suffolk's house.'

I sighed. 'She's been ill. She'll go to Wingfield when she's strong enough.' Grizel fixed her eyes on mine. 'She lost a baby.'

'Oh, Harry, why didn't you say so? It's not uncommon with a first but you must be so sad. She can always come here if she needs a refuge – but maybe being with the children wouldn't be tactful.'

It was a generous offer because Grizel had not taken to Kate. I held out the pot I was still holding. 'Thank you. Listening to your calm common sense might help her.'

Thomas and Rendell appeared at the door to the workshop as Grizel chuckled. 'D'you hear that, Thomas Chope, Harry's praising my calm common sense?'

'Oh Christ, if he only knew!' Thomas thumped me on the shoulder. 'Meant to stick together, husbands are.'

315

'If you ask me, husbandhood is a state best avoided,' his brother-in-law said. 'Makes a man feeble-minded.'

'We'll remind you of that one day,' Thomas laughed as his wife passed little Margery into his arms.

I turned to Rendell. 'Grizel says Kate's still at the Manor of the Rose. Do you know how she is?'

He winked. 'Heard the steward arranging for a litter to take her to Wingfield next Tuesday so I reckon she's all right. Will you come and see her before she leaves?'

'I'm not sure I can,' I said, inventing desperately. 'We're not always free to leave the Tower. Kate knows that. We said goodbye.'

Rendell opened his mouth but he must have glimpsed his sister shaking her head and, unusually, he stayed quiet.

Before I set out on my return I mentioned to Thomas my encounter with Stephen Boice at the house on Tower Hill and his long campaign of menaces against me. If I were to suffer death in unexplained circumstances, my friend would know where to look for an explanation.

*****

I felt guilty that my friends' uncomplicated happiness made me depressed and I did not leave the Tower precincts for the next twelve days. I spent much of my time talking with Suffolk and found him increasingly philosophical about his prospects, recognising that his time of ascendancy was over. To escape with his life was as much as he could hope for and even that was ambitious. He continued to have faith in the goodwill of the King and Queen but he understood how limited was their ability to save him without incurring the wrath of nobles and Commons alike.

The Duke received letters, scrutinised first by the Constable, and it was one from the steward at the Manor of the Rose which brought my days of peaceful inertia to an end. I was with Suffolk as he scanned the short communication and watched his expression darken.

'This concerns you, Harry. I'm sorry. Something is very wrong. Mistress Kate is missing.'

I took the letter he held out and read it with increasing horror. As planned, Kate had departed, with old Syb attending her, conveyed by litter and escorted by three armed men. The steward sent a messenger ahead to Wingfield to inform the Duchess that Mistress Somers was on her way and it was only after several days, when the travellers did not arrive, that a courier was sent back to London recording concern. The steward had now initiated enquiries to trace my wife's whereabouts but he suggested I might wish to call at the Manor of the Rose to discuss what more could be done.

'You must go at once, Harry,' the Duke said. 'God grant there is some harmless explanation.'

'Most likely Kate was ill again on the journey,' I said with composure I did not feel. 'Although it's strange no message was sent to explain the delay. I'll return as soon as I can, your Grace.'

I ran and stumbled my way across the City and when I reached the Duke's house I was panting. The steward did nothing to allay my fears but took me to his room and poured wine with a shaking hand.

'Forgive me, Doctor Somers,' he said. 'I did not put all I've gleaned into my letter. There are delicacies which I thought best not to commit to paper.' He saw my alarm and shook his head. 'No reason to think your lady's come to harm but something strange has occurred. Maybe I should have realised it was odd from the beginning.'

I had no idea what to expect. 'Tell me everything, please.'

The steward swallowed some wine and brushed his sleeve across his mouth. 'Mistress Somers seemed much recovered and Syb told me she was fit to make the journey to Wingfield. I gave permission for the old woman to go with her and said I would order a litter and provide armed attendants. Then Syb brought me a message that Mistress Somers was making her own arrangements, using people she knew. She used your name, Doctor, to satisfy me that the men were reliable. True enough they were neatly turned out when they came and most respectful to me. I know Mistress Somers can be a forceful lady, begging your pardon, so I never questioned what she'd done. Dear God, I should have done.'

He took another gulp of wine and I waited, my mind churning with outlandish fears which I tried to calm with logical thought. 'When the ladies of the Suffolk household travel to Wingfield there are standard places they stop overnight. The first is near Enfield so the sergeant sent one of his men to check whether Mistress Somers had arrived there. I had in mind to make enquiries all along the route if necessary but it seems she did not get that far. I'll never forgive myself, Doctor, if she's been abducted.'

'That doesn't seem likely. Is it possible she stayed the night elsewhere?'

'The man made enquiries at several establishments. He's one you know, Doctor: Tonks.'

I sighed with relief, assuring the steward he was in no way blameworthy, and asked that Rendell join me. He came quickly and gave me details he had not included in his report to his superiors.

'There ain't many places a lady could stay within five miles of Enfield. I went to them all. After I came back and saw the steward I made some more enquiries without telling him. I went round the gates of the City in case anyone remembered a litter with an armed guard leaving. I didn't think there was much hope but I found a fellow who recollected seeing a party that fitted the description. He knew one of the escort and they exchanged a joke or two so it stuck in his memory.' He paused.

'Which gate?'

'The far side of London Bridge.'

'So they were heading south?'

'Can't be sure it was Mistress Somers.' Rendell bit his lip. 'The men were wearing livery.'

'Whose?'

'The gatekeeper weren't certain because some noble families have a dozen variations but he thought the crest belonged to the Nevilles.'

I shut my eyes. 'It's very likely to be Kate.'

Rendell did not query my assumption. 'Are the Nevilles your enemies? Have they carried off Mistress Somers to spite you?'

'No, no, she went voluntarily. She organised it all to deceive us, so she could get well away before we traced her movements.' I stood straight and tried to look unperturbed. 'She's left me, Rendell,' I said and my quivering voice betrayed my desolation. 'She's left me.'

Chapter 26

Although I firmly believed what I had told Rendell I had to prove it to myself before I could consider the implications. There was one obvious place to start but it posed a difficulty because I dared not go in person to the court at Westminster while Suffolk was held in the Tower. There was too great a risk I would be recognised and rumours set running: that I was sent to plead for a pardon, or organise a surreptitious escape, or that I had abandoned the Duke and was laying evidence against him. I would not wish to make his position worse and would achieve nothing of use in my private quest by blundering in without warning. I needed to make an appointment in a place removed from Westminster.

It could also be self-defeating for Rendell to make enquiries at court on my behalf. There was a danger he could be identified as one of Suffolk's guards and if he did succeed in accosting Baron Thornton he might be brushed aside as a presumptuous nobody. Philip Neville would be alerted to my suspicions without condescending to meet me. My messenger must be a person of more substance, whom Thornton would not dismiss so readily.

Reluctantly I turned to Thomas who had helped me so often in the past. Now he was a family man with a prosperous workshop I hesitated to embroil him in problematic matters but in this case there seemed no risk to him. Indeed when I met him at the hostelry beside the Thames, where we had drunk together for many years, I found he had already engaged himself in my affairs.

'I asked around my contacts about the house on Tower Hill, where you met Master Boice,' he said. 'It's not rented in his name. Men come and go there all the time – watching the Tower, I suppose – but the lease has been taken by one Roger Egremont. I've never heard of him.'

'I have.' I set down my cup of ale and pulled a face. 'He has a title which he's chosen not to use. He's the Earl of Stanwick now. I had the misfortune to meet him in

Ireland. He's one of York's followers but unreliable and dissolute; I don't think the Duke has much time for him.'

'But he might have his uses to York's less respectable friends?'

'Exactly.' Then I explained the mission I wanted Thomas to undertake and of course he readily agreed. He went home to collect his horse and set off at once, arranging to meet me later at the Manor of the Rose, on his way home.

I told Rendell what Thomas was doing and after an initial complaint that he could have undertaken the task he acknowledged the good sense of what I had arranged. We waited together for his brother-in-law to return and he did so more speedily than we expected. It was easy to see from Thomas's expression that he had been unsuccessful in arranging a meeting for me but the reason was a surprise.

'Baron Thornton's not been at court for at least three months. I'm told he left well before Yule and is with most of the Neville clan at Raby Castle, far in the north of the kingdom.'

I nodded. 'I've been there. Do you trust what you've been told? Could you have been sold a packet of lies?'

'Not unless there's been a conspiracy involving gatekeepers, marshals, watermen and laundry maids. I asked half a dozen people after the chamberlain told me and it all added up to the same story in different terms. Philip Neville is at the other end of England. Do you think they're carrying Kate there? It would take weeks in a litter.'

'Hardly likely to set off by crossing the Thames to go south,' Rendell said. 'Even if they meant to put to sea, they could have done that from the wharves north of the river. The road from London Bridge leads into Kent.'

Kent. It was plausible. I should have thought of it. She had fled there when she wanted to escape her brother. But I had no idea where in the county her uncle's house was located and I knew of only one person who could tell me. 'Tom,' I said, 'do you know of a notary in the City, called Edward Devereux?'

His bushy eyebrows shot up in mock horror. 'Keep away from notaries as much as I can. I want to look after the money in my purse. But I'll find out, Harry. Give me a day and I'll find Master Devereux – provided you count me in for the next instalment of the search.' He glanced at his wife's brother. 'Not a word to Griz, Rendell.'

*****

In the event I went to the house on Ludgate Hill alone, pleading it was family business and I was hardly likely to run into danger in a notary's office. The obstacle to be overcome was Edward Devereux's unsmiling clerk who said his master was out and offered to book me an appointment in a week's time which I declined rather loudly. I sat down on a hard bench and declared I would wait. The disagreeable fellow glowered at me while he pretended to concentrate on the papers he was copying but eventually, when it was clear I was not going to move, he got up and sidled through a door behind his desk. Shortly afterwards he returned and, with minimum courtesy, beckoned me to follow him.

The thin-faced notary I remembered was not pleased to see me but he possessed a veneer of graciousness which his clerk had not learned to emulate. 'Doctor Somers, this is unexpected. Is there some bad news concerning my sister?'

'I hope not but I need your help. Kate had been unwell but was recovering and was due to travel to join the Duchess and her companions in the county of Suffolk. I have been in attendance on the Duke while he is lodged in the Tower but, as you see, I am not required to remain there permanently. It seems that Kate decided not to make the journey through East Anglia when she set out from the City. I believe she has gone to her uncle's house in Kent but I don't know where that is. I'd be grateful if you would tell me so I can contact her.'

Edward's strangely flecked eyes glinted as he gave a sarcastic smile. 'Kate has not informed you?'

'Communications have been difficult.' It sounded lame and I was irritated by his manner.

He fingered the lappets of his gown and adjusted it on his shoulders. 'I seem to recall advising you not to enmesh yourself with my sister. She has an affliction in her mind and has the capacity to cause you grief. Yet she is your wedded wife. You have every right to know her whereabouts and require her presence at your side. I cannot dispute that. The law upholds your rights and permits you to chastise her for disobedience.'

'I've no wish to chastise her. I want to help her recover a tranquil mind.'

'Bah! Such foolishness will only encourage her wayward behaviour. A birching would bring her to her senses.'

I bit the inside of my lip compelling myself not to rise to his provocation. 'I note your advice. I understand your sister has caused you annoyance in the past and I don't want to waste your time. If you would let me know where your uncle lives, I will leave you to your business.'

'Unfortunately, Doctor Somers, I do not have details of the location. I have never been close to my uncle, unlike my sister. His manor is in the vicinity of Canterbury: that is all I can tell you.'

'That may be sufficient for me to make enquiries. I'm obliged. His name is Devereux, I take it?'

His satisfied smirk was offensive. 'I'm afraid not. It is my late mother's brother we are speaking of: her younger brother. They and another sister were children of a Neville mother but their father had a less distinguished name. You may even have encountered Uncle Boice?'

My mouth fell open at the monstrousness of what he had said and I could not hide my revulsion. 'Stephen Boice?'

'I thought you might know him. He's a well-travelled merchant with a wealth of interests. Kate always had a fascination with him since she was little. We didn't see him often but he would laugh, bounce her on his knee and call her his creature. I hoped she had grown out of her discipleship but it seems she still turns to him for comfort. He has an amiable, patient wife, who's everything Kate is not; she would make her niece welcome at the manor-house. I shouldn't worry. She's in good hands.'

Our meeting was at an end and I left my good-brother's office without glancing at the affronted clerk hunched over his desk when I passed through the ante-chamber. I was unable to credit all I had heard, yet pondered deplorable possibilities. At least I was clear what I must do to resolve my doubts.

*****

I hammered at the door of the house on Tower Hill like the frantic madman I had become. If I had been capable of rational reflection I would have realised it was rash to call there unattended and in so agitated a frame of mind but I had no choice. The compulsion was overpowering and I must yield to it. Belligerently I demanded to see Master Boice and gave my name whereupon, with no demur, the servant admitted me to the entrance hall, bidding me sit on a cushioned form while he fetched his master. The ease of my reception calmed me a little.

Not long afterwards I was shown upstairs to a small and simply furnished room where a fire was burning in the grate, with a pair of chairs set each side of the hearth. A flagon of wine and two finely cut glasses stood on a table by the window. I was about to sit when I heard shuffling footsteps in the corridor so I remained standing and faced the door.

'By Christ and all the saints, it is you. God in Heaven has sent you here.'

Roger Egremont, Earl of Stanwick, lurched towards me, the wine on his breath noticeable from several feet away, the flush on his cheeks unhealthily angry. 'You snivelling, filthy swine, you tricked me out of my inheritance. You let them steal my promised bride, marry her to some Norman bastard.'

The effort of delivering this speech caused him to draw breath and he leaned against the table to steady himself.

'My Lord, I assure you I had no hand in the marriage of Mistress Eleanor. I beg your pardon, it's Master Stephen Boice I've come to see.'

The Earl snatched up a glass. 'But it's me you're seeing and me who'll teach you a lesson you'll not forget.' He smashed the bowl of the goblet against the table-top and with remarkable agility hurled himself forward with the jagged edge directed at my face. I side-stepped but one of the chairs was in my way and I blundered into it and was thrown off balance. I reached out with one hand to fend off my attacker and with the other attempted but failed to draw my dagger from within the folds of my gown. Roger Egremont threw himself onto me and we crashed to the floor where, with his considerable weight, he pinned me down. My cap fell off and I felt a trickle of blood run down my chin where the glass grazed me.

'Born with the Devil's mark on one cheek, weren't you. I'll match it with my carving on the other.'

I twisted my head as he jabbed at me, catching the broken glass in the neck of my jerkin, and I reached back to grab a log I glimpsed lying behind me. I had not realised it was smouldering at one end and when I brought it down on the Earl's head we were showered with sparks. Roger Egremont growled with fury and, seizing my throat, pushed my head towards the leaping flames. I heard the sizzle of scorched hair and began to panic.

'Stop this instant, you drunken sot!'

I had not heard the door latch but was suddenly aware of hands hauling my assailant off me so I could roll free and allow an attendant to press a cloth on the back of my neck.

325

'Take the Earl to his chamber and confine him there.'

The voice was familiar, one that in the past had sent me to be tortured and threatened my death, but now Gilbert Iffley, Baron Glasbury, was my improbable saviour and I struggled to my feet to thank him.

'The Earl is a liability we have to bear if we are to keep his support. His name counts for something even if his person is worthless. I hadn't expected you to enter the house. Is it possible you've experienced an epiphany and come to join us?' He gave a satirical smile but did not appear hostile.

'I'm afraid I must disappoint you. I came to see Stephen Boice. I believe my wife is at his house in Kent but I only know it is near Canterbury. I wish to write to her.'

Iffley adopted his most urbane manner. 'Ah, Harry, you and I have both married into that house of misbegotten Nevilles. I sympathise if Mistress Somers is at times wilful. Lady Glasbury is her aunt, you know, and inclined to be self-willed.'

'Is your lady in good health?'

He narrowed his eyes but did not change his tone. 'She is fully recovered from her misfortune nearly two years ago. It was completely accidental that you became involved in that sorry occurrence. I do not hold you in any way culpable for delivering that aberrant child. Only the ignorant spread that story.'

'Yet as I recall you struck me to the ground, had me thrown into a cell and left me to drown.'

'I had fathered a deviant monster and my wife might have died. I was distressed.'

He poured wine into the remaining intact glass and held it out to me but I shook my head. His riposte was outrageous but, given my relief at escaping Stanwick's violence, I found it amusing. 'Is Stephen Boice here?'

'Alas, no, Doctor Somers. He journeyed to St. Edmundsbury, where he has business interests, a week ago. If your lady is at his house in Kent, she is with his wife who is supposed to be level-headed and practical. I'm sure you need have no concern for Mistress Somers' welfare.'

'I'm grateful for the information. Do you know the exact location of Boice's house?'

'Alas, no.' He drank from the glass of wine and set it down. 'Heaven has willed this encounter between us, it seems, and I must use the opportunity it provides. I've made friendly overtures to you before, between the less agreeable episodes of our acquaintance. Trust me; I make this approach now in complete sincerity. William de la Pole will not survive his disgrace. One way or another you will soon be stranded without a master or a livelihood. Although I have found your stubbornness irksome and imprudent, I have a grudging respect for your foolish loyalty to your lord. But when Suffolk's head is off, perhaps you will come to your senses. Richard of York will overlook your earlier refusal to take action if you ask to join his household at that point. It is a generous offer, which I endorse. Bygones will truly be bygones if you join him then. Think about it, Harry.'

'I hear what you are saying but my service remains to the Duke of Suffolk.'

'Of course – for the moment. Let me escort you from the house to be certain Roger Egremont has not evaded his attendants. Remember what I've said. I wish you good fortune in finding and taming your passionate and impulsive wife.'

His description of Kate was all too apposite. I thanked God that Syb was with her.

*****

I regaled Suffolk with an account of my enquiries to distract him from frustration at the continuing silence from the King, although I did not mention Glasbury's renewed effort to entice me into York's camp. The Duke was immediately sympathetic and bade me go to Canterbury to locate Boice's manor and find Kate. He

327

wrote an instruction to his sergeant-at-arms that Rendell be allowed to accompany me on such an expedition and I hired horses for our departure two days hence.

In the meantime news came that Sir Thomas Kyriel with a force of three thousand men, mainly our famed English archers, had landed in Normandy. This cheered the Duke who retained hope that a victory across the Narrow Sea and the recovery of lost territory would change his fortunes and secure his resumption of power at the King's side. I was less sanguine but glad to see him in better spirits and easier in my mind at the prospect of leaving him without the attendance of his physician for perhaps a week.

Then later that day, on the eve of my intended departure, I received a letter, brought by hand from the Manor of the Rose, and it changed everything. It was from Kate although in a clerkly hand and I could not find an echo of her voice in its words.

Most honoured and esteemed husband, you will have learned by now that I chose not to join Duchess Alice at Wingfield but to seek respite elsewhere. I have found refuge at my uncle's house where I received succour once before. All is calm here and I welcome the gentle pace of life. My aunt is kind and I have the inestimable services of a physician, who has helped me previously, arranged by my dear uncle. He gives me physic which brings me rest and dulls my fears.

I wish to let you know that I am well cared for and more at peace than hitherto but I beg you not to try to find or contact me. My physician advises I should not be excited or disturbed as I would be if you were to come before I am totally freed from the devils which torment my mind. God keep you.

Above her untidy signature and the Devereux seal she insisted on using, a few words had been scored through so they were indecipherable.

I stared at the missive, full of apprehension. I did not question the facts it gave but the language was too cool and collected to reflect Kate's inner turmoil. Had it been dictated by someone else? What was this physic her doctor was supplying? Who was this unknown physician and what did he know of her condition?

I read the letter again and the horrible supposition became stronger. Boice had arranged for Kate to be attended by a physician with whom he was acquainted – and of course I knew one such, an admitted murderer, a suspected poisoner. Could it possibly be Willison? My mind raced with theories. The letter spoke of the physician helping Kate previously. Did that refer to her ostensible miscarriage? I had wondered how she was able to make up the dangerous mixture to abort our child. Had Willison directed her? And what was the nature of Kate's link to her uncle, disparaged by her brother? Edward referred to her 'discipleship' and called her his uncle's 'creature': could this have an atrocious connotation? Had she been placed in Suffolk's household to carry out her uncle's instructions? To suborn innocent pages, inducing them to spy on and steal from their master? To seduce me and seek to bend me to her will? Was Boice's threat to harm her simply a pretence to alarm me or had he consigned her to Willison's care to destroy her mind as my punishment?

I could not bear to speculate further. I was tempted to rip the letter into pieces, as if it had never existed, but instead I held it to the light and peered at the scrawled out words above her signature. By tilting it to catch the dying sunlight I could just distinguish them. They were in a different hand from the rest of the letter, Kate's jerky round hand which had signed her name. They said *I love you.*

Someone had tried to obliterate the message she had added and that terrified me. Had she scribbled over it herself or had someone censored her addendum?

But what was I to do? If I went careering to the countryside around Canterbury, as I had intended, I could be certain news of my presence would soon become known to Kate's keepers. What were the implications? If Willison

329

was with her, did he plot to kill her if I appeared? Or was he slowly destroying her with some foul medication that would fatally unbalance her disturbed mind? Would travelling there accelerate his despicable plans or could I thwart them? Was all my anguished speculation rubbish? Was I inventing bizarre scenarios which had no basis? Could Kate's physician be some benign fellow committed to curing her? Could my sudden arrival cause a relapse in her condition? I needed to think more clearly than I was capable of doing while in shock.

I sent a message to Rendell to delay our journey by one day to give me time to think and, during those twenty-four hours, although the uncertainties remained unresolved, my mind became more focused. I was satisfied that whatever the dangers I must go to Canterbury to discover the truth. Then, as evening drew on, visitors were admitted to Suffolk's chamber for private discourse and shortly afterwards I was summoned to join him. I was to be rapidly jolted out of my self-obsession.

Chapter 27

The strangers were royal officers come to require Suffolk's attendance before the King on the following day when, we were told, judgement would be given on the charges against him. He would inevitably take his retinue with him from the Tower and it was my duty to attend him. It meant a further postponement of my venture into Kent but, as it was to be expected that the sentence passed on the Duke would be implemented without delay, the likelihood was that I would soon be masterless and free to journey where I chose. Whatever mixed feelings I had towards William de la Pole, I could not begrudge him a further day of service.

We were taken by water to Westminster to avoid passing through the excited crowds gathered in the streets. Word was out that Suffolk was to be condemned and the citizens of London were avid to hear his doom and witness his execution. Even boatmen and their passengers hissed and made obscene gestures as our barge passed them and the air was redolent with antagonism. As always the Duke bore himself bravely in the face of so much hatred, his stance upright and his head high, but he winced and put his hand to the small of his troublesome back when he stepped ashore.

We were not conducted to the throne-room this time but to the King's innermost chamber where the assembly of lords and bishops was crammed into every space between furniture and wall hangings. I squeezed into position beside Suffolk's chaplain as the outer doors were shut and the King emerged from his private entrance. There was scarcely space for us all to bow to him. His face was gaunt and his knuckles blanched as he gripped the armrests of his chair. No one could doubt how painful the occasion was for our sovereign lord compelled to judge the misdemeanours of his friend.

King Henry signalled to Archbishop Kemp, the Lord Chancellor, and the long list of Suffolk's alleged misdeeds was read out: as before, a jumble of serious crimes and ludicrous inventions, all recited with equal solemnity. Then the King rose and William de la Pole dropped to his knees.

'My lord Duke,' the King said, 'I have formed my judgement on these accusations but it is your right to claim trial by your peers in respect of them. What is your will?'

Suffolk looked steadily at the King and it occurred to me that this exchange might not be spontaneous, their speech predetermined. 'Most puissant Highness, I am content to waive my right of submission to my peers and humbly accept your judgement.'

The King inclined his head. 'Then be it known that I find the group of accusations against you, which allege treason in your dealings with the French, not proven. There is no sufficient evidence for them. I do however uphold the lesser charges of interfering with the course of justice in our land and peculation in some dealings with our Treasury. In respect of this judgement, I therefore banish you from all our lands for five years, commencing from the first day of May in this year of grace. My officers will conduct you once again to the Tower.'

The intake of breath across the room was audible and almost drowned Suffolk's abject acceptance of his sentence. The King cast a regretful glance on his erstwhile adviser and turned away, leaving the chamber by the door behind him. At once a hubbub of muttering broke out, some lords welcoming Suffolk's reprieve from execution while others showed by their frowns and exclamations that they saw the King's intervention as a trick to preserve the life of his favoured counsellor. A neatly staged drama, I thought it, with a cleverly arranged but hazardous result. I recognised from his expression that the Duke thought so too. He knew King Henry's clemency would be criticised and his own safety would remain in jeopardy until he had sailed into exile from the land of his birth and pre-eminence.

We returned to the Tower and only then did I learn that the day's activities were not over. We were instructed to be ready to leave and take horse for Wingfield immediately. Late at night the Duke and his retinue were to be let out of the Tower in the hope that they could make good their escape without attracting the attention of pugnacious Londoners. Once in his own domains, Suffolk would be able to organise his crossing of the Narrow Sea, securing passage to a country willing to give him sanctuary.

Two emissaries from the court had joined us. The Frenchman, Jacques Blondell, came from the Queen's household. He had been detailed to serve the Duke in his exile and no doubt to report back to his mistress. Master Henry Spenser, a yeoman of the Crown, had a more specific and crucial role because he carried letters of safe conduct to the commanders of the garrison at Calais ordering them to assist Suffolk if he needed to make landfall there. Preparations for an orderly retreat from the realm were thorough and my companions were optimistic all would go well. I found myself a solitary voice of caution, reminding the Duke that all exits from the Tower were being watched and a departure, even at dead of night, might not secure him from attack. Nevertheless, there was no possibility of my concerns influencing his plans – through intermediaries they had been settled with the King and Queen and could not be amended.

The Duke seemed more alert to the perils facing him than many of his henchmen, handing out generous allowances of gold and urging his followers to have a care for themselves. Any of us who lost touch with the main party was to make his way to Wingfield as soon as possible. This suited me well. I did not question that I would start out in Suffolk's entourage but I hoped I might reasonably leave him when he was clear of London and its dangers so I could double back and head for Kent. I could not know how long I would need to find Kate and settle my mind about her welfare but the Duke would not be leaving the country for six weeks and I should have time to re-join him. Only when I was sure of Kate's safety would I be able to decide whether to accompany him across the sea.

I hoped I would have the opportunity to take Rendell with me into Kent and I was re-assured to see him in Suffolk's bodyguard drawn up in front of the Tower as we departed. We were an impressive company, mounted on horses selected for their speed, and we set out at a pace which was uncomfortably fast for me. For a few minutes it seemed the ploy was to be successful and our progress unhindered. I noticed a light was burning in a downstairs room of the house on Tower Hill but there was no sign of anyone leaving the premises to pursue us so I concentrated on controlling my powerful mount which demanded all my attention.

At the front of our troop torchbearers lit the way and there was fleeting moonlight from a cloudy sky. We were close-packed in the narrow streets and it was only necessary to see enough to keep head to tail with the rider in front and avoid bumping the riders to each side. Unfortunately my restless horse seemed irked by the dark rump under his nose and I needed to rein him back from trying to overtake with no space to do so. Then a more acute problem shattered the false respite we had been granted for, as we cantered towards Cheapside, from every side lane and alley furious citizens emerged, brandishing weapons and screaming their fury. Our speed quickened to a gallop as missiles were hurled by our pursuers and from windows above us. Stones cracked against metal of the armour worn by our soldiers and sticks landed at our horses' hooves, threatening to unseat the less experienced from their saddles. When an arrow whistled past my ear to bounce off the cuirass of a guard, ripping his cloak, I felt blind terror. I was unprotected by mail or plate armour or even a quilted jacket and I would stand no chance against steel. All I could do was ride faster than I had ever attempted and pray.

The ground was wet from earlier rain and as we pounded over uncobbled surfaces the mud became churned, sending gobbets of filthy clay to splatter our faces and impede our sight. I knew I could not sustain the pace for much longer while, conversely, my horse seemed invigorated by the chase and frustrated by my efforts to keep him constrained. A mouldy cabbage landed on my lap but while I rejoiced it was nothing more lethal the creature beneath me swerved out where the road widened and we hurtled past half a dozen serving men who shouted their annoyance at this undisciplined behaviour.

I recognised that we were approaching Newgate and when I realised from our increasing speed that the gates must be thrown open for us, I began to hope we might escape with only minor injuries. Despite the disorderly conduct of a few riders, or their horses, we had kept our compact formation and if the gatekeepers were vigilant they should be able to slam the gates shut without letting through more than a handful of pursuers in our wake. In more open country beyond the walls of the City we should be able to shake them off and, although I dreaded the prospect of giving my exuberant horse his head, I longed to be free from men bent on doing us injury.

My moment of hope was short-lived. We thundered through the gates into St. Giles without Holborn, an area of shabby dwellings housing impoverished labourers and their families but also feckless and untrustworthy rogues. I had not expected to encounter organised opposition there but I was wrong. Awaiting us as we rounded a bend, were serried ranks of armed adversaries wielding staves and swords, pick-axes and cudgels. It was cleverly arranged, catching us as we relaxed a little on escaping the City, and they exploited their advantage, falling on us with fury.

My horse had carried me towards the front of the troop and I saw the Duke pulled from his saddle but promptly hauled onto his sergeant's mount and carried off to safety. Some of his servants did not fare so well, manhandled onto the ground and beaten where they lay, while our orderly progress became a scrummage. I tried to direct my horse round two men tussling on the earth but their contortions must have disturbed him. The animal suddenly whinnied and reared, throwing me from my seat to crash among thudding hooves in a panicked stampede. I flung my arms over my head, trying to roll into a ball, but my thigh was kicked with such force than I felt sure the bone was fractured. I managed to drag myself painfully into a stinking runnel by the side of the road when hands grasped me and my chin was wrenched up to face a ruffian intent on brutal theft.

'Give me your purse.'

I had no intention of resisting but my pouch had slipped on my belt when I tumbled down and lay beneath me. I tried to wriggle and reach for it but my assailant mistook my movement and whacked me across the head with his cudgel so I fell back, half-stunned. Mysteriously, at the same time, he screamed and crumpled by my side as I heard a vaguely familiar voice saying, 'he's mine'. With a sickening squelch a sword was withdrawn from the thief's neck and in my befuddled state I thought Rendell had rescued me. Then I realised I had been preserved only for a more murderous foe to take his place when Roger Egremont, coldly sober, seized my shoulder and raised his bloodstained sword ready to slash my throat.

'I'll send you to hell unshriven, vile quack, and thank the saints for giving me my revenge.'

He lunged forward as I squirmed and his weapon slashed my upper arm. He lifted it again and grabbed at my hair to hold me still but then he doubled up with a groan and toppled sideways. I fancied my senses were disorientated causing me to imagine Rendell as my rescuer once again but this time it was true. He whipped his dagger from his victim's back and pushed the Earl aside.

'Got to get you out of this shambles before a third comes after you. Christ knows what they see in you! That bump on your head's swelling as I look at it and your arm's bleeding.'

'My leg,' I mumbled as he dragged me upright and slung me over his shoulder. Before he transferred me to his horse I had lost consciousness.

*****

I knew where I was when I came to myself, not by recognising the room or the roof outside visible from the window but because of the small interloper who had crawled onto my pallet and was peering into my battered face.

'Mam, Mam, his eyes are open,' Hal called and Grizel scurried into the attic with a baby under one arm and two squabbling infants at her heels.

'Thank the Lord, Harry. We've been worried about you. Do you remember the skirmish?'

My thoughts seemed to take up where I had left them. 'My leg,' I said, feeling my thigh and finding no splint.

'There's a bruise with the fine impression of a horseshoe but the bone's not broken. You'll be up and about within the week.'

'Rendell brought me here?'

'I did, God knows how many times I've saved your life. Fair monotonous, it is.'

He had followed his sister into the room and intermittently over the next two days I pieced together from him all that had happened since the encounter at St. Giles without Holborn. It appeared that Suffolk and most of his followers had got away safely into East Anglia and Rendell had left a message about my condition with the steward at the Manor of the Rose who was to act as the hub of communications for the Duke and his scattered entourage.

337

While Grizel was out of earshot I asked Rendell if he knew what had happened to the man he stabbed. 'Did you see? Had you killed him?'

'Dunno. As I rode off with you I saw blokes run over and bend down beside him. Why should you be bothered? He'd have done for you.'

'He's a contemptible wretch but it happens he's a belted Earl and if he's dead there might be a fuss.'

'Christ! What was an Earl doing in that rumpus?'

'Looking for me, I imagine. Best lie low for a while until things quieten down.'

Rendell rubbed his nose. 'Reckon they'll get worse first. There's been more rioting in the City since Suffolk got away. Men are angry at being robbed of their prey. Some are acting stupid. There's a vintner's servant to be executed for going round shouting daft words. How'd it go? *By this town, by this town, for this array the King shall lose his crown'.*

I shivered at that chillingly treasonable sentiment, which turned the City's recriminations directly towards King Henry himself. 'Best not repeat those words. It's a chancy time.'

Rendell was no longer clad in livery and he had permission to attend me until I was sufficiently recovered to go to Wingfield. When I could limp from my bed and tentatively put weight on my sore leg I explained the journey I must make before I went north and my young friend insisted he would accompany me. I gave no details of what I feared to find but Grizel knew of Kate's miscarriage and accepted that a delicately built lady might need some time to recover from such an ordeal. I prayed in my heart that the loss of a further week before I was able to ride would not prove disastrous but as I grew stronger my mind resumed its frantic imaginings with my wife as victim of her own inner turmoil and her Uncle Boice's devious schemes.

I did not relish the prospect of spending several days in Kent which had a long-standing reputation as a hotbed of dissension against the King's advisers and was a centre of opposition to Suffolk. Baron Saye and Sele who filled the position of High Sheriff in the county was the Duke's friend and I had heard he was unpopular among the people of his fiefdom. I wondered if it was entirely coincidental that Boice held land in that breeding ground of uprisings. Certainly it was important we did not draw attention to ourselves as we pursued our mission and I tried to impress this on Rendell.

The journey to Canterbury took us three days because my discomfort in the saddle was great but we were able to locate Boice's manor house without difficulty. It was a sprawling building to the west of Canterbury, set in the midst of orchards and pasture land, with an appearance of well-maintained prosperity. I could not be sure of a friendly welcome and when I presented myself at the entrance and gave my name I was not surprised to be kept waiting while the maid servant spoke to her mistress. The fact that the door was firmly shut in the meantime, and I heard a bolt creak into place, was not encouraging so I feared I might be denied admission. Before long, however, the door opened a crack to reveal a stout little lady with an elaborate head-dress and a sturdy retainer, carrying a club, at her shoulder.

'My name is Anne Hopgood, wife to Master Stephen Boice. Are you indeed Doctor Harry Somers?'

'I am, mistress. I understand you've been caring for my wife and I'm concerned to know how she's progressing. I've no wish to excite or disturb her with my presence but I've been deeply worried since she left London. I needed to trace her.'

Mistress Boice bit her lip and then exhaled. 'Are you armed?'

'I have a small dagger for my own protection. Nothing else.'

'Please hand it to Wilfred here, until you leave.' She waved a hand towards Rendell skulking by the outer gate. 'Your man must remain outside.'

'As you wish, mistress.'

Rendell had taken a step nearer the door but I indicated he should comply with the lady's demands. My heart missed a beat as I crossed the threshold and I entered what might prove to be hostile, dangerous surroundings but I had no choice if I was to find Kate. It was re-assuring to realise that Anne Hopgood was as nervous of my intentions as I was for my safety. She led me to a comfortably furnished parlour, offered me a window bench and indicated that the stalwart Wilfred should stand by the door. She seated herself at a table covered with a fine Turkey carpet. Her manner was inquisitorial.

'Why have you come when Mistress Somers wrote asking that you should not contact her?'

'Because I need to satisfy myself she is safe. She hasn't been well and she is prey to strange fancies. Old Syb, her serving woman who is with her would vouch for me.'

Mistress Boice folded her hands in her lap. 'The old woman died soon after they arrived here.'

This truly alarmed me. 'How? She seemed in good health.'

'She developed a fever. The journey was probably too much for her. She was elderly.'

Her dismissive attitude added to my worry. 'Kate trusted Syb. It must have been appalling for her to lose a loyal servant. I want only to protect my wife.'

'You have reason to think she would not be safe here?'

'Mistress, I will be open with you. Kate spoke of being cared for by a physician, arranged by Master Boice, who was seeking to free her from the devils which torment her mind. I don't believe her affliction is caused by devils. The church may hold to that doctrine and resort to exorcism but medical knowledge suggests different treatment may be more apposite. I would be happier to know the physician treating her agreed with me.'

'Do you know this doctor?'

'Kate didn't name him in her letter but I am aware that Master Boice is acquainted with Doctor Bertrand Willison whom I've met.'

'And you don't trust Doctor Willison?'

'I regret to say I can't be confident about his methods. Did he treat old Syb in her fever?'

'Indeed, he gave her medicines but all to no avail.'

I dared not express my fear that Willison had disposed of Syb because he saw her as an obstacle. Unquestionably she would have defended Kate from his ministrations if she suspected his intentions. There was a pause before Ann Hopgood spoke again.

'Do you trust my husband, Doctor Somers?'

I would gain nothing by being mealy-mouthed. 'Master Boice has shown himself inimical towards me in the past and he has threatened Kate's safety in an unsuccessful attempt to bend my actions to his will.'

The lady gasped. 'Can that be true? Kate has always adored her uncle.'

'I know. I can't give you a sensible explanation but the situation is distressing.'

Anne Hopgood stared at me intently as if trying to probe my soul. Then she rose and dismissed Wilfred from the room, ordering him to wait in the vestibule. She exhaled with a sigh 'I think you are an honest man, Doctor Somers. I didn't expect that when I heard of you from my husband and Doctor Willison but your assessment accords with my own. I will be equally honest with you. Master Boice and I are not close. He pursues his own concerns and I stay here in my family home rearing our two children. We are content with this arrangement and I will trade with you, confidence for confidence, by saying I would not be happy to have it otherwise. I think you understand me.'

She paused and I nodded, appreciating that this homely-looking matron juggled loyalty with astuteness. 'I suspect my husband's dealings would not always charm me if I knew of them – I choose not to – but I will not permit him to harm Kate. I've grown to love her. Her condition has deteriorated since she has been here, despite my efforts to help her. Perhaps it was aggravated by losing her serving woman. What do you suppose my husband plans?'

'I'm not sure. How is Willison treating her? Is he in the house now?'

'He gives her potions to make her sleep and that seems to me good for she is very weak. She hardly eats more than an infant – all slops – she resists the tasty delicacies I prepare. Willison isn't here for a few days. He's gone to London. He said he must obtain some instrument which he can use to help Kate.'

'An instrument?' For a moment I was puzzled then I shot to my feet, suddenly remembering a conversation in Wolvesey Castle when the Cardinal was nearing his end. 'Dear God, he doesn't propose to attempt trepanation?'

Anne Hopgood paled. 'He did use a word like that. What does it mean?'

'Trepanation involves drilling a hole in the patient's skull in the belief that this may evacuate the devils inside the head. I hold it to be of unproven value and profoundly dangerous. Willison has expressed an interest in experimenting with the procedure previously and I believe Master Boice condones his plan because he wishes to punish me by harming Kate.'

'That is horrible, horrible.' Her hands shot upwards to her headdress as if seeking to keep out the sound of my words and protect her own head. 'What can we do?'

I was delighted that she associated herself with the need to rescue Kate from Willison's vile purpose. 'I must take Kate away from here; place her somewhere secure.'

'She's too fragile to journey far and she needs constant care. Where could she go?'

I thought for a moment. 'Is there a convent nearby where the nuns might look after her? Where she could be guarded and Willison would be refused access? I could provide fittingly for the cost of her upkeep.'

342

Mistress Boice did not reply immediately and I feared there was no such suitable establishment. Then she seemed to come to a decision and stood. 'There is a sisterhood not two miles from here, at Thanington, where they care for the infirm of the locality, under the charge of Sister Michelle. The house is well esteemed in the neighbourhood and I'm sure the sisters would give Kate all the attention she needs. If they were willing to accept her, they would have Holy Church's protection in refusing admission to anyone bent on harming her. But I can't be certain they would be able to accommodate her as she comes from far away. Generous payment would be helpful in persuading them but is there any reputable connection you could mention to strengthen your request? Not the Duke of Suffolk or his associates; they are widely disparaged in this county.'

I smiled. 'I would be vouched for by the Abbot of Peterborough, the Prioress of St. Michael's Convent in Stamford and, though I would hesitate to trouble him, Bishop Waynflete of Winchester.'

The lady gave me a mischievous grin which quite changed the contours of her face. 'I think that will suffice.'

'I will visit the sisterhood at once but could I see Kate before I go? Will you permit it?'

'Are you suggesting I would bar a man from seeing his lawful wife? Doctor Willison might wish me to but he is not here.' Ann Hopgood opened the door and beckoned me. 'Come. She will be sleeping, no doubt, but come.'

Kate was indeed peacefully asleep, the remains of an evil-smelling draught in a flask beside her bed, but at the sound of my voice she stirred and I took her hand. Her eyelids fluttered but those wonderful green eyes were opaque and devoid of intelligence.

'Don't be angry with me for coming,' I whispered. 'I won't harass you. I only want to be sure that you're safe and shielded from those who might harm you. Your aunt will ensure your protection. I know you have confidence in her. When you're stronger, we can talk.'

The edges of Kate's mouth twitched so I knew that she had heard me and I felt the faint pressure of her fingers on mine. I leaned forward and kissed her brow lightly before following Ann Hopgood from the room. It was crucial I should not appear threatening to either of the women.

Mistress Boice insisted that I took refreshment before I set out for Thanington and went so far as to admit Rendell to the kitchen to eat under Wilfred's watchful eye. I could not resist asking her what it was that had persuaded her to trust me after her initial caution.

'I could tell you loved your wife and wanted what was best for her. You did not bluster and proclaim your conjugal rights. Although she is frail and troubled, I envied her for your selfless devotion. It is not an experience with which I am familiar.'

She tossed her head, dismissing any vestige of self-pity, but I imagined the life she must lead as Stephen Boice's wife, however separate their existences, and I was sorry for her.

While we sat at table I glimpsed a servant riding from the house and deduced that my hostess had thoughtfully sent him ahead to advise the sisters at Thanington of our intended visit.

Chapter 28

Disbursement of gold I had received from Suffolk and judicious name-dropping secured me the support I needed from Sister Michelle. She had come to Kent many years previously from Normandy and was overjoyed to find I knew the city of Rouen and some of its prominent inhabitants. She also responded with enthusiasm to the idea of defending Kate from a vicious doctor who planned to drill into her skull and we arranged for my wife's removal to her care the next day.

Mistress Boice accompanied me in escorting Kate's litter to Thanington with Rendell and Wilfred, both fully armed, riding side by side behind us. We saw the patient comfortably installed in a small cell adjoining a larger dormitory which reminded me of the Sustern Spital at Winchester and I felt confident that the cordial Sister Michelle mixed to soothe Kate into slumber was innocuous. I stayed an hour watching over my wife and I prayed in the chapel where the infirm were taken for God's blessing. It seemed to me an extravagant request to Heaven that she might be restored to full health but I made my petition all the same. At least my mind was eased that Willison's scheme had been thwarted.

Rendell and I set out to return to London without spending a second night at Stephen Boice's manor, although his wife urged us to stay and I was sorry to leave our congenial hostess's company. We could not be sure when Willison would reappear and my duty now was to return to Suffolk's service. I remained uncertain whether I would travel with him into exile for much would depend on the reports Sister Michelle had promised to send me, addressed to the Manor of the Rose, on the prospects for Kate's recovery. Experience as a physician told me that there was small chance of significant improvement in a mind and body so battered and abused but, as a husband, I could not abandon hope that my wife might be restored to me in perfect health.

We reached Rochester and sought a night's accommodation at the hostelry frequented by most travellers into Kent including pilgrims on their way to St. Thomas's shrine at Canterbury. The yard was bustling with arrivals and we had to wait until an ostler could attend to our horses so Rendell, ever restless, flung me his reins and sauntered over to a hatch where flagons of ale were available. When he returned he looked pensive.

'A bloke scarpered into the inn when he saw me. He wasn't in livery but I'd swear he was at the Boices' manor.'

'Over-active imagination,' I muttered as the ostler approached on my other side to hold the bridle while I dismounted. Rendell shrugged and I pretended to be unconcerned but I was well acquainted with his powers of intuition. I entered the tavern cautiously, peering around me, but there was no sign of the man Rendell had spotted or anyone else I recognised. I paid an extortionate amount for pallets in a tiny chamber, to be shared with only one other wayfarer, then returned to the public area to sup on some indifferent broth and highly seasoned but tough mutton. Rendell spent some time bantering with a buxom serving girl and was evidently pleased with himself when he joined me at the table.

A bundle of possessions stood on the third pallet when I returned to our room but the owner was absent and, as I was weary, I flung myself down on the scratchy mattress, trusting his arrival would not disturb me. Rendell said he was going to relieve himself in the yard and when he did not return I wondered if he had made an assignation with the maid who had dallied with him. I was soon asleep.

I must have slumbered soundly despite movement in the room and it was Rendell's distant cry which roused me from oblivion although I did not open my eyes at once. I grunted and turned over, only then becoming aware of a presence close to me. Before I could react a hand clamped over my mouth and in the gloom I distinguished the glint of steel above my face.

'If you resist or call out, you're a dead man, Harry Somers. My servant's dealt with your retainer so you won't be rescued. Just do as I say and you'll both be able to join Suffolk's exile unscathed. Sit up.'

Doctor Bertrand Willison pulled at my shoulder which was still sore from the wound I received at St Giles without Holborn and I jerked away from him. Instantly his knife was at my throat.

'I saved your life once, as you saved mine. Now we are quits and I owe you nothing. I'll have no qualms about slitting your windpipe if you're foolish. But it will serve us both better if you do as I say. You'll live and I'll have your mad wife to release from her demons. I need your seal on this paper, that's all.'

He had put a taper in a wall-sconce but it gave little light where I lay and the window showed only a blackened sky. I felt a sense of unreality as if the episode was simply a bad dream but I knew I must play for time. 'What does it say?'

'It authorises me to convey Mistress Somers from the convent where you placed her and to resume my treatment of her unfortunate condition.'

'Don't be ridiculous. I refuse to have her trepanned.'

'It could free her from her devils, Harry.'

'It could kill her.'

'What use is she to you as she is? A burden you'll carry until one of you dies. Let me open her skull and God will decide whether she'll be healed or you'll be relieved of a lifetime's encumbrance.'

'No! I refuse.'

The tip of his knife jabbed my cheek. 'I'm fascinated by phenomena, Harry, by distortions of nature, by the Devil's intervention in our world. We are linked together in pursuing this destiny, don't you think? We stood side by side to observe that freakish birth in Dublin and now you have the power to let me free your wife from possession by Satan. If you don't co-operate, I'll slice this

347

mouldy skin from your face before I kill you. Your vivid birthmark is Hell's handiwork and I'm intrigued to see what lies beneath it. Will it bleed scarlet juices like a normal man or will black bile seep upwards out of your foul intestines?'

I saw a brief flicker of light outside the window. It was quickly gone but Willison had seen it too and his voice became peremptory. 'Either sign the paper yourself and go free or you're a dead man and I'll sign it for you. Where's your seal?'

'I haven't got it with me,' I lied.

'Rubbish. It'll be in the purse at your waist. Get it out.'

'Get it yourself.'

He clouted my cheek with a blow that opened the scratch his weapon had made. 'So you can catch me off guard and find the dagger under your pillow? You think me a fool? Give me your seal.'

I groped in the folds of my loosened shirt and pulled the belt round so my purse was resting on my stomach. A glow outside the window intensified as I fumbled to undo the buckle.

'Fire! Fire!' The shout echoed from the courtyard, taken up by several voices.

'Quickly! Damn you, quickly!'

Willison seized my purse, trying to yank it from my belt but the leather was too tough and he was disconcerted by running feet on the internal staircase and much shouting both inside and outside the inn. His attention wavered only for a moment but it gave me my opportunity and I butted his belly with my head, causing him to drop his knife. I jumped off the pallet but he sprang back at me with another implement in his hand before I could extricate my dagger. I dodged to the side but stumbled over my bundle of clothes and in an instant he had me in a headlock with a fearsome pointed instrument aimed at my forehead.

348

'How ironic, Harry: a trepan through the eye seems fitting.'

'No you bloody don't!'

The door crashed back, Rendell's furious yelp rang out, Willison screeched and I found myself dragged to the floor as he collapsed. I was drenched in his gushing blood.

'Here throw his travelling cloak round you. I've got your things. We must get away before they find two bodies, neither due to a footling little fire in an outhouse. The horses are ready.'

Cool and collected, as a soldier is trained to be, Rendell extracted his sword from the back of Willison's neck and dragged me away from the gruesome scene.

In the yard men were passing buckets of water from hand to hand to douse the remains of a blaze in a storehouse which had not spread to the main building or the stables. No one heeded us as we scuttled under the archway into the road where a curvaceous young woman was waiting with two bridled horses. Her dress was somewhat disarranged. Rendell gave her a smacking kiss, slapped her affectionately on the bottom and leapt into the saddle.

We rode at speed to a postern gate out of the town where Rendell spoke briefly to the guard who let us through without demur. When we were clear of the walls he looked over his shoulder and winked.

'Baron Saye is High Sheriff of Kent and a mate of Suffolk's. Lucky I've got me de la Pole badge with me – as I ain't wearing livery. I thought we'd best head down to Chatham and get a boat. Reckon they'll be after us by daybreak.'

Out of breath, I nodded.

'Who was the geezer I did for? Why'd he want to kill you?'

'Doctor Willison. He'd been tipped off we were coming. What happened to his servant?'

'Guess.' Rendell drew his hand brusquely across his throat. 'Thought to catch me unawares but I was ready for

349

him. Had a bit of a chat first, we did, once I'd disarmed him. He'd been left at the manor-house in case you turned up there when his master went to London. Mistress bloody Boice knew all about it. Fucking women! Never trust them.' He urged his horse into a gallop. 'Mind you,' he shouted back at me. 'That pretty maid was a bit of all right.'

I was unsure how to construe Mistress Boice's role in alerting Willison. The arrangements for Kate's care at the convent seemed secure enough, else there had been no need to seek my authority for her release. I could believe Ann Hopgood feared her husband and dared not thwart his instructions but surely her dislike of Willison was genuine. Perhaps she did what she had to and relied on Heaven to determine who would prove victorious in the encounter at Rochester. I found it difficult to blame her.

I had no need to ask who started the fire at the inn, as a distraction, or to be surprised by the ease with which my young friend had learned to kill. He would defend himself and me without hesitation, at whatever cost to assailants, but I feared we had become marked men. There would be a price on our heads once those corpses were discovered for we were the obvious suspects. Despite the often unchecked lawlessness in the King's realm, orders would be given for us to be apprehended and I could have no confidence in persuading a Kentish jury that the dead men had been the attackers, not us. Suffolk's physician and a member of his bodyguard would be deemed guilty by association. We would be wise to lie low for a while. My uncertainty about joining the Duke in his exile had been resolved.

*****

We were lucky in securing the use of a fishing smack at Chatham, with a master content to sail for Ipswich, in Suffolk's own county, and we arrived there next day. On the quayside, as we anchored, we recognised some of the Duke's servants and the yeoman of the Crown, Henry Spenser, whom I had met when he came to the Tower of London with the King's safe-conduct. He told me they had been sent to hire ships to convey Suffolk's party into exile at the end of the month.

Suffolk made me welcome when we arrived at Wingfield and told me he had agreement from the Duke of Burgundy for him to sojourn in the Low Countries during the period of his banishment. He expressed delight that I intended to accompany him but I thought him preoccupied and not wholly relaxed. I wondered if he feared some last minute hitch in his plans but he shrugged off my tentative enquiry.

'We are in God's hands always,' he said. 'But it behoves us to put all our affairs in order before crossing the sea. Alice will care for our son on the estates which will be his one day but I shall miss watching his development into manhood. I have in mind to write advice for him, to guide him into the paths of virtue and avoid the pitfalls his father has blundered into.'

'I'm sure the Duchess will ensure young John keeps his father's precepts well in mind.'

Suffolk smiled and for a moment looked misty-eyed. Then he drew himself erect and slapped his fist into his other palm. 'I am forgetting, Harry. There is a message come for you – special messenger this morning.'

I quailed. 'From Kent?' I had not yet shared details of my journey with the Duke.

'No, no, from Norfolk, from Attleborough, from Lord Fitzvaughan's wife.' He handed me a sealed packet which I opened.

I read the short letter and held it out to the Duke. 'Lady Fitzvaughan announces the birth of her grandson. He is a healthy child and his mother, the young Dame de la Tour, is apparently recovering well from her ordeal.'

'The lady invites you to visit them while you are in the vicinity and you should do so, Harry. You've been a good friend to the family and it may be some time before

351

you see them again. Go tomorrow and spend a few nights there. I propose to leave Wingfield soon and reside at my manor of East Thorp near Saint Edmundsbury until it's time to sail. You can join me there when you've made your farewells at Attleborough.'

I bowed and thanked the Duke. The diversion would occupy my time while waiting to flee the country and it would be pleasing to confirm that the new mother and her baby were thriving.

'Commend me to Lady Fitzvaughan. Her husband is fighting with Sir Thomas Kyriel's troop: Gaston de la Tour as well. I still have hopes that they may beat the French back into their own domain and rescue Normandy for our King. Who knows, if they succeed, might I be rehabilitated?'

He gave a mirthless laugh and I knew he had no such hopes.

*****

I stayed a week at Attleborough and for most of that time I was pleasantly at leisure, rejoicing for Eleanor de la Tour's happiness and coddling her sturdy infant without dwelling on the sadness in my heart for my own lost offspring. Maud was more contented than I had known her but I parried the innuendo which was a covert invitation to her bed. I spoke cautiously about my wife's health and led them to believe she was recuperating from an ailment. I could tell Maud wanted to extract details but I did not encourage discussion of the subject. Eleanor at least respected my privacy.

And then the royal messenger rode through the entrance gate and the world changed for those I accounted my friends. Maud received the communication in her own chamber but her wailing could be heard throughout the house. I presented myself to her trusty serving woman, Marian, and was admitted to her room while others were barred from entering. I had never seen Maud so extravagantly distraught, her hair loose, torn from its headdress, as she stumbled back and forth between the window and the door.

'Walter is dead, Walter is dead,' she repeated over and over. 'At a place called Formigny, with four thousand others. He's dead, Harry. He's dead. I am a widow.'

She snatched at me and I put my arm round her, wondering at the sincerity of her emotion. 'Were King Henry's men defeated?'

'Oh, yes, utterly. Sir Thomas Kyriel and the remnants of his army are in retreat. All of Normandy is lost. What shall I do, Harry, where shall I go?'

'Is there news of Gaston de la Tour?'

'The letter comes from him. He was wounded but not seriously. He speaks of his devastation, his love for my husband. I could almost feel sorry for him, his grief is so profound.'

'Eleanor will be joyful and her son will have his father. That is a blessing.'

'But I am a widow! Gaston will hold Attleborough in the name of his wife. He has no fondness for me. I shall be ejected from this house. I shall have nothing but a modest dower house. Widows are meant to live secluded from society. It will be a thousand times worse than living at Ravensmoor. What shall I do?'

Even in the face of this appalling news I could not suppress a smile at her self-absorption. 'Many widows marry again. You will be sought after, Maud. You are still beautiful.'

'But barren. I cannot repeat the trick I played on Walter, allowing him to believe I might bear a child. Oh, Harry, is it my punishment for all I did to deceive him? Has he been taken from me in retribution?'

'That seems a little unfair on Lord Fitzvaughan.'

'Oh, you beast, you beast! You are mocking me in my despair.' She pummelled my chest with her fists. But I took her wrists and led her to a chair.

'You must try to be calm, Maud. I'll mix you a potion to help rebalance your humours. But I should go to tell Eleanor that Gaston is safe. You owe your daughter that.'

'You make me sound like the crone I am meant to become. A widow! Bereft, abandoned, widowed in my prime. Oh, the misery that is my lot!'

I slipped from the room to find Eleanor, white-faced, outside the door, and was able to give her the reassurance she longed to hear. Then she entered her mother's room and I heard the tones of youthful common sense battling with the agitated exclamations of Lord Fitzvaughan's relict. I crept upstairs to reflect with sadness on the loss of a man who had been more than ordinarily wise and fair-minded and who had served his King with loyalty. My own relationship with him had been chequered but I had reason to be grateful for his support and always respected him. I mourned his loss and also the last futile hope that Suffolk's fortunes might be restored by a victory in Normandy.

*****

Earlier in my visit to Attleborough I had renewed acquaintance with Robin Willoughby, the Fitzvaughan bailiff, and his family. Bess, whom I remembered with affection from our tentative courtship nearly ten years previously, was now the mother of boisterous little Anne, approaching her third birthday, and a two month old son named for his father. I had tried not to envy them their domestic contentment or contrast it with the trammels and disappointments of my own marriage. They were aware of my changed status and I spoke to them about Kate without disclosing anything of her troubles. They were at ease and happy but for me it was a bitter-sweet meeting.

As the news of Lord Fitzvaughan's death spread round the demesne I was asked to call on Mistress

Willoughby in the dower-house across the courtyard from the manor, where she and her husband had been permitted to live while there was no other call on these lodgings.

Bess was loading her cooking pots into a chest while sustaining the movement of the cradle on its rockers with an occasional tap of her foot. Her daughter sat beside the coffer clutching a beaker to her chest. 'Not put it in box,' she protested fiercely as I entered.

Bess brushed back a tangle of hair which had escaped from her cap and swallowed the reproach she was about to deliver to her child. 'Doctor Somers, thank you for coming. Anne, you can hold your cup while I talk to our visitor but then it must be packed.' She indicated a chair piled high with garments. 'Put those things on the table and sit down, Doctor.'

We were always formally correct in addressing each other and I guessed she found our infrequent encounters less awkward than I did. 'Mistress Willoughby, are you already preparing to vacate the dower-house?'

'Of course, Lady Maud is now the dowager and has the rightful claim to it. We're to move to a pleasant enough dwelling out on the estate, near the woods Robin tends. It will be convenient for him.'

'But less so for you, perhaps. You'll be away from friends at the manor house.'

'It's only a mile or so distant. We'll manage.' She put down the basin she was holding and spoke in a low voice. 'I wanted your advice as a physician, before Robin returns.'

'Are you ailing – after your son's birth?'

She shook her head. 'No, I'm fortunate. I've had no problem. But Robin has hurt his knee and I wondered if there was some poultice which would help it heal more quickly. It hurts him to crouch. I have a tincture of cinquefoil which I rub into the joint but it still pains him.'

'I have a special mixture which the Duke of Suffolk has always found helpful in easing the muscles of his back.

I'll fetch you some. You can rub it on the knee just as you've been doing with your tincture. It's a bit stronger than cinquefoil on its own.'

'Thank you.' She rapped the cradle with her toe as a whimper came from its occupant and bent down to lift her daughter. 'Look, Anne, you can pack your beaker yourself. Would you like to tuck it between those platters? It'll be quite safe and you'll have it again tomorrow at the new house.' Reluctantly the child leaned forward and placed her precious possession carefully in the chest. Bess petted the infant and set her down before turning to me. 'Robin needs to be so active. He's always on his feet around the estate and he disguises his discomfort. He'd hate to think I'd bothered you on his behalf. He regards you as an eminent physician.'

'And you don't, Mistress Willoughby?'

She blushed. 'You shouldn't tease me, Doctor Somers. It isn't fitting.'

There was no annoyance in her gentle reprimand and I bowed to her with a smile. 'I'll send a page with a pot of my mixture. I'm leaving Attleborough in the morning and I'll be crossing the sea with the Duke. I hope I may return and visit you again but I cannot tell when that might be. I wish you well in your new home.'

She reached out and touched my forearm lightly. 'God go with you, Doctor Somers. May He bless you and Mistress Somers with children, as Robin and I have been so richly blessed.'

I choked back tears as I crossed the courtyard, stung by the innocent irony of Bess's appeal to Heaven on my behalf. I rejoiced in her happiness but her capable good sense and serenity diverged painfully from the effects of Kate's mental affliction and I found the comparison almost too much to bear.

All I had to trust in was Kate's verbal admission, even in the disturbance of her mind and despite attempts to erase her written declaration, that she loved me.

Chapter 29

I accompanied the Duke to his house at East Thorp where we stayed until we moved to Ipswich where vessels were waiting to convey us to the Netherlands. Two small ships and a pinnace had been hired and manned for the crossing while safe conducts from King Henry and the Duke of Burgundy were intended to ensure there were no obstacles to our progress. Nevertheless the whole household was in sombre mood, disheartened by news of arrivals from Normandy at ports on the south coast: lines of bedraggled and wounded soldiers forced to retreat in ignominy from the scenes of their defeat, cursing the King's advisors who were responsible for this disgrace. Their plight angered the local populace as they came ashore and it was reported that in the counties of Kent and Sussex discontent threatened to turn to violence.

At Ipswich we waited for a favourable wind to carry us to the Low Countries and on the eve of our departure Suffolk called together his household and leading gentlemen of the neighbourhood. He took the Sacrament before them and swore on the Host that he was guiltless of treason and the crimes attributed to him. He then retired to his chamber to write a letter to his young son, which he allowed me to read, and I was touched by its dignity and the virtue of its sentiments. I commended it but was struck by the sorrow in his eyes.

'You fear you will not be reunited with your son, your Grace?' It was a presumptuous question but he did not rebuke me.

'My heart tells me I will never see Alice or John again. I trust I shall reach the Duke of Burgundy's domains without harm but five years is a long time for a man of my age and I intend to offer my services in the field to the man giving me sanctuary. I may well fall in battle, in Burgundy's service, and I will be satisfied to die in armour with my honour intact. You are free to leave me, Harry, whenever you wish.'

357

'That's generous, your Grace, but my enemies, the men you know of, will be seeking to have me arrested after a skirmish in Rochester in which one of their number was killed.' There was no need to give Suffolk details of Willison's death and Rendell's part in it. The Duke's eyes were glazed as he mulled over his own miserable prospects. 'There's much work for a physician on the battlefield. It's experience I've not yet acquired.'

'True enough. You would be welcome.' He stretched and peered into the darkness through the open window. 'Get some sleep, Harry. The master of my ships was hopeful the wind would change over-night and I feel a breeze which may prove him right. Make sure you are at my side when we embark, with stocks of your valuable embrocation.'

I bowed and left him. I was pleased to think that Duke and bailiff alike might benefit from my liniment.

*****

We set sail on the day before Suffolk's exile was due to begin and the wind carried us briskly down the coast past the estuaries of the Thames and Medway. Suffolk's entourage was divided between the two ships with a small contingent on the pinnace which could move more speedily to take messages and bring us news from other craft or the shore. The Duke had asked me to travel with him and, as evening approached, I was glad to see Rendell on the deck of the same vessel. We exchanged greetings and remembered how less than a month earlier we had sailed in the opposite direction after our escape from Rochester.

'Dunno if there are search parties looking for me over there.' He pointed to the line of the north Kent coast. 'D'you reckon the justices are that diligent? Was that Doctor Willison important?'

358

'His friends might think so and they may include Richard of York but Willison was a devious rogue – a murderer.'

Rendell whistled. 'You have a habit of attracting nasty enemies. By the way, I heard from a mate who stayed in London for a bit after the scuffle at St. Giles: that bloke who went for you there and I knifed hasn't died. Earl what's his name survived. Seems I didn't stab hard enough.' He sounded rueful.

Although the Earl of Stanwick was no great ornament to the realm, I did not wish him dead. 'One less on your conscience then.'

'Soldiers can't afford the luxury of a conscience. That's why we're shriven before we go into battle. Shouldn't think physicians can either? How many of their patients do they kill rather than cure?'

He dodged my playful cuff and hurried over to his sergeant who had just left Suffolk's cabin on the forecastle and was summoning his men.

I joined the Duke who was in discussion with the master of the small convoy and Henry Spenser, yeoman of the Crown, who was clad in royal livery representing King Henry.

'We've rounded the North Foreland now and the wind will take us straight to Calais if we let it but it's getting stronger. We'll not make Middelburg directly in these conditions. I recommend we make for Calais and shelter there until the breeze slackens or changes direction. Then I'll be able to take you up the coast without a problem.' The master spoke confidently, accustomed to acceptance of his professional judgement.

'I'm not certain I'd meet with a welcome in Calais.' The Duke was staring ahead as if he could see something invisible to his companions.

'I have the King's safe-conduct.' Master Spenser sounded irritated. 'No commander will disregard it – at his peril.'

'I don't doubt the integrity of the commander in Calais but men in his garrison may think differently. Bishop Moleyns was put to death by disgruntled soldiers, as I remember. I'd be happier to have assurance from the commander that his men were under firm control.'

The yeoman of the Crown puffed in disgust at such a suggestion but the master adjusted his short gown on his shoulders and cleared his throat. 'Your Grace, I'll send the pinnace on to Calais to ask how you would be received. We can heave to in the straits while it flits there and back. Then if all's well we'll make a speedy crossing. Otherwise if the wind rises to a gale we might need to put in at Dover.'

'Impossible. That would breach the order for my exile. Send the pinnace at once, master.'

The seaman bowed and left the forecastle. I surveyed the scene through the cabin window as signals were given for the pinnace to approach, receive instructions and set off towards the French coast. We were nearer the English shore and could see Dover Castle standing proudly on its ridge of white chalk but I knew that from the other side of the deck, if there was still enough daylight, France would also be visible.

'There's a large ship out to sea,' I said as we began to turn into the wind and come to a standstill.'

'There must be dozens of vessels on the Narrow Sea at any one time.' Suffolk was composed. 'Let's get a little rest before the pinnace returns. If the wind increases the last part of our crossing may be rough.'

I rolled myself in my travelling cloak and curled up on the deck with Suffolk's household retainers. I dozed intermittently, feeling the movement of the sea, but it did not seem to me that the wind increased. I came to myself as the first streak of light came in the east and I thought at once that the pinnace could not yet have returned or I would have heard the clamour of shouted messages. Then I realised that there was shouting and this must have roused me. I sat up and saw, not the pinnace, but a large vessel which had come within hailing distance. Its deck was lined with armed men. I could just make out its name: *Nicholas of the Tower*. This meant nothing to me. We all bustled to our feet as Suffolk appeared at the door of his cabin and we watched while two rowing boats were lowered from the alien-ship and drew alongside. From the Kentish shore I fancied I heard the sound of a horn.

A fellow stood in the bow of the front boat and demanded to know our identities and business. His tone was peremptory and it was unclear whether the *Nicholas* was manned by privateers, common on the Narrow Sea, or commissioned to keep peace on the water in the King's name. The Duke himself answered the enquiry with courtesy, explaining that he was sent to Calais by command of King Henry and requesting free passage past the great ship. The spokesman below us conferred with another man in the rowing boat.

'We've no authority to let you pass, your Grace. We've no knowledge of your mission.'

'I have the King's safe-conduct to ensure my journey is not obstructed.' Suffolk's tone was measured.

Master Spenser delved into his robe and waved the folded paper. 'It bears the King's personal seal,' he called. 'I am here to represent the King as yeoman of the Crown.'

Further discussion took place on the boat at it rose and subsided on the swell of the tide and the speaker steadied himself before responding. 'We know who you are, my Lord Duke, you and your companions. We have taken your pinnace in tow. You must come aboard the *Nicholas* and present yourself to the master of our ship. I advise you against any resistance.'

Suffolk glanced round and I followed the direction of his eyes. He took in the sight of our crew, clustered in the stern, sullen-faced and passive. They were pressed men with no interest in the fortunes of their principal passenger; at best they were likely to mistrust him, more probably they wished him ill. They would not intervene on his behalf.

Suffolk stood tall, stretching the unreliable muscles of his back. 'I am at your service,' he said. 'I wish Master Spenser and some other of my followers to accompany me.'

Permission was granted and the Duke signalled that I should be one of the six men who clambered down the rope ladder behind him to take our places in the rowing boats. I dreaded slipping during this athletic feat but reached the deck of the *Nicholas* without mishap in time to see the master of the vessel stride forward and address Suffolk.

'Welcome traitor,' he said with a sardonic bow. 'Welcome to *Nicholas of the Tower*. You have enjoyed cossetted captivity in the Tower of London. Now you shall experience the hospitality of its namesake.'

The Duke controlled his momentary flinch but I could tell he understood from this greeting what fate awaited him. His objective now must be to retain his dignity in the face of whatever provocation he encountered and the role of his small band of retainers must be to bolster his resilience. We trooped behind William de la Pole as he was led into the master's cabin and once again I heard the distant sound of a horn while mariners on board the *Nicholas* hauled up some kind of signalling pennant. This was no accidental encounter at sea between the exile and the *Nicholas*; there was collusion with his foes on land who were aware of his movements.

Inside the cabin we were confronted by a range of seamen standing in front of us: an impromptu and illegal jury ready to hear the charges brought against the Duke. These were read out by the master of the *Nicholas,* the familiar rodomontade mixing absurd accusations and plausible misdeeds, all given equal credence. The scowling faces of the self-styled jurors indicated how they rated the indictment and the roughest looking fellow spat noisily at the prisoner's feet. Naturally Suffolk refused to plead before this irregular tribunal but he calmly displayed his safe-conduct and asked if they were intent on defying the

King's decree. The ship's master took the paper, unfolded it and showed its contents to his crewmen but one of them seized it with an insulting guffaw and ripped it in half.

'No fucking paper's going to stop common men's justice. The crown of England rests on our favour.'

I caught my breath at these seditious views and at my side Master Spenser blew out his cheeks in disgust at such effrontery. No one dared speak. The seaman held up the torn pieces of the safe-conduct and ripped them again and again, letting the fragments fall to the floor before he trampled on them.

This parody of legal process continued and after several speeches infused with venom Suffolk was found guilty. The sentence was then a formality. The master ordered that the Duke be allowed until the following day to prepare himself for death and gave permission for his companions to attend him until that time. Writing materials were to be put at his disposal. The Duke's chaplain had accompanied us on board the hostile ship and was able to shrive him but we all in turn were granted the opportunity to make our farewells.

Suffolk faced me, hand on chin, clear eyed. 'I've made provision in my will for you to hold the manor of Worthwaite, in future, free of encumbrance and Duchess Alice will see you are recompensed for your loyalty with a fitting reward. You'll have adequate resources to live as you wish, Harry. I trust you can find happiness with your pretty Kate and that she will be restored to health. I'm grateful for your dedicated service and regret the burdens I've placed upon you.'

'Your Grace, that's generous.' My voice was husky. 'I'm deeply sorry you're facing such an ignominious end.'

He patted my shoulder. 'Courage, physician. I have my honour and I scorn their derisory judgement. I die a martyr for serving my King with diligence and sincerity. You've been a retainer who has given me unbiased advice and I value that. God save you, Harry Somers.'

Out on deck I wiped away a tear while more men from Suffolk's ships were brought on board the *Nicholas of the Tower*. Among them was Rendell and we exchanged brief greetings before he and his colleagues were relieved of their possessions and herded together at the bow.

'These bastards have been checking if there'd be any trouble from the crew of the Duke's ship,' he said. 'Bloody cowards! They won't lift a finger to save him.'

'They'd have no chance against the numbers on the *Nicholas* and they see him as their enemy. There's nothing to be done. Just get yourself out safely – they'll have no interest in holding so many prisoners once Suffolk's dead.'

After this I was hauled aside, made to empty my purse and told to hunker down on the deck until daylight. It was a dark night with only a sliver of moonlight and I slept not at all but I prayed for the man I had served, whose strengths and flaws of character I knew as well as my own.

At dawn on the second day of the month of May in the year of Our Lord 1450, William de la Pole, Duke of Suffolk, was forced into one of the ship's boats and allowed to take his chaplain and another companion with him. It was a privilege that he asked me to go with them but I crouched at his side in terror at the thought of what I must witness. We pulled towards the shore until we were in shallow water and, when the rowers had shipped their oars, the wretch who had spat at the Duke during his travesty of a trial ordered Suffolk to kneel and lean over the gunwale. Then the villainous fellow took up a rusty sword.

Kneeling in such an uncomfortable position would be acutely painful for a man with damaged muscles in his back and the Duke grimaced as he lowered himself, giving a quick glance at me as if to say he had need of my poultice. It was a kind thought, in extremis, to relieve the tension I felt but the horror of what followed drove such comfort aside. The eager executioner had no skill with his broken-down weapon and no care for the finesse of his actions. Six blows through flesh, sinews, blood-vessels and bone it took before William de la Pole's head was fully detached from his neck and by that time I was spewing into the foam. Even the hostile seamen turned their eyes away from the sight until the splash alerted them to the fact the deed was done. Then the executioner reached out, thrusting spattered fingers into Suffolk's greying hair, darkened by the water and spread out on the sea like a tarnished aureole, to haul his head into the boat.

Next the sailors dragged both head and torso onto the beach while the chaplain and I were put ashore beside the body parts. The boat pulled away immediately, the oarsmen exerting their strength against the incoming tide, and I heard shouting out at sea where the *Nicholas* was waiting. Pedantically I lifted Suffolk's head to place it neatly above his ragged neck and I could not prevent a moment's fascination to see the severed cords and windpipe in his throat but this was not an anonymous dissection, such as I had witnessed at the university in Padua. This was a man I had come to account my friend and it was his blood dribbling over the shingle and being washed back, diluted, with the skeins of seaweed.

'We must send word to Dover Castle,' I said, thinking that I must go while the chaplain knelt to say the prayers for the dead but he was more observant than I was.

'One of our soldiers has just swum ashore. He must have dived off the ship.'

'Something I learned in France,' Rendell said, squelching across the strand and crossing himself at the sight of the Duke's body. 'I'll climb the cliff and report to the garrison. You stay here, Doctor, you look done in.'

'I'd be grateful. Didn't they try to stop you escaping?'

'They weren't bothered. They're going to land all Suffolk's men along the coast. Probably thought I'd drown anyway.' He waved and set off at a run up the beach to the bottom of a steeply angled path ascending the cliff.

I joined the chaplain on my knees but I saw in the distance, down by the harbour, a small cluster of people who seemed to be looking in our direction and I kept my eye on them. It did not take Rendell long to return with half a dozen soldiers from the castle because the watchman on the gate-tower had already sent them out to check what had occurred below the cliffs. They wrapped the corpse decently in their cloaks and with the chaplain intoning his dirges beside them, they set out to return uphill. I told Rendell to go with them.

'There's a party of spectators making their way across from the harbour. They must have seen something and we don't want fanciful accounts being spread around before we've reported to the Warden at the castle. I'll have a word with them and send them on their way. Then I'll catch up with you. You need to get out of those wet clothes.'

Rendell rubbed his nose. 'Getting as fussy as Grizel, you are. Mind your step on the path up the cliff with your wonky leg.'

He hurried off and I was glad to see him go because I did not want him to meet the man I had identified from afar with his companions. I wondered if I would be able to make good my promise to join Rendell at the castle but I did not expect the further events of that dreadful day to be even more personally searing than those I had just witnessed. I walked towards the newcomers.

*****

'I'm greatly obliged that you have come to meet us. It might have been awkward for me to call at the castle where Suffolk's friend, Baron Saye and Sele, is Warden.' Stephen Boice's manner was ingratiating. He was leading his horse with his wife seated on the saddle. A veil fixed to her head-dress covered most of her face but I recognised her build. Her eyes were cast down as if she was ashamed to confront me. A step behind his master came a man carrying a horn and further back a posse of well-armed horsemen provided a formidable bodyguard.

'What do you want?'

'My dear fellow, why do you suppose we're here?'

'I deduce you have just played a part in contriving Suffolk's capture and murder. As you made no secret of your wish for his death, I'm hardly surprised.'

Boice sniggered. 'He was destined to be judged by the people he had despoiled. Perhaps that was appropriate but it would have been quicker and tidier for everyone involved if you had complied with my suggestion and delivered him several weeks earlier from his troublesome life.'

I said nothing and he looked annoyed. 'I warned you what would happen if you refused to assist. I don't take kindly to those who try to thwart my will.' He twitched the bridle of his horse and turned it so Mistress Boice was facing me. 'You have met my wife. Remove your veil, woman.'

Ann Hopgood trembled when he addressed her and lifted the corner of the material to show half her battered countenance. Her left eye was swollen and below it her cheek was discoloured but it was not enough for her husband. He seized her arm and jerked the veil aside completely so I could see the vivid weal across her other cheek where heated metal had branded her.

'You're a barbarian, Boice.'

'Oh, come now, she tricked you too, did she not? She's a devious bitch and too full of her own notions. She deserves every chastisement she's received. But I didn't seek you out to display my wife's discomfiture. I have business to conduct for the benefit of the King's realm. When you join your friends at Dover Castle you can tell them Suffolk's death is but the taper to set alight the kindling of indignation and defiance built up in Kent. Wait a week or two and you will find the whole county blazing with men's fury. Well, what do you say to that?'

'I hear you. I have nothing to say.'

367

'Perhaps you will have something to say when you see the conflagration. You were a fool not to join our cause, Harry Somers, and you've brought great suffering to one you professed to care for. I warned you I would harm your wife and, with the unfortunate Willison's assistance, I have done so. He may not have succeeded in opening her head in the pursuit of medical knowledge but I believe he made free with her in ways I would not wish to describe. She has been martyred for your foolishness.'

He signalled to the group behind him and two horses were led forward, emerging from the knot of Boice's followers to reveal a nun riding pillion on one animal and a slender, motionless woman flung across the saddle in front of the second rider. Men with drawn swords took up position around me but there was no possibility that I would attack their master. I was numb and rooted to the ground.

'Since Suffolk is dead I have no need to detain your witless wife. Take her, Harry. She was always my creature, ready to do my bidding. I think you know that. I had her placed in Suffolk's household, instructed her to entrap you and latterly ordered her to leave London and find sanctuary at my manor house. Now she is no further use to me but you must live with the knowledge of what you have caused her to suffer. The balance of her mind was always fragile, wasn't it? Now the humours are in turmoil and she is lunatic.'

He unfastened the buckles which held Kate on the horse and lifted her to the ground, gripping her wrists as if he expected she would attack him with her nails. 'Good Sister Michelle has come with her from Thanington and has a potion and straps to quieten her if she grows frantic. I've no doubt you will want to put her away securely where she can be restrained but you are shackled to her by the Sacrament of Holy Matrimony and must carry the burden of her affliction until one of you dies. Here now, pretty niece, don't look so scornful. You must go to your husband. You are his chattel. I bid you goodbye.'

He kissed her on the lips, causing her to scream and writhe, until Sister Michelle took hold of her and led her towards me. At this Boice leapt into the saddle, beckoned his followers to do likewise and they set off at a gallop along Dover Sands towards the harbour. I ignored them.

Kate clung to Sister Michelle, hiding her face in the nun's robe, and I waited until they were two steps from me. Then I dropped to my knees. 'Kate, Kate,' I said softly. 'You are free from your abusers. You will get well again. I am your husband and I love you.'

She sank to the ground in front of me and the nun took a step back, satisfied that her charge was not about to behave violently. I did not touch Kate but gazed into her beautiful, blank eyes until faint light came into them and tentatively she put out her hand to brush the birthmark on my distorted cheek with her fingertips.

'I remember you,' she said in a far-away voice. 'I knew you once.'

'And you will come to know me again, I promise you, Kate. We will be together and I will protect you.'

Then I put my arms round her and she let me hold her close.

HISTORICAL NOTE

Most characters in *The Martyr's Scorn* are fictional but many events which provide the background to the story are factual. The death of Cardinal Beaufort, the rise of William de la Pole, Marquis of Suffolk, and the ambivalent position of Richard, Duke of York towards King Henry VI are all recorded in the annals. So too are the deteriorating relationship with France, the loss of territory in Normandy and the growing antagonism towards the King's advisors, especially Suffolk. This antagonism culminated in the dramatic events affecting William de la Pole during the first few months of 1450 described in the book.

Richard of York did not actually take up his post in Ireland until 1449, although he had been appointed to it, two years earlier. There is no record that he made a preliminary visit there in 1448 but it was convenient to assume he did!

The Martyr's Scorn continues the story of the young physician, Harry Somers, which began in *The Devil's Stain,* followed by *The Angel's Wing and The Cherub's Smile.* Several characters in it (both factual and fictional) appear in the earlier books.

THE AUTHOR

Pamela Gordon Hoad read history at Oxford University, and the subject has remained of abiding interest to her. She has also always loved the drama and romance of characters and plot in historical fiction. She tried her hand at such creative writing over the years but, due to the exigencies of her career, she mainly wrote committee reports, policy papers and occasional articles for publication. After working for the Greater London Council, she held the positions of Chief Executive of the London Borough of Hackney and then Chief Executive of the City of Sheffield. Later she held public appointments, including that of Electoral Commissioner when the Electoral Commission was established.

Since 'retiring', Pamela has been active in the voluntary sector and for three years chaired the national board of Relationships Scotland; she continues her involvement with several voluntary sector organisations. Importantly, during the last few years, she has also been able to pursue her aim of writing historical fiction and she published her first three novels in a series about the young physician, Harry Somers: *The Devil's Stain*, *The Angel's Wing* and *The Cherub's Smile*. Harry's story is continued in *The Martyr's Scorn and* a fifth book in the series is planned for publication in 2019.

Pamela has also published short stories with historical backgrounds in anthologies published by the Borders Writers Forum (which she chaired for three years). She continues to chair or be a committee member of various organisations concerned with the creative arts and history.

Other books by Silver Quill writers:

For adults:

The Devil's Stain by Pamela Gordon Hoad: '*A tense fifteenth century English murder mystery, full of twists and turns*', which introduces Harry Somers, physician and investigator.

The Angel's Wing by Pamela Gordon Hoad: '*The action and drama of the first book continue in this compelling sequel as Harry gains a reputation for his medical skills whilst becoming embroiled in the politics of fifteenth century Italy...*'

The Cherub's Smile by Pamela Gordon Hoad: Harry Somers is torn between allegiances. '*I felt I was there, caught up in the turmoil of fifteenth century England, and the characters were totally "real" – as well as intrigue, there is friendship, passion and disappointment... and pathos.*'

Crying Through the Wind by Iona Carroll. '*...Sensitively written novel of love, intrigue and hidden family secrets set in post-war Ireland... one of those books you can't put down from the very first paragraph...*'

Familiar Yet Far by Iona Carroll. Second novel in *The Story of Oisin Kelly* trilogy follows the young Irishman in *Crying Through the Wind* from Ireland and Edinburgh to Australia. '*The author has a genius, bringing you into whichever country she is writing about. You can smell the rain in Ireland and the dust in the Outback...*'

Homecoming by Iona Carroll: Third novel in the series. '*A deeply moving novel about the struggles facing a wounded soldier on his return to his family*'.

The Manhattan Deception, The Minerva System, Seven Stars and ***Bomber Boys*** by Simon Leighton-Porter. '*...Fast paced thriller with a plot which twists and turns.*' '*I loved it...*' '*As soon as I picked this book up I knew I wouldn't be able to put it down...*'

Voices by prize-winning author, Oliver Eade: a tale of murder, family love and child abuse seen through the eyes of a grandfather, father and young girl.

The Parth Path by Oliver Eade: In a post-apocalyptic world ruled by women, one brave young man seeks to recapture the happiness of his childhood.

For young readers:

Shadows from the Past series by Wendy Leighton-Porter. '*...Wendy has written a fantastic series of books (Shadows from the Past) filled with mystery, suspense, and adventure.*'

Firestorm Rising & ***Demons of the Dark*** by John Clewarth '*...Children learn that there are far more terrifying things in the universe than they ever learned at school, as a terrifying monster is awakened from a long hot sleep.*'

For young adults:

Golden Jaguar of the Sun by prize-winning author, Oliver Eade: first book of a trilogy, spanning the USA and Mexico: a story of teenage love and its pitfalls and also a tale of adventure, fantasy and the merging of beliefs.

The Merging by Oliver Eade is the second book in his *Beast to God* trilogy and continues the story of the young protagonists in *Golden Jaguar of the Sun*.

Revelation by Oliver Eade completes the *From Beast to God* trilogy. No one could have guessed whom Pepe, Adam's and Maria's son, would find in Xibalba, the land of dead souls.

And others...

Visit www.silverquillpublishing.com

Lightning Source UK Ltd.
Milton Keynes UK
UKHW02f0248151018
330565UK00002B/37/P

9 781912 513611